THE PARIS PILGRIMS

THE PARIS PILGRIMS

a novel

CLANCY CARLILE

Carroll & Graf Publishers, Inc.
New York

To Herbert Blau

First Carroll & Graf cloth edition 1999
First Carroll & Graf paper edition 2000

Carroll & Graf Publishers, Inc.
A Division of Avalon Publishing Group
19 West 21st Street
New York, NY 10010-6805

Excerpts from "They all Made Peace—What is Peace?" and "The Soul of Spain with McAlmon and Bird Publishers" from 88 POEMS by Ernest Hemingway, copyright © 1979 by The Ernest Hemingway Foundation and Nicholas Gerogiannis, reprinted by permission of Harcourt Brace & Company.

Excerpts from *The Making of Americans* by Gertrude Stein courtesy of Dalkey Archive Press.

Library of Congress Cataloging-in-Publication Data is available.

ISBN: 0-7867-0753-4

Manufactured in the United States of America

1

Sylvia

WHEN SYLVIA BEACH was fourteen years old, her father was sent from his Presbyterian parsonage in Princeton, New Jersey, to serve as pastor of the American Church in Paris, and Sylvia knew that Paris would be her home forever. During the years of the World War of 1914–1918, she served in Serbia as a *volontaire agricole,* working in the fields alongside peasant women, gathering crops for the war effort, but when the war was over, she came back to Paris to start a bookstore that specialized in selling works of literature in English. In her search for a suitable location, she went into a bookstore at 7 rue de l'Odeon called La Maison des amis des Livres, which was owned by a young Frenchwoman named Adrienne Monnier. Sylvia and Adrienne fell in love, and soon Sylvia moved into Adrienne's apartment at 18 rue de l'Odeon. The second-floor apartment was just a few doors up the street from 12 rue de l'Odeon, where Sylvia opened her own bookstore. She called it Shakespeare and Company.

Ernest Hemingway came into Shakespeare and Company one blustery January day in 1922. From behind her desk, where she was proofreading a set of galleys, Sylvia glanced at Hemingway as he moved around the room looking at photographs of the masters of modern literature on the walls: Walt Whitman, Edgar Allan Poe, James Joyce, Joseph Conrad, Ezra Pound, D.H. Lawrence, Sherwood Anderson. As though he were paying his respects, he stared at the pictures for a few minutes, and then he approached Sylvia's desk. He asked if she was Miss Sylvia Beach. She nodded. He took an envelope from the pocket of his plaid mackinaw and handed it to her.

"A letter of introduction," he said. "From Sherwood Anderson."

Anderson had visited Paris the year before. Sylvia had first seen him standing outside her shop, gazing through the window at the display copy of the book that had recently made him famous, *Winesburg, Ohio.* He had come into the store, introduced himself, and he and Sylvia quickly became friends. With tousled straw-colored hair and lively hazel eyes, he was an avuncular bear of a man, as warm and open as the American Midwest from which he had sprung. During Anderson's stay in Paris, Sylvia had been able to introduce him to James Joyce, Ezra Pound, and Gertrude Stein. Now Anderson had sent one of his young writer friends from Chicago to meet her. She recognized his generosity in the text:

> This will introduce Mr. Ernest Hemingway. He is a young fellow of extraordinary talent and, I believe, will get somewhere.

"Well, welcome to Paris," Sylvia said. "And welcome to Shakespeare and Company. We're always glad to see another writer. Have you published anything that I might read?"

"Naw, not yet," Hemingway said, as if made a little uneasy by his lack of credentials. He was dressed in the scruffy attire of a lumberjack, and his friendly grin and swagger gave him the appearance of a grown-up Huckleberry Finn still running from the phoniness of civilization. Quite handsome, too, in a rugged, unshaven, masculine way. He had brown eyes, a ruddy complexion, brownish-black hair, beautiful teeth.

"Just newspaper stories so far, but I'm working on some of my own things."

"Well, Mr. Anderson obviously thinks you're good, and I trust his judgment completely. Would you care for tea? Come on back, I have a kettle on."

Turning the sales desk over to her young assistant, Sylvia led

Hemingway to the back of the bookstore, walking down aisles of bookshelves crammed with hundreds of volumes that reached to the ceiling and stretched to the back room. There were many tables about, most of them covered with books. Sylvia and Ernest sat at a table near the coal-burning stove, and Sylvia poured two cups of strong tea.

"So, is this your first trip to Paris?"

"Oh, no, I was here once before. During the War. Nineteen seventeen."

"As a soldier?"

"I came over with a bunch of volunteer ambulance drivers, on our way to the Austrian front in Italy. They gave us three days leave here, before we had to board a train for Milan."

"And did you like it? Paris, I mean?"

His chuckle was one of naughty-boy embarrassment. "Well, I didn't get to see much of it, tell the truth. The first night I was here, I met a woman. . . ."

"Ah, a woman! The plot thickens."

"Met her at a party at a Red Cross canteen. There was a bunch of high muck-a-mucks there, and this . . . this beautiful woman, she took a shine to me, and took me home with her and . . ." He chuckled again, then shrugged, as if enough had been said.

But Sylvia, seeing that the memory brought joy and pride to his face, encouraged him to keep talking.

"A French girl, was it? And you fell madly in love?"

"She was a woman, not a girl. Belgian. She told me her first name, that's all. Mata, it was. She wouldn't tell me anything else about herself. But she took me home with her and wouldn't let me leave for three days. Hid my uniform so I couldn't leave. Kept me supplied with caviar and champagne and cigarettes, and she was very affectionate, but after three days, I had to beg her to give me back my uniform and let me go. Otherwise, I'd miss the train to Milan and probably be court-martialed for desertion. So she finally did." He fell silent for a moment, sipped his tea, lit a cigarette, and in a voice that reflected all the awe and mystery of the experience, added, "But I finally found out what her last name was. I read it in the papers. It was Hari." A slight dramatic pause, then he supplied the punch line: "Mata Hari."

Sylvia was agog. "*The* Mata Hari?"

Hemingway nodded gravely. "But I never knew it till they put her on trial."

This was a real revelation for Sylvia—not because she was awed by Hemingway's exploits, but because she knew that the story had to be a barefaced lie. Sylvia had heard a lot about Mata Hari at Natalie Barney's lesbian salon, to which the German spy had once belonged.

"And how old were you then?" Sylvia asked, trying to give Hemingway the benefit of the doubt.

"Nineteen. She was in her early thirties, I think."

Yes, Sylvia thought, if you can guess the age of a corpse, because Mata Hari had been dead for two years before Hemingway even got to Paris. He had probably been no more than a seventeen-year-old high school student when Mata Hari had been stood up against a wall and shot by a firing squad.

What was she to believe after such a whopper? And the worst part of it was she felt baffled and maybe even a little insulted by Hemingway's obvious assumption that she knew nothing about an historic event as sensational as the trial and execution of Mata Hari. Did he take her for a fool? Or did his fantasy life simply overwhelm his common sense? Was he one of those people for whom fantasies become facts?

By the time they were on their second cup of tea, he had told her that, after arriving in Italy, he had transferred from the Red Cross to an Italian infantry unit and fought on the Italian-Austrian front. And what was she to believe? Service in any army, she knew, required a pledge of allegiance to the country being served, and an American who pledged his allegiance to another country automatically lost his American citizenship; and presumably Hemingway hadn't lost his. He even claimed that he had been wounded in battle. Sylvia tried not to show her skepticism, but perhaps it was too acute to conceal entirely, and perhaps that was the reason Hemingway removed his right shoe and sock and hoisted the leg of his pants to show her the dreadful scars of his war wounds.

"Oh, dear," she said, and her dry but warm maternal sympathy caused him to become more vivid in his descriptions. He said the Italian army doctors had taken 227 pieces of shrapnel from his legs, and that a machine-gun bullet had torn off his right kneecap. His kneecap, he said, had been replaced with one made of steel. He held out his right hand for her to see the signet ring he wore on his finger. It had a peculiar-looking stone.

"It's set with a piece of shrapnel from my legs."

"Oh, my God . . ." She examined it closely. She thought it still might have blood on it.

He had received the wounds, he said, while leading a patrol of Arditi troops in the battle of Monte Grappa on the Austro-Italian front in northern Italy in 1919—the Arditi being Italy's toughest, fiercest fighting troops. He claimed he had been the first American volunteer to be wounded in Italy during the war, and that he had killed twenty-seven Austrians before he had been wounded.

"All in one day?"

"No, but I did kill ten in one day."

"And it doesn't, uh, bother you to . . ." She stumbled into silence, wondering if she were being too probing in her questions, but because her curiosity was greater than her tact, she finished the inquiry: ". . . to, uh, talk about the men you killed?"

"Naw. I'm going to write about it someday anyway, so I can't be at all squeamish about it. And I always killed them clean. On the day I shot the ten, I was leading a patrol, and when the Austrians spotted us, they sent a big outfit out to get us. We got behind some tombstones in a walled cemetery. I got the first one as he climbed over the wall." He aimed down an imaginary rifle. "*Pow!* He was loaded down with equipment, and he fell over into the cemetery. By then more were coming over at another part of the wall. We shot all of them. I got ten."

"I see," Sylvia said. "Why, you must have a chestful of medals."

"Only five." He pulled two from his jacket pocket. "Including these, *La Medaglia d'argento* and *Croce di Guerra,* which I got for trying to carry one of the wounded Italian soldiers to safety after I'd had my kneecap shot off by the machine gun."

"I see. Well, your parents must be very proud of you."

"My parents are dead," he said.

"Oh. Oh, dear. Both of them?"

Sadly but stoically then, he told her how his mother and father had died when he was sixteen, how he had been on his own since then, riding the rails across America, supporting himself by working as a cowboy, a fruit picker, a barroom bouncer, and how he had even been a sparring partner for some of the best boxers of the time, naming Sam Langford and Harry Greb as examples.

"Well, I know practically nothing about boxing, but I've heard those names. They were champions, weren't they? You must be very good."

"Pretty good," Hemingway admitted. "And getting better. On the ship coming over, I had a bout with Young Cuddy, he's a light-heavyweight contender, and I whipped him. I'm thinking about turning pro."

"Really? But what about your writing?"

"Oh, my writing is nothing, my boxing is everything. If it hadn't been for the injury to my eye, I'd be heavyweight champ before it's over."

"You've been injured in the ring?"

"Harry Greb, the bastard, a real dirty fighter, he put his thumb in my eye when we were sparring once, left me almost blind in my left eye."

He didn't explain how a man who was nearly blind in one eye could become a soldier in the fearsome Arditi, and Sylvia wasn't going to dampen his enthusiasm by asking him for an explanation. Besides, even if he was stretching the truth or telling outrageous lies, she couldn't resist the enthusiasm of the telling. In him, she recognized one of those rare people who generate excitement in others. No matter what he said, his enthusiasm gave the experience a heightened quality, an excitement that almost made truth irrelevant.

"Well," she said at last, "for a young man, you've certainly had a full and colorful life, Mr. Hemingway. And I must say, I've certainly enjoyed our chat. It's been *very* enlightening."

There was no irony in her tone; she was speaking the truth. It wasn't every day that a ruggedly handsome young man came thundering out of the American West and into Shakespeare and Company and went to such mendacious lengths to impress her. He was like a boy doing handstands and walking on top of a fence to bedazzle her.

But didn't this imply that his interest in her betrayed more than a desire for admiration? Could it be that his boasts and lies also betrayed a sexual attraction to her? Was that credible? She wasn't sure. There were, after all, many factors that mitigated against such an attraction. Age, for instance: he was only twenty-three years old (which didn't appear to be a lie), she was thirty-six—a big difference. And it wasn't as if she were a ravishing femme fatale. On the contrary, she had descended from a long line of puritan clergymen back thirteen generations. This tradition would stop with Sylvia because she had renounced her father's religion; but a Victorian childhood had left her with a disdain for makeup and other means of making herself attractive to men. All her life, her mother had taught her and her sisters to fear and detest the touch of men, especially those men who made such a show of manhood. "Brutes," her mother had called them in warning whispers. And Sylvia had been faithful to her mother's admonition, "Never let a man touch you in *that* way."

Sylvia had lately come to the conclusion that her mother must have been a repressed lesbian who had been trapped by tradition and religion in a marriage that she hated. And she had tried to pass that hatred on to her three daughters.

Still, even though Sylvia didn't mind being plain and unattractive to men, and even though she had always been physically afraid of men, she had to admit that she was sometimes guiltily drawn to them. Yes, and sometimes she was unaccountably flattered when a man tried to make himself a hero in her eyes, paying court to her with boasts and lies. But it puzzled her. Hadn't Hemingway noticed the mannish style of her clothing and gestures? Had he no inkling at all that she was a lesbian? She had to wonder, too, if he was aware that Mata Hari had been a lesbian.

Hemingway was a married man. Practically a newlywed, in fact. And his tone of voice when he spoke of his wife made it clear that he was very much in love with her. Well, then, maybe he hadn't really been trying to get a sexual response from Sylvia, after all. Maybe this urgent application of masculine charm was just second nature to him. Or maybe he was the kind of man who needed to be admired by every woman he met, regardless of his marital status and her sexual bent.

"Her name is Hadley," he said of his wife, putting his shoe back on. "She's swell. You'll like her."

Sylvia could hardly keep from noticing that his socks were soiled and his feet rather smelly. And as the heat from the stove steamed the winter dampness from his clothes, she became aware of a rather strong, rancid body odor.

"Well, I look forward to meeting her," she said. "Where is she now?"

"Fixing up the apartment."

"Oh, you managed to get an apartment already—how very fortunate!"

"A friend of Sherwood's found it for us. Lew Galantiere. American. Works for the International Chamber of Commerce here in Paris. Know him?"

"Oh, yes, he belongs to our lending library. Well, weren't you lucky he was able to help!"

"It's not much of an apartment," he said with—what? Modesty? Disparagement? A tone meant to minimize any gratitude he might owe Galantiere for finding it? "Hallway toilet. No bath, no running water, no electricity."

Yes, that would help explain the manly ripeness of his smell; poor man, he had no bathroom. Well, neither did Sylvia, for that matter. Affordable apartments in Paris were usually without plumbing, electricity, or heat. When she and Adrienne wanted to take a bath, they placed a galvanized washtub in front of the fireplace, filled it with hot, sudsy water, and took turns in the tub, scrubbing each other's back.

"Where? On the Left Bank?"

He nodded. "Rue du Cardinal Lemoine. Number Seventy-four, up near the Place de la Contrescarpe."

"Oh, sure, I know that area well. Valéry Larbaud has an apartment near there. Number Seventy-one. Mr. Joyce and his family lived there for a while, in Larbaud's apartment."

"Joyce?" Hemingway said with a sparkle of excitement in his eyes. "James Joyce? *He* lived there? Why, that's just across the street from us"—as if that fact raised the quality of the neighborhood considerably in his estimation.

"For a few months, yes, last year."

"I have a letter of introduction to him, too. From Sherwood."

"Well, you can leave it here, if you like. Mr. Joyce comes in nearly every day for his mail. Shakespeare and Company is publishing *Ulysses,* you know? And Mr. Joyce is very apprehensive about it. That's what I was doing when you came in, reading proofs."

"Golly," he said, nodding toward the front desk. "Those were the proofs of *Ulysses?*"—as if he could hardly believe that the galleys of what was already considered a masterpiece were right there, touchable. "Gee, that's swell. I've read the parts published in *The Little Review*—the ones the post office in the States didn't burn, that is—and I can hardly wait till the whole novel comes out. When will that be?"

"Next month, on Mr. Joyce's fortieth birthday—if all goes well. Which means," she added pointedly, "I'm going to have to tear myself away from your delightful company, Mr. Hemingway, and get back to my proofreading."

"Oh, gee," he said, jumping to his feet, guilty of having kept her away from such an important task. "I'm sorry. I was enjoying your company so much—the fire, the tea—I guess I just rattled on. I'll be going now."

"Don't feel you have to leave just because I have to get back to work. Stay around. Pick out some books from the lending library, if you like."

At Shakespeare and Company you could buy most of the important literary works in English, as well as literary periodicals from England and America—*Poetry, The Dial, The Little Review, The Egoist*—but Sylvia had also created a lending library, which one could join for a fee.

Hemingway nodded toward a notice on the wall stating that membership cost fifty francs for a year, seven francs for a month. "I'm sorry, but I don't have enough money with me."

Ordinarily one might think that a proud man might be

embarrassed by such an admission of poverty, but Hemingway wasn't. On the contrary, he seemed to take a sort of sneaking pride in being poor, as if he expected to be admired for it. This caused Sylvia to wonder if he ever in his life had really been poor.

Well, even if he were faking it, he obviously wasn't loaded with money, and she would have bet that he wasn't a thief, either. So she said, "That's all right, you can join on credit. Take what books you like. Just have Myrsine, my assistant, make out a card for you."

Hemingway went wolflike among the stacks, snatching up the books he would take with him.

Sylvia went back to the sales desk in the front room, sat down to the *Ulysses* galleys once more, found the place where she had stopped proofreading, and began again. She had already read the novel in manuscript and therefore wasn't surprised by anything, but the language of the book still made her blush and giggle. The lines above which her red pencil presently hovered contained some of Molly Bloom's bawdiest ruminations.

> . . . I wanted to kiss him all over also his lovely young cock there so simple I wouldn't mind taking him in my mouth if nobody was looking as if it was asking you to suck it. . . .

Passages such as that sometimes caused Sylvia to get migraine headaches. The tension came from the inner battle between thirteen generations of puritan clergymen and her intellectual freedom. She remembered that her grandmother, Nancy Orbison, that pious woman, had once burned a copy of *Hamlet* because she had come across a passage that "wasn't nice." Sylvia wondered what would have been Granny's reaction to *Ulysses*. Probably she would have fainted dead away or had an apoplectic fit. And if she had learned that her granddaughter, her favorite, was actually *publishing* the book . . . why, she probably would have keeled over dead.

Sylvia laughed. It was more of a nervous laugh than a mirthful one, but it brought Hemingway up short as he was passing her desk.

"Is it funny?" he asked with lively interest, grinning, his arms full of books.

"Oh, yes! The book is wonderfully funny, yes, yes, but I was laughing at my own thoughts. So! You've found some books, have you?" She could see the titles of three of them: *Fathers and Sons, Sons and Lovers,* and *War and Peace.* "Heavy stuff," she said admiringly. "Well, Myrsine will check them out for you, and you can keep them for three weeks."

"Oh, but I'll be back before then. I'll come back with the money tomorrow, and bring Hadley with me."

"I look forward to meeting her," Sylvia said, smiling, and turned back to her proofreading. But her thoughts kept returning to Hemingway. She watched him as he left the store and went out into the night, hunching his shoulders, and after he was out of sight, she replayed in her mind their long conversation. She was still trying to figure out why he would tell such whopping lies. He had seemed to welcome her maternal solicitude, of course, but was it all mixed up with seduction? Still, he was awfully young.

She couldn't keep from wondering if he had actually been attracted to her in ignorance of her being a lesbian. Or in spite of her being a lesbian? Or—more intriguing still—because she was a lesbian?

This last hypothesis, as novel as it was, actually gained some credence the following day when Hemingway came back to the bookstore, accompanied by his wife. Sylvia was arranging some books in the window when she saw them coming across the street, and at first she couldn't tell whether the person following Hemingway was a man or a woman. They were both wearing pants and were holding the collars of their coats tight against the icy wind of a Paris winter.

When Hemingway reached the door, he opened it and came in without waiting for his companion to catch up, but once inside the store, he beamed with pride and love as he put his arm eagerly, possessively around the shoulders of his follower, and said, "Miss Beach, I'd like you to meet the feather cat, my wife, Hadley."

Smiling radiantly, Hadley tugged the mittens from her hands and shook Sylvia's hand with a firm and friendly grip. "How do you do, Miss Beach? Ernest told me about you and your wonderful store, and I want to thank you for letting him have the books yesterday. We brought the money for the library fee."

It took Sylvia a while to respond to Hadley, preoccupied as she was with her androgynous looks. She had lovely red hair that was cut as short as her husband's, she wore no makeup, her baggy coat and sweater were those of a man, and her smile was that of an eager, bashful boy—quite like Hemingway's smile. In fact, from a distance, they could have been taken for big brother and little brother. Up close, though, it was apparent that Hadley could never have passed as Hemingway's younger brother, for she was at least seven or eight years older than he.

If this, then, was the kind of woman Hemingway was attracted to, maybe Sylvia had been correct when she wondered if his lies and boasts betrayed an attraction for her.

However, if Hadley was masculine in appearance, she was just the opposite in attitude. It was obvious from the way she looked at her husband that she adored him. She had the awed admiration of a girl and the indulgence of a fond and foolish mother. This attitude brought with it a deference to her husband that any man would have envied. Whenever she was saying something and Hemingway interrupted with some remark of his own, she would say, "Excuse me," and fall silent, not saying another word until her husband had finished. Though Hadley was not petite, she reminded Sylvia of a little brown pheasant hen, shy and submissive, adoringly devoted to her beautiful and bold and adventurous cock.

When they left the store, Sylvia watched them through the window until they were lost to sight, marveling at the continuing arrivals of the young people she and Adrienne had begun to refer to as the Paris Pilgrims: the artists who were flocking to Paris by the hundreds—by the thousands—from all over the world. Only yesterday she had read in the Paris edition of the *Chicago Tribune* that Americans alone accounted for at least

35,000 of the foreigners now living in Paris. Most of the Americans—along with Russians, Swedes, Italians, Irish, Japanese, Rumanians, and various other nationalities—were living in Montparnasse or Montmartre or the Latin Quarter, and most of them were aspiring artists of one kind or another. Among them, of course, were the countless ones who would never be famous, but there were some who had already laid their claim to distinction, and many who held the promise of greatness, and they were all there on the tree-shaded boulevards and café terraces. Like the Hemingways, they had come, not just for the good food and good wine and good art and good books and good companions—though those things were important, as well as inexpensive—but for the things they could never find at home: the freedom to be who they were, to live out their sexual and artistic fantasies, unhindered by pressures and expectations from society, family, friends.

And the writers and poets among them always, sooner or later, came to Sylvia's Shakespeare and Company or to Adrienne Monnier's La Maison des amis des Livres, where Sylvia and Adrienne loaned them books and money if they needed it, collected and forwarded their mail, helped them find rooms and apartments and doctors and abortionists, if necessary, and published a masterpiece, *Ulysses*.

For these reasons, Sylvia and Adrienne often laughingly called themselves vestal virgins in the cult of culture, high priestesses in the religion of literature, the keepers of the flame in the temple of books, whose duty it was to welcome those pilgrims who came in search of artistic fulfillment and even salvation in Paris, the cultural mecca of the world.

2

Hadley

WHEN THEY LEFT the bookstore, Hadley and Ernest had two more books with them. Hadley had chosen a Henry James novel for herself and Ernest had found a copy of Havelock Ellis' *The Third Sex,* which had been banned back in the States. So, clutching their books, they headed for home. Patches of dirty, slushy snow made walking messy, and now and then an automobile would come along the narrow street and they would have to jump back to avoid getting splashed by the slush. Sometimes when they passed the lighted windows of small bars and bistros and bakeries, they stopped to put their noses against the windowpanes, and smiled at each other because the bistros looked smoky and inviting and the smells from the bakeries were warm and yeasty.

"What a wonderful stroke of luck that Sherwood gave you that letter of introduction to Miss Beach," Hadley said. "We are lucky, aren't we?"

"We're always lucky," Ernest said.

At Hadley's suggestion, they stopped in one of the bakeries and bought oven-fresh croissants that warmed their hands as they ate them. Hadley wanted to stop for coffee, too, but Ernest worried that they were spending too much money—which was absurd, of course, because Hadley had a trust fund that paid three thousand dollars a year in interest, so they could have croissants and coffee anytime they liked without any danger of putting themselves in the poorhouse. The problem was that Ernest had no money of his own except what he could earn as a correspondent for the *Toronto Star.* He had been a freelance feature writer for the *Star* before leaving for Europe, and had been told by its editor that he could act as the *Star's* first foreign correspondent, provided he would accept occasional freelance assignments at seventy-five dollars a week, plus expenses. For every unassigned piece that the paper accepted, he would be paid at the rate of a penny a word. Since arriving in Paris, he had sent three unassigned pieces to the *Star,* which had established his bona fides as a foreign correspondent, but the articles hadn't earned him much money, and he was embarrassed to be spending Hadley's. It hurt his pride. Where he came from, a man wasn't a man unless he could support his family. However, because he loved her and she loved him, he was willing to let Hadley help out until he could get started as a writer—a real writer, that is, not just a hack reporter for a small Toronto newspaper.

"I'll go down to Leida's Gym next week, hire out as a sparring partner. The heavyweights pay ten francs a round here, I'm told. Hold this," he said, giving her the Havelock Ellis book to carry, and he, perhaps envisioning wonders to come, began shadowboxing as he walked along. People they met along the street gave Ernest strange looks and plenty of room.

"Oh, Tatie, I wish you wouldn't do that—be a sparring partner, I mean. I don't want any injuries to your lovely brain. If you get your brains beat out, how are you going to become a great writer?"

He snorted, blowing plumes of vapor in the cold air, and swung short, chopping rights, then shot a long left jab at the bastard's face, saying, "Ah, don't worry, Feather Cat, I won't let them hurt me. I can take care of myself. You saw what I did with Young Cuddy, and he's ranked sixth in his division. Never laid a glove on me, hardly. Huh! Huh!" he snorted as he swung and jabbed and did some fancy footwork. "Might even turn pro. Get a few good fights under my belt. Make some money that way. I mean, if I could beat Cuddy, why not?"

Hadley groaned with guilt and regret. It was only because she had interfered in the shipboard boxing match between Ernest and Young Cuddy that Ernest believed he had won fair and square, whereas, in truth, she had prevailed upon Cuddy to take it easy. She hadn't wanted him to throw the fight exactly; just refrain from knocking Ernest's brains out.

It had happened on the *Leopoldina,* the ship they took from New York to Le Havre. On board was Henry "Young" Cuddy, on his way to Paris for three bouts. Ernest struck up a friendship with Cuddy, and when it became known to them that one of the passengers on board was a nice young Frenchwoman who was returning to France because her husband, an American soldier she had married during the War, had taken her back to America and then deserted her, leaving her with no money and a young baby to care for, Ernest thought of a way to help her.

"She's in third-class, steerage, so I haven't seen her, but they say she's down to her last ten francs," Ernest told Young Cuddy after a workout in the ship's gym. They were in the cocktail lounge with Hadley. "So why don't we talk to the captain about putting on a little sparring match as a benefit for the poor woman? We could rope off part of the dining room, bring up a couple of mats from the gym. Go three rounds. Charge the passengers a buck or two. Maybe raise enough money for the woman and her baby to get home from Le Havre. I got the gloves. Twelve ouncers."

"I wouldn't want to hurt you."

"You don't have to worry about that," Ernest said. "I was a sparring partner for Sam Langford and Harry Greb in Chicago."

Cuddy gave Ernest a skeptical look, then shrugged. "Okay. If you've got the gloves, sure, why not?" He had a deep dent in his nose.

"We'll make handbills," Hadley said, catching Ernest's eagerness and excitement, "and I'll distribute them all over the ship."

"You'll have to be my cornerman, too, Hash," Ernest said. "In case," he added in a goadingly ironic voice, "in case someone has to throw in the towel for me."

"Oh, I'm sure it won't come to that," Cuddy said.

But Hadley wasn't so sure. She worried. She didn't want to see her handsome young husband—quite the handsomest man she had ever seen in her life—get hurt. A broken nose she could live with, if she had to, though Ernest did have an exceptionally fine nose, and if it were broken, he would probably no longer look like a young Greek god, and that would be an awful shame; but not nearly so bad as losing an eye, say, or getting knocked nut-ward. After all, he had told her the story of how Harry Greb, the famous middleweight champion, had poked his thumb in his left eye when they were sparring, causing Ernest to be almost blind in that eye. What if this Cuddy fellow stuck his thumb in his other eye? Maybe blinding him? What, then, would become of the great writer he and she expected him to be? No, it was just too dangerous. It was like allowing a great violinist to risk his hands chopping wood.

So Hadley had a talk with Young Cuddy. She found him in the games room three days before the fight, playing alone at a pool table. He was lining up balls and shooting them as he smoked a big after-dinner cigar. And once more observing his bashed-in nose, Hadley wondered how much he could have received in compensation from the fight in which he'd had it broken like that. Had it been worth it?

"I would have thought you'd be with Ernest down in the gym, working out, getting ready for the big match," Hadley said for openers.

"Me? Naw. Don't want to overtrain for a bout. Leave your fight in the gym—know what I mean? Anyway," he went on after making a fancy shot, "it's no big deal. Three rounds with an amateur, what the hell? And he *is* an amateur," he said as he knocked the ash off his cigar and lined up the next shot, "ain't he? A young, smart, good-looking kid like that, he's never been knocked around."

"No, he hasn't, and that's the way I'd like to keep it," Hadley said confidentially. "Now, if he knew I was talking to you like this, he'd probably divorce me, but I have to tell you that my husband . . . well, he's not as experienced in the ring as he likes people to believe."

"I know," Cuddy said. "I seen him work out." Aiming along his cue stick, he asked, "But he was a sparring partner for Sam Langford and Harry Greb—right?"

"Well, you see, Mr. Cuddy—"

"Call me Henry," he said. "Or just Young."

"Henry. Yes. Well, you see, Henry, it's hard to explain, you see, but as a writer my husband has a rich fantasy life, and his fantasies are every bit as real to him as our real experiences are to us. So he's not really telling a lie when he says he sparred with Greb. He has sparred with him—in his mind, and that makes it real to him."

"Writers do that, huh?"

"Well, he does, anyway. And I'm telling you so you'll . . . well, so you'll take it easy on him in the fight. I mean, it can't be very important to you, a little shipboard benefit fight like this, so . . ."

"You asking me to throw the fight?"

"Oh, I didn't say that. It's just . . ."

"You play pool, by any chance, Hadley? All right to call you Hadley?"

"Yes, please do. And as a matter of fact, I do play a little pool. Ernest taught me how. Our friends, the Smiths, had a pool table in their apartment in Chicago, and—"

"Any good at it?"

She shrugged modestly. "Not bad, I guess. I got to where I could beat Ernest at it, anyway."

"Ah. An amateur pool player, too, is he? Well, I'll tell you what, Hadley, let's me and you play a game, what d'you say? You beat me, I'll take it easy on Ernest. Okay? Might even let him win."

Hadley considered the offer for a moment. "And if I lose?"

"Well, I might not take it so easy on him. I should put on a pretty good show. There's a newspaper sports reporter on board, you know? Could be a bad thing for me if he wired ahead to Paris, saying Young Cuddy had been beaten in a shipboard fight by an amateur. See what I mean?"

She shrugged. "Rack 'em up."

"That's the spirit," Cuddy said, and racked the balls.

She took off her coat, tossed it on a chair, and chose a cue stick from the rack. She sighted down it to make sure it was perfectly straight. She was dressed in a tweed skirt, a turtleneck sweater, thick stockings, and sensible shoes.

"If a steward comes by, grab him, will you?" she said. "I could use a drink to steady my nerves."

Deferring to a lady, Cuddy allowed Hadley to break the balls, and he seemed pleasantly surprised by the force of her thrust, the beautiful spread she got, and the two balls that rolled into pockets. Then, chalking her cue stick and talcum-powdering her hands, she sank another ball, and the reverse English she put on the cue ball to bring it into a good position for the next shot brought a grunt of admiration from Cuddy.

She sank two more balls before she missed. Cuddy sank his first few balls with confidence and dispatch, but when he was only a few points behind Hadley, he made a bad shot, the shot of a clumsy beginner. Hadley commiserated with him, then settled down to her game. She actually had hopes of running the table, but the cue ball sank on a hard shot and it went to Cuddy. He made a nice shot, but failed to position the cue ball, and so missed the next shot, and Hadley finished it off.

"You're really good," Cuddy told her. "How about another game?"

Hadley glanced at a clock on a bulkhead. "Haven't got time. Ernest'll be finishing his workout in a few minutes, and I have to give him a rubdown." She looked at Cuddy for confirmation of their agreement. "Well? I won, right?"

He nodded. "You won. Okay, I'll carry him for three rounds, try not to do any damage. Who knows, he might even win."

"Thank you, Henry," she said, replacing her cue stick in the rack. "You're a swell guy." She started away, but turned back. "Oh! And if . . . well, you know, I'll be in his corner, and if I yell, 'Kill the bum,' or something like that, don't take it personally. I'll just be trying to keep my man's spirits up."

"All that, and rubdowns, too? Listen, if there ever comes a time when he don't want you, I'll hire you as my manager and trainer at double what he's paying."

"Which would be exactly nothing," she said, pulling on her coat as she went out, feeling relieved and reassured by her win over Cuddy—though she had to wonder if he had deliberately let her win.

Well, it didn't matter. All that mattered was that now she could rest easy about the fight. Knowing that Ernest wasn't going to get knocked cockeyed by a professional boxer, she could even allow herself to cheer him on. And this would be the perfect time to give him those boxer's trunks she had been knitting for him over the last few months. She had been ambivalent about them, afraid of encouraging him to participate in such a dangerous sport, but since this bout with Cuddy was going to be nothing more than some sparring fun, it seemed appropriate that she should give Ernest the trunks.

"Lavender?" he said. He had been lying facedown on the bunk while she rubbed him down and gave him a massage, but when she dug the knitted trunks from one of her suitcases, he came up on his elbows, then sat up on the edge of the bunk, staring at the lavender trunks. "You don't think they'll make me look like a fairy?"

"Oh, no, honey, nobody's going to mistake you for a fairy. Try them on. Over your jockstrap."

Ernest pulled on his sweat-damp jockstrap, then tugged on the knitted lavender trunks. The fit was quite tight in the crotch.

"My, my, my," Hadley said, impressed. "They do show off your manly form, don't they?"

He liked that, and he liked it that Hadley liked it, so he wore them.

For the next three days, Ernest and Cuddy trained together, shadowboxing in front of the gym's mirrors, jumping rope, doing roadwork on the promenade deck, and wherever Ernest was, there Hadley was, too, with a towel or a stopwatch.

Ernest and Hadley had gotten drunk every night of their first five days on the ship, but he slacked off a little during training, and he didn't have a drop of alcohol the night before the fight. He went into the ring cold sober, without a hangover.

The captain of the ship, who had liked the idea of a benefit for the destitute Frenchwoman, had ordered the crew members to unbolt and remove three tables from the floor of the second-class dining room, and three strands of rope had been strung on portable stanchions to make a square ring, and some mats had been brought up from the gym.

All the seats had been sold out. More than a hundred passengers and crew came to see the fight, and the young French-woman and her baby, the beneficiaries, were given a ringside seat next to the captain.

Ernest climbed into the ring in his tight lavender boxing trunks, and Hadley, very much in the spirit of the thing, carrying a bucket and a bottle of water and a couple of towels and some Vaseline, took her place in Ernest's corner. Ernest waved a gloved hand in response to the cheers from those in the audi-ence who were impressed by his manly form. Mixed in with the cheers, however, were a few whistles—wolf whistles—from the sailors, and Ernest wasn't sure how to respond. Hadley hoped he would ignore the whistles, or respond with humor, but she knew how much he hated fairies, and how he would be furious to be mistaken for one, and those lavender trunks . . .

"It's me," she said, trying to distract him.

"What?" he said. "What d'you mean?"

"They're whistling at me," she said, hoping he would believe her. "Now, listen. . . ." She tried to recall from the fights that Ernest had taken her to in Chicago just what a handler was supposed to do for his boxer. She smeared Vaseline over his eyebrows and cheekbones to prevent cuts, saying hurriedly, ner-vously, "Now, listen, remember our fight plan—"

There was a stool in each fighter's corner, but, unlike Cuddy, who climbed through the ropes with an air of nonchalance and sat down on his stool, Ernest preferred to keep moving around, dancing, shadowboxing, flexing his muscles.

"He's a pro, and he's fast, so stay away from him. Use your left jab and don't get him mad. You've got at least twenty pounds on him, so if he hurts you, tie him up, lean on him. And, listen, now—"

The captain climbed into the ring and made a small speech explaining the occasion for the bout, and while he was doing so, Hadley happened to glance toward Cuddy's corner, and Cuddy, catching her eye, winked at her. It was a very obvious and con-spiratorial wink. Ernest saw it.

"Hey," he said, "he winked at you."

"What? What're you talking about? He didn't wink at me."

"Then he must have winked at me," Ernest said, perhaps still confused by the wolf whistles. "Why would he do that?"

"Oh, who knows? Maybe he's a fairy."

The instant it was out of her mouth, she knew she had said the wrong thing.

"No, he isn't, I'm sure he isn't," she said. "Now, don't get him mad, Tatie," she pleaded.

The captain announced that the timekeeper would be the ship's purser, and the referee would be one of the ship's crew. Then he introduced the fighters: "In this corner, wearing white trunks, a professional boxer from Salt Lake City, Utah, on his way to Paris for a series of bouts, is . . . Henry 'Young' Cuddy!"

The audience cheered. Cuddy responded with a languid wave of his gloved hand.

"And in this corner, wearing what looks to be . . . lavender trunks, a Cheyenne Indian from the wilds of Michigan—"

Hadley said, "What? A Cheyenne—? Did you tell—?"

"Ernest 'Warpath' Hemingway!"

"Warpath?" she said. "Did you tell—?"

Ernest turned to face every segment of the audience, holding his hands up like a victorious gladiator, to receive their cheers. And once again mixed in with the cheers were a few wolf whistles, which caused Ernest to glare in the direction of the whistlers.

When the captain left, the referee called the two fighters to the center of the ring. Hadley stayed with Ernest during the instructions, massaging the muscles of his neck, and when the referee told them to shake hands and come out fighting, they went back to their corners to await the bell. Hadley took the stool from the ring. She was tempted to give Ernest a good-luck kiss, but she knew that would only bring more whistles from the sailors.

The bell rang. Hadley was shivering with excitement and fear as the two boxers squared off in the middle of the ring and began dancing and shuffling around each other. They threw a few jabs, but nothing with any power. They were just feeling each other out, and by the end of the round, the action began to get faster and meaner. Ernest was going in and mauling Cuddy when he got a chance, and Cuddy would snap a sharp left into

Ernest's face now and then, throwing him off stride, breaking his rhythm.

But it wasn't until the second round that Ernest began throwing punches with all his weight behind them. If one had landed, Cuddy would probably have gone down, maybe even been knocked out, but he slipped Ernest's punches easily enough and remained unhurt, though it was obvious by the end of the round that he was beginning to be annoyed by Ernest's mauling style and increasing aggressiveness.

"I think I can take him," Ernest said, panting with exertion and excitement, when he came back to his corner. "I think I can knock him out."

"No, no, no." Hadley gave him some water from the bottle and held the bucket for him to spit in. "Remember our fight plan. Stay away from him. You're winning it on points. Besides, this is only a sparring exhibition, remember?"

"But I think I can take him," Ernest said again, agog at some unrestrained fancy of actually winning by knockout over a high-ranked professional boxer. "Think of the publicity! There's a sports writer on board, he'd cable Paris, maybe I'd get a few fights out of it."

"Tatie, listen to me, you've got the fight won on points, don't take any chances."

In spite of her fear that Ernest would anger Cuddy and suffer the dire consequences, however, Hadley found herself becoming excited when Ernest went out in the third round and began swinging. He was obviously going for a knockout, and for a while Cuddy seemed defenseless against his overwhelming bulk. The audience, sensing an upset, began to shout encouragement to Ernest, and soon Hadley found herself joining in.

"Kill him! Kill the bum!" she cried, quite beside herself.

But when Cuddy delivered a sharp left hook to Ernest's jaw, Ernest's attack came to a sudden, stunned stop. His eyes instantly glazed over and his legs went wobbly. From the audience came a collective intake of breath, then a moan of pleasure at seeing that Ernest was hurt. And for a moment it seemed that the smallest shove would topple him to the canvas. But rather than take advantage of Ernest's condition, Cuddy went in and, under the guise of clinching, caught him under the arms and steadied him. The referee tried to separate them, but Cuddy held on until Ernest had regained some sense of balance, then Cuddy broke the clinch, and as he stepped back, he shook his glove at Ernest as if shaking a shame-on-you finger, and warned loudly enough for Hadley to hear, "This's supposed to be a sparring match, pal, not a knock-down-and-drag-out."

And that's what it was for the last minute of the round, a sparring match. Ernest kept Cuddy at arm's length, peppering him with light jabs, his hopes of a knockout gone.

At the end of the fight, the captain climbed into the ring again, announced that the bout had raised one hundred and sixteen dollars for the young Frenchwoman, who clapped her hands to her mouth with joyful surprise at the news, and then the captain declared that Ernest "Warpath" Hemingway had won the bout by a unanimous decision.

Ernest was elated. His boyish grin stretched across his whole face, though he tried to assume a ponderous mien when the sports reporter approached him as he climbed out of the ring. The reporter asked Ernest if he was a pro.

"Well, I'm not registered in anybody's book as a pro, no," he said. "But I've had a few bouts."

"Maybe you ought to think about turning pro," the reporter said. "You were doing great till you got tagged there in the last round."

"Yeah, I got too eager, wanting to put him away before he was ready. If it'd been a ten-rounder, I would've waited till he was ready to go, then knocked him out."

"Well, anybody who could have Young Cuddy in trouble like you did might have a future in boxing."

Hadley wanted to scold the reporter for putting such ideas into Ernest's head, but there it was now, another fantasy to be lived out.

"You going to write about the fight for the Paris newspapers?" Ernest asked hopefully.

"Naw," the reporter said. "If you'd knocked him out, sure, that'd be a story, but winning on points in a three-rounder . . ."

He shrugged. "I'll keep my eye out for you, though, in case you turn pro."

"You could be my second all the time," Ernest said to Hadley on their way back to their cabin, he shadowboxing as they went. "We'd make a great team, wouldn't we, Hash, you and me?"

"We'd make a great team in anything we do," Hadley affirmed. "And whatever we do is okay with me. I'll be in your corner, always. You can count on me. But I do wish you'd give up the idea of being a boxer, Tatie. I want you to become the writer you know you can be."

"Why not both? Make some money boxing, so we'll have enough to live on in Paris while I get started writing."

"But aren't you afraid you'll get your brains scrambled?"

"Afraid?" he thundered disdainfully, and then in a little boy's voice, with a little boy's belligerence, he said, "Fwaid of nothin'!" This was a frequently repeated remark from Ernest's childhood, something he had said as a very small boy that became a sort of coda for his life. It had happened that for the first four years of Ernest's life his mother had tried to pass him off as a girl, keeping him in dresses and long curly hair and bonnets—had actually told people that Ernest was a girl, and in her sweetest, motherly voice had called him "My little summer girl." She had once shown Hadley a photograph of Ernest taken when he was two years old, dressed in a flowery little hat and frilly little dress, the cutest, darlingest little girl you ever saw, and under the picture, in Mother Hemingway's handwriting: "My little summer girl." God only knows how long this would have gone on if Clarence Hemingway, Ernest's henpecked but finally desperate father, had not at last put his foot down and bravely, in the face of his wife's protests and tears, insisted that Ernest get a boy's haircut and wear boys' clothes. He wasn't going to raise a sissy, Dr. Hemingway said. And so the little summer girl, having been hauled off to the barbershop, emerged not just as a boy, but as a real toughy, too, and when he came out of the haberdashers in his new cowboy clothes, that boy had *balls*. And from then on, whenever the new and belligerent little Ernest dressed in his cowboy clothes, he became Buffalo Bill, a terror to the Indians and buffaloes. He loved to go out and kill them with his toy guns, and when he was asked if he wasn't afraid the Indians might scalp him, he would always answer with a snarl, "Fwaid of nothin'!"

And he was no more afraid of getting hurt while boxing than he had been of being scalped by Indians or run over by buffaloes. He was invulnerable. Life was his to take and dominate and enjoy, and nothing could stop him. All he needed to feel such self-confidence was constant admiration, and he never had to look far for that. Hadley's adulation was always there, of course, freely and gladly given, and he had no trouble finding others who were willing to repay him in homage for the sense of enthusiasm and excitement he generated in them.

Two of their shipmates, for instance, Betty and Irene, a couple of young Americans on their way to Europe to party and ski, gravitated toward Ernest. They obviously came from wealthy families, were experienced travelers and independent young flappers, but they were still drawn to Ernest because his enthusiasms were contagious. On the night of the fight, after Ernest had showered and dressed and returned to the ship's lounge, Betty and Irene approached his table and introduced themselves. They said they wanted to tell him how much they enjoyed the fight and his lavender trunks. But rather than accepting their compliments and then dismissing them, Ernest sat them down at the table, ordered drinks for them, made introductions, and had their life stories in fifteen minutes. And before the night was over, he was planning their futures and they were hanging on his every word. They had fallen in love with Ernest, really, but Hadley didn't mind. She wasn't jealous of their attentions to him. She knew that what he wanted from them wasn't sex. He was getting enough of that from her to keep him faithful; what he wanted from others—men or women—was adulation. That was one thing he couldn't get enough of. And when he, being a take-charge guy, came in contact with people who were less sure of themselves than he was of himself, they were often pulled into orbit around him like stray planets around a sun.

It had been that way with Hadley, too. She had put herself in his hands—not just her physical self, but her very identity. She had despised the person she had been before she met Ernest, and so was happy to become whatever he wanted and expected her to be. She had been trained in such adaptability by her mother, who had coerced Hadley all her life into being what she—her mother—wanted her to be. The trouble was, her mother—a neurotic, joyless, bluestocking shrew—had wanted Hadley to be nothing more than a timorous, mousy old maid, hardly more than a servant in her own home. The youngest of six children, Hadley had never been close to her father, an alcoholic and a bankrupt who killed himself with a bullet to the head when Hadley was fourteen years old, so she had grown up under the complete domination of her man-hating mother, who blamed sex for the subjection of women and taught her daughters that if they married and enjoyed sex with their husbands, they were no better than prostitutes. Fonnie, the sister closest to Hadley in age, had been permanently warped by their mother's teachings, but Hadley had somehow escaped irreversible damage, although until she was twenty-eight years old she seemed to have little chance of ever being anything other than—as she put it herself—"a born wallflower."

Then, after a long and agonizing illness, her mother died, and Hadley was left free for the first time in her life to escape from her puritan prison in St. Louis. As a student in St. Louis' Mary Institute, an elite private school for middle- and upper-class girls, Hadley had become best friends with a girl named Katherine Smith. Upon graduating from the Mary Institute, Katherine—Kate to her friends—moved to Chicago, to live among her brothers and their cronies. And after Hadley's mother died, Kate had invited Hadley to visit her in Chicago. At the time of the invitation, Hadley had been contemplating suicide, so hopeless and dead did she feel, so she decided she had nothing to lose by accepting Kate's invitation. Indeed, as it turned out, she had everything to gain, for she found among the cronies of Kate Smith's brothers a young man named Ernest Hemingway. Though she was eight years older than he, they fell in love, soon married, and Hadley's life changed completely.

Instead of a wallflower, a woebegone blossom wilting on the vine, she learned to laugh and to love. Under Ernest's tutelage, she learned to go after life with gusto, to explore all the pleasures imaginable. So she became wholly his. She wanted to serve him, to lose herself in him, to be him. In her love-filled eyes, he could do no wrong. He was perfect.

So she didn't object to the sighing flattery that young women such as Betty and Irene showered on her husband. He was their hero, too. She understood. After all, what woman with a grain of sense wouldn't adore him? She only objected to the way that the two young women treated her. They were closer in age to Ernest than she was, and their natural reaction was to treat her with the respect and politeness that children accord the mother of a friend, with that look of always asking, "Please, ma'am, can Ernie come out and play?"

Of course, he could. He could do anything he wanted.

Well, almost anything. She wasn't keeping notes for a brief, of course, but she had to admit that now and then—just once in a while, mind you—Ernest did something that didn't meet with her unqualified approval. Once in a while he seemed to betray a streak of brutality that dismayed and disappointed her. It was usually just a momentary thing, something shadowy that she saw in his eyes, the gratuitous meanness of a bully stepping on a bug.

It was Young Cuddy who put a name to the characteristic. On the day the *Leopoldina* was due to dock at Le Havre, they— Ernest, Hadley, Cuddy, and the two girls, Betty and Irene—had met for a last drink in the cocktail lounge. Ernest and the girls had gone off to find out which of the passengers had won the time-of-arrival lottery, leaving Hadley and Cuddy alone at the table, and Hadley said, "I never got a chance to thank you for taking it easy on him during the fight. I know his aggressiveness must have made it hard for you to keep your end of the bargain, but you did, and for that I'm grateful."

"Maybe it wasn't such a good idea, though," Cuddy said, lighting her cigarette with a silver lighter. "He tells me he's thinking of turning pro. Thinking if he could hold his own with me, he could do it with others."

"I know," Hadley groaned. "Look, tell me the blunt truth, will you? What kind of a chance would he stand as a pro?"

Cuddy snorted through his bent nose. "Not much. Some guys would use him as a punching bag a few times, and that'd be it."

"He's got nothing going for him as a fighter?"

"Sure. He's clumsy, but he's strong as an ox. But that's it. No. Wait. There is something else that could make a difference in a few fights."

"What?"

"A killer instinct."

"A killer instinct?" Hadley tried to reconcile that with the boyish, baby-talking lover that she knew.

"That's it," Cuddy said. "That boy's got it, a real killer instinct."

"How can you tell? Was it something he did in the ring?"

"Watch his eyes," Cuddy said.

Hadley began to look for signs of this killer instinct in Ernest's eyes, wondering what it might look like, and it was a few days later, in Paris, that she got a glimpse of what Cuddy was talking about.

They had taken the boat train and arrived in Paris on December 21, 1921. After saying good-bye to Cuddy and Betty and Irene at the Gare du Nord, they took a taxi to the hotel that had been recommended to them by Sherwood Anderson, the Hotel Jacob et Angleterre, at 44 rue Jacob. They rented room 14 for twelve francs a night, not quite a dollar at the current exchange rate. It was a rather shabby room, but they didn't intend to spend much time in it. They went out to walk the streets of Paris. Night and day, arm in arm, they poked about Montparnasse, peering into courts and shop windows. They drank hot rum over a charcoal brazier on the terrace of the Café du Dôme, keeping an eye out for famous writers and artists. They had lunch at the Closerie des Lilas, then went upstairs to play billiards. They attended an art exhibit at the Café du Parnasse, the catalog of which declared that "Montparnasse is the center of the world."

But the weather was beastly cold, the sky unrelentingly leaden and dark, and Christmas brought with it a homesickness that belied Montparnasse's claim to being the center of the world. Hadley even shed a tear or two over their Christmas dinner, which they ate in a small, dingy second-story restaurant. The fare was tough, gristly chicken and greasy fried potatoes. No dressing or cranberry sauce. Half drunk, they began to feel sorry for themselves. They envisioned the home folks gathered around Christmas tables of abundant, steaming, savory turkeys and hams and roasts and stuffing and vegetables and fruits and puddings and pies and good cheer and presents piled high under decorated Christmas trees.

"Let's not think about it," Ernest said.

So they got drunk to keep from thinking about it. They drank so much that they both got sick and went back to the hotel and threw up together.

Their homesickness was alleviated a little by the receipt of a letter from Sherwood Anderson. They had only known Anderson and his wife, Tennessee, briefly in Chicago, and they were amazed that he was turning out to be such a helpful and supportive friend.

"Isn't he a wonderful man to bother with us!" Hadley said.

"A good man to have in your corner," Ernest said with pride.

Lewis Galantiere showed up at their hotel the next day. He said that he'd been sent by his good friend Sherwood Anderson to see how the Hemingways were getting along during their first days in Paris. And when he learned what an awful Christmas dinner they'd had, he invited them to be his guests for dinner that very evening at Michaud's, a well-known and expensive Left Bank restaurant.

"It's where James Joyce and his family frequently eats," Lewis said, as if he were privy to everything.

Lewis was a native Chicagoan, an elegant dresser who projected the image of the witty and sophisticated man-about-Paris. He was twenty-six years old and had a well-paying job in Paris with the International Chamber of Commerce. Though neither an artist nor a writer, he prided himself on being conversant with the literary and artistic scenes in Montparnasse. He was a small trim man, not more than five-foot-three, balding, and wore small, round rimless glasses. Physically he wasn't someone who would attract notice in a crowd, but he was charming and had a talent for mimicry. Hadley found him amusing; Ernest was more grudging in his acceptance. Indeed, so entertaining and self-assured and knowledgeable did little Lewis appear during their fine dinner at Michaud's that Ernest began to be noticeably jealous. The Joyces were not there that evening—"That's their table over there, by the window"—but Lewis did such a good job of mimicking each of the four Joyces in turn—the dour James; his voluble wife Nora; their glum daughter, Lucia; and vain, vacuous Georgio, their son—that Hadley declared she was glad the real Joyces weren't there, so amused was she by Lewis' imitations of them.

At any other time Ernest, too, might have been amused, but now he grumbled that Joyce was a goddamned good writer and hinted that he deserved respect, not ridicule, from people who didn't appreciate how hard it was to write well. It was as if Ernest had begun to look for things in little Lewis that offended him, and he didn't have far to look. Lewis' size and Bantam rooster cockiness, not to mention his twittering mimicry, could be considered an affront to real manhood, but the worst thing was that he had made himself the center of attention, a position that was usually conceded to Ernest. In his expensive clothes, with a wallet full of money, Lewis spoke French fluently, knew the best restaurants, boasted that he knew everyone in Paris who was worth knowing, and made Hadley shake with peals of laughter—all these enviable attributes constituted a kind of treachery to Ernest.

Still, everything might have gone off all right had not Lewis, as soon as Ernest sought to reclaim center stage by telling how he had beaten Young Cuddy in the boxing match on the ship, mentioned that he, too, had once been something of an amateur boxer.

"Oh, yeah?" Ernest said. "Flyweight?"

"Bantamweight," Lewis said. "At Princeton."

Which was another mark against him. Ernest had never been to college and was jealous of those who had, especially Ivy Leaguers. So it was with unconcealed sarcasm that he said, "Oh? A college-boy boxer, eh? Well, I have some gloves at the hotel, how about coming up and sparring a round or two? Show me some of the things you learned in college."

Chipper as usual and now a little drunk, Lewis agreed to the suggestion. Hadley wasn't enthusiastic about the idea. She tried to convince herself that there was no reason to be apprehensive; after all, what could Ernest, who was six feet tall and weighed nearly two hundred pounds, be wanting to prove by boxing little Lewis Galantiere. Nothing, surely. It would be just a little fun.

When they returned to the hotel room, Lewis put his rimless glasses aside, put on the boxing gloves, and took the classical boxer's stance, mimicking a fighter rather than being one. This brought another laugh—albeit a nervous one—from Hadley. From Ernest he got nothing but an offended frown and a terrific punch on the nose. He almost went down, and two more blows to the top of his balding, bowed head must have brought him to the realization that Ernest was trying to knock him out.

Lewis could have conceded defeat and quit, but, still the clown, instinctively trying to quit in a comic way in order to save his pride and dignity, he held up his gloved hand like a traffic cop; then, using both gloved hands, reached out for his glasses. He put them on, then thrust his face toward Ernest with a pix-ieishly goading expression, and said, "You wouldn't hit a man with glasses on, would you?"

For an answer Ernest hit him. Hard. And it was then that Hadley saw what Cuddy had been talking about. Thwarted in his revenge, Ernest's eyes suddenly became the eyes of a killer. His face took on a scornful expression, and there was a dark look of brutality in his eyes as he swung and hit Lewis with a right hand to his face. The blow knocked him down and broke his glasses.

Hadley cried out and ran to where Lewis sprawled on the threadbare rug, groping for his glasses. To her great relief she saw that the lenses had not shattered. Had they done so, Lewis might have been blinded. But the frames had been broken in two.

"Oh, Tatie!" Hadley said reproachfully. "Look what you've done."

Ernest seemed stunned for a moment, as if he were as sur-prised as anyone else, and then he began apologizing as he jerked off his gloves and went to help Lewis to his feet.

"Oh, gee, I'm sorry. I . . . You said you knew how to box. I thought you would duck. I'm sorry. You okay?" His remorse was genuine, no doubt about it. It was as if he didn't know what had come over him to cause him to hit Lewis so hard.

"Yes, sure, I'm all right," Lewis said, getting to his feet and taking the boxing gloves off.

Hadley put the broken pieces of his glasses in his hand. "We'll pay for them, of course," she said, and Ernest quickly concurred, "Yes, of course," but Lewis said, "Oh, that's all right. Accidents happen. I have another pair at home, so don't worry about it. I'm just glad the lenses didn't break in my eye," he added, and that was as close as he came to being reproachful.

He went away with Hadley's and Ernest's profuse apologies and their warm thanks for a wonderful dinner, and after he was gone, they worried that Lewis might bear a grudge and have no more to do with them. Hadley worried, too, about the killer instinct that she had seen so briefly in Ernest's eyes. How could such a good-natured, compassionate man, a man of such puppylike friendliness and joy, actually want and intend, however momentarily, to kill someone?

"I don't know what came over me," he said. "I hope he won't hold it against me. I was counting on him helping us find an apartment."

He needn't have been concerned. Lewis came around again the next day, this time wearing a pair of glasses with tortoiseshell rims, and offered to be their guide and interpreter as they looked for an apartment. They accepted his offer and were grateful for his suggestions as they made their way around the Left Bank in search of *à louer* signs.

After looking at a few flats, they settled for a small, third-floor walk-up apartment in a working-class district of the fifth arrondissement at 74 rue du Cardinal Lemoine. True, it wasn't near the good cafés and nightlife of Montparnasse, and it had no running water or bath or inside toilet, but it was cheap—250 francs a month, about twelve dollars. To take a bath, they had to use a warm pan of water and washcloths—a whore's bath, as the troops in the War had called it—or go to the cold-water public bathhouse at the place where rue du Cardinal Lemoine met the Seine, the Pont de Sully. This was inconvenient enough, but the toilet was even worse. On the landing on each floor was a W/C *turc*—a Turkish toilet, which was nothing more than an enamelled metal crater in the floor, with a circular hole at the center at floor level, with raised, cleated, shoe-shaped elevations on each side of the hole. The user placed his or her feet firmly on the footholds and squatted. From the soggy wall on a nail hung a supply of cut-up newspapers. To flush, one pulled a chain that deluged the enamelled crater to a depth of a few inches. The practiced users could get out of the compartment before their feet got wet; those who weren't speedy soon learned. The toilets flowed into cesspools that were emptied at night by horse-drawn tank wagons. In the night one could hear the tank wagons pumping, and the stench was overpowering.

"We'll have to buy a chamber pot so we won't have to go out to the toilet on cold nights," Ernest said.

"And get a *femme de ménage* to carry down the chamber pot," Lewis suggested.

For heat, the apartment had a small coal-burning fireplace with a black mantel. There was no electricity. They had to read by the light of gas lamps. There was a big mahogany bed with gilt decorations of medieval manor scenes, and the mattress was good. Hadley insisted on renting a piano, but where would they put it? Since the tiny dining alcove wasn't big enough to hold the dining table and a piano, too, they decided to move the dining table into the bedroom and use the alcove for a small, upright Gavian piano. This made the place livable for Hadley.

She was an accomplished pianist. As a child she had demonstrated a definite musical talent, and the teacher said she might even have been of concert caliber had she possessed the requisite ambition and self-confidence. But, no; she was willing to play for Ernest and perhaps a few friends, but her greatest satisfaction came from playing for herself, not for an audience. It was one of her greatest joys, and the little piano made the smallness and lack of amenities of the apartment bearable.

Marie Rohrbach also helped make it bearable. The concierge recommended Marie to them as a *femme de ménage,* and they hired her for two francs an hour to haul buckets of water up the stairs, empty the chamber pots, take down the garbage, and do the laundry and shopping. Marie, a Breton peasant girl—soon affectionately called Marie Cocotte by the Hemingways—knew her way around the rough, rundown neighborhood and the shops and stalls of the nearby market street, rue Mouffetard, where fishmongers called to buyers and housewives shouted and shoved to get to the cheapest goods.

In gratitude for Lewis Galantiere's help, Hadley invited him to come for a good dinner as soon as they were settled in and functioning properly, which she supposed would be in no more than a few days.

"As soon as the weather clears up," she said, ignorant of Paris winters, little realizing how long the sky would continue to be overcast and the air cold. And while they waited for better weather, the windswept streets and the crowded and uncomfortable apartment dampened their spirits, and soon Hadley came down with a cough and a fever and had to sit by the puny fireplace all day while Ernest wrote his first article for the *Toronto Star* while lying in bed with his small Corona typewriter—a present from Hadley on his last birthday—resting on his thighs, and the last thing they felt like doing was having someone over for dinner.

On their first Sunday in the apartment, Marie Cocotte went to church, so Hadley had to go out and buy a bundle of twigs to start the coal *boulettes* in the fireplace. Ernest was still in bed, reading *The Third Sex,* the book by Havelock Ellis that attempted to explain lesbianism—a subject that seemed to interest Ernest inordinately. He was boning up on the subject, he said, in preparation for meeting Gertrude Stein.

"This Havelock Ellis is really something," he said aloud but as if to himself. "Bill Smith used to keep a copy of one of Ellis' books—the one on love and pain, Volume Three, I think it was, of *Psychology of Sex*. Kept it under his mattress at Horton Bay. We used to sneak it out and read it every now and then. If his Aunt Charles had ever found out, she would've skinned us alive. But this one's a lot better. Listen to this, Bones"—Bones being his latest pet name for her. He shifted in the bed, propped his head up with one arm, and read from the book. " 'A congenitally inverted Englishwoman of distinguished intellectual ability was attracted to the wife of a clergyman, who, in full cognizance of all the facts of the case, privately married the two ladies in his own church.' How d'you like that! I wonder what he got out of it? Did he watch them on their wedding night? Did they all sleep together?"

"Must have been a ménage à trois," Hadley said absently, snuffling. "Otherwise, why would he do it?"

"Does that sound like fun?" Ernest said speculatively, then dropped back on the bed and resumed reading with a ravenous interest.

Hadley banked the birch twigs around the *boulettes* and lit a piece of newspaper and blew gently a number of times until the smoldering twigs cracked and spat and flames leaped up. She held her hands over the fire, rubbing the cold and stiffness out of her fingers. She was trying to get her hands limber enough to play the piano, but she knew the moment she touched the keys her fingers would once again be too cold to play, and soon, in one of her rare fits of hopelessness and self-pity, she began to cry.

"What is it, Bones? What's the matter?"

"I'm sorry. It's just that . . ." She fell silent, ashamed to complain.

"What, honey? What's the matter? Are you getting your period?" When she didn't answer, he took his notebook from the bedside table and checked the dates for her menstrual cycle. "Yeah, you're due day after tomorrow. Is that what it is?"

"No, no, no, it's not that, it's just that I . . . I didn't know this is the way Paris would be. I thought Paris was supposed to be full of light, and gay, and beautiful, and . . ."

He got up, braving the cold, to crouch beside her in his pajamas and put his arm around her. "Bones, listen, I been thinking. I've finished the *Star* article. Why don't we go for a skiing holiday in Switzerland? In that place Betty and Irene told us about—remember? Chamby. We could buy some boots and skis secondhand, and third-class train tickets couldn't cost much, and we could eat as cheaply in the mountains as we can here in Paris. Why not? It'll be good for your cough, and by the time we come back, the weather here will be better. Let's do it!"

And as usual his eagerness and enthusiasm buoyed her, swept

her along. "But I don't know how to ski," she warned, drying her tears. "I don't even know if I could."

"Oh, sure you can," he said. "I'll teach you. You'll learn fast, you'll see. You're a natural athlete."

She had never been much at sports. When she was a child she had fallen out of a window and hurt her back and had to spend a year in a wheelchair. During that year her mother, in order to gain complete dominance over her, convinced her that she would never be anything but a frail invalid. Now Ernest was once again encouraging her to prove that her mother and sister had been wrong. Once again he was opening her life up, offering her the key to the world, and she worshipped him for it.

"Wonderful!" she said. "Let's do it!" But in a token effort to be a levelheaded helpmate, she said, "But aren't you afraid we'd spend too much money?"

"To hell with it," he said.

"All right," she said, throwing caution to the winds. "Let's!" She gave him a hug, and he, with his enthusiasm growing, said, "Don't worry about the money. I'll go down to Leida's Gym and hire out as a sparring partner for a few days. I've been wanting to do it, anyway, and now's a good time. I can make nearly a dollar a round, and sharpen my skills while I'm at it. Maybe get in good enough shape to turn pro pretty soon." He feinted a left jab to her chin.

"Oh, shit," Hadley said, the enthusiasm leaving her like air from a slowly deflating balloon.

3

Sylvia

FEBRUARY 2, 1922, was James Joyce's fortieth birthday and the official publication date for *Ulysses*. On that morning Sylvia Beach got up before dawn to go meet the train from Dijon, on which was arriving the only two complete copies of the book thus far in existence. The printers in Dijon, who had only received the final page proofs two days previously, had worked night and day to get the first two copies ready so that Joyce could have one for his birthday.

While Sylvia bustled about in the cold room, getting ready to go, Adrienne lay in bed, yawning, stretching, sighing, saying, "My God, it's not even light yet! You're going to ruin your health."

"All in a good cause," Sylvia said.

As Adrienne watched her dress, she sighed with tenderness and said, *"Ah, ma petite fleur de presbytere."* It was a phrase that seemed to describe Sylvia perfectly, "My little flower of the parsonage."

Sylvia said, "A daisy, no doubt." Since she spoke fluent French and Adrienne spoke only broken English, they nearly always conversed in French. "Something plain and unpretentious?"

"Not so plain as that. A pansy, perhaps." It never ceased to amuse her that Sylvia, a libertarian and a lesbian, had never lost the look of her missionary ancestors. And it was true that, removed from the bohemia of Left Bank Paris, Sylvia might easily have been mistaken for a missionary, or at least a schoolmistress, or perhaps a managerial secretary—someone who could be forceful and resourceful, someone of unimpeachable rectitude. She never wore makeup, her hair was cut short and tightly crimped, and the steel-rimmed glasses that pinched the bridge of her thin nose added to the severity of her countenance, while her clothes were always mannish and sensible: an Edwardian-style velvet jacket, a silk foulard flowing from a large white collar and tied into a droopy bow, a plain brown woolen skirt, sturdy American shoes. This ensemble had virtually become a uniform for her.

"Must you hurry off?" Adrienne asked. She had a booming voice, perhaps the legacy of alpine forebears who hailed one another from peak to peak. "Aren't you going to eat any breakfast?"

"I'll get coffee and a croissant at the Café Voltaire. You go back to sleep."

"Give us a kiss, then," Adrienne said in English. When she was seventeen, she had spent nine months in England with the young woman who had been her first love, but the only English she had learned were a few amusing idiomatic expressions, such as "Geeve us a keys."

Sylvia sat down on the side of the bed, leaned over Adrienne's ample, warm, soft body, and gave her a kiss on the forehead. Sylvia's body was all angles and knobs, Adrienne's all rounds and mounds.

"Is that all? I meant a passionate kiss, my darling—a French kiss, not the peck of a Yankee Calvinist."

Sylvia ruffled Adrienne's thick beautiful chestnut hair and gave her a quick kiss on the tip of her nose. "You know I can't, my darling. Destiny and James Joyce await!"

"I hate James Joyce. His damned book has taken you away from me."

"No, you don't hate him, and his book hasn't taken me away from you. The necessity to work takes me away, and as long as I have to work for a living, I'd rather be doing what I'm doing than anything else in the world. And the same is true for you."

Adrienne surrendered to the inevitable. "Yes, yes, of course. Very well, then, off you go—off, off, off! I will go back to sleep and dream of you here beside me in the warm bed."

"Sweet dreams, then." Sylvia kissed her forehead once more, then grabbed her satchel and great coat and headed for the door.

Had she turned left on leaving the apartment she would have been at the door of Shakespeare and Company in a few steps. But this morning, rather than going to her store, Sylvia turned right, going up the street toward Place de l'Odeon, in the center of which was the Theatre de l'Odeon, with its imposing classical facade and lofty columns. Performances of classical plays and music brought crowds to the theater nightly and on Thursday and Sunday afternoons, and around its arcade during the day would be little bookstalls and vendors selling roasted chestnuts; but now, in the cold predawn light nothing moved in the area except a ribby dog, sniffing in the gutters for food, and an occasional working man or a drunk or a taxi driver heading for the Café Voltaire, which was just across the street from the theater.

The Voltaire had been a landmark nineteenth-century café whose patrons had included Whistler, Mallarmé, Rodin, Anatole France, Rimbaud, Gauguin, and Verlaine, and now it was a gathering place for the moderns, the dadaists, and the surrealists, although at this hour most of the patrons were people who had stopped for a quick coffee and a pastry before going to work. The sidewalk tables would be used in the summer, but now everyone was crowded into the smoky, steamy, noisy interior.

Sylvia made her way to the counter and ordered coffee and a croissant with orange marmalade. After devouring the croissant, she took a cigarette from a packet in her coat pocket, and before she could find a match to light it, a flame appeared in front of her. It was Louis Aragon who held the match.

"Ah, good morning, Louis," she said, speaking English, puffing on the cigarette. "Thank you. My, you're up early, aren't you?"

Speaking excellent English without an accent, he said, "No, I'm up late. I haven't been to bed yet."

He was a handsome young Frenchman and ordinarily very presentable, but now his pasty pallor, bloodshot eyes, disordered brown hair and soiled clothes attested to a night of dissipation, or artistic discussion, or both. He smelled rather . . . well, rotten.

"Another wild night?" she asked.

"We had a poetry reading in Montmartre, had eggs and tomatoes and rotten cabbages thrown at us. A wonderful night! I read two poems and only got hit with one rotten tomato." He reached into the inside pocket of his overcoat and brought out some wrinkled scraps of paper. "Here, I was on my way to the bookstore to leave these." From among the papers he sorted out five subscription forms for *Ulysses*. As usual when he brought back subscription forms that had been filled out by drunks in the wee hours of a wild night, the signatures and addresses were hardly decipherable. With thanks, she took the forms from him, leaving him holding two torn sheets of notebook paper covered with scribbles and what appeared to be some food residue.

"These are the two poems I read last night," he said. "Would you like to hear them? I was taking them down to Adrienne, to see if she would want to publish them, but perhaps I could try them on you first?"

"Shoot," Sylvia said, with more noblesse oblige than enthusiasm. She didn't really understand dada—which of course was the very object of the literary movement: not to be understood. The dadaists believed that any work that could be understood was the product of a bourgeois hack. Since the War had destroyed all morals and values, the dadaists believed that all art or literature that was conventional, rational, or understandable was *merde*. Sylvia could not take them seriously, but they were young and fired by the flames of revolution and therefore amusing.

Louis smoothed the wrinkles from one piece of soiled paper, and with what seemed to be a tone of admiration, he indicated a big splotch on the paper. "One of the rotten tomatoes," he explained. He cleared his throat. "It's called 'Words', and it's the poem of ultimate organic unity." He read,

"words
words

words
words,"

and then turned to her with a look of pride and triumph. "There! Of course, it goes on for hours like that, just that one word, over and over. I'd been reading it for about thirty minutes last night when I got hit with the tomato. What do you think?"

"Well," she said, circumspect, not wanting to go overboard before she had a chance to think about it. "I especially like the rhyme scheme."

His face suddenly fell. It was as if she had brought about a dramatic revelation. *"Sacré bleu,"* he groaned. "It's true, isn't it? It rhymes. Who would have thought that I could do something so conventional! No wonder someone threw the tomato." He tore the poem into confetti and dropped the pieces on the floor.

"Oh, I am sorry," Sylvia said.

"No, it's all right. You were right to bring it to my attention. But here," he went on, smoothing out the other piece of wrinkled paper. "This one is better, I'm sure you'll agree."

Sylvia glanced at her watch. "I don't want to be rude, Louis, you know I love your poetry, but I have to find a taxi to the Gare de l'Est to meet the seven o'clock train from Dijon. The first two copies of *Ulysses* will be coming in on it."

"Oh, wonderful," Louis said. "No, this won't take long, it's a short poem."

As Louis read his poem, Sylvia drained her coffee cup and turned her collar up in preparation for leaving the café.

"It's called 'Alphabet'," he said, and read.

"A, b, c, d, e, f, g,
h, i, j, k, l, m, n,
o, p, q, r, s, t, u,
v,
w,
x, y, z."

Finishing, he gave her an expectant look. "Well, what do you think?"

"It's good. It's very good, Louis. Quite original." But there was a hint of reservation in her voice and expression. "But, uh—" She took the paper from his hand. "Maybe you could change the scan of a couple of lines, to keep the *z* and *v* and *g* from rhyming."

"*Alors, bien sur!*" he said. "Yes! Definitely, I'll do that. Thank you so much." Then he added slyly, "Sylvia, I was wondering. . . ."

"Yes? Was there something else?" she asked, and knew almost for a certainty that he was trying to summon the courage to mention Cyprian, Sylvia's younger sister, and . . .

"I was wondering," he said, "if Cyprian might be in the bookstore sometime today."

"Afraid not. She's in Berlin, trying out for a role in a film."

"Ah, that's right," he said. "She mentioned it. A Fritz Lang film, I think. *Alors,* when you write to her, please give her my regards, will you?"

"I'll be sure and do that," she said, and left the Café Voltaire. Walking along rue Racine toward Boulevard St. Michel, where she would flag a taxi, she pondered the plight of Louis. For a long time the poor man had been involved in a tumultuous on-again, off-again affair with Nancy Cunard, the heiress to the Cunard shipping fortune, and during their off-again times he frequently came to Shakespeare and Company, where Sylvia's sister could usually be found when she was in Paris. His hopes of a romantic relationship with Cyprian, however, had never come to fruition, and were, indeed, rather far-fetched, for the simple reason that Cyprian, too, was a lesbian. And Louis must know it. Her name alone—not her given name at birth, which was Eleanor, but the one she had adopted for herself, Cyprian—should have alerted him, if nothing else, Cyprian having been a beautiful young woman of Lesbos, one of Sappho's lovers whom Sappho had praised in her poems. Or perhaps Louis did know it but didn't think it mattered. Perhaps, like many men, he believed that all a lesbian needed was a good man to make her see what she had been missing.

As Sylvia was nearing Boulevard St. Michel, who should she run into—literally—but Ernest Hemingway. He came out of a small side street, jogging and shadowboxing, panting long plumes of vapor into the air, and bumped into her. It was only a glancing collision, so Sylvia was not knocked off her feet, but she staggered, and Hemingway, profusely apologetic, grabbed her and steadied her.

"Miss Beach! It's you! Oh, I'm sorry," he said. "I'm so sorry. I—"

"It's all right," she assured him. "No harm done. My, my, what're you doing out this early in the morning?" She noted that he was unshaved, dressed in worn, shaggy clothes and tennis shoes, and had a swollen black eye.

"I'm in training," Hemingway said, and went through a few more shadowboxing motions to demonstrate. "I went down to Leida's Gym and got some work as a sparring partner for the pro boxers who train there. Trying to make enough money to take Hadley and me on a skiing trip."

"Is that where you got the black eye?"

"Yeah," he sheepishly admitted. "I wasn't in shape, couldn't move fast enough."

"Oh, my goodness," Sylvia said.

"That's why I'm getting in shape now, and as soon as this eye goes down, I'll show 'em." He sounded like a humiliated child seething with a volatile mixture of self-pity and vengeance.

Unable to work up any real sympathy for him, and anxious to be gone, Sylvia said, "Oh. Yes. Yes, I'm sure you will. Well, I must be off. Have to meet the express from Dijon. The first two copies of *Ulysses* will be on it."

"Listen, I've had an idea. . . ."

"Yes?"

"About Joyce's book. I understand you can't get copies into the States."

"That's right. We have a hundred or so subscriptions from America that we can't fill. If we send them by freight or mail, the customs or the post office police will seize them and burn them."

"I know how to get them in."

"You do?"

"I know some bootleggers in Chicago. Used to work with

them, bringing booze in from Canada. Nick Neroni, alias Pickles McCarty. Once was a prizefighter. I worked as his sparring partner a few times. Anyway, he got wounded in the War, and couldn't fight anymore, so he became a smuggler, hauling booze in from Canada. I'll tell you what, you send the books to an address I can give you in Canada, and Pickles will have them picked up and smuggled into the country with the booze."

"Pickles?" Sylvia said. "Will you never cease to amaze me, Mr. Hemingway? Bootleggers! You used to work with a bootlegger named Pickles McCarty?"

"That was his alias," he said, as if reluctant but willing, given the need, to speak about himself. "I got into that after my old man died and I became the sole support for my family. A mother, three sisters, and a brother I had to feed. Had to quit school at sixteen and go to work, and Pickles got me some jobs as a sparring partner for some of the heavyweights who were training around town. When he started smuggling, he took me along for a couple of rides."

"When you were—? But I thought—" She faltered and fell silent. She distinctly remembered him telling her that *both* his parents had been killed when he was sixteen, and that he had gone out into the world to earn his living as a rodeo cowboy and a boxer. He hadn't mentioned that his mother had survived the nameless calamity that had claimed his father, and that he had had to become the sole provider for a family of five. She was quite curious to know such things, but she thought it better not to embarrass him by catching him in a lie. Because if he really did know some rum runners . . . "That would be very exciting," she said. "If you can really get them to do it. . . ." She tried not to sound too skeptical.

"Consider it done," Hemingway said. "I'll bring you the address tomorrow." He gave her a parting salute, and continued jogging down the street, shadowboxing as he went.

Sylvia stood and watched him for a few seconds, bemused and puzzled, trying to figure out if Hemingway was a truly amazing young man, or simply the biggest phony she had ever met.

4

Hadley

THERE WAS TO be a party that day, one of Gertrude Stein's famous Saturday evening soirees. Ernest and Hadley had been invited to come early so they could get acquainted. The letter of introduction from Sherwood Anderson had brought the invitation; any friend of dear Sherwood's was a friend of Gertrude's.

Sylvia Beach warned Hadley what would happen. She explained the protocol at the Gertrude Stein–Alice B. Toklas household. Alice had strict orders to keep wives out of the way while Gertrude talked to the husbands. When husbands were invited to 27 rue de Fleurus, wives naturally assumed that the invitation extended to them, but if wives could not be prevented from coming, they were not allowed to interfere with the serious discussions of the masculinefolk.

Hadley had been looking forward to meeting Gertrude Stein, but Alice didn't even allow her an introduction. With ruthless dispatch, the wiry, raptor-looking little woman with a soft voice and dark, piercing eyes took Hadley by the elbow and separated her from Ernest, who had been summoned to approach Gertrude's chair by a wave of her long, scepterlike cigarette holder, the smoke from the cigarette leaving trails of evanescing curlicues in the still air. At two hundred pounds and five-foot-two, Gertrude was almost as wide as she was tall, and she made an imposing figure in the low, thronelike Renaissance chair, her bulk buttressed by brocaded pillows, her legs crossed at the ankles, one sandal dangling from a big toe.

A cast-iron stove in a corner warmed the room admirably, a few shafts of pale winter sunlight seeped through the high windows to illuminate works of art and books and bric-a-brac, and past festivities had left the room redolent with smells of good tobacco and the potpourri of fading bouquets. An ornate bullfighter's cape lay open on a small table, a carved African mask hung from an umbrella stand, and the walls from floor to ceiling were covered with paintings: here a Picasso, there a Matisse, a Braque or two, a pair of Cezanne compositions, a Renoir nude. Directly above Gertrude's chair was a portrait of her that Picasso had painted. It was not a good physical likeness, but the painting did capture her soul, revealing that the real Gertrude Stein was the one in the painting.

A sturdy Florentine table surrounded by Renaissance chairs was drawn close to the stove—Gertrude's worktable, obviously—and sideboards and bulky chests and small tables lined the walls, all loaded with objets d'art and curio shop bric-a-brac: cheap porcelain figurines, costly Renaissance plates, tiny alabaster urns with tiny alabaster angels balancing on the rims, bronze Buddhas, and fragments of bas-reliefs.

Hadley's instinct was to resist being so aggressively maneuvered by Alice; if she was not to be allowed to talk to Gertrude, she felt she ought at least to be allowed to listen to the conversation between her and Ernest, even if it meant being a nice, submissive, silent wife. But this was not a household where you got away with breaking the rules. In spite of being a lesbian household, everything seemed to have a heavy, patriarchal feeling. There was an unmistakable contempt for femaleness implied in shuffling the wives off to the kitchen, where Gertrude no doubt believed they belonged.

Hadley stopped in the kitchen door and turned to get a look at Gertrude and Ernest. Apparently Gertrude was conducting a quick tour of the room's art treasures for Ernest's benefit. They were standing below a Cezanne painting, she lecturing with operatic gestures, while Ernest looked on with rapt attention. Gertrude was telling him that she sat under the painting every night to do her writing, hoping that she could somehow transfer Cezanne's technique of painting to the written word.

"Come along, now," Alice said, retrieving Hadley. "I want to get another woman's opinion of these canapés we're making for the soiree this evening."

The kitchen was a marvel of copper pots and hanging garlic and well-scrubbed cleanliness, the kitchen of a gourmet cook. Now it smelled richly of onion soup and garlic bread. The maid was at a table, preparing the canapés.

"We're expecting twenty people this evening," Alice said, and perhaps there was a hint of social vanity when she let drop, "Georges Braque . . . Picasso, of course . . . Jean Cocteau . . . Mildred Aldrich . . . Here, try this soup, will you, and tell me what you think."

Hadley took the soup spoon, tasted, and said, "Oh, that's wonderful. I'll have to get your recipe," expecting that this was what Alice wanted to hear.

"I can give it to you right now," Alice said, quick to seize on a subject that would keep Hadley in the kitchen.

"Oh, don't bother with it now. I'll get it—"

"No, no, it's no bother," Alice said. Taking a small loose-leaf notebook from her skirt pocket, she began jotting down the recipe, mumbling and frowning as she remembered the ingredients, as an actor might strain to remember dialogue he had memorized for some long-ago performance. Meanwhile, Hadley kept one ear tuned to the conversation in the next room, snatches of Gertrude saying, "Paris is the place suited for those of us geniuses, geniuses together, who are creating the art and literature of the twentieth century. Paris is—"

She could tell by Ernest's eager assent that he had found someone who could spellbind him. And a little later, while suffering through a lecture from Alice about how and where to shop at the outdoor markets in Paris for the best and freshest food, Hadley strained to hear what Ernest was saying, and was not surprised to learn that he was once again telling lies about his childhood. He was telling Gertrude that his father had died when he was nine, leaving him nothing but a pistol and a family of five to feed. Gertrude's maternal "Ahhhhs" of sympathy kept him on about how he had ridden freight trains across America, had been a cowboy, had boxed as a sparring partner for famous heavyweights, and he was diverted from the subject of himself only when Gertrude, confessing she knew nothing about boxing, revealed that her and Alice's favorite blood sport was bullfighting. Gertrude told him how she and Alice had gone to Spain the previous summer and followed the bullfight festivals, and how wonderful they had been, and Hemingway should go to Spain and see a bullfight sometime. Still stuck in the kitchen with Alice, Hadley could imagine Ernest absorbing Gertrude's every word, and she could hear the inflections in their voices that seemed to have a flirting undertone. Alice also seemed to detect this, and after casting a few apprehensive glances toward the other room, she made some excuse to take Hadley back into the studio. Gertrude was in her huge chair now, and Ernest sat on the ottoman at her feet, obviously entranced.

Hadley never failed to find it curious that Ernest always got on so well with lesbians. Had Gertrude been an effeminate male homosexual, for instance, Ernest would probably have refused to enter the house, let alone be found sitting at the homosexual's feet, hanging on his every word. And to go even further, it seemed that Ernest was interested in Gertrude, not in spite of her being a lesbian, but possibly because of it. It was an interest that exceeded mere curiosity. He had studied Havelock Ellis' book on lesbianism, *The Third Sex,* and he had long ago queried Hadley about all her own thoughts and feelings on the subject, however secret. He had been particularly keen to learn about the times when the issue of lesbianism had entered her life. The first time had been back in the dark days when Hadley, depressed and on the brink of a nervous breakdown, had attended Bryn Mawr for a short while and met a classmate named Edna Rapallo. A thin, dark girl, bright and ambitious, Edna had sensed how unhappy Hadley was and had tried to help her. Edna had lived alone with her mother, Constance, in a town house in Manhattan. Edna's father, a successful Manhattan lawyer and railroad official, had been separated from Constance for years. On weekends and holidays Edna took Hadley home with her to Manhattan, and during Hadley's first summer vacation from Bryn Mawr,

Edna and Constance took her with them to their family vacation home in Windsor, Vermont.

Hadley had been fascinated by Constance Rapallo, a beautiful and highly intelligent woman, a feminist, chic in a mannish way. And Constance, recognizing in Hadley an emotional cripple, had mothered her with compliments and embraces, with kisses. Was there a time when the embraces and kisses became less maternal and more sensual, more carnal? Hadley, bewildered and frightened by her own sensual excitement, couldn't tell. All she knew was that she liked to lie in Constance's arms, liked to feel Constance's kisses, comforting and affectionate, on her forehead, her eyes, her lips. . . .

After years of being indoctrinated by her mother to regard sex with men as horrifying and disgusting, Hadley hardly knew how to regard sex between women. But she must have been acting under some uncertainty, perhaps some guilty compulsion, when she wrote something to her mother that brought the summer vacation with the Rapallos to an abrupt end. She couldn't even remember what she had said in the letter, but whatever it was, it was enough to set off alarms in her mother's moral firehouse. She ordered Hadley home immediately, and when she arrived and asked her mother for an explanation of the recall, her mother said she had begun to suspect that the Rapallo mother and daughter were unnatural women.

"Lesbians!" her mother had said in the face of Hadley's confusion. "You know what that word means, don't you? Unnatural sex between women!"

"Well, to hear you tell it," Hadley responded, "all sex is unnatural."

"And am I to gather from your reaction that my fears are well-founded—that you have lesbian longings for those Rapallo women?" And in the face of Hadley's stunned silence, her mother had added, "That's it, isn't it? You, too, harbor lesbian lust for other women. Don't you? Don't you?" Her tone was not one of accusing cross-examination, but a tone of commiseration, as if her mother was ready to forgive her the worst if only she would confess it. Her tone struck Hadley as being strange, though at the time Hadley was so devastated by the words that she couldn't think of anything else. Being very suggestible, Hadley could only wonder if her mother's concerns had implanted the idea in her mind, or if she was, indeed, a lesbian.

Later the same night, after she had gone to bed in her old room in the St. Louis house, Hadley, pondering the perplexing mystery of her mother's reaction, had suddenly sat up in bed with a revelation. It occurred to her, without any preliminary thought, that her mother had been projecting her own feelings onto her daughter. That, it seemed to Hadley, was the only thing that could explain her mother's reaction and oddly commiserating tone: she herself must have had a repressed attraction for women, and imagined that Hadley, too, felt it. Yes; that would help explain the irrational hatred and contempt her mother had for men, especially very masculine men.

Hadley had related all this to Ernest one hot, muggy summer night on the roof of his apartment building in Chicago. Trying to keep cool, they had carried a mattress up to the roof. Lying on it and gazing at the stars, they talked and kissed and told secrets. It was that night, and in response to Hadley's story about the possibility that her mother had been a repressed lesbian, that Ernest confessed to her in hushed tones that he, too, had reason to believe that his own mother, Grace, had had a long-term lesbian affair. Ruth Brown, the daughter of a salesman, had come to the Hemingway house as one of Grace's voice students when the girl was only twelve years old. A year later Ruth moved into the Hemingway house as a part-time cook and mother's helper. She called Grace "Muv," and washed Muv's hair and combed it and stroked her forehead when she had a headache. And before long Ruth and Grace had become quite loving, inseparable. They slept together. Nobody thought anything of this at the time; it was as if Grace finally had a daughter whom she could love wholeheartedly. But then one day Ernest's father, Dr. Clarence Hemingway, had come home and found the two women together, doing something unforgivable.

Ernest was sixteen at the time, and sexually curious, but he never learned what his father saw that night. All he knew was that his father, in a loud and peremptory voice, had ordered Ruth Brown to leave the house immediately and never come back.

And for perhaps the first time in his life Ernest had heard his mother begging—begging his father to let Ruth stay.

"That's how I knew it had to be real serious," Ernest told Hadley. "Something real nasty had to be going on between Ruth and my mother to make a henpecked coward like my father ignore his bitchy wife's commands and pleas and throw the woman out of the house. Just like that. He never said a word about it to anybody, but it wasn't hard to figure. I always had the feeling the old bitch was an androgyne. My sisters, too, they thought Ruth and Mother were lovers."

So maybe that was the reason Ernest showed so much curiosity about lesbianism? Although when Hadley thought about it, she concluded that it couldn't have been the only reason, or even the main one, because his interest seemed to go past mere curiosity. When Hadley had first told him about Constance Rapallo, for instance, she had held back because she feared Ernest might criticize or judge her harshly, might even accuse her of immorality or depravity; but when she perceived that the details of hers and Constance's touching and kissing somehow excited him, she found herself dredging up repressed memories, or making up memories, in order to excite him more. She even embroidered a little on the truth when she went on to tell him about Elsa Blackman, her second lesbian "crush," as she called it.

Elsa was the daughter of one of Hadley's mother's oldest friends. Six years older than Hadley, Elsa had supplied the comfort and consolation that she so desperately needed after she had dropped out of Bryn Mawr because of the sorry mess of the Rapallo affair. Returning to the family home in St. Louis, Hadley had suffered attacks of insomnia, despair, depression. She was well on her way to a madhouse or an early grave, she said, until she found in Elsa Blackman someone she could confide in, without fear of being accused of being an evil degenerate. They went for walks in the woods, smoked cigarettes in long holders, cried, laughed, and kissed.

Hadley felt that her experiences were grist for Ernest's fantasy mill, and that these crushes posed no threat to his masculine pride. Nothing she said about Constance Rapallo and Elsa Blackman seemed to cause him any jealousy. It was only when she told him—confessed, under questioning—that she'd had two very short and badly botched love affairs with men before she met Ernest that he showed any signs of jealousy. Sullen and grudging, he wanted to know who the men were, wanted to know in detail when and where she had given herself to them. She said she regretted not being a virgin for him, and hoped she hadn't alienated him by her confession, but he only sulked for a day or two before he forgave her. In exchange, however, he required her to swear that she belonged to him now and would never again give herself to another man.

"Of course not," she assured him. "It's not that I'm something outside of you that belongs to you and can be given away to others; I am you. We're the same fella now, remember?"

She didn't require him to say, in return, that there would never be another woman in his life. In fact, she had occasion to wonder if there weren't one or two other women still in his life, left over from before they met. Katherine Smith, for instance, known as Kate to her friends and family, who was Hadley's chum and classmate from the days of the Mary Institute, the elite St. Louis girls' school they had both attended. It was Kate who brought Hadley to Chicago after Hadley's mother died. It was Kate who introduced her to Ernest. Hadley gathered from the banter and oblique references among the many friends who swarmed around the apartment at 63 Division Street, where Ernest lived with—among others—Kate's two brothers Bill and Y.K. Smith, that Ernest and Kate had once been lovers, perhaps still were, occasionally. They had known each other since they were children at Horton Bay, up in Michigan, where the Smiths and the Hemingways vacationed together at Lake Walloon. But because Kate was six years older than Ernest, he was still a gawky, barefoot adolescent boy when she became a young woman entering adulthood, and so there was no attraction between them then. It wasn't until Ernest returned from the Great War, a full-grown man, handsome and dashing in his Italian lieutenant's uniform and officer's cape, a hero with medals and wounds and boots of Italian leather, that Kate fell in love with him. And before Hadley found out about Kate's feelings, she herself had already fallen in love with him.

Even then Hadley would have considered stepping aside, had she thought she was breaking up a love affair between Ernest and Kate, but Ernest flatly denied that he loved Kate. He loved Hadley, and only Hadley, he said, and Hadley loved Ernest, and they were going to get married, and Kate, realizing that she had lost, decided to be gracious and civilized about it, and so had agreed to be the bride's maid of honor. The whole thing appealed to Ernest's sense of drama, and fed his vanity to be the object of so much female attention.

"But she says she thinks you ought to allow her to wear half mourning," he had told Hadley in a teasing way, chuckling. This was on the Saturday that he took Hadley out to Oak Park to meet his family, and they were returning to Chicago on a streetcar, talking about the upcoming wedding.

"Really?" Hadley said. "Well, if she's going to advertise her heartbreak—"

"No, no," he said. "She was only teasing. She said she'd try to act as if there weren't anything much between us, to keep people from talking. Said she'd try to remember that it's your wedding."

"I don't think I have the right to criticize her, because I feel so guilty about taking you away from her, but how long is she going to carry a torch for you? When is she going to face the facts?"

Ernest chuckled again. "Maybe never. She says she gives us a year at the longest. She thinks you'll be fed up with me by then, and then she'll come to Italy and live with us to hold the home together."

That seemed to appeal to Ernest, the idea of the three of them living together. But just how would she hold the family together? By making it a ménage à trois, perhaps? And the same question arose when Kate, at Ernest's request, agreed to play chaperone during Ernest's first visit to Hadley in St. Louis. Ernest was to come down to meet Hadley's friends and what was left of her family, to see if he could pass muster for the marriage. Since her mother's death, Hadley had lived alone in the large two-story red brick Richardson house on Cabanne Place in St. Louis' strait-laced, Victorian West End, where it would have been fatally scandalous for a young woman living alone to have a young man for an overnight visit without a chaperone. Ernest said, sure, he could understand that, scandal had to be avoided at all costs, but apparently he saw nothing odd about asking Kate, a former lover who was still in love with him, to be that chaperone.

It became even more complex when Ernest made it clear that he expected to make love to Hadley in her house during the visit. They had made love once already, on the roof of the apartment house in Chicago, and now Ernest expected that they would do so at any convenient opportunity, and what better opportunity, with only Kate for a chaperone?

Hadley put Ernest in her bedroom, it being the most comfortable room in the house, though Ernest teased her about it being frilly feminine. She said she would sleep on the living room sofa for the duration of Ernest's visit. Kate was put in the guest room. With that arrangement, Hadley had a perfectly plausible excuse to go back into the room two or three times a night to get something—some medicine, a garment, a cosmetic cream—that she had forgotten there.

But as for making love, the first time she went into the room, Ernest proved to have a slight problem with what Hadley's Bryn Mawr sex education books called "insufficient tumescence." This surprised Hadley, who was not sexually experienced enough to know that a man like Ernest, the epitome of take-charge manhood, might sometimes find it difficult to perform. She was worried—even horrified—that it might be her fault, until she went back to the room a second time. By then Kate had gone to bed and was—presumably—sleeping. Then Ernest performed with such ardor that Hadley was afraid Kate would be awakened by his loud moaning and the squeaking of the bedsprings, and before it was over, Hadley had to wonder if Ernest wanted Kate to hear them. She wondered because what seemed to be the most thrilling moment came just when there was a sudden, sharp rapping on the bedroom door.

"Wemedge," said Kate's voice through the door, using one of Ernest's childhood nicknames, "are you awake?"

"What do you want?" he grunted.

"Hash isn't in the living room. I got worried. She used to talk about suicide a lot, and—"

"She's all right," Ernest said. "Go back to bed."

"Is she in there?" Kate asked, as if she didn't know.

"Of course not," he said, and it was this moment that seemed the most unbearably erotic for him. He climaxed, and the noises he made left no doubt of their cause.

"Oh, I see," Kate said in a hurt, self-pitying voice. "Well, then, I guess I'll go back to bed."

But she waited around outside the door, as if half expecting Ernest to invite her to come in. Was that what gave him such a sudden rush of erotic power? To know that Kate, standing just outside the door, listening, knew what they were doing? And sometime later Hadley wondered if Ernest's climax neutralized the dynamic that had been bringing the three of them together in one bed. Or maybe in Ernest's mind all three had indeed been in the same bed at the same time.

And how would Hadley have felt about that? She couldn't imagine. The only thing she knew was that, with Ernest, she would probably, sooner or later, explore all the possibilities of sexual passion. Just as he had come along during her most need-ful hour, to rescue her from suicide or insanity with joy, with love, so, too, he would open up for her all the wild, dark, incomprehensible thrills of erotic ecstasy. And how could she say no to that? How could she say no to anything Ernest suggested? Even when he playfully suggested that she cut her waist-length hair like Kate's, Hadley hesitated only for a moment before saying, "But won't that make me look like a . . . ?" She didn't finish the comparison. Instead, she sat down in front of a mirror and held her long, copperish red hair up and away from her head, trying to imagine what she would look like if it were short. Women had been shortening their hair only since the Great War, as a way of rebelling against stuffy Victorian values, but it was only girls and young women who were considered to be "fast," of loose morals—the flappers, the liberated women of the big cities—who had cut their hair in boyish bobs. Kate had cut hers years ago, and prided herself on her image. And it was she who turned Ernest's playful suggestion into a serious proposition.

"For God's sake, yes," Kate said, her green cat eyes twinkling with visions of beauty. She stood behind Hadley and raised her long, thick hair in her hands. "Why, it'd do you a world of good. It'd make you look like a new person."

"Oh, but I'd be afraid."

"Of what?" Kate asked.

"But, Ernest," she said to Ernest's reflection in the mirror. He was slumped in an overstuffed chair, smoking a cigarette and drinking coffee, watching with interest. "You said your father told all your sisters that if they ever got their hair bobbed, they'd better not come home."

"What better reason for cutting it?" Ernest asked.

Kate volunteered to do the cutting, and after a little more debate, Hadley, her heart fluttering with fear, experienced a great release of tension when she summoned up all her courage to say, "All right! Let's do it!"

With a pair of shearing scissors, Kate cut huge handfuls of Hadley's hair. She placed it on the dresser in front of Hadley, and when it was all done, when her hair had gone from being about twenty-four inches long to only a few inches, Hadley, though slightly aghast, felt the promise of freedom, even of abandon, welling up in her like a wave that would wash away her old, timid, unhappy, wallflower self and leave her joyously free to be whomever Ernest wanted her to be.

Kate halted for a moment to survey her handiwork. "So what do you think, Wemedge?"

Ernest got up to give Hadley's hair a closer inspection. He ran his fingers through it, grinning, and said, "Maybe just a little more off the back?"

"Hash?" Kate queried.

"Whatever he says," Hadley said. "Why not make it just as short as his? I want to look like him. Only one of us blond, the other dark." To Ernest she added, "And if you let yours grow long, I'll be your boy and you'll be my girl."

And after a few more judicious snips, Kate stepped back for an appraisal. "Well, you do look like a boy, sure enough."

"Good. Wonderful. I'm still a woman, but now I'm a man, too, and I can do anything." And to mark this new attitude, this turning point in her life, she gathered up the great mass of hair that Kate had placed on the dresser and ceremoniously dumped it into a wastebasket. "Good-bye to girlhood," she said.

"Well, it's true, you two look enough alike to be brother and sister," Kate said, which proved to be an observation commonly repeated by people who didn't know quite what else to say about Hadley's new hairdo. But as long as Ernest liked it, Hadley didn't care what anybody else thought or said.

However, she would have thought that the woman of words, Gertrude Stein, could have come up with something more original. But, no, during the whole afternoon and evening of Ernest's and Hadley's visit to 27 rue de Fleurus, the first and only words that Gertrude directed to Hadley were, "When I first saw you together, I thought perhaps you were brother and sister." Then, without even waiting for Hadley's response to that doubtful sop, the Buddha-like Gertrude turned back to Ernest and they resumed their lively tête-à-tête, leaving Hadley once more to the mercy of Alice's conversational diversions, from which she didn't escape until the first guests began to arrive.

Most of the guests seemed to know one another. They all seemed to be regulars, or at least occasional guests, at the Saturday night soirees. Gertrude and Alice made a special effort to include Ernest in the crowd by introducing him to the most important visitors.

"Pablo, this is Ernest Hemingway, a writer, a friend of Sherwood's," Gertrude said. "This is his wife."

Picasso was surprisingly short. Hadley had somehow gotten the idea from his paintings that he must be a big man, maybe even a giant. But he was only about five-foot-four in his high Spanish heels, about two inches taller than Gertrude herself, but not nearly so massive as she. He was short but muscular, like a peasant laborer, and was dressed in a style that indicated a total indifference to clothes. However, tonight he had obviously spent a lot of time on his hair, greased it with something—lard, perhaps, or shoe polish—and sculpted it into a sort of pompadour.

"Americans?" he said, and when Ernest said, "Yes, Chicago,"

Picasso became excited. He spoke a polyglot of good Spanish, fair French, and bad English.

"Chicago! Illinois! Land of Lincoln, *n'est-ce pas?* Tell me truth—" He turned to Ernest and Hadley in profile, like an actor, and ran his hand over his hair to call attention to it. "Am I like anyone you recognize? Eh? Eh? Americans say I look like Lincoln. You know—Abraham. *Qu'est-ce qu'il y a?* I fix my hair just like Lincoln's in the pictures, *n'est-ce pas?* I think I look like him—don't you?"

"Not very much, I'm afraid," Ernest said apologetically. "For one thing, he was about a foot taller than you are."

"Tall? *No dicí* 'tall'." His gesture of disdain was truly Spanish. "I say how I look like him, your Lincoln, I think so. Don't you, Miss Stein?"

"Whatever you say, Pablo, but do come here for a moment, will you, and see this new painting by Picaba. I have it on consideration from Vollard's. You think I should buy it?"

"Pardon," Picasso said, answering Gertrude's summons.

Left alone for the first time since their arrival at the soiree, Hadley finally got a chance to say sotto voce, "Well, you and Miss Stein had quite a chat, didn't you?"

Ernest tilted his head in a gesture of hard-earned admiration. "Amazing woman. Wonderful woman. Said she'd come by our place sometime next week and read some of my work."

They were interrupted by Alice, who introduced them to Jean Cocteau. Ernest tried valiantly to turn a natural snarl into a polite smile as he shook Cocteau's ever-so-elegantly limp fingers. To judge from Ernest's expression, he was probably wondering where that hand had been lately.

"This is his wife," Alice said as an afterthought, then excused herself to greet another guest at the door.

"Hadley Hemingway," Hadley said.

"Comment allez-vous?" Cocteau asked, taking her hand as if it were a proffered rose, raising it halfway to his rouged lips, as if smelling it, and then giving it back to her. *"Parlez-vous français?"*

"Un petit peu," Hadley said.

"Americans," Cocteau said, with the hooded lids and large

pupils and dreamy amiability associated with opiates. "American jazz you like?"

"Oh, yes, we love it," Hadley said.

"My wife plays piano," Ernest said.

"Ah, then you must some evening come, play with us at Le Boeuf. I play drums in jazz band. Le Boeuf sur le Toit, 28 rue Boissy d'Anglas. Please come. You play *le jazz hot?*" he asked, but went on without waiting for her answer. "All best people come to Le Boeuf. Eric Satie plays. Kiki sings. Not a bar, a kind of club, meeting place for all the best people in Paris—writers, musicians, artists, loveliest women, poets . . ." His voice trailed off, as if his opium vision was perhaps doing a kaleidoscopic rearrangement of thoughts, and then—perhaps at last sensing Ernest's antipathy, which plainly showed in his grimacing smile—Cocteau drifted away, floating like a wreath of smoke back to where his lover, Raymond Radiguet, sat with Bernice Abbott, the photographer, on a divan. Radiguet was eighteen years old and had already become well known in Paris for his writing, as well as for his tempestuous love affair with Cocteau.

"Prissy pervert," Ernest said under his breath after Cocteau had gone, and once more Hadley was struck by his double standard of homosexuality: Why would he consider Gertrude Stein a wonderful woman, but dismiss Cocteau as a prissy pervert? Cocteau was gaining fame as a poet and writer, and certainly had more claim to being a genius than Gertrude Stein did. And certainly he was a lot prettier than she. Indeed, in spite of being effete, Cocteau was an exquisitely handsome man. So what was the difference? Only their gender, it seemed. But Hadley didn't ask Ernest to explain himself, not only because she didn't want to get into such a personal discussion while at the soiree, but because Ernest did not like being asked to explain his contradictions. Besides, the issue was only a matter of curiosity to Hadley, not something of vital interest.

Georges Braque, a more normal specimen of manhood, came in holding a young woman in one arm and a concertina in the other. Djuna Barnes was the next to arrive, a beautiful woman with dark red hair—hair a shade darker than Hadley's own. Having read some of her poetry and short stories in *The Little Review* in Chicago, both Hadley and Ernest thought she was a brilliant writer. With Djuna was her lover, Thelma Wood, a silverpoint artist and sculptress of some note, an American. Physically, they seemed an incongruous pair: Djuna, with her stern, alabaster beauty, a natural aristocrat, wearing green, purple, and blue makeup, dressed in a chic ensemble of cape and pearls and silk turban and long ebony cigarette holder; and Thelma, without makeup, a tall, slouchy, freckle-faced, masculine woman, the closest thing to an amazon Hadley had ever seen. Thelma had short, uncombed hair and big feet and was dressed in slacks and a sloppy sweater, as befits a woman who had a reputation for being good with her fists. Hadley hoped Ernest wouldn't invite Thelma down to the gym to spar a few rounds with him.

She needn't have worried. Of that pair, it was Djuna Barnes who stirred Ernest's interest. Ernest left Hadley sitting in a corner with a canapé in one hand and a cup of lukewarm tea in the other while he pursued Miss Barnes around the room and finally finagled an introduction to her. He proved that he had not altogether abandoned Hadley when he brought Miss Barnes to her and introduced them. Up close, Miss Barnes (and one tended to think of her as Miss Barnes, rather than Djuna) was even more bizarrely beautiful than from afar, a beauty that had turned Ernest into a grinning, flushed, excited suitor.

But Hadley didn't have to worry about Ernest getting too friendly with Miss Barnes, for always there, somewhere close by, was Thelma Wood, studying the paintings or slouching against a wall, a cigarette dangling from the corner of her scowling mouth and one eye squinted against the upcurling smoke, the look of a street tough ready for a ruckus.

Gossip around Paris had it that Thelma Wood and Djuna Barnes sometimes got into fistfights, and it was said that Thelma wasn't adverse to engaging men in fisticuffs, either. And so it was with a little trepidation that Hadley saw Thelma approach them from across the room as Ernest and Miss Barnes carried on a little literary chitchat about Miss Barnes' good friend James Joyce.

"I read your piece about him in *Vanity Fair,*" Ernest was saying as Thelma approached. "Damned good. You must know Joyce well. I've got a letter of introduction to him."

Thelma didn't wait to be introduced. With the bravado of being drunk, she simply stepped up to Ernest and said without preamble, "Sylvia Beach told us you're a professional boxer—that true?"

"This is my friend Thelma Wood," Miss Barnes said, trying to blunt with politeness the sharpness of Thelma's tone. "This is Mr. Ernest Hemingway and his wife, Hadley."

Thelma was at least six feet tall, with broad shoulders; big hands; and long, limber arms. Hadley recognized in her husky voice a Missouri accent, and guessed that Thelma had been a rakehell tomboy in her day. She shook hands with Ernest and Hadley—big hands, firm grip—but wasted no words on conversational pleasantries.

"Are you?" she demanded of Ernest. "A professional?"

"Oh, well, I've had a few fights," Ernest answered with guarded modesty and a little confusion, obviously uncertain of Thelma's motive for asking.

"Would you teach me?" Thelma asked.

"You?" Ernest said. "You want to learn to fight?"

"I was raised on a farm with a bunch of brothers, used to stand toe-to-toe with 'em and slug it out. So I know how to fight. What I want to do is learn how to box. Could you teach me?"

"Well. Sure. Okay. If you want to learn, okay, I guess," Ernest answered in a voice that betrayed some of his old prickly combativeness. "But if you think you can take advantage by being a woman, I might have to knock you on your ass."

"I'll look forward to that," Thelma shot back, then drained her glass of liquor and went to get a refill.

5

Joyce

WHEN JAMES JOYCE came to Shakespeare and Company one day in late March to pick up his mail and perhaps put the touch on Sylvia for another small loan, he found among his letters one that not only had no postage or postmark but had the soiled, wrinkled look of having been carried around by hand for a while. It was from Sherwood Anderson, a letter introducing a young American writer recently relocated to Paris. Joyce thought the letter was somewhat presumptuous, since he had only met Anderson himself briefly the year before and, although friendly enough for mere acquaintances, they had hardly become friends, hardly indebted to each other for favors. He asked Sylvia about this young man, this Hemingway fellow, and was told about Hemingway's plan to smuggle copies of *Ulysses* into the United States from Canada in trucks hauling bootleg whiskey. Joyce was amused by the idea. When asked what sort of man this Hemingway was, Sylvia said guardedly as she lit another cigarette, "Brawny. A boxer. Or so he says. And a skier. Intelligent. Aggressively charming, though not too pushy. He had that letter to you for over a month."

"Rich?" It seemed to Joyce that most Americans he met were rich and were therefore usually good for a touch. Robert McAlmon, for instance—now there was the kind of American Joyce liked: young, unlearned, glad to be of use, brash, a good drinking companion, and rich—rich enough to send Joyce 150 dollars each and every month. This stipend was always referred to as a loan, but Joyce had never repaid any of it, and McAlmon obviously didn't expect him to.

Sylvia smiled and made a lightly dismissive gesture with the hand that held the cigarette. "Not to hear him tell it. He'll lead you to think he's a starving orphan, but he comes from Oak Park, Illinois, a wealthy suburb of Chicago, so his family must have at least a little money." She paused, uncertain. "If he comes from Oak Park, that is." Another brief pause. "And if he has a family." She tapped the ashes from her cigarette into the ashtray on the table. "With him, it's hard to tell."

Joyce sat across the table from her, smoking, toying with an empty tea cup. Beneath his rimless glasses, he wore a black eye patch over his left eye. He wore a small, snap-brimmed felt hat, and smoked his cigarettes from a long, ivory holder held in long, limp fingers. On the fingers were a number of ornate rings. One of the rings, made of many metals, Joyce wore as a good-luck charm against blindness. His clothes—an odd mixture of bow tie, brocaded vest, and canvas tennis shoes—made him look like a barber who had fallen on hard times, but the rings and the cigarette holder and the blackthorn walking stick he carried established his dignity and his aloofness from the common herd. He sat with his legs crossed, his right foot entwined behind the calf of his left leg.

"He has a jolly wife," Sylvia continued in the face of Joyce's momentary preoccupation, "a few years older than himself. Mrs. Joyce might like her."

"Might she?" he asked, still preoccupied.

"Yes. How is Nora?"

"Nora? Oh, as fine and strong as ever. Sends you her regards."

"Has she gotten used to Paris yet?"

"No, I fear not. She and the children haven't much French yet. Nora speaks English and Italian, but the children speak only Italian, and sometimes, when we have guests who speak only French or English, the apartment sounds a little like the Tower of Babel must have. Just the other day Nora said to the concierge, 'I don't want to make you an experience.' " He made small, almost inaudible, chuckling sounds in his throat. "What she meant was, she didn't want to put him to any trouble. The man gave her a fishy look, I can tell you. 'I don't want to make you an experience'!" Another dry chuckle, savoring the incident. But then his face abruptly turned somber. As he took the butt from his cigarette holder and stubbed it out in the overflowing ashtray, he said, "But the truth is, the poor woman is worried. I had another attack of iritis recently." He held both hands over his eyes. "The pain was nearly unbearable. I rolled around on the floor, weeping like a child. I had to be taken to the hospital in Neuilly."

"Oh, I'm so sorry," Sylvia said with heartfelt sympathy. "I hope the doctors were able to help."

"They applied leeches to drain the blood from the eyes, and then an injection of the cocaine solution into the eyeballs to stop the pain, as usual. But the prognosis . . ." His voice faded into a despairing silence.

"Yes?"

"Not good." He was softened by the warm, comforting vibrations of Sylvia's sympathy, which made it easier for him to broach the subject of borrowing more money from her. His dignity made this disclosure of his affairs a complicated and grave procedure. "Another operation is indicated, I fear. An iridectomy, the doctors say."

"Oh, no, Jim." It was one of the rare times she addressed him by his first name, and—also a rare intimacy—reached across the table to place a hand on his forearm. "Not another one, so soon."

He nodded. "They fear glaucoma *foudroyant*—the disease that is believed to have caused Homer's blindness." He snorted. "What cruel precision—eh?—that Fate, it seems, is striking me, as it did Beethoven, in the very organ necessary for the practice of my art! Well!" he said, trying to summon up the strength to bear his misfortunes. "But, there, I do have the faithful support of a good wife, to say nothing of your own patience and sympathy, Miss Beach."

The use of her last name reestablished the formality that banished the familiarity of her touch; she withdrew her hand from his arm.

"Even so," he went on, "I find of late that there are more and more moments when I have nothing in my heart but rage and despair—a blind man's rage and despair."

"Well, I'm sure you know you will always have my sympathy and support," Sylvia said. "Is there anything I can do?"

He tipped his head resignedly, and finally came to the crux of the matter. "Well, there is the expense of the doctors and hospitals. . . . How much am I indebted to you now, Miss Beach?"

She shrugged slightly, trying to make it seem a matter of indifference, though her tone took on a businesslike edge. "About forty thousand francs, the last time I looked."

"Would it be possible, do you think . . . ?"

He didn't have to say more. As she lit another cigarette, she said, "Of course we can do something for you. I've asked my sister Holly for a loan of ten thousand francs. She's having a little trouble raising it on such short notice, she said, but I expect it'll be here in a day or two. Will that be soon enough?"

"Yes, and I'm sorry to . . . to make you an experience." A momentary smile, thin and mirthless, flickered on his thin lips, then vanished. "I was hoping that the subscriptions would have brought in enough by now. . . ."

"The subscriptions for *Ulysses* are pouring in, as I mentioned, but the books themselves are not. We're only getting about fifty a week, and the printer insists that his contract payments be kept current with the deliveries, which means he has to be paid off before we begin paying royalties." She shrugged again.

He untwined his legs and rose unsteadily to his feet. "So be it. I have every confidence in you, Miss Beach . . . Nora and I will be grateful . . . finances always a burden . . ."

"I understand."

They parted company on that note. He gathered his overcoat and blackthorn walking stick, tucked his mail into the inside pocket of his coat, and set out for the Café Voltaire on the Place de l'Odeon, where he would dine on an omelette accompanied by a glass of white wine. He seldom drank any alcohol during the day while he was working. The doctors had ordered him not to drink any at all, because it was very bad for the glaucoma, but to give up drink entirely was simply beyond him. He was an

Irishman, after all. Besides, how many pleasures did a blind man have? So his daily consumption usually amounted to several bottles of white wine between eight o'clock in the evening and the wee hours of the morning, and though it was still early, he felt that he might indulge himself in a glass or two. After sixteen years of thinking about *Ulysses,* and seven years writing it, he believed he was entitled to disregard constrictive habits of time. And this prospect, combined with the relief he felt at receiving Miss Beach's promise of more money in a day or so, made him feel almost jaunty. He twirled his blackthorn every few steps, and hummed a bit of "Finnegan's Wake."

> Tim Finnegan lived in Walking Street
> A gentleman Irish mighty odd.
> He had a tongue both rich and sweet
> . . . Tum tum tee tum. . . .
> With a love of the liquor he was born. . . .

Ah, he loved to sing the old songs. And how much gayer was a singer's life than a writer's! Nora had probably been right, always telling him that he should have stuck to singing and let the writing go. He'd be rich and famous now, she said, if he had. Sure, and wouldn't she be proud to see him standing on a musical stage, singing his heart out? Ah, Nora had no love for the literary life. But she was a good woman, a strong woman, just what he needed, someone to take him in hand.

He always smiled whenever he used that expression with regard to her, remembering that night so long ago in Dublin—June 16, 1904—when he first took Nora Barnacle out walking toward the harbor, to Ringsend, which was deserted at night. Nora, a chambermaid at Finn's boardinghouse, had to be back at her job by half past eleven, and so she wasted no time. After a few kisses, she took him in hand, thereby revealing that she knew how to please a man without losing her virtue. This discovery caused Joyce much jealous torment in the years to come, wondering how she knew what to do to him—by experience or intuition? But for those moments at Ringsend he felt only grateful astonishment as she unbuttoned his trousers, slipped her hand in, pushed his shirt aside, and jerked him off into her handkerchief. But why into the handkerchief? Perhaps she had taken the handkerchief back with her as a remembrance? But he had always been afraid to ask her that; what if she had such souvenirs from other men? It might be better not to know.

The Café Voltaire was not crowded in the early evening. Joyce found a table by a window and had his omelette and was enjoying a second glass of wine when he caught sight of something peculiar. He couldn't be sure of what he was seeing through the steam-clouded window, but it appeared that a man was approaching the café in the grip of some sort of spastic movement—a dance, perhaps? But then, just before the man entered the café and ceased his jerky, flailing movements, Joyce recognized what the man had been doing: shadowboxing—walking and skipping along the street, throwing punches at an imaginary opponent. Joyce found this quite curious, and then to his curiosity was added a distinct shiver of excitement and dread as the strange young man came into the café, looked around for a moment, and then came straight to Joyce's table.

"Hello," he said. "You're Mr. James Joyce, aren't you? Sylvia Beach said you might be here." He held out his hand. "I'm Ernest Hemingway."

"Ah," Joyce said, struggling to disentwine his legs and stand up to shake hands. Hemingway motioned him to stay seated, for which Joyce was grateful. And because he was slightly afraid of the mighty paw sticking out toward him, he only offered half of his limp fingers for the shake. Hemingway frowned and grunted with what could have been construed to be disapproval of such a sissified shake. A burly American, he no doubt would have preferred a firm, manly, hard-pumping handshake, but such robust friendliness was beyond Joyce. He asked the young man if he'd care to sit down and join him in a drink.

"Thanks," Hemingway said. "I just wanted to tell you I read *Ulysses,* and I think it's a goddamn wonderful book."

"Ah," Joyce said, and that was all, and it was not a response conducive to conversation. He had very little capacity for chitchat. He felt ill at ease with new acquaintances, and envied men like Hemingway and Ezra Pound, those raw, blustering men from the heartland of America, who seemed afraid of nothing.

When the waiter came and asked what the young man would have, Hemingway asked Joyce, "What's that you're drinking?"

"The only thing I ever drink," Joyce said. "A Swiss wine, *Fendant de Sion,* which nobody seems to like but me." Amused by his own cast of mind, he added with a flicker of a smile, "It's quaintly comparable to urine, I think—an archduchess' urine, to be sure, but urine nonetheless."

Hemingway ordered another glass of piss for *le monsieur* and a whiskey for himself. Joyce's inclination was to decline, thinking he might have had enough, and that Nora would be angry, but he couldn't summon up the courage to say no. He had to admit that he was a little frightened by this young man—frightened and, at the same time, fascinated, as big, extroverted men always frightened and fascinated him. He saw himself as a passive man who was, in one way or another, in retreat before threatening masculinity.

"I read *Dubliners,*" Hemingway announced.

"Ah," Joyce said.

"Nobody's ever written better short stories. How old were you when you wrote them?"

"Twenty."

Hemingway seemed slightly incredulous for a moment, even speechless. "Twenty!" He seemed mentally to be counting on his fingers. "But I thought they only came out about five years ago."

"They were turned down by twenty-two publishers, that's why it took so long to bring them out."

"No shit?"

"The same for *Portrait of the Artist as a Young Man.* It was turned down by every publisher to whom it was offered—a dozen or so, at least—until Ezra Pound persuaded the *Egoist* in England to bring it out, and even then about twenty printers in England and Scotland refused to set the type for it. Have you read it?"

"Yeah, sure," Hemingway said unconvincingly, then chuckled and hurried on. "Well, gee, you sure do stir 'em up, don't you? I hope I can stir 'em up a little, too, with my novel."

"Ah. Yes. Well, Mr. Anderson did mention in his letter that you were a writer. You're writing a novel, then?" With each glass of wine, Joyce found it easier to chat, and it helped that Hemingway's robust masculinity was proving to be more boyishly charming than threatening.

"That's what I came to Paris for. 'Course I have to keep writing for newspapers to make a living, but . . . well, have to eat and pay the rent."

"Impossible to make a living writing literature, of course. I had to teach languages for Berlitz schools around Europe for years, starving all the time." Pause. "Still am, for that matter. Starving, I mean." He was automatically softening Hemingway up for a small loan. It was true that Hemingway looked poor—quite poor, as a matter of fact—but Joyce guessed that to be only camouflage. All Americans were rich.

"Yeah, I know," Hemingway said. "Sometimes we get so broke I have to go down to the Luxembourg Gardens and catch a few pigeons just to have something to eat. But thank God writing isn't the only way I have of making a little money now and then. I go down to Leida's Gym now and then and hire out as a sparring partner for the pro boxers."

"Good Lord," Joyce said, genuinely impressed. "You must be the only writer I've ever met who's also a boxer."

"Me? Oh, I'd say it was the other way around. I'm a boxer who's also a writer. My writing is nothing, my boxing is everything."

Joyce could find nothing else to say.

"Say, I hear you used to live over on rue Cardinal Lemoine, in Larbaud's flat," Hemingway said. "That's just across the street from where we live now, at 74, next door to the bal musette." When Joyce affirmed this with only a nod, Hemingway continued, trying to find a subject that would counteract the alcoholic stupor that Joyce seemed to be sinking into. "That's not where I do my work, though. The apartment proved too small. No privacy. My wife likes to play the piano, and—"

"Ah, the piano," Joyce sighed.

Hemingway waited for a moment to see if Joyce was going to pursue that. When he didn't, Hemingway went on, "So I rented a studio on rue Descartes. It's at 38, the studio where Paul Verlaine was supposed to have died in 1896."

"Ah," Joyce said. "I know the place. Verlaine, yes. Odd fellow."

"Queer, you mean."

"A bugger, yes." Joyce smiled. "When I lived in Paris the first time, some years ago, I used to practice my French, and make a few francs on the side, by translating Verlaine's poetry." And without any encouragement, he began reciting in a soft, poignant, Irish voice:

I think upon
A day gone by
And I weep.
Away! Away!
I must obey
This drier wind,
Like a dead leaf
In aimless grief
Drifting blind.

"Say, that's great. 'Aimless grief.' That's great. Remember any more of his stuff?"

With a small, piquant smile, Joyce said, "Someday perhaps I shall recite to you his greatest masterpiece." He raised his glass in salute to Verlaine's unseen presence. "His incomparable 'Ode to the Arsehole'!" He finished his wine. "But it would only be appropriate if it were recited in the bal musette where he wrote it—the Gipsy Bar, in the Latin Quarter. Have you been there?"

Hemingway ordered another whiskey for himself and another glass of wine for Joyce. He was obviously beginning to enjoy being with Joyce and was trying to keep him talking. "So you lived in Paris before? This is not your first time?"

"I lived here for four months in 1904. By myself. Studying medicine and starving to death, making myself repellent to all and sundry, cursing God, the Catholic Church, myself, the day of my birth." Though Joyce's voice was still soft and there was more mockery in his words than anger, he became aware that he was becoming more voluble than usual. This he attributed to a subtle change in his feelings toward Hemingway. He was beginning to feel comfortable with the young man, beginning to see that the young man's masculinity, rather than threatening, could actually be protective. "Had I not been challenged to a duel," he continued, "I might have stayed here, in which case I'd be a doctor today. Such are the vicissitudes."

"A duel? You were seriously challenged to a duel?" Hemingway seemed to find this most exciting. "How come? Over a woman?"

"No. Over the Holy Catholic Church. One day in a café, much like this one, well into my cups, I was making some remarks about the buggering Pope to an excitable young man who took offense. He challenged me to a duel."

"What did you do?"

"Being without funds, I ran to find my fellow Irishman John Millington Synge, who was staying at the Hotel Corneille at the time, begged him for some money, and took the next boat back to Dublin."

The excitement and admiration that had been gathering in Hemingway's expression faded into disappointment, though he did seem to reserve a readiness to be convinced that Joyce was joking. "You ran?"

"Just as fast as I could," Joyce said, and in response to Hemingway's look of disappointment: "Literary courage I have; physical courage, none."

"You were never a soldier?"

"Good God!" Joyce hooted softly, and then, sensing that Hemingway was once again taking on a vaguely threatening quality, he added in a tone intended to avert offense, "You were?"

"I was," Hemingway asserted, like an Irishman—not just "Yes," but "I was"—as if the assertion itself might snatch some pride of manhood from the taint of Joyce's disparagement.

"Ah," Joyce said, retreating into his customary timorousness. "Well! I must be going, I believe," he added in a beg-pardon tone.

"Oh, I'm sorry," Hemingway said, repenting his assertiveness, seeing that he was scaring Joyce away. "I was hoping you could show me where the Gipsy Bar is, where Verlaine used to hang out. I'd like to buy you a drink, and maybe get you to recite 'Ode to the Arsehole.' "

As Joyce tipsily struggled to his feet, Hemingway jumped up and reached out to touch his elbow and steady him, once again with a boyish, ingratiating grin. "You okay? Here, let me give you a hand with that." He helped Joyce into his overcoat. "Come on, how about it? Shall we get you a taxi to the Gipsy Bar?"

At first Joyce was inclined to forgo a visit to the Gipsy Bar. It was a notorious gathering place for sailors, *poules,* apaches, hoodlums, and street toughs, many of whom might see in Joyce a defenseless victim, easy prey. But Hemingway's assumption of a caretaker's role caused Joyce to reconsider. Maybe Hemingway would be a protector, after all. And Joyce did feel a tug of nostalgia for the old bal musette. He hadn't visited the place in almost twenty years now, and he did remember it fondly as just the kind of low, sordid place that he and Verlaine loved.

"You wouldn't be afraid of the lowlife clientele there?" Joyce asked as he tottered toward the door, with Hemingway providing a steadying hand on his arm.

"Fwaid of nothin'!" Hemingway said in a comic tone, jutting his jaw pugnaciously.

"Well, but you must promise to see me home safely if I become incapacitated by drink."

"I promise."

"Otherwise I'm likely to pass out in the gutter," Joyce said, recalling those days in Trieste when he would get drunk and pass out on the street and remain there until some policemen came along to roust him, or until Nora, poor Nora, big with child, angry and weeping, would find him sometime in the wee hours of the morning and get him home. Sure, those were hard times for Nora, bless her heart, and now if he happened to pass out while on his way home, he was confident that Hemingway would carry him the rest of the way. Besides, it was good to have company, and while he himself had no need to fill every silence with words, Hemingway seemed willing to do so, and all it took to keep the garrulous young man going was a grunted response now and then, a nod of interest, a question.

Hemingway had to hold Joyce's arm to steady him as they

went to the curb and flagged a taxi. He helped Joyce into the
backseat, then went around and got in the other side. They both
lit cigarettes and felt the buoyancy of being on an impromptu
adventure as the taxi made its way through the thick, loud traffic
along Boulevard du Montparnasse. Making conversation, Hemingway asked Joyce if he had ever been skiing.

"Skiing? Good God, no."

"My wife and I just got back. Went to Chamby. In the Swiss
Alps, above Montreux. We're going back next winter. Maybe you
and your wife would like to join us? We've got a wonderful
pension there, and it's cheap."

"I'm sure it would be very hard on the trees when I went down
the mountain, blind as I am. And Nora . . . !" The thought of
Nora on skis almost brought a laugh of delight. "Sure, that would
be a sight to see, that would, Nora going slippity-bang down a
mountain on a pair of skis."

"But we could bobsled, the four of us could," Hemingway
suggested. "We could be a team. It'd be swell fun." He managed
to control his growing excitement for only a moment, and then
rushed on, as if the memories were as intense as the experiences. "We climbed Cape du Moine, my wife and I did—seven
thousand feet—and then just sat down on the bobsled and let go
and coasted down the mountain. A wonderful ride. The four of
us could do that."

"Nora would like that, I expect," Joyce said, wondering if she
would be attracted to young Hemingway. She was a handsome
woman still, Nora was, a woman who had grown handsomer
with time, and her body had become fuller with the warm juices
of life swelling to overflowing behind her usual facade of fussy
matronhood. Joyce had heard her sigh in the nights with the
boredom of being unfulfilled. And because his own desire
seemed to be failing fast, he had of late begun to take a certain
shadowy pleasure in observing her attraction for other men. To
see other men want her made him want her.

"You're a happily married man, are you?" he asked Hemingway as the taxi bumped along. It was merely a conversational
question, not a prying one, but it seemed to have struck an
untuned chord in Hemingway.

"I don't know," he said. "This married life, sometimes I wonder about it. My friends back in Chicago warned me not to get married. Don't get me wrong, Hadley's the best, but . . . goddamn, sometimes I miss being free. Don't you?"

"Free?" Joyce didn't even quite understand the concept. But, drunk enough now to be getting a little talkative, it pleased him to say, "I think I'm much freer now than I was before Nora and I became a couple. The tyranny of sex, that's what I finally escaped, with her help. Going about with a hard-on half the time, looking for something to put it in—that's not what I call freedom. Not I. Slavery, more like. Sex, that's the real slavery."

"Yeah, I guess I can see what you mean."

"No, young man, you'll pardon me if I doubt that you do, unless you were born and raised in a Catholic country like Ireland, and since there's no other country like her, I doubt you can imagine to what lengths a supposedly civilized people will go to stamp out lustful thoughts. Why, my mother, bless her soul, good woman that she was, could spot a lustful thought in my head as easily as she could spot a louse on it. And for both I'd get a good dousing: kerosene for the lice, the toilet bowl for the lustful thoughts."

"The toilet bowl? You mean . . . ?"

"I mean she'd stick my head into the toilet bowl."

Hemingway supplied a sympathetic groan.

Puffing on a cigarette through its long holder, Joyce said in an amused voice, "If the critics are correct who say that I confuse sex with the excretory functions, perhaps that's why."

"Is that what they say?"

"Among other things." After a moment of silence, he added, "And I suspect they may be correct in that, at least."

"They said that about Verlaine."

"Yes, yes, just like our friend Verlaine. How is it to work in his studio, by the by? Does the ghost of the old bugger ever visit you?"

"No. Too bad. If he did, I'd try to get him to recite that smutty poem of his you translated—what was it? 'Ode to the Arsehole'?"

Joyce smiled one of his rare smiles. Drunk enough now to be

totally relaxed, and feeling secure in Hemingway's presence, he allowed a smile to reflect the merriment he sometimes derived from reading Verlaine's lewd poetry. "Ah, sure," he mused, "it's a lovely little lyric, that is. You'll see when we get there. I'll recite it in honor of Verlaine, the bugger, in the place where he wrote it—perhaps at the very table."

"How late does this place stay open?"

"All night—or until the last customer leaves. Later, if you like, we can go to Les Halles for a breakfast of onion soup."

"If I stay out all night, my wife will worry. Won't yours?"

"Perhaps, but over the years I have built up an immunity to her scolding."

"And you like married life?" Hemingway asked, as if he couldn't quite believe that anyone would. "I mean, you don't get tired of it sometimes? The same old shit?"

"No, no, I can hardly get through the routine of one day without Nora. I don't believe there's been a day in our marriage that would've been better without her."

"Damn, how I envy you! How long you been married?"

"We've been together now since June 16, 1904, but . . ." He gave a little shrug and paused for a moment, wondering how much openness and confidentiality might be warranted by the circumstances, and then decided to confide in Hemingway, though what he had to confide was not really a secret, and was never intended to be. "Officially, of course, Nora and I are not married. We've never had a license, and no priest has performed a ceremony, and I'm proud of her—proud of her courage to stand with me in open defiance of both the church and the state."

As the taxi made its way through the crowded traffic of Boulevard St. Michel, Joyce was becoming downright garrulous. Most people thought of him as being dour and taciturn, as indeed he was most of the time, but talking was like singing: it was something he loved to do, but seldom did in public. Once in a while, however, he felt like doing a conversational aria, as it were.

"Why not? I mean, if you're going to live together . . ."

"But why should I require her to go before a priest or a lawyer and vow to love, honor, and obey me for the rest of her life?

How could I ask her to swear away her life to me? The ignominy and slavishness of it all! Who are they to tell us who we can love? And when and how and in what positions to have sex? How dare they!"

They had turned into rue Cujas and were going by the Pantheon as Joyce was saying, "No, no, no, I totally reject the whole present social order and Christianity—all religious doctrines, in fact. My mind rejects the recognized virtues, the idea of home, of social classes, and especially—most especially—the poppycock of popery. How could it be otherwise, coming from the home I did? There were fifteen of us children—*fifteen*—got upon my mother between my father's beatings. Ill treatment by my father, that's what killed her—that, and the Church's insistence that she breed, breed, breed. 'More Catholics! Give us more Catholics,' the priests cry! And I did not make her dying any easier with my own cynical frankness of conduct. I wouldn't kneel beside her bed, you see, as she begged me to do, when she was dying. Sure, I had left the Church, hating it most fervently, and I would be damned before I would go down on my knees, even if it was my mother's dying wish. And when she lay in her coffin and I looked upon that face, gray and wasted with ill-use and suffering, I saw that she had been a victim all her life, a pathetic victim. And I cursed the system that made her that."

The taxi had stopped in front of the Gipsy Bar. Joyce was still talking as he refused to let Hemingway pay the taxi fare, carelessly pulling out a handful of loose francs and coins from his pocket, spilling some on the street, and still talking as he, with Hemingway holding him by the arm to steady him, shambled rubber-legged into the Gipsy Bar.

The barroom was loud, crowded, smoke-filled, stinking of sweating bodies and overflowing urinals and spilled wine, the ceiling festooned with multicolored streamers that moved languidly in the air stirred by the ceiling fans, with a big ball made multifaceted by mirrors that hung from the center of the ceiling to cast flickering reflected lights like confetti over the dancers and drinkers. This was Joyce's kind of place. To hell with the barons and ducs and princes that Proust was so enamored of.

Here were the sailors and servant girls and chambermaids and whores among whom Joyce felt at home.

Of course he would never have come without Hemingway, for there were often fistfights in the place, and sometimes even knife fights. But he felt fairly safe with Hemingway. He had Hemingway pegged as a man who liked to show off, a man who could be manipulated into playing the hero, allowing Joyce the possibility of escaping without injury, should there be a fight.

Most of the customers were at the bar, where drinks were half price, but Hemingway and Joyce found a table—solidly bolted to the floor against its use as a weapon in brawls—in one corner of the room away from the small bandstand. Accompanied by an accordion player, a chanteuse sang rowdy waltzes and languorous tangos and bawdy sea chanties.

A waiter brought Joyce a bottle of *Fendant de Sion*. Hemingway ordered cognac. They drank a toast to Verlaine.

"May his spirit be among us," Joyce said. "By any chance do you feel him near?"

"No," Hemingway said, quite droll. "Maybe he needs an invocation. Try calling him up by reciting some of his poetry."

"Splendid idea! Yes. What, though? I know!" Joyce began reciting in a voice loud enough to be heard above the musical duo on the bandstand, but the music suddenly ended after only a few words of the poem, and nearly everyone in the barroom heard Joyce as he, with liquored gusto, continued at the same volume.

> O fairies, O buggers,
> Eunuchs exotic!
> Come running, come running,
> Ye anal-erotic!
> With soft little hands,
> With flexible bums,
> Come, O Castrati,
> Unnatural ones!

"How's that?" Joyce asked. "A sufficient invocation for the old bugger, do you think?"

"That's one of his?" Hemingway asked, and when Joyce nodded, he added, "Is it part of the 'Ode to the Arsehole'?"

"Oh, no, that's another one. That's—"

They were interrupted by two girls—poules, probably—who had heard and been impressed by Joyce's recital. Even though they couldn't understand English, they knew poetry when they heard it.

One of them asked in French, "Is the poet someone whose English cannot be translated?"

The girls were dressed in the latest lower-class fashion: skirts with suspenders, satin blouses, and spit curls—kiss curls, some called them—that seemed standard for tarts and poules, like identification badges. The kiss curls were small coiled locks of hair flattened onto their foreheads or temples and held in place by a pomade as shiny as shoe polish. One was wearing a beret on the side of her head, the other a cloche hat.

"No, no. Verlaine. One of the great French poets," Joyce said, speaking French. "Would you like to hear it in French? Sit. Join us. Order a drink. I'll do it in the original French."

Eager for free drinks and the company of big-spending foreigners, the two girls were quick to accept the invitation, and they listened with scandalized smiles as Joyce recited Verlaine's poem in French.

"Oh, mon Dieu! What filth," they said. "He must be French all right, this Verlaine."

"Here's another one for you," Joyce announced. "First in English for my friend here, then in French for you."

This was about as close as Joyce would ever get to being manic. With Hemingway for protection; with enough alcohol in him to put him on the cusp where the upward curve of euphoria would reverse directions and plunge him into torpor or even unconsciousness; with poetry in his mouth and attractive young women hanging on his every word, all that was joyous in Joyce arose.

Because the musical duo had taken a break, Joyce was noticed by everybody in his close vicinity. Even from across the dance floor came the sardonic comment of a man who was clearly

another Irishman: "Bedad, how do you like that! A paddy spouting poetry in Paris!"

"Wait," said Hemingway, who was also drunk by now and
getting into the spirit of helping Joyce to make a fool of himself.
He patted the tabletop and said, "You need a stage. Can you
stand? Come on, we'll help you—won't we, girls?" he added in
French.

Joyce was a little uncertain about this sort of daredevilry, but
before good sense could prevail over his drunkenness and rare
manic extravagance, Hemingway and the two poules had
cleared the table of drinks and ashtrays and were physically tug-
ging Joyce's limp body out of the chair.

"We'll support you! Don't worry, we'll support you," said the
girls in French. "The table is bolted down."

"Use the chair as a step, up you go," Hemingway coaxed.

And before Joyce quite realized what was happening, he found
himself standing on the table, weaving back and forth, with
Hemingway and the laughing girls propping him up.

"Okay," Hemingway announced to the audience, "here we go,
a poetic recital, 'Ode to the Arsehole.' "

Once it became clear that they weren't going to turn loose and
let him fall, Joyce was glad enough to become the cabaret per-
former. Using his walking stick as a stage prop, he struck poses
as he recited his translation of the poem.

> That female arse, oh, such a nest for our caress!
> I hug it kneeling, and then lick its puncture, while
> My fingers play in the other moist defile
> Or tease the fine breasts' loose and lecherous laziness.
> But to compare the arse of man to this good bum,
> This coarse posterior less for pleasure than for use
> To the male buttocks, joy of joys and view of views—

That was as far as he got. His legs began to wobble out of
control, he tottered and fell off the table. Hemingway caught
him. His hat came off and his glasses were knocked askew, but
Hemingway's strength saved him from any injury. Hemingway
deposited his body onto the chair. The laughing poules put his

hat back on and straightened his glasses over his eye and eye patch. And hardly had the scattered applause for his poetry recital died down than he was jolted by an apparition appearing in front of him. As bad as his eyesight was, and as close to besotted numbness as his brain was, he could still spot a fellow countryman. Bandy-legged little bastard, he was, with the map of Ireland on his gob.

"Aye, another paddy a long way from home, is it?" the man asked, holding out his hand for a shake. He, too, was quite drunk and unsteady on his legs.

Joyce was reluctant to deliver his hand into that work-hardened claw.

"Yes, happy to—*oww.*"

"Me mates and me," the Irishman said, gesturing toward three more drunk Irishmen sitting at a table across the room "have been on a merchant ship for ages now, and, sure, we long for a sight of the old sod. We're from Dublin, how about yourself?"

"Dublin, also," Joyce croaked, and cleared his throat with another gulp of wine. "Damn the place to hell."

"What?" the cocky Irishman said. "You don't like our Dublin?"

"Dublin," Joyce said with uncontrollable venom, "is the gray, sunken cunt of the world." But he immediately regretted it, seeing the quick, combative look come over the Irishman's face.

"Oh! The gray, sunken cunt of the world, is it? Well, now, boy-o, I won't be allowing that to be said of me hometown by the likes of a Paris fairy like yourself, see? Even if you are a paddy." In a quick, jerky way, he planted his feet and assumed the classic pose of the great bare-knuckle heavyweight champion John L. Sullivan. He was so drunk that he probably could have been knocked down with a small thump, but he was as combative as he was drunk. "On your feet, boy-o! Prepare to defend yourself."

Joyce clutched at Hemingway's arm and pleaded, "Deal with him, Hemingway, deal with him."

Hemingway got to his feet and slowly brought himself to his full height, with a half smile on his face, as if, true to Joyce's assumption, he enjoyed the chance to show off. But instead of socking the Irishman, Hemingway said in a calm and reasonable voice, "My friend doesn't fight." He towered over the Irishman by about eight inches and outweighed him by at least fifty pounds.

"And who the hell are you?" the Irishman asked.

"My name is Ernest Hemingway, known professionally as War-path Hemingway, and I'm the tenth-ranked heavyweight boxer in the world," he said, and sounded convincing.

"Glory be! Well, my argument's not with you, Yank."

"But my friend can't stand up to fight, and being an honorable man that I'm sure you are, you wouldn't want to hit a fellow Irishman who was too drunk to defend himself and blind, to boot, would you, now? In spite of his opinion of Dublin." Hemingway was speaking in a winking, conspiratorial tone, as if he and the Irishman were friends behind Joyce's back, making it easy for the Irishman to back down from his threat.

"Aye, you're right, no doubt," the Irishman conceded, giving up his John L. Sullivan stance. "He ain't responsible. Well, good luck to you in your fights, Champ." He shook hands with Hemingway before he turned and strode cockily back to his seamen friends, leaving Joyce relieved but puzzled.

"You didn't hit him," Joyce said, wondering if he had been wrong in assuming that Hemingway would use such an opportunity to show off his prowess.

"It would've been a pleasure, but if I'd hit him, I'd've had to fight all of them, him and his three friends, at the same time. Bad odds."

"Yes," Joyce said with a shudder of apprehension. "Let's get out of here, shall we? They're Irishmen, they'll likely want to fight before the night's over, just to complete the evening, and I don't want to be here when it happens."

But the poules didn't want them to go. "We like poets. You don't like us? There's a room upstairs. We could all go up and have a good time. The rough sailors won't bother you there."

As Hemingway finished his drink, Joyce apologized to the girls and gave them a few francs to appease them, then found that he was too drunk to stand up, close to passing out. Hemingway assessed the situation. He pulled Joyce up, held his skinny body against his own, and maneuvered him toward the door.

Once outside, Hemingway looked around for a taxi, but the bleak, twisting street was without any kind of traffic. Whores and their customers and their pimps stood in the dark doorways in the vicinity of the bar, the glow of their cigarettes lighting their faces, but otherwise the late-night street was without signs of life.

"How are we going to get you home?"

"It's paralyzed, I am," Joyce said, finding that he couldn't even stand without Hemingway's help, let alone walk. "Don't abandon me, Hemingway. Those Irish dogs will come out and tear me apart."

"Well, then, I'll have to carry you over my shoulder, I guess, like a sack of oats."

"Oh, no," Joyce said, feeling his gorge rise. "Upside down, I'll lose me hat, me glasses, and everything I've drunk tonight. The blood will rush to me head, I'll be ruined entirely."

"Well, we can't do it like this, it'd take all night. Here, sit here for a minute." He sat Joyce down on the curb and leaned him against a lamppost.

"You're not going to abandon me, surely?"

"No, no. Wait a minute." He had spotted a wheelbarrow among some building materials under a stairwell. He brought the wheelbarrow out. "This'll do. After I get you home, I'll bring it back. It'll be on my way home, anyway."

He sat Joyce in the wheelbarrow, facing forward, his legs dangling over the sides, his back resting against the rear rim. It was quite serviceable. And as Hemingway was getting Joyce's hat firmly on his head and his eyeglasses straight, who should come out of the Gipsy Bar but the bantamweight Irish sailor, almost too drunk to stand up, looking for a place to puke. His sailor friends were not with him.

Hemingway was ready to wheel Joyce away, but then he saw the sailor and watched him. The sailor staggered around the corner of the building and leaned against it, vomiting. Hemingway went over to him. At first Joyce thought that Hemingway was perhaps going to see if the poor wretch needed some help. But after glancing over his shoulder to make sure the sailor's friends hadn't come out of the barroom, Hemingway drew back his fist, took leisurely aim, and hit the man a good thumping blow on the side of his head. The sailor dropped. Returning to the wheelbarrow, Hemingway said, as if quite pleased with himself, "That'll teach the bastard to have more respect for poets."

The violence, though short and one-sided, threw a bit of a scare into Joyce. He acted as if he hadn't seen it. And to keep himself from getting sick to his stomach from the bumpy, lurching wheelbarrow ride, or keep himself from fading into unconsciousness, he managed to sing a few verses of one of his favorite songs as Hemingway wheeled him toward 9 rue de l'Université. In his fine Irish tenor, loud enough to wake the sleepers in the houses along the way, Joyce sang as he rode along:

> Who is the tranquil gentleman who won't salute the
> State
> Or serve Nebuchadnezzar or the proletariat
> But thinks that every son of bitch has quite enough to
> do
> To paddle down the stream of life in his own damned
> canoe?
> Mr. Dooley, Mr. Dooley,
> The wisest wight our country ever knew,
> Something . . . something . . .
> Says Mr. Dooley-ooley-ooley-oo.

"What do you think, Hemingway?" he asked, soliciting compliments. "It's me own version of a fine old Irish folksong."

"You're a good singer. I didn't know you could sing."

"Oh, I once studied to be a singer," Joyce said, making an effort to keep from slurring. "Nora, bless her heart, thinks I should have been. A singer. Thinks I'm a better singer than I am a writer. Fact. She says if I had listened to her I would now be a rich and famous singer, instead of poor and infamous writer. Oh, I love that woman, Hemingway. She doesn't understand me a whit, it's true, and is as ignorant as an Irish potato, but I love that woman." He was becoming maudlin, on the point of tears.

"She's a wonderful woman. I love that woman, I tell you! I say, are we going the right way to Avenue Charles Floquet?"

"We're keeping to the side streets to avoid the cops."

"Ah, yes, the bloody peelers," Joyce said, and sang another verse.

> Now, who's the funny fellow who declines to go to
> church
> Since pope and priest and parson left the poor man in
> the lurch,
> And taught their flocks the only way to save all human
> souls
> Was to pierce their bodies through with dumdum bullet
> holes?
> Mr. Dooley, Mr. Dooley,
> The mildest man our country ever knew
> 'Who will release us
> From Jingo Jesus?'
> Prays Mr. Dooley-ooley-ooley-oo.

He tried to sing another verse, but his words soon became nothing but drooling mumbles, and he rode the last few blocks in a sort of semiconsciousness. He only came awake again when Hemingway shook his shoulder.

"Is this where you live?"

"Do I live here? Hmmmm. Looks vaguely familiar, yes."

"You got the key?"

Nora appeared on the second-floor balcony, dressed in a robe, her hair in curlers, with the light from the apartment behind her.

"Sure," she said, "here's the famous writer, James Joyce, is it? Drunk again, being brought home in a wheelbarrow in the wee hours of the morning by a stranger. Sure, and if you keep this up, Jim, I'm going to leave you, so help me, I will. I'll take the children back to Ireland and have them baptized."

"Mind your manners, woman. This young man is a friend of mine. Invite him up for a cup of tea."

Nora disappeared from the balcony and soon appeared in the doorway.

"The devil of a man you are for drinking, Jim," she said. "You're after falling down dead or blind in the gutter someday, I'm thinking. And who is this?"

"This is my new friend, Ernest Hemingway—a Yank."

"I thank you for bringing hisself home," Nora said as she maneuvered to get Joyce out of the wheelbarrow.

"I'll help you get him upstairs," Hemingway said.

With Joyce's left arm over Hemingway's shoulder and his right over Nora's, they began hoisting his thin, noodle-limp body up the stairs. They got him into the apartment and lowered him into his favorite overstuffed chair. Then Hemingway, declining a cup of tea, said good night and departed. Nora continued staring at the door for a moment after Hemingway had gone, and then said with marked interest, "A handsome young lad, that one. A bit of a brute, though, I'm thinking."

"A brute?" Joyce said, trying unsuccessfully to insert a cigarette into his long ivory cigarette holder. "That's not the half of it. That head-bashing boy-o is the tenth-ranked heavyweight boxer in the world."

6

Hadley

With the approach of April and the coming of intermittent sunshine, Hadley began to like Paris more. She could buy fresh vegetables at the markets on rue Mouffetard, and she was learning the language well enough to do a little gossiping on the sidewalks and stoops with the local housewives, getting to know their names. Unfortunately, the warmer weather brought with it a rougher neighborhood. There were more drunks on the street, some of whom slept in doorways, passed out in their own urine, and sinister-looking gypsies loitered in the shade of the horse chestnut trees in the Place de la Contrescarpe. The police often had to come to the *Bal du Printemps,* a noisy and rough bal musette on the ground floor of the building next door to stop fights and make arrests. A hangout for poules and apaches and sailors and a few American expatriates who nicknamed it "Bucket of Blood," the crowded bar was a colorful but dangerous place.

To balance these drawbacks, Hadley could now grow red and pink geraniums in her window boxes, and the apartment could be aired out, and she could play the piano without wearing fingerless gloves to keep her hands warm. Sometimes she went out into the street in the early morning to meet a goatherd leading his flock of goats down from the Place de la Contrescarpe. Playing a little pipe to announce his arrival, the goatherd would sell milk from the udder. The housewives along the street came out with pots and pans, into which the goats were milked. Hadley enjoyed chatting with her neighbors in her awkward French while waiting in the frosty morning air for her pan to be filled, and she loved the scene because it was so picturesque, so very . . . *Parisian*. And she loved taking the pan of warm, steaming milk back up to the apartment and serving Ernest, while he was still in bed, a breakfast of warm goat's milk and croissants and orange marmalade.

On the whole, she was happy—happier than she had ever been in her life, happier than she had ever dreamed of being—even though she was becoming worried about Ernest. Where Ernest was concerned, the approach of spring had failed in its promise of a resurgence of breeding fever. Or if he was lusting after someone lately, it wasn't Hadley. Actually there was no reason to suspect that he was lusting after anyone at all. He was often sick, his complaints ranging from an infected throat to hemorrhoids to spasms in his back, and during those times when he felt good enough to make overtures, inviting her encouragement for him to be frisky, wouldn't you know it? Hadley herself came down with a cold or a sore throat or an abscessed tooth or her period.

Ernest was dissatisfied with his writing, too. He wasn't getting enough time to write what he wanted to write, and what he wrote wasn't much good. This shaky state of affairs had begun when they came back from their skiing vacation in Chamby, Switzerland, and Ernest wrote a couple of articles for the *Toronto Star*. One of the articles was about the people who came to Paris to be writers and artists and ended up spending more time in the cafés and at parties than they did at their art. In the article, Ernest called these people the "scum of Greenwich Village," who had been "skimmed off and deposited in large ladles" in the all-night cafés of Montparnasse. "You can find anything you are looking for at the Rotonde," he wrote, "except serious artists."

Hadley felt this was an unfortunate thing to say, and told Ernest so, because they themselves had spent some time on the Rotonde's terrace getting drunk with such friends and acquaintances as Man Ray, Kiki, James Joyce, Picasso, John Dos Passos,

Djuna Barnes, Hart Crane, Jules Pascin, Marsden Hartley, and many others, all of whom could certainly be called serious artists.

"Look, that was written for a stodgy Canadian newspaper," Ernest answered, annoyed by her reaction, "and that's the kind of stuff they want to hear. It's called slanting, for God's sake."

Hadley didn't voice any further objections, but she felt that Ernest's willingness to peddle such hokum was more than just an opportunistic willingness to slant his article for money; it was a betrayal of their friends and fellow artists. By pandering to such touristy prejudices, he was being no better than a guide on one of the tour buses that had lately begun driving through Montparnasse, telling the gawking tourists, "There they are, the drunken bums who pass for artists, the phonies, the so-called expatriates."

Hadley suspected that this betrayal bothered Ernest, too, and his guilty conscience made him irritable. And certainly the article he wrote for the *Star* about the hotels in Switzerland should have bothered him. Using scathingly sarcastic language, he wrote about rich, older women in the Swiss resort hotels who pay the bills for the "utterly charming young men" who act as their consorts and gigolos. And while this was not a substantial distortion of the truth, Ernest must have been bothered—at least subconsciously—by the hypocrisy of his accusations, for while he was disparaging the young men who lived off older, wealthy women, his own hotel and bar bills in Switzerland were being paid for with his older wife's money.

These things were the source of some discord in their marriage, but they didn't diminish Ernest in Hadley's eyes. To her, he was still the handsomest, most charming, most loving and lovable man in the whole world—not to mention the greatest writer. And the fact that Gertrude Stein read his stories and his unfinished novel without any whoopee-like enthusiasm didn't in the least diminish Hadley's confidence in his talent.

Gertrude's reading took place a week after Ernest and Hadley had first visited 27 rue de Fleurus. True to her word—and to Hadley's surprise—Gertrude did come to lunch with the Hemingways on the day she had said she would. Hadley felt it was a tribute to Ernest that Gertrude—a celebrated hostess, after all, who no doubt had to turn down dozens of invitations every week—had been sufficiently impressed with Ernest to keep her luncheon date at the small, uncomfortable Hemingway apartment on rue de Cardinal Lemoine.

On the day of Gertrude's arrival, Hadley had been watering her geraniums in the window boxes and called Ernest to come and look when she saw Gertrude approaching in her Model-T Ford. It was a topless touring car that roared through the small streets of Paris like a war wagon, preceded by the rudest horn imaginable, going *Uhuuuggha, Uhuuuuuggha,* warning the pedestrians to get out of the way. And Gertrude Stein, sitting in the driver's seat, obviously enjoyed the power conferred upon her by the most peremptory automobile horn anyone had ever heard, enjoyed the way it parted the pedestrians in front of her car the way the Red Sea must have parted for Moses.

Little Alice Toklas was there in the passenger's seat, probably scared out of her wits, as the car careened to a stop in front of the apartment house. After honking the horn once more for the benefit of the neighbors and onlookers, Gertrude began extricating her monumental heft from the car. Alice, as quick as a little brown bird, jumped out and put chockblocks under the Ford's front wheels.

With Alice close at her heels, Gertrude pulled her two hundred pounds up the three flights of stairs and arrived, out of breath but chuckling, at the opened door of the Hemingway apartment, with the Hemingways and their *femme de ménage,* Marie Cocotte, scurrying about inside, getting ready for their guests. After exchanging grinning hellos and handshakes, Gertrude sniffed the aroma of the food cooking on the two-burner gas stove, and said, "Ah! The wonderful smell of food, to replace the odor of what happens to it"—nodding toward the stinking hallway toilet.

"Yes," Hadley agreed, "with the warmer weather, I'm afraid the toilets are getting rather overpowering, aren't they? And how are you, Miss Toklas? Come in, come in."

"And except for the plumbing, how are you liking Paris?" Gertrude asked, which was the first time she had ever said anything directly to Hadley.

"Oh, we love it," Hadley said. "It suits us fine."

Gertrude took off her leprechaun hat and made herself comfortable in the front room, saying, "Yes, Paris is the place suited for those of us who are creating the art and literature of the twentieth century."

This made Hadley feel important, as if she were a participant in a movement of world-shaking importance, but it also made her more apprehensive about Gertrude's intention to read some of Ernest's work. What if she didn't like it? Was that possible?

"The apartment is not all we could wish," Ernest said, "but it's all we can afford. A few paintings like you have on your walls would help enormously, of course, but God knows we can't afford them. We could barely afford the boots and clothes we needed for our trip to Switzerland."

"If you want to buy paintings, forget about clothes, forget about them," Gertrude said. Look at us, we have pictures, some that cost no more than a dress. Who cuts your hair?" she asked Hadley.

Slightly flustered by the bluntness of the question, Hadley said, "Oh, well, the last time . . . a coiffeur on rue Monge. . . ."

"No more coiffeurs," Gertrude commanded. To Ernest, as if from one husband to another, she said, "I myself cut Alice's hair. I'll show you how to cut your wife's, save the money to buy paintings."

"Yeah, sure," Ernest said. "That'd be swell, thanks."

"What is that cooking?" Alice asked timidly.

Marie Cocotte had made her speciality for lunch: frogs' legs Provençale, with a garlic and butter and lemon-juice sauce, topped with chopped parsley, and Ernest had chilled in a bucket of ice a bottle of his favorite Pouilly-Fuissé. The four of them sat around the small table next to the bed in the main room as Marie Cocotte served.

"Oh, it's delicious, you must give me the recipe," Alice said, which, coming from her, was the ultimate compliment.

"Wonderful," Gertrude concurred. "Marvelous. If the Hemingways ever fire you," she said to Marie Cocotte in French, "we'll give you a job."

Marie Cocotte, vaguely aware of the nearly legendary status of the two odd-looking American women, blushed and made a little curtsy.

Too bad Gertrude wasn't as enthusiastic about Ernest's stories. After lunch, the table was cleared except for coffee cups and ashtrays, and Ernest brought out, at Gertrude's request, his novel-in-progress, called *Along with Youth,* which Ernest had begun before leaving Chicago. Gertrude zipped through the pages, and kept up a running commentary, then passed the pages on to Alice, who read them without comment. Gertrude said, "You have it in you to be a good writer, Hemingway, but I do not care for the novel. In it you raise more expectations than you fulfill, you must see what its what is. Also a great deal of description, and not particularly good description, no, not good descriptions, not good."

Ernest was baffled. "But what do you mean, its 'what is'? What is its 'what is'?"

"Its 'what is' is its 'what is,' " Gertrude insisted. "It's what it's about, its meaning. Concentrate on that. Start over. Descriptions are not literature, Hemingway."

Ernest did not take criticism easily, and this criticism was especially hurtful because he was proud of his ability to describe the natural world. Indeed, this was the one thing that Sherwood Anderson himself, after reading a few of Ernest's first short stories in Chicago, has praised in his work, and yet Gertrude Stein was telling him to throw it away? To start over? What Ernest needed was approval and help, neither of which Gertrude seemed willing or able to give.

Hadley sensed some vengeance in the next thing Ernest offered for Gertrude's critical eye: a short story he had written before leaving America and had rewritten a few times since then, a story called "Up in Michigan," the most graphically sexual story he had ever done. It was about the irresistible desire that women feel for men, written from a woman's point of view, and not likely to be appreciated by a lesbian. And though she seemed riveted to the story, Gertrude dismissed it by saying that it was unprintable, and Alice was made so uncomfortable by the sex scene that she didn't finish the story.

"It shows promise, but promises, promises, what's the use wasting your time writing stories that nobody will print?" Gertrude asked.

Hadley tried to keep herself busy in the small kitchen while the reading was going on, but she didn't miss a word that was said, and, more importantly, her furtive glances caught their crucial facial expressions, and she was saddened to hear the story called unprintable. Of all the stories Ernest had written, "Up in Michigan" was Hadley's favorite, because it was about a woman who loses her virginity to a loutish, insensitive lover, and it was written from the woman's point of view. It was the only time that Ernest had written from a woman's point of view, and she felt that he had succeeded wonderfully. In the story Ernest had really become the woman reluctantly submitting to a man's importunate and painful mastery. Given Ernest's extreme masculinity, Hadley had been very surprised to find hidden in him such a true feminine sensibility.

But there it was, unprintable, and Alice couldn't finish it. And it struck Hadley as terribly unfair that Gertrude, whose only publications had been at her own expense, would advise Ernest to stop wasting his time writing stories that no one would print. No one would print hers, either, but she kept writing them, didn't she?

As she was preparing to leave, Gertrude summed up her criticisms by saying, "Go to Spain, Hemingway, see some bullfights, the matador will show you how to concentrate. Concentrate on the bull, Hemingway, concentrate on the bull—the bull! the bull!—to the exclusion of everything else. But," she continued, "you'll have to give up the newspaper writing, if you're going to succeed as a fiction writer. Too much of the newspaper's telling gets into the fiction's showing. Well, good-bye. Thank you for the delicious luncheon, and feel free to drop by rue de Fleurus anytime in the late afternoon or evening. Come along, Pussy."

"Yes, Lovey," Alice said.

Ernest escorted them down to their car. Hadley watched from a window as Gertrude and Alice climbed into the car—Gertrude, from an overhead perspective, looking like a two-hundred-pound dwarf in a leprechaun's hat—and Ernest cranked the car for them, and then, with a blaring of the horn, *Uhuuugghha,* the car shot off down the street, with Gertrude sitting high and mighty in the driver's seat, oblivious of the chaos and curses she caused among the pedestrians who had to scramble to get out of her way.

Ernest was very demoralized when he returned to the apartment. He picked up the manuscript of the unfinished novel and squeezed it, as if wanting to wring its neck.

"So it's shit," he said in a tone that allowed no contradiction, though Hadley did contradict him.

"No, it isn't, she didn't say that at all, she—"

"That's what she meant—shit, shit, shit!" He flung the pages to the floor and stamped on them.

"No!" Hadley cried. She fell to her knees and snatched the scattered pages from underneath his feet. "And it's not shit! You know it's not. Some of it's wonderful."

"Yeah?" he jeered. "Well, the last time I read it to you, you didn't seem to think it was so damned hot."

"That's not true! I thought it was captivating," she said, but without much conviction, because it was true, she hadn't thought it was so hot, though it was also true that she had found it captivating—indeed, she was fascinated by all of his work, and especially by anything autobiographical, which *Along with Youth* was. "All I said was I didn't get it—or something like that. Look, you always want to read me stuff after we've been to a movie, or after we've made love, when I'm very tired, and I like to take time with all good things. But listen, all I said was, I didn't get it—you know, like you're supposed to 'get' the punch line of a joke. I didn't 'get' it, that's all."

"Oh, yeah? You didn't get the 'what's it,' huh? So what do you want me to do, make a joke out of it, so you can 'get' the punch line?"

"Oh, Tatie, now, that's not fair and you know it. I love you, and I'm living for you, and it hurts me when you jeer at me like that."

He sighed. "I'm sorry." He sat down on the bed, holding his head in both hands. Hadley put the gathered manuscript on the table and sat down beside him and put her arm around him, coddling him in a there-there sort of way.

"It'll be fine, you'll see," she said. "Do like Gertrude says, begin again. And stop wasting your time writing for the newspapers. Devote all your time to your fiction."

"Sure, that's easy enough for her to say, she's got a nice, fat Jewish trust fund to live on, she can afford to write from now till doomsday and never have to earn a penny. *I do.*"

"But you don't," Hadley insisted. "Damnit, darling, you have to let me back you in this. It's like in our tennis games, you know? From the way I play backcourt in doubles, you know I'm good at backing up my partner's serves. That's what I do best, back up my partner, and that's what I want to do for you and your writing. My annuity will keep us going till you can get started selling your fiction, and you'd be doing me a favor if you used it for that. I need to be necessary to you, Wemedge. Please."

"You don't know," he murmured. "You never know how long it might take me to be successful—or if I ever will be."

"Oh, come on, that's not my Wemedge talking. Where's that self-confidence you radiate so well? Where's that indomitable spirit I so much admire?"

"We can't live on confidence and spirit."

"Of course we can! As long as I have three thousand dollars a year coming in, we can."

But Ernest would not be consoled. "But, goddamnit, I can't keep living on your money and keep my self-respect. I got to make some money as a writer, and you heard what Gertrude said, I'm no good."

"She didn't say that! And even if she did, so what? Who is she? You know what Leo Stein—her own brother!—said about her, don't you? He said she was the biggest literary fraud of the century. Said her writing was like a child playing in its own shit. The only things she's ever published are things she published with her own money."

"Yeah," Ernest agreed. "Where does she get off, anyway, telling me to concentrate on what its 'what is'? Sounds like some of that childish gibberish in *Tender Buttons* that she claims is the work of a genius. You know that she claims that she and

Shakespeare are the two greatest geniuses in the history of literature? Ha!"

"There you are! You can see that she's so out of touch with
reality that you shouldn't be discouraged by anything she says."

"Yeah." Ernest's disappointment seemed to be evolving into
defiance and anger. He flexed his shoulders as if preparing for a
fight. "And, anyway, who cares? I can always go back to boxing." He began shadowboxing around the room.

Hadley groaned. Ernest's one visit to Leida's Gym had resulted
in his coming home with nothing more to show for his services
as a sparring partner than 50 francs—about three dollars—and a
big black eye. Since then Hadley had managed to dissuade him
from going back to the gym to earn money as a sparring partner
for professional boxers, but not a week went by that Ernest
didn't spar a few rounds with friends and acquaintances, all of
whom were base beginners, or—at best—rank amateurs, and his
easy victories over them continued to feed his delusions of pugilistic grandeur.

When the *Star* asked Ernest to cover an international economic conference that was due to take place in Genoa, beginning in the first week in April. The newspaper would pay him
seventy-five dollars a week, plus expenses, the cable said, but
such expenses didn't include a travel allowance for a wife. So
Hadley wasn't invited.

Not that she could have gone, even if she had been invited.
The day the cable came, she was too sick to get out of bed. Since
coming to Paris, their lives had fallen into a pattern of late-night
hours and heavy drinking. Most nights of the week they were at
the terrace tables of the Dôme or the Rotunde or the Select,
drinking and partying with friends and strangers, and these
strenuous pastimes, combined with the cold, miserable weather
of a Paris winter and spring, had lowered their resistance to
respiratory illnesses—bronchitis, flu, sore throats—that one or
both of them had about half the time. And both had been sick—
Hadley with a bad cold, Ernest with an infected throat—when he
left for Genoa. She tried to get him not to go, but he said they
needed the money.

She was in bed when he left, and she stayed there after he had gone. No longer needing to keep up with Ernest, she got plenty of rest, but it still took a couple of weeks for her to recover. After that, she began to miss Ernest terribly. This was the first time they had been apart during their eight months of marriage, and Hadley hadn't realized until now how dependent on him she had become—not just for company and emotional support, but for her very existence. And it was truly a matter of dependence, not just sentimental attachment. Ernest had busted her out of the jail of her self, where she had languished as a prisoner of timidity, defeat, and hopelessness; but when she escaped from her old life and family home in St. Louis, she had left her old self behind. She had become Ernest—become an appendage of him—and in being parted from him, she experienced the phantom feelings that an amputee is said to feel about a missing limb: she could still feel it there, throbbing and itching, but when she reached out to soothe it or scratch it, it wasn't there.

And out of this feeling of incompleteness, she began to experience the incipient panic of feeling her new identity dissolving. She felt as if she were sinking back into the old Hadley she hated so much. She wanted to be the person Ernest had made of her; without him she was nothing. She needed him, and from his very first letter to her from Genoa she could tell how much he needed her.

> I have a fever, and I can see big white patches at the back of my throat, and I'm gargling with alcohol and water, but it doesn't do any good. I hate being sick, and if it ain't one thing, it's another. Sometimes my hemorrhoids are so bad I can hardly sit down to work. I wish I was home with my mums, my feather kitty, and to hell with this assignment.

She recognized the black, self-pitying mood that Ernest so often fell into, and she knew the baby talk and feather kitty pity that would help bring him out of it. She tried to do this in her answer to his letter, but she had barely got her consolations in the mail before she received another letter from him, this one telling her about an accident he'd had involving a gas water heater. The pilot light had gone out, and when Ernest tried to light it with a cigarette, the gas that had seeped out exploded. Ernest described his injury as an eight-inch gash in his right shin, a badly bruised left hip, a sprained wrist, and a burn that had taken the skin off his right hand.

"Oh, my God," Hadley groaned in sympathy, and wrote in a letter, "Oh, my poor tiny wax puppy, I can't bear to think of you there all alone with all your misfortunes and injuries. Come home and I'll kiss them and make them well."

But he wasn't there all alone—not entirely, anyway. As he explained in his next typewritten letter, he had met and made friends with a few other American correspondents at the conference. All of them liked him, he said, and they had volunteered to share their notes with him until he could once again hold a pen in his injured hand. In addition to the well-known Paul Mowrer of the *Chicago Daily News,* these friendly and helpful correspondents included Lincoln Steffens, the famous muckraker himself, who was covering the conference for the Hearst Newspapers, and William Bird, the head of the Consolidated Press in Paris, as well as the famous Max Eastman, the former editor of the monthly *Liberator.* Ernest was cultivating these influential men for the purposes of advancing his writing career, and he said in his letter that Max Eastman had read some of his sketches and thought they were terrific and had sent them to the man who had succeeded him as editor of the *Liberator.*

The present editor of the *Liberator* ultimately rejected the sketches, but even so, the conference was not a loss. Ernest had made some important friends, and by the time the conference stalemated at the end of April and Ernest returned to Paris, he had earned nearly 300 dollars. His injuries from the gas heater explosion had nearly healed, but his throat was still inflamed, he was exhausted, and his hemorrhoids were giving him hell. It took a lot of Hadley's hugs and coos, as well as aspirin and cups of tea, to get him on the mend, and her job wasn't made any easier by the chilly winds and rains that ushered in what they had hoped would be the merry month of May.

"Let's make it merry by getting the hell out of here," Ernest suggested. "Let's go back to Chamby, shall we? For a few weeks? The mountain air would do us both good."

Hadley thought that was a wonderful idea. She had very fond memories of their previous trip to Switzerland. She often remembered the ancient chalet in which they had rented a room, and how they were warm in bed together at night with the windows open and the stars bright, and how Madame Gangswisch, the wife of the pension's owner, came into their room every morning and closed the windows and got a wood fire roaring in the big porcelain stove, then brought them breakfast in bed.

But though it was a wonderful place for a romantic idyll, it hadn't taken Hadley long to realize that she wasn't enough for Ernest. As good as things were between them, he had needed something more. He needed an audience, men and women who could appreciate his struts, who could be impressed when he showed off, who would listen when he bragged, who would serve as foils in his games of conquest. He, too, recognized the need.

"I know what," he said as they were making their plans. "Let's invite some people along. Maybe James Joyce and his wife— what d'you say? Or maybe Bill Bird. I got to know Bird in Genoa, and he's a hell of a chap. You'd like him. He's got a swell wife, too. Named Sally. And I told Lincoln Steffens about Chamby, too—maybe he'd like to come along."

Hadley agreed to have any or all of them along on the trip, what the hell, the more the merrier.

But it turned out that all of them had other things to do, or—in the case of the Joyces, at least—simply didn't think it was a good idea. Ernest wanted to take his boxing gloves with him, but who was he going to box with if nobody could be persuaded to join them for a holiday?

The only person who finally agreed was an old friend of Ernest's from the War, a British officer named Chink Dorman-Smith, who was now stationed with the British forces in Cologne, Germany.

7

Chink Dorman-Smith

HIS REAL NAME was Eric Edward Dorman-Smith, but Hemingway, with his predilection for tagging his friends with nicknames, began calling him Chink soon after they met. They had been talking about what they would rather be more than anything else in the world, and Hemingway had said he would like to be a sultan with a harem. In the same vein of liquor-loosened fantasy, Dorman-Smith had said that he would like to be a Chinese emperor, and from that day forward Hemingway called him Chink. Less fanciful in his choice of nicknames, Dorman-Smith called his new friend Hem.

Chink first met Hem in Milan at the end of the War. Although only twenty-three years old at the time, Chink was an acting captain and had commanded British infantry troops of the Northumberland Fusiliers on the Italian-Austrian front. He had been in combat since 1914, had been decorated with a military cross for extraordinary bravery, and had been wounded three times. But it was a severe case of gastroenteritis, not a wound, that got him transferred to Milan, where, after recovering from his affliction, he was given command of the British troops stationed there. That's where he met Hem, in Milan's Anglo-American Club, on the day—November 3, 1918—that Italy and Austria signed an armistice, bringing the war between them to a close. Hem and Chink happened to be occupying adjacent tables in the Club when someone came running in with the news of the armistice, and soon Hem had joined Chink at his table and they were celebrating the event with many toasts of champagne.

Hem could hold his drink. Though wounded and walking with the aid of a cane, he could still maneuver well enough to avoid staggering as the two of them left the Anglo-American Club and walked to Biffi's restaurant in the Galleria, where Hem was to meet a Red Cross nurse for dinner, she being the love of his life. Hem was an eager young man and brash, as so many Yanks were, and acted as if he and Chink, in the space of a few hours, had become lifelong chums. During those few hours Hem flattered and amused Chink by his relentless interest in Chink's wound stripes and in his career as a veteran British army combat officer. He told Chink a good deal about himself, too—told him that he had been orphaned when he was sixteen years old, and thereafter had made his living as a boxer, a cowboy, and a lumberjack. Chink got the impression that Hem very much wanted to be admired for being a daredevil and a dashing fellow, but after he said he had been wounded in the legs and scrotum by 229 pieces of shrapnel while he was leading Arditi troops on Monte Grappa, Chink wondered how much of his story was pure cock-and-bull. A nineteen-year-old American Red Cross ambulance driver, leading Italy's most famous shock troops into battle? Now, really! This was a bit much to swallow without the customary grain of salt. Still, Chink didn't challenge him, or try to pin him down. Hem was such a jolly fellow and friendly and flattering, and Chink, after all, was beyond being surprised by the war stories told to him by noncombatants, and he had no desire to embarrass Hem by exposing him as a liar.

Hem had obviously been wounded, whether in combat or not Chink didn't know or care, though he had to admit that he was a bit curious about Hem's alleged scrotum wound. As they were walking toward the Galleria, Hem limping with his cane and Chink with a cigarette in one hand and a swagger-stick in the other, Chink asked Hem, with utmost delicacy, whether the, uh, the testicles had remained intact. Hem assured him that he was still in possession of his balls, although he'd had to keep them resting on a pillow for two months while they healed. The only awkwardness caused by the wounded scrotum, Hem volunteered, had been on those occasions when he made love to his nurse, the young American woman they were on their way to meet at Biffi's.

Her name was Agnes von Kurowsky, and she was, as Hem had boasted, quite a good-looking woman—"damned beautiful," Hem had said rapturously, but she didn't quite fit Chink's criteria for beautiful. Handsome, yes, but beautiful? Not quite. When they met at a table in Biffi's, Miss Kurowsky was with another nurse whom she introduced as Miss Macpherson. Both were dressed in their white dress uniforms, with capes and flat-brimmed hats. They were members of a contingent of American nurses from Bellevue Hospital in New York who had volunteered to come to Italy for the duration of the war, to nurse the sick and wounded in American Red Cross Hospitals.

What surprised Chink about Miss Kurowsky was her age. She was at least seven or eight years older than Hem, Chink guessed, and did not at all act the part of the passionate lover. On the contrary, she seemed more maternal toward him, rather indulgent but basically indifferent, and seemed slightly discomfited by his eager familiarity. Her attitude might have been explained, of course, by her efforts to keep her friend from suspecting that there was any kind of intimacy between Hem and her, since it was strictly forbidden for nurses to fraternize with their soldier patients.

In whatever case, Chink soon became skeptical of Hem's claim that he and Miss Kurowsky were actually lovers. He didn't doubt that Hem was in love with her—that much was obvious to anyone—but it didn't seem that she reciprocated the feelings, and as for them being carnal lovers . . . well, Chink knew how men seemed inclined to boast about such things, just as they boasted about dubious war experiences.

Still, they all had a jolly dinner at Biffi's, and drank a great deal to celebrate the armistice, and smoked and talked about the things they would do now that the war was over. Hem boasted that he was going back to America and become the heavyweight boxing champion of the world, his war wounds permitting, and if his war wounds kept him from accomplishing that, he would settle for becoming the world's greatest writer.

"I may not be able to knock Kipling out, but I could take him in a fifteen-round decision," he said, and added pointedly as he placed his hand over Miss Kurowsky's, "as long as I have Ag in my corner."

Miss Kurowsky freed her hand from his by reaching for her glass, and forced a smile as she gave her nurse friend a sidelong glance, signaling that such comments by Hem should not be taken seriously. And to reinforce the notion that they were merely being silly, she said, "Sorry, Ernest, my dear, but I have every intention of going to England and marrying the Prince of Wales."

Hem seemed disappointed that he couldn't maneuver her into a public acknowledgment of their relationship as lovers, but her reserve—condescension, really—was never breached by Hem's boyish enthusiasms. Indeed, the only time Miss Kurowsky showed any sign of flirty warmth, it was toward Chink, not Hem, and was occasioned by her learning that Chink came from an old Anglo-Irish family with an ancestral estate in Bellamont Forest, Cootehill, County Cavan, in Ireland.

"How interesting!" she said, batting her eyes as if to clear her vision and see Chink better. "And will you inherit?"

"Afraid not," he said, sorry to disappoint her. "Second son. Laws of primogenitor, you know. Afraid it's the Army for me."

And even though it was in an atmosphere of jesting, Chink fancied that Miss Kurowsky's sudden loss of interest in him betrayed the characteristic of a rather transparent fortune hunter. If that were indeed the case, he surmised that she would never marry Hem, since Hem obviously had no fortune.

The next time he saw him, Hem claimed that Miss Kurowsky had agreed to return to America with him as his wife. But as his departure date drew near, she said she changed her mind and promised to follow him and marry him after he had found a job and showed that he could support a family. He was apparently not sophisticated enough to see that she was merely easing him out of the picture, but there was no doubt in Chink's mind that that was the case. Chink said nothing about it, however. It was not his place to disillusion the poor chap. And when Chink and Hem said good-bye the day before Hem boarded a train for Naples and a ship that would take him home to America, he promised to send Chink a wedding invitation. Chink said he would look forward to receiving it, and they even joked about Chink being the godfather to Hem's first son.

It was about a month later that Chink saw Miss Kurowsky again. She came to the Anglo-American Club in the company of an Italian major whom she introduced as Domenico Carracciolo. About her own age, the major had a pencil-thin mustache and carefully coiffed wavy hair and aristocratic airs. Had it not been for his uniform, he might have passed for a pimp with an air of prickly self-importance, but the four wound stripes on his sleeve and the medals for heroism on his chest were proof enough that he was the real thing, all right, a line officer of Italy's fierce and much feared Arditi shock troops.

"Ah, yes," Chink said after they had accepted his invitation to join him at his table for a drink. "I recently met another Arditi officer. A lieutenant. Hemingway, his name was. Wounded rather badly near the Piave River, I believe. One of Miss Kurowsky's patients. Nice young American chap. Know him?"

It was as if he had poked the major with a stick. With a withering look at Miss Kurowsky, who obligingly withered, the major, speaking Italian so fast that Chink had trouble keeping up with him, said, "Unfortunately, I did not meet this . . . this Hemingway. But when Agnes told me about his preposterous claims, I made it my business to look into the matter, and what do you think? I have the duty to tell you, sir, the puppy was a liar, a braggart, and an impostor. An Ardito? Good God, it was against the law for him to carry a gun, let alone fire it! The truth is, he was in Italy for only one month, and always with the Red Cross. Never once did he carry a gun. Wounded? Yes, yes, it's true, he was wounded by an Austrian mortar, but he was on canteen duty at the time, riding along the front lines on a bicycle and passing out candy and cigarettes to the fighting troops— women's work! That's what he was doing, women's work. Captain, please! Forgive me being so upset by this, but you are a combat officer, you understand. The honor of the Arditi is at stake!"

"But there were the medals," Chink said weakly, knowing how worthless medals were, how little they proved. His only hope was that Major Carracciolo was ignorant of what medals Hemingway had received. However, as the major said, he had looked into the matter.

"Medals!" he sneered. "Yes, the records show two medals! What medals? La Croce al Merito di Guerra—the War Cross of Merit. It was awarded to all who were engaged in action during the war. Every clerk, every ambulance driver, every canteen attendant—all received the Cross of Merit. The Medaglia d'Argento al Valore—the Silver Medal of Valor, this was given to every man wounded in battle, not for brave deeds, but for being wounded. Ah, Captain, I must ask you, sir, not to dishonor great fighting men by believing the absurd lies and empty boasts of a snot-nosed schoolboy like this . . . this Hemingway." Again he gave Agnes a withering look, as if to ask her how dare she consort with such a lying blackguard, and again she hung her head as if in shame.

Of course Chink understood the major's concern—what professional soldier wouldn't? Cheapening the experiences of war for those who have done the fighting and dying is a brazen kind of theft, a sort of sacrilege. Still, Chink thought the major's reaction extreme. But then Chink caught the smoldering look that passed between the major and Miss Kurowsky, and he realized that there was more at stake here than the honor of the Arditi. The major was a jealous lover. Miss Kurowsky had apparently told him that Hem had been in love with her, wanted to marry her, and Hem's vulnerability as a demonstrable liar and fake proved to be very convenient for the major.

"Now, Nicky, dear," Miss Kurowsky whispered in a soothing voice. "Don't upset yourself so, darling. He's gone." And by the look she gave him—a look of awe and admiration and melting love—it was clear that Hem had lost the woman he had claimed was the love of his life.

"And a good thing, too!" the major said, talking with his hands.

Chink would not have been surprised if the major had suddenly broken into a recitative, a jealous operatic hero swearing sweet revenge. "If he were here, I would give him a good beating, that liar! That fake!"

Chink thought the major was being rather hard on poor Hem. It was natural enough, after all, for young men to stretch the truth a bit about their war experiences, wasn't it? And if it was done to satisfy some desperate need to be admired and re-spected, where was the great harm? Certainly Hem's deceptions had not been for purposes of crime or fraud; he had merely been trying to steal somebody else's glory. So Chink made allowances for him, and because Hem continued to hold Chink in high re-gard (how can you think badly of someone who thinks well of you?), he and Hem continued to be friends in the letters they exchanged after Hem had gone back to America.

Chink never met Miss Kurowsky and her Italian major again, but he was kept abreast of the story of her love affair with Major Carracciolo by Hem himself. After the war, Chink was sent to Cologne, Germany, to serve with His Majesty's Fifth Northum-berland Fusiliers in the army of occupation, and Hem's first letter to him there contained the bad news about Miss Kurowsky.

> Ag, the lovely nurse you met, the love of my life, has dropped me. She met an officer of the Arditi, and then she wrote to me in the States that what we had was just infatu-ation. She said I was a kid and she was too old for me. She hoped I would understand and not hold it against her. She's going to marry the wop major in the spring, she said. On receipt of such wonderful news, I went out and got drunk and picked up a girl and yenced her and a week later I came down with the clap.

In subsequent letters Chink learned that Miss Kurowsky had not married her major, after all. As Hem related it, the major turned out to be the heir to a dukedom. As soon as his father died, the Arditi major would become the Duke of something. When the future duke took Miss Kurowsky to his ancestral home in Naples to meet his family, his mother immediately put a stop to any talk of marriage. She pegged Miss Kurowsky as an upstart foreigner in search of a title. Miss Kurowsky had written to tell Hem about it, apparently hoping to rekindle his love for her, but he was having none of that.

> She is in a hell of a way mentally and says I should feel revenged for what she did to me. Poor damned kid. I'm sorry as hell for her. But what can I do? I had loved her and she gypped me and now it's gone.

Next Chink got a wedding invitation from Hem, announcing that he was marrying a Miss Hadley Richardson. In a handwritten note on the invitation, Hem said that he and his new wife were going to save their money and move to Italy, where they could live cheaply and he could devote all his time to writing. He asked if Chink would come down to Italy and visit them. Chink promised he would, but before those plans came to fruition Hem met the well-known American writer Sherwood Anderson, who advised him to move to Paris, not Italy. Paris was where the twentieth century was being born, Anderson told him.

But no sooner were Hem and his wife settled in Paris than they were off on a trip, a skiing trip, to a place called Chamby in the Swiss Alps, seeking to escape in ten feet of dry, sunlit Swiss snow the gray, wet cold of a Paris winter. Hem wrote to Germany and asked Chink to join them there, but Chink had no furlough time coming until May. Coincidentally or not, that was when Hem and his wife took their second trip to Chamby, and this time Chink was able to accept their invitation. The skiing conditions were not good so late in the season, of course, but Hem knew that Chink considered himself something of a mountain climber, so he promised plenty of mountains, and trout streams, too, if Chink cared to fish.

Hem and his new wife, Hadley, met Chink at the train station in Montreux. Chink's English reserve withstood Hem's bear hug greeting with only slight embarrassment. Although Chink tried not to have any expectations of Mrs. Hadley Hemingway, he was nevertheless surprised that she was about the same age as Miss Kurowsky had been—that is, about eight years older than Hem.

Other than that, however, she seemed physically to have very little in common with Miss Kurowsky. Whereas Miss Kurowsky had struck Chink as being conventionally good-looking and feminine and something of a flirt, Hadley had a face covered with freckles rather than makeup, her hair was short and red and windblown, giving her a masculine, athletic look. It became clear before they got back to their pension in Chamby that she was a jolly good fellow—just one of the boys, as she herself said while they were having beers before taking the tram.

It was Hem's suggestion that they have the beers. Chink'd had enough to drink on the train and didn't want any more at the moment, but as soon as Hem got his hands on Chink's luggage, he took charge. He led the way to a tavern near the tramway station, and ordered them each a beer, and it soon became apparent that there was more to the beer drinking than mere physical satisfaction or a celebration of their reunion. Hem finished his first beer in a few gulps, as he did his second, and his third, and each time he ordered himself and Hadley another beer, he ordered one for Chink, too. Chink kept up with them for the first three, but on the fourth he declined, and Hem challenged, "What? You're not ready for one? Come on, drink up."

And even though Chink kept his half-filled glass in his hand where Hem could see that he wasn't ready for a new one, Hem said goadingly, "Sure you won't have another one? Sure?"

Hadley tried to keep up with Hem, and almost succeeded in matching him beer for beer, but Chink refused to compete—for that's what it had become, a competition. By his behavior Hem was making it plain that Chink's refusal to match him drink for drink was not simply a matter of choice, but an admission of defeat. Hem had assumed the role of the leader, the one who set the pace, the one who was in charge, the host, the champ, and this was something new in their relationship. In the short time Chink had known Hem in Milan just after the War, he had always treated Hem as a younger brother, and Hem had always played that role, never challenging Chink in anything. But beginning that day in the tavern in Montreux, and becoming clearer during the time they spent in the Gangswisch pension in the old hamlet of Chamby, Hem was no longer playing the younger brother role. Now he needed other men to test himself against, and an audience to applaud him.

The Gangswisch pension was the same one where Hem and Hadley had stayed during their previous visit to Chamby. It was a lovely old chalet, filled with warm fires and lamplight and smells of good food and drink, with flakes of soft spring snow falling through the pine forests all around, and a lovely view of Lake Geneva in the distance. The dining room had a low ceiling of smoke-darkened timbers and tables made smooth and dark by years of use and spilled wine, and it was here that Hem's need for an audience assumed bizarre proportions. Every morning when he and Hadley came down for breakfast, they disturbed Chink's bachelorhood with detailed descriptions of their sexual exploits during the night.

"We had a fine time in bed last night," Hem announced as he and Hadley sat down to a breakfast of steaming porridge and coffee and bread and eggs on that first morning. The three of them were wearing dark goat's wool robes and heavy skiing socks that the pension supplied to its winter guests, which gave them a passing resemblance to monks.

"Hope we didn't disturb you," Hadley added, smiling.

Chink had the room directly beneath theirs, and their rather rambunctious lovemaking during the night had made him wonder if they had intended for him to hear them. But not wanting to embarrass them, he lied.

"You didn't hear us?" Hem was slightly incredulous and—could Chink be mistaken?—a little disappointed.

"Well, I heard something," Chink said, discreetly evasive. "A couple of yowling cats, I supposed."

"That was us, all right," Hadley said.

"But that was only during the first time," Hem told her. "When we were doing it the second time we were on the bed and you were on top of me—remember? The cat cries had tapered off by then, but"—addressing Chink—"we thought you still might hear the bedsprings squeaking."

This seemed pretty explicit for Hadley not to get Hem off the subject, but she didn't seem to mind.

"Ah," Chink said. "Perhaps I supposed it to be the squeaks of mice."

"Sorry if we disturbed you," Hadley said.

But of course they weren't sorry. Chink doubted that they were consciously aware of the significance of their actions and admissions, but by then he knew that they had intended to disturb him, for the same reason that they related their nightly sexual escapades to him every morning at the breakfast table. Once again Chink was supposed to be functioning as the audience that Hem needed, the envious admirer of his manly performances.

Each day after breakfast, they packed food and wine in their knapsacks, and climbed the Cape au Moine, a 7,000-foot peak, or the 6,000-foot Dent du Jaman, with Hem leading the way, reconnoitering the countryside, choosing the trails, saying, "Let's eat here," or "Let's make a huge snowball and roll it down the mountain," with Hadley and Chink following him without dispute or argument, even though Chink was the more experienced mountaineer. They fished for trout in a stream called the Stockalper, near the juncture of the Rhone River and Lake Geneva, and it was Hem who said, "Here, you'll have better luck if you use this fly," or, "Let's fish that hole, I'll bet that's where the big ones are." They drank a lot of beer and brandy at night around the pension's fireplace and smoked cigarettes and sometimes argued and sometimes played poker with local woodcutters who came to the chalet on snowy nights to drink the hot rum punches, and Hem got mad as hell if he didn't win the arguments or the poker games. Hem couldn't stand to lose. Chink, on the other hand, refused to compete in anything. If it were up to him, he would let Hem win in whatever competitive game he wanted to play.

Except boxing. Hem had brought his boxing gloves and gym shoes with him, and urged Chink any number of times to spar a few rounds with him.

"Come on. Just for the fun of it. I won't hurt you."

Chink declined. It was no skin off his nose if Hem won the luge races, caught the biggest trout, drank the most beers, or was first to the top of the highest peaks; Chink entered into those activities for pleasure, not for winning. But he knew there would be some skin off his nose if he boxed Hem without the intention to win. From the moment he first met Hem, Chink had been the superior officer, the older brother, the decorated combat veteran, the unflappable Brit that Hem so much admired and emulated; but now he sensed in Hem the strong need to get the best of him in some way, a compulsion to establish dominance. So even if Chink boxed Hem and won, he would lose, for their friendship would never be the same. Hem needed to be the champ more than he needed friendship, and Chink didn't need to prove anything, to himself or anybody else. So he declined.

But he was not to be let off so easily. Determined to have some sort of supreme contest before their vacation ended, Hem came up with the idea of the three of them hiking over the St. Bernard Pass into Italy.

"We could send our luggage on ahead to Milan on a train, pick it up there," he suggested. "Just carry knapsacks with the bare necessities. What do you think, Hash? Think you could do it?"

"If it's doable, I can," she said.

"And then I could show you the hospital where I stayed in Milan after I was wounded," Hem said, growing excited by the possibilities. "Maybe we could even go on to Schio, where I was stationed during the War, and then—why not?—on to Fossalta di Piave, see the place where I got wounded. Would you like that?"

"Oh, very much," Hadley said. "I can't wait."

"What do you say, Chink?"

They spread the maps out on the table in the dining room.

"Railroad could take us across the Rhone Valley and part way up the pass. To here. Bourg St. Pierre," Chink said, as if planning a military reconnaissance. "Have to walk from there. Have to reach St. Bernard Hospice at the summit before dark. If we got caught in a freak spring snowstorm, might not make it at all. Could be dangerous, this time of year."

"It's thirteen kilometers from Bourg St. Pierre," Hem said, examining the map, "and we'd be climbing from five thousand to more than eight thousand feet. Sure you can do it, Hash?"

"Sure," she said. "As long as we take plenty of cognac in our knapsacks."

But what items they carried in their knapsacks besides cognac almost caused the mission to be aborted. After they had packed all their unnecessary gear and shipped it to Milan by train, they went back to the pension to get a good night's sleep and leave for Bourg St. Pierre at dawn. But the next morning, as Chink was waiting in his room for Hem and Hadley to finish packing their knapsacks and come down to meet him, he began to hear them in the room above, arguing. He went up to find out what was wrong, and found them squabbling about Hadley's toilet articles. She had refused to ship them ahead with their other gear, and Hem refused to pack them in the knapsacks.

"Bare necessities! Isn't that what we agreed on?" he asked Chink. "But look at these things!" He waved scornfully at Hadley's bottles and jars of unguents and lotions and creams. "Well, they're not going," he announced.

"Oh, gee, Wemedge, don't be that way!" Hadley begged.

"Well, who the hell's going to carry them?" Hem demanded.

"I'll carry them myself."

"But then you won't have room to carry your share of the necessities, and I'll have to end up carrying them, and I'm not going to do it."

This was the first time Chink had seen them in an argument, and he was surprised that Hadley, who always seemed the sweet, subservient wife, would provoke an argument over such trifles—trifles, which, as far as he knew, she never even used. He had never seen her use beauty aids, and the complexion of her freckled, rosy face was that of an outdoor girl, not the peaches-and-cream complexion that came from bottles and jars. It occurred to Chink that the toiletries had become symbols of some sort in a much deeper argument, and since any argument about symbols is essentially an irrational one, he knew it would never be settled unless he removed the symbols.

"I'll take them," he said. "I have room."

Both Hem and Hadley accepted that solution, but seemed grumpy about it, as if they had been robbed of a chance to settle something, as they traveled to Bourg St. Pierre by train. There they secured lodgings for the night in a small inn. Although there was no snow in the village, they learned from the concierge that the snow line was low that year, at about 6,000 feet altitude, and that the road was not open. As yet no one had crossed the St. Bernard Pass this year from the Swiss side. They were advised not to go.

"Snow a few kilometers up the road," Chink said as they discussed the matter over dinner that night at the inn. "Still two to three feet deep, they say, and mushy. Hard walking. Snowstorm might blow up. Dangerous if we get caught in one."

Hem was quick to probe for a weakness. "What're you saying?—that we shouldn't go? That we should turn back?" He made it sound like an act of cowardice rather than mere caution.

"Might be best."

"Well, I don't know about you two," Hem said, "but I'm going to do it, if I have to do it alone. That's the pass Napoleon and his army used to cross the Alps in 1800, and I want to be able to say I crossed it, too, and I'll probably never get another chance."

"I, too," Hadley said in a voice that pledged to stand by her man. "I'm going."

"In those shoes?" Chink asked.

Otherwise she was well dressed for the trip, with riding breeches and golf stockings and wool sweaters, with fur mittens hung around her neck on a string, a tam that could be pulled down over her ears, but on her feet she wore low-cut saddle oxfords. Chink hadn't mentioned the footwear before because he hadn't wanted to seem to be taking charge of the expedition; Hem clearly wanted that role for himself. However, Chink had assumed that they intended to buy some hobnailed hiking boots for her in Bourg St. Pierre before they started, and now the boot stores had closed for the night and they had planned to leave at dawn the next day, before the stores would be opened for business, so what did they have in mind? Chink gathered from their sulky reactions that this subject had been touched on before.

"They'll do," Hadley said defensively. "It's a road, isn't it?"

"Not a good one, they say," Chink said. "Probably hasn't improved much since Napoleon's time. And there'll be snow. What happened to your boots?"

"She sent them on ahead with our other gear," Hem sneered. "Can you beat that? And you know why? Tell him why," he ordered, but she kept a defiant silence, and Hem added, "She said she wanted you to admire her trim legs."

"Ah," Chink said quickly and noncommittally to keep Hadley from having to respond. "Maybe we'd better wait for the store to open tomorrow. Buy you some."

"No," Hem said. "If she's dumb enough to send her boots on ahead, she'll just have to hike in those."

Hadley didn't seem offended by such scorn, but nodded her head as if in agreement, as if accepting it as her due, so Chink said no more about it. Actually he expected them to become sensible about buying some boots the next morning, but Hem insisted that they stick to their plan and leave at first light of dawn, and Hadley seemed willing to bear whatever punishment Hem deemed appropriate for her lack of preparation.

Hem took the lead for the first few kilometers, but by the time they began slogging their way through one or two feet of slushy spring snow, and had reached an altitude where the air was becoming noticeably thinner, Hem began panting heavily from the struggle. He suggested they take a break.

By this time Hadley's shoes were filled with melted snow that squished with every step she took, so they sat down on an out-cropping of rocks and had their first swig of cognac to warm them up while Hadley took off her shoes and massaged her feet, which she said were so cold that she could hardly feel the blisters that were beginning to form on her toes and heels.

It was lovely country. They had not yet reached the timberline, so the mountainsides were dotted with pines, the limbs of which were loaded down with snow, and as the day warmed up they could hear, in between the panting sounds of their own labored breathing, the occasional *shish* sound of melting snow sliding off a pine bough and plopping onto the crusted, crystalline snow that covered the ground and glinted with eye-piercing brightness in the morning sun. An occasional chilly breeze swept up the draws toward the summit of the awe-inspiring mountains, swirling the dryer snowflakes at higher elevations through the crevices of solid granite escarpments, the towering spires of barren stone. Fearful of seeing a gathering of the dark-bellied clouds that could portend a spring snowstorm, Chink's eyes were always drawn upward toward the summit by the passing shadow of any cloud.

"Better go," he suggested, stamping out his cigarette. "Have to reach St. Bernard's before dark. You all right?"

"I'll do," Hadley said, putting her wet shoes back on.

They trudged on. The snow got deeper, and every slogging step took them into the thinner air of the higher altitudes, and soon the climb became so arduous that they began to feel dizzy from lack of oxygen. They staggered, they stumbled, they gulped air like fish out of water.

During their noon rest period, while they ate sausage sandwiches and hard-boiled eggs and warmed themselves with swigs of cognac, Chink gingerly broached the subject of turning back, but Hem wouldn't hear of it.

"We've gone almost halfway," he said.

"The easiest half," Chink said.

By now Hadley's feet were a mass of blisters, some of which had burst and were bleeding. She walked behind Chink so she could step in the tracks he had made in the snow. It was useless for her to follow Hem's tracks because his dizzy spells were causing him to stagger like a drunken man. And, indeed, he had probably become a little drunk, too, with all the cognac he had been gulping on their rest stops, and soon his dizzy spells began to bring on heart palpitations. They had to stop, panting and blowing, and wait for Hem's heart to regulate before continuing. Still he didn't suggest going back. Chink thought Hem was waiting for him to turn back, so that he could escape the humiliation of being the first to quit, but Chink wasn't the one who was having the dizzy spells and heart palpitations. It wasn't his wife whose feet were covered with blisters. He kept going.

It was Hadley who first dropped in the snow, gasping for breath, and jerked off her knapsack as she said, "No! To hell with it, I can't go any farther. You two go on ahead, send one of those St. Bernard rescue teams back for me."

They rested for ten minutes, and Chink said, "We can't just leave you here. If a snowstorm came up, or we didn't get back before night . . ."

"Maybe if I just leave the knapsack here, I can go on . . .

maybe send somebody back for it. My feet are swelling so much, I can hardly move them." She was near tears of exasperation and exhaustion.

It was true, her feet had become so swollen that one of her shoes had split. Chink used his pocket knife to cut the other one open.

"Take a little of the pressure off, make it easier to walk," he said. "And I can carry your knapsack."

"I can't let you do that," she demurred, but she had neither the interest nor the energy to protest further as he slung her knapsack over his shoulder and they struggled on, up into the thinner and thinner air of the now treeless crags and snowy peaks of the Alps, and perhaps they would have made the last two or three miles to the Hospice of St. Bernard before darkness descended had not Hem suddenly been seized by altitude sickness. He developed a terrible headache, one whose pain was so acute that it caused him to hold his head in both hands and drop to his knees, groaning, and then he vomited his lunch and cognac into the snow, and kept retching even when there was nothing left to vomit. Hadley crawled through the snow to him and held his forehead as he convulsed, saying, "Oh, my poor poo. Oh, poor darling poo."

"My head! My head!" Hem groaned. "I must be having a stroke."

"Altitude sickness," Chink said, coming back to where they had fallen in the snow. "Not much you can do about it." He took his knapsack off and took some aspirin and brandy from it, and when the retching tapered off, he gave Hem the tablets. "Here. Take these. Won't cure it, but it'll help."

Hadley helped Hem shed his knapsack and then used the pack as a pillow for his head as he lay in the snow. He groaned and cursed, waiting for the pain to subside.

"Can you go on?" Chink asked finally.

"I don't think I can," Hem said. "Should turn back. Can't make it to the top."

"Sure, you can. Anyway, can't turn back now. Take us longer to go back than it would to get to the summit."

"Jesus," Hem said, holding his head. "You go on, send a stretcher back for us, will you? I'm sorry, but . . . I can't. Jesus, I can't without feeling I'm passing out, or dying."

Chink shook his head. "Too dangerous. What if I broke a leg, couldn't get to the Hospice? We'd all freeze out here tonight."

"Jesus, am I dying?" Hem asked. "Jesus, I don't want to die here."

"Come on," Chink urged. "Have to keep going. No choice. But we'll make it easier. Walk twenty minutes, rest ten, walk twenty, rest ten. Leave your knapsack, I'll come back for it."

From then on Chink carried two knapsacks forward at a time, then returned for the odd one. Hem and Hadley struggled on in in the snow. They were unable to understand what had happened, unable to understand how their plans for a brisk daylong hike over a mountain pass had slowly turned into a nightmare of sickness and pain, unable to understand that their predicament carried with it a possibility that they might not survive. Night was coming on, and small flurries of snow began to sweep across them now and then, threatening disaster.

"Come on, we've got to make it to the Hospice before it gets dark," Chink kept saying to them. "Come on, you can make it a little farther. Maybe only a mile or so. Come on, Hem, get on your feet."

But the pale sun disappeared into the mist and mountain peaks and the weather suddenly turned freezing. They had brought along extra sweaters, which they struggled to get on, but they weren't enough to keep them from shivering in the icy cold gusts of mountain air.

Two or three times Hadley and Chink had to pull Hem to his feet after a rest period. He was panting as though his lungs would burst, and the altitude sickness still gripped him, causing his muscles to cramp from lack of oxygen and his head to ache.

"Feels like my head's in a vise," he groaned.

Chink, too, was nearing exhaustion and was ready to abandon the knapsacks completely when, finally, in a moonscape of tortured and desolate terrain he caught sight of the barracks-like building that was the Hospice of St. Bernard. A few of the frost-encrusted windows glimmered with the soft yellow lights of lanterns and candles.

"There it is," Chink said as encouragement to Hem, who was at the point of total collapse. "Just a little farther now. Keep going. In a little while we'll have hot food and beds."

Chink left two of the knapsacks so that Hadley and he could support Hem, one on each side, as they stumbled the last hundred yards toward the thousand-year-old sanctuary. They were met by a couple of very curious St. Bernard dogs as they approached the front entrance, and they could hear other dogs barking from their shelters as Chink rang the almoner's bell. Soon a robed and tonsured monk came to let them in. He was quite surprised to find foot travelers on the pass so early in the season, and he and his monastic brothers quickly shepherded them to a roaring fire in a dining hall, where they, under the watchful and curious eyes of the monks and dogs, were served soup and bread and wine and mugs of steaming hot chocolate.

The Hospice had forty-five beds for travelers and a connected inn with eighty more beds, all of them empty, so the three of them—the first tourists of the season—were given royal treatment by the many idle monks who acted as servants, cooks, and medics. After dinner, Chink went back to pick up the two knapsacks that he had left on the road. When he took Hem's to him in his and Hadley's room, he found Hem immersed in a big copper tub in front of a roaring fireplace, groaning with relief and pleasure as a monk added another bucket of steaming water.

"Hadley's in the infirmary, having her feet looked after," Hem said. "The medic said my case of altitude sickness was one of the worst he'd ever heard about," he added in a tone that was both justifying and boastful.

"How you doing? All right?"

"Yeah, 'cept for the hemorrhoids."

"Hemorrhoids?"

"Yeah. They were so bad on the way up, I could hardly walk, but . . . what the hell," he said, cavalierly dismissing the martyrdom of hemorrhoids.

"Ah," Chink said. "Well, I'll leave Hadley's toiletries, in case she wants them." He dug the beauty aids from his knapsack and left them on the dresser, bidding Hem good night, and went to his own room, where a monk was filling a big copper bathtub for him in front of a blazing fire.

8

Hadley

THEY HAD PLANNED to hike all the way to Milan, but the condition of Hadley's feet required them to stop in Aosta, the first little Italian town they came to after hiking down from the summit. There they took rooms at an inn, and Hadley spent two days in bed, flat on her back, while her blisters healed and the swelling in her feet went down. This delay chafed Ernest, but he was robbed of a chance to feel superior because he, too, had to spend the days in bed, nursing his hemorrhoids. Then, with Hadley's feet swathed in gauze, and wearing a pair of very loose house slippers to accommodate the bulk of the bandages, they caught a train for Milan.

Chink was with them for two more days before he had to report back to his base in Cologne, and Ernest was glad to have him. It meant a lot to him to have someone who could share his wartime memories of Milan, someone he could talk to about Agnes von Kurowsky without discomfort. And perhaps out of his gratitude to Chink, Ernest began growing a mustache just like his. By the time they got to Milan, it had been five days since Ernest had shaved, and after they had gone to the railroad station and picked up the baggage that they had sent on ahead from Montreux, they checked into the Continental Hotel and Ernest left his mustache untouched when he shaved. His was dark brown and Chink's was light brown, but other than that, they were the same. It even made him and Chink look more alike, as if they were brothers.

But while most of Ernest's comments about Agnes were meant for Chink's ears, it was Hadley's heart that was most affected. At first she didn't see the significance of Ernest, on their first hours in the city, taking her and Chink to the open tables at Biffi's in the Galleria and ordering for Hadley a cup of fragrant wild straw-berries chilled in a frosted glass and laced with Capri, but Ernest enlightened her with his comment, "It was Ag's favorite dish."

"Really," Hadley said.

To Chink, Ernest said, "She and I used to come here in the afternoons, and she would have the wild strawberries. We used to sit at this very table. Then we'd go over to the Cova and have cappuccino and brandy before going back to the hospital."

Hadley had to wonder if she were sitting in the same chair in which Agnes had sat.

After the strawberries, Ernest insisted that they have cappuc-cino and brandy at the Cova, and then he wanted to show Had-ley the Red Cross Hospital where he had been taken to be cured of his wounds—wounds that had been so bloody, he said, that a priest in the frontline aid station had baptized him as a Catholic and given him the last rites, fearing that he would not live; but after being transferred to the American Red Cross Hospital, he had been nursed back to health by his first great love, Agnes von Kurowsky.

"We always went back to the hospital this way," he said.

From these reminiscences, Hadley was beginning to realize that her husband was a budding—if not already a full-blown—egoist, since egoists believe that anything they say or do must be inherently interesting to everyone else. She didn't want to be the one to disabuse him of that notion, so she kept her mouth shut, even though she often felt like telling him that his preoccupation with his first great love was beginning to be a bore.

When they reached the old four-story mansion at 4 Via Cesare Cantú that had been the American Red Cross Hospital, a frown of disappointment settled over Ernest's face. The structure had the decayed look of a mansion that had been turned into an apartment building. The paint on the large rectangular window frames had flaked and fallen away, the varnish on the huge doors had cracked and peeled, and patches of stucco had fallen off the walls. Wet clothing had been hung over the balcony railings to dry, and the cries of children and fretful mothers could be heard in and around the building. But the fourth-floor balcony on which Ernest had sat in his wheelchair in the bright summer sunlight for many an afternoon, being fussed over by his nurse, Agnes, was still there, though disappointing in its shabbiness and disarray.

Next he showed Hadley and Chink the Ospedale Maggiore, the Italian hospital where he had undergone the physical therapy for his leg and knee, a procedure, he said, that saved him from being a cripple for the rest of his life.

The next morning, after a big breakfast in the hotel's dining room, all three of them went to the San Siro racetrack just outside of Milan, where, Ernest said, he and Agnes used to go nearly every Saturday.

"All the races were fixed in those days," he said. "And maybe they still are, but we had a lot of fun working the field."

He tried to work the field again that day, but there seemed to be no fun in it for him, no excitement, as if he had long ago seen the last of the good times. Once, between races, when he went to the toilet, Chink caught Hadley's eye, and said, "I admire the way you're taking all this. Just childhood memories he's reliving, you know, all this Agnes nostalgia."

"Is it? I don't know," Hadley said, glad that he had brought it up so that she could speak to someone about it. They were standing at the fence near the finish line, waiting while the horses for the next race got lined up in the starting gates. Chink offered Hadley a cigarette and gave her an encouraging smile as he lit it for her. Chink was a handsome man, and Hadley had become quite fond of him. He was tall and spare, with a nicely trimmed mustache, blue eyes that almost crinkled closed when he smiled, and he had the fine manners and studied nonchalance of a well-bred upperclass Englishman.

"Whatever it is, I don't understand it," Hadley said. "It's like when we got married, one of his former lovers—Kate Smith her name was, an old friend of mine from St. Louis, who introduced me to him—he wanted her to be the maid of honor, and all his ex-girlfriends were invited to the wedding, and the first person we went to visit after the wedding was the girl who had been his first lover, named Marjorie Bump. Maybe he wanted to show me all his old conquests, maybe show me all the girls he'd turned down for me. Or maybe he wanted us—all his lovers—to know each other, so we could all worship him together, I don't know."

"A harem," Chink said.

"I don't know," Hadley said. "Maybe so."

"He once told me he wanted to have one. Wanted to be a sultan, have a harem. Quite right not to take it too seriously. He's idealizing this Miss Kurowsky, you know. The one that got away. Longing for the unobtainable. If he had gotten her, he wouldn't have wanted her. Shouldn't worry about her, if I were you."

"Worry? Oh, I'm not worried about her. I've got him; she hasn't."

"You're the lucky one."

Hadley heard no British irony in his tone, but she looked to see if there was any in his face. There wasn't. In spite of the huge differences between them, Chink truly liked Ernest. He considered him a genuine friend, and Hadley was thankful for that, and for the way he always declined to play Ernest's competitive games. It was as if he were an older brother, nonjudgmental, standing above the sibling fray.

After the last race was over, the three of them returned to Milan. They had dinner at the Grand-Italia, the finest restaurant in Milan, where Ernest and Agnes had dined a few times, at the very table at which they had sat. Then they roamed the streets and piazzas for half the night, and Ernest must have found a hundred other things that reminded him of Agnes. And even the next morning, while he and Hadley were saying good-bye to Chink at the Garibaldi Station, Ernest had to share with them his memory of Agnes saying good-bye to him four years ago at this very same train station, on this very same platform, on that cold day of December 27, 1918.

"It was the last time I saw her," he said.

After waving good-bye to Chink as the train pulled out of the station, Ernest and Hadley caught a bus for Schio, the small Italian town in the Trentino Hills, the foothills of the Dolomites, where Ernest had been stationed as a volunteer Red Cross ambulance driver during the War. And the disappointments for Ernest that had begun in Milan, due to the differences between what he remembered and what he saw, increased with every kilometer they traveled in his pilgrimage to the scenes of his Red Cross service.

As they left the bus station and walked along Schio's muddy, trash-strewn streets, carrying their knapsacks and suitcases, Ernest shook his head sadly and said, "I used to consider this town one of the finest places on earth. It had all the good cheer, liveliness, and relaxation a fella could want. Now it's . . . Why, I wouldn't have recognized it now. It's like going into the gloom of a theater where the charwomen are sweeping up."

They found the hotel he was looking for, the Due Spadi, which had served as an officer's trysting place during the war, a place where an officer could bring his inamorata for a night of discreet fornication.

"But it isn't anything like I remember it," he said after they had checked into one of its drab and shabby little rooms. "Or at least I remember it being very different," he added. "It was jolly then, and had lots of colors, and there would be music and the sounds of champagne corks popping and girls laughing."

"Did you ever bring Agnes here?"

"No, no." He seemed slightly offended that she would have to ask. "I only met her after I was wounded. Why do you ask?"

"I just didn't want to end up sleeping in the same bed you two had used." And after a moment's hesitation, she added, "Who did you bring here?"

"Why do you want to know that? I don't ask you questions like that about the affairs you had before you met me, do I?"

"Nothing that specific, I guess," she said. "But, then, I've never taken you on a tour of my old trysting places, either, have I?"

But he ignored her, too overcome by the contemplation of his own past to get involved in Hadley's.

That afternoon, they hired a car to take them to see some of the old sites and scenes that Ernest remembered from the days of his ambulance service. They began at the woolen mill that had been converted into a barracks for the Red Cross ambulance drivers, which the drivers had referred to as the Country Club. Now it was once more a woolen mill, spewing toxic dyes into the river where the ambulance drivers used to swim and frolic in the clear blue water. Then on to Fossalta di Piave, which Ernest remembered as a town heavily bombarded and almost destroyed; now it was an ugly little town with nothing to remind him of the War except the scars on the trees. He even complained that the dead soldiers, whose graves had made the site holy and real, had been dug up and reburied in graveyards miles away. It seemed that he considered the villages to be far more beautiful when they were bombed out than they were now. It was as if the recovery of the land and villages had robbed him of his personal past.

When he and Hadley stopped on the banks of the Piave River and found the place where Ernest had been wounded by the Austrian mortar, Ernest reached the nadir of his depression, seeing that the trenches had been filled in, the fortified bunkers had been blasted out and smoothed over, and the battlefield covered over by what he called a green smugness.

As they were walking through the tall grass and flowers, Ernest stopped at one point and looked around carefully, then said, "I think it was about here. Maybe at this very spot. The mortar."

"Where you were wounded?"

Preoccupied, he said, "There was a coughing sound, like a locomotive starting up, and then a flash like a blast furnace door swinging open. I couldn't breathe, I couldn't see for the white brightness, and I couldn't breathe because of the blast and the heat, and I felt my soul leaving my body, floating out, and . . . I knew I was dead. I knew it, so I must have still been alive to know it, but I was dead, and I knew it. My soul floated out and hovered for a moment, and then . . . instead of floating on, I felt it slip back into my body, and I was alive again."

"Oh, poor Nesto . . . Poor Nesto."

"For a long time after that I couldn't sleep at night. If I did . . . if I even shut my eyes in the dark and let go of myself, I was afraid my soul would float out of my body and never come back, and I would be dead."

In the interest of letting him purge himself of such memories, Hadley kept quiet and waited for more revelations. None came. The two of them stood on the sunny slope leading down to the blue Piave River, amid the grass and weeds and wildflowers of another spring, trying to imagine that July day four years ago when Ernest had died and been reborn. And finally he shook his head and said, "I wish I had never come to see it. It's a bum show, chasing yesterdays."

They both got drunk that night. They ate at a small trattoria where the food was bad and the waiter dour and indifferent. In answer to Ernest's questions, the waiter said, yes, he had been in the War, but he didn't want to talk about it.

"Best to forget the bad times," he said.

"I was here in Schio during the War," Ernest said.

"Yes? Well, many people were," the waiter said, and took away their dirty dishes.

After they staggered back to the hotel, with Ernest carrying a bottle of brandy in each hand, Hadley took stock of their room, and asked Ernest, "Are you sure this hotel is any different than it was when you were here four years ago? It looks to me as if everything has been here for at least that long, probably a lot longer. This bed's probably been here for twenty years, with its lumpy mattress and squeaky springs."

"I don't know," Ernest said. As he got undressed, he stopped now and then to take a pull from the brandy bottle. "But it sure looks different."

Hadley thought about it as she drunkenly fumbled out of her clothes and got into bed beside him, and by the time she thought she finally had it figured out, he was too close to passing out to appreciate it.

"You know what I think your trouble is, Tatie, my dear?" she asked, and had to be satisfied with a grunt as a response. "The trouble with you is, you can't distinguish between memory and imagination."

All she got for her observation was another grunt, but she was satisfied that she had finally found an explanation for Ernest's endless lies about his past; for the way his fantasies seemed as real to him as genuine experiences seemed to ordinary people; for the way he remembered this shabby, third-rate little hotel as being a classy and exciting love nest.

She could only hope that his memories of Agnes von Kurowsky were equally at odds with reality, and that someday he would meet his long-lost love again and realize that she wasn't who he had thought she was. Failing that, she would probably always be first in his heart—indeed, even in his drunken dreams. That night he reached out for Hadley and groaned "Ag!" In her own alcohol-sodden sleep, Hadley could have mistaken the name for just another grunt, a meaningless night noise, but there could be no mistake when Ernest rolled over on top of her, his breath quickening with growing sexual excitement, and groaned, "Agnes . . ."

She didn't correct him. She waited for him to realize that she was not the girl of his dream, but if he did come awake enough to be aware of who he was making love to, he didn't mention it, then or ever.

9

Hadley

THEY GOT BACK to Paris on June 18, having been gone for a little more than a month, and the Paris they returned to was one they had never seen before. It was a Paris of heat and flowers and leafy trees swirling with sparrows, a city of lovers sitting on the banks of the Seine, of café terraces crowded with people laughing and drinking and arguing through the nights under bug-swarmed lights. Hadley was glad to be back in their little apartment, and would have been glad to resume their lives as struggling Left Bank writer and wife, but after their trip to Milan and Schio, things were never again quite the same between them. In the heat of a Paris summer, Ernest began to take on some of the qualities of a city besieged with heat and tourists. He became edgy, short-tempered, restless and yet listless, and suffered long bouts of depression and impotence. He spent a lot of time in his Verlaine studio on rue Descartes, writing stories and poems, which he would read to Hadley as soon as they had taken shape. "My Old Man" was one of them, a story about a boy and his beloved father, a crooked jockey. It was a good story, in spite of being very derivative of Sherwood Anderson's stories about horse races and racetrack touts. Indeed, if Hadley hadn't known better and someone had asked her to identify the author from a reading of the text, she would have named Sherwood Anderson instantly. Unfortunately, however, she told Ernest that it reminded her of Sherwood. She meant the comparison to be a high compliment, but Ernest didn't take it that way. He became sulky and spiteful.

"Oh, for Christ's sake," he grumbled, "just because Anderson wrote about racetracks doesn't mean he has a monopoly on the subject, does it? You think nobody else should write about murder after *Crime and Punishment?*"

"No, no, of course not, it's not that," Hadley said, conciliatory and repentant. "I only meant that . . ." She started to mention the style and tone were very much like Anderson's, too, but realized in the nick of time that that would only make the matter worse. Ernest's ego would not let him be like anybody else. He even hated to admit influences. As far as he was concerned, he was original, and woe to the wife or critic who told him he wasn't.

And perhaps it was this response that caused her to hold back on her comments about the next story he wanted her to read, the latest chapter of his novel-in-progress called *Along with Youth*. It was without question a very autobiographical novel, and, as usual with him in his first drafts, he didn't bother to change the names of the real people he was writing about. So the hero of the novel was a young man called Wemedge who wanted to be a great writer, and his girlfriend's name was Kate Smith.

As Hadley read it, she was never quite sure what kind of a response he wanted or expected from her. The writing was very revealing, and he must have known that she couldn't be a totally detached observer, not when he depicted in such raw and graphic details the lovemaking between him and Kate. He knew that she knew that he and Kate were the characters in the story, and the setting was a perfect rendering of Lake Walloon in the summertime, so what kind of message was in that for Hadley? What was she expected to feel as she read about Kate and Wemedge making love outdoors after everyone else has gone to bed?

Hadley asked him if he intended to change the names of the characters before publication, and he sneered, "Of course," as if that went without saying, so she confined herself to telling him that it was a good addition to his novel, and to keep up the good work, although that was something of a lie, since she didn't, in fact, think the writing was very good. Back when they had first gotten together, Ernest had been writing short stories like those he read in *The Saturday Evening Post,* formula stories with stereotyped characters, rendered in a style that would not offend the little old ladies in Dubuque. It wasn't until the *Post* summarily sent the stories back to Ernest with stock rejections that he began to adopt higher standards of writing. In such stories as "Up in Michigan" and *Along with Youth* he had certainly graduated to subject matter that would have horrified the editors of the *Post* and the little old ladies, but he had not as yet found his own style. He was trying to develop a voice that was his own, but that didn't come until he began his tutelage under Ezra Pound.

10

Ezra

EZRA POUND HAD been living in Paris at 70 *bis* rue Notre Dame des Champs for a little more than a year when Hemingway came to see him for the first time. That was in June 1922, just after Hemingway had returned from a trip to his old battlegrounds in Italy. He brought Ezra the letter of introduction from Sherwood Anderson.

"That was nice of the old fart," Ezra said, meaning nothing personal in his characterization of Anderson. It was just his way of speaking. Ezra was aware of *Winesburg, Ohio,* of course, and thought it commendable, but he had met Anderson only once. That had been last year, in Sylvia Beach's bookstore, and he had accepted Anderson's invitation to have dinner with him and his wife that same evening. It was during dinner that Ezra had sized up Anderson as a fuddy-duddy old fart who was long on niceness and short on intellect. The basis for this judgment was Anderson's silly notion that Gertrude Stein was a literary genius. Ezra knew little about Gertrude Stein, but he knew enough to be certain that she was sure as hell no literary genius.

"Why, cat piss and cucumbers," Ezra had said to Anderson, "that woman—to use the word loosely—that woman is nothing more than an addlepated old fraud, the pages of whose innumerable unpublished manuscripts might better be used as ass wipe."

But Anderson prided himself on being a big man, both physically and spiritually, so he forgave Ezra his bitter opinion of Gertrude. He seemed to dismiss it as being some personal antagonism between Ezra and Gertrude, and in that, he was certainly correct. When Ezra had first moved to Paris in 1921, he came in like a whirlwind from out of the West, determined to stir up the Paris literati. Very quickly he had become friends with the likes of Jean Cocteau, who was a good friend of Gertrude's, so he soon had an invitation to one of Gertrude's Saturday evening soirees. But whirlwinds were not appreciated in Gertrude's house, and Ezra's manner—proudly opinionated, exuberant, flamboyant, domineering, high-handed, pontifical, erudite, condescending, contemptuous, cantankerous, restless, and raucous, as befitted the superior being that he considered himself to be— did not sit well with Gertrude Stein. It was obvious that she, after all, wanted to be the star of her soirees, and she did not brook any competition from people who knew more about everything than she did. However, it wasn't until his second visit that Ezra made himself persona non grata forever in Gertrude Stein's museum. That was when he flung himself into one of Gertrude's Tuscan antique chairs, leaned back on its hind legs, and, in response to one of his own witticisms, laughed so hard that the poor little chair collapsed.

Gertrude had apparently been so furious she could not trust herself to speak, so it was left to Alice Toklas to escort Ezra to the door and suggest to him that he never return to 27 rue de Fleurus.

And did Ezra give a damn? Hell, no!—especially after hearing that Gertrude had referred to him behind his back as a "village explainer—which might be of interest if you're a village," she had reportedly quipped. "If you're not a village, not."

Well, being a village explainer was better than what Ezra called Gertrude. Sometimes he called her old tub-of-guts, but mostly he called her a fat kike dyke. Not that he was anti-lesbian. On the contrary, the women he liked and admired most were, in fact, the ones who were masculine, the real lesbos—Sylvia Beach, for instance, and Natalie Barney, Margaret Anderson, and Jane

Heap, Djuna Barnes, Hilda Doolittle, and—on and on. So he had nothing against lesbians.

But he did have something against Jews. He believed that Jews were the corrupters of Western civilization—or syphilisation, as he liked to call it—and he had coined words that reflected the way Jews had gained control of the Western economies. Stinginess, for instance, was a characteristic he called *kikeitis*. Usury was *kikery*. A greedy person was *kikefied*. Bankers were *kikerds*—or, in polite company, bamboozling Yids, or, in scholarly print, international Jewry.

Ezra liked to think that he had come by his dislike of kikes honestly, through his extensive knowledge of economics gained by studies of cultures and by personal experience. His wife, Dorothy, on the other hand, while in complete accord with him on the Jewish question, had inherited her opinions from a long line of English aristocrats. Her maiden name had been Shakespear— Dorothy Shakespear, of old English stock. Not a descendent of William, who spelled his surname differently, but she had something that old William had never had: money. She had a nice, tidy trust fund, a substantial family home in London, and a charming, cultured mother—Olivia by name—who had once been the mistress of William Butler Yeats, the man who was considered by some to be the world's foremost living poet. Ezra had known from the time he was six years old that someday *he* would be known as the world's foremost living poet, and by the time he met Dorothy Shakespear and W.B. Yeats in London in 1909, he was sure that he, at the tender age of twenty-four, had at least acquired in his short life more knowledge about poetry than any other man in the world. And by the time Yeats came to the fullness of his years and was ready to pass on his laurel crown of supremacy, Ezra intended to be that poetic heir.

In the meantime, however, he recognized the imperative to acquire himself a wife—a wife who had money. That was the reason he had set his sights on Dorothy Shakespear. To be sure, she had qualities other than a trust fund to recommend her as a wife. She was shy, for instance, and picture-pretty. She was soft, submissive, and slightly ethereal. She had wisps of honey-yellow hair upswept into a *fin de siecle* crown, hair that encircled her head like a golden diadem. With such looks and such aristocratic bearing, in addition to the trust fund that would pay enough interest every year for her and Ezra to live on, if they were kikey with her money—well, with all that, what more could a poor country-boy genius like Ezra want in a wife? Famous people for friends and relatives? He had them. Dorothy's mother, Olivia, had sponsored him as a member of an elite group that met at W.B. Yeats' house in London every Monday evening for serious group discussions about mysticism and the occult, about astrology, telepathy, alchemy, ghosts, reincarnation, sex, creativity, spiritualism, and communications with the dead, among other things. But because sex was discussed at the meetings, sometimes in blunt terms of equating orgasms with mystical states and coitus with creativity, Olivia Shakespear did not permit her daughter, Dorothy, to attend. She believed that Dorothy's virginal ears were not ready for discussions of such topics, and especially after Ezra, happily finding himself among kindred spirits during his first meeting, advanced his own theory that the brain itself was, in origin and development, only a sort of great clot of coagulated genital fluid.

May Sinclair, novelist and feminist and one of the regulars at these meetings, had taken exception to Ezra's theory. "Oh, dear," she had said snidely, "do I once again hear the caveman intellectual howling in the wilderness?"

Ford Madox Hueffer and D.H. Lawrence, the other two male guests present, had been ready to listen, but May Sinclair went into the kitchen for more tea.

"I offer this as an idea, not as an argument," Ezra had said, leaning back on the two rear legs of his chair, the legs groaning under the jerky movements of his contorting body. He was wearing a pince-nez attached to the lapel of his green coat by a red ribbon. "Don't you see? If we consider that the power of the spermatozoid is exactly that of exteriorizing a form, and if we consider the lack of any other known substance in nature capable of growing into a brain, we're left with only one conclusion: that the spermatozoic substance—*jism,* in short—"

"Ezra. Your language," Olivia quietly scolded, but to no effect.

"—must have changed from a lactic to a coagulated condition, and—"

"Oh, poppycock," said Violet Hunt. She was the third female in the group, a novelist, the mistress of Ford Madox Hueffer, and she, like May Sinclair, played into Ezra's hands by refusing to sit around and listen to some damned man spouting off about jism. This was the first time Ezra had met Violet, and she obviously concluded rather quickly that he was a crazy, irascible, eccentric American, and—also obviously—only the requirements of civility kept her from telling him what she thought of him. But she evidently didn't think a good "Poppycock!" or two would be amiss, and she even threw in a "Balderdash!" now and then. "This is sheer balderdash, Mr. Pound, and you know it! Jism indeed!"

"Violet," Olivia said. "Your language."

But the fact that he was shaking things up encouraged Ezra to go on: "—and I suggest the ancients realized this, for in the symbolism of phallic religions, man—really the phallus—the spermatozoid charging, head-on, into the female chaos. You've felt it, haven't you, Ford? When you're driving a new idea into the great passive vulva of London, a feeling analogous to the male copulating?"

"Oh, I say!" Ford said in a tone of feigned shock, smiling behind the overhang of his walrus mustache. "Oh, I say! Do you really—"

"Oh, do shut up, Fordie," Violet said. "What I want to know is—"

"Ezra," Olivia chided, "I really must ask you to—"

"What's this I hear?" cried May Sinclair, returning from the kitchen with a cup of tea. "More patriarchal puke?"

Ford Madox Hueffer snorted his objection to being told by Violet to shut up, D.H. Lawrence tried to interrupt with an opinion, and everyone except Yeats and Ezra talked at once.

Ezra loved to stir things up. Even as a boy, he loved to throw rocks at hornets' nests, then run like hell. He loved a good dustup, as they used to call such commotions back in Idaho. He hardly considered a meeting a success unless he had offended, outraged, or rattled somebody. Of course, with lesbians and feminists, it was easy pickings, they being so damned touchy about their bugaboos; but any sort of dustup would do. And this one brought a gloating smile to his face, which caused his pince-nez to become askew. He righted the pince-nez and glanced at Yeats to see if he, too, was enjoying the disturbance. But Yeats sat in his overstuffed armchair like the reincarnation of some somber Druidic poet, which he believed himself to be, and surveyed the brouhaha with the mixture of amusement and disapproval of a patriarch studying his rowdy offspring.

As the uproar continued, Ezra leaned farther and farther back in his chair, until he was as near to the horizontal as he could manage. It was a sitting posture that he had developed in order to facilitate the flow of spermatozoa from his balls to his brain. He smirked, but the smirk gave way to sudden astonishment and fear as the tortured rear legs of his chair finally broke, sending Ezra crashing to the floor.

An astonished silence followed the crash, and when it became obvious that Ezra had not been injured in anything except his dignity, May Sinclair laughed. The others glanced at Yeats to see how he felt about his chair being smashed, and when he recovered from his astonishment and saw that Ezra was unhurt, he, too, laughed. Then everyone laughed, including Ezra. The sound of his laughter was like that of a goat coughing.

Ezra knew when to laugh at himself. As a schoolboy he had always been made the laughingstock of whatever school he attended. The other students had called him four eyes, because he wore glasses at his mother's insistence, or called him professor because of the polysyllabic words in his vocabulary that his mother had taught him, and because he had long, dark curly hair, which his mother wouldn't let him cut off. And it didn't take him long to learn that there were times when it was better to laugh at himself, rather than give the laughers the satisfaction of seeing that he was angry and outraged. So he laughed at himself that night in Yeats' home when his chair collapsed beneath him, and turned the accident into an occasion for humor.

"Ah," he said accusingly as he got to his feet, "the kike termites have been at it again. They're always undermining everything."

Yeats called the meeting to order by saying in a gravelly, Irish voice, "I suspect that I have the only chair in the room capable of supporting Mr. Pound." He pushed himself to his feet and signaled for Ezra to take the chair. "There, sir, you'd better take it."

Perhaps he expected Ezra to demur out of respect for Yeats' greatness and advanced years (he was, at forty-four, the oldest person in the room); if so, he was mistaken. Ready to claim the master's chair at any opportunity, Ezra accepted the honor. He sat down and rubbed his bottom around on the seat.

"Perhaps some of your genius will rub off on me," he jested.

"That, sir," said Yeats, "is not where my genius is."

This brought another laugh at Ezra's expense, and he couldn't think of a retort. Though he often tried hard, Ezra was simply no good at repartee. He could perform verbally with consummate skill when he had the chance to construct his aphorisms in advance, but he had never been able to respond nimbly to witty remarks made by others. It was only later, after he had departed the scene, that he could think of the devastating ripostes he should have made.

Yeats took one of the wooden chairs, and said, "I am still of the opinion that only two topics can be of the least interest to a serious and a studious mind—sex and the dead. I congratulate our young guest, Ezra Pound, on a vigorous presentation of a sexual theme, and I'm sure we could sit around all evening, stamping out Jew vermin, but now, let us return to our agenda, shall we? Let's talk about the dead."

And that ended any more talk that evening about the handicap women had to bear because they lacked the capacity to produce spermatozoa. The next day, however, as Ezra was walking along the street with Ford Madox Hueffer, headed for the office where, every few months, more or less, Ford put out a literary magazine called *The English Review,* Ford cleared his throat and said, "I say, Pound. That bit you got off last night about the brain being just a sort of—what did you call it? A lot of coagulated jism? Not serious were you? Not just having the women on?"

"Absolutely serious!" Ezra cried, sometimes twirling his malacca cane, sometimes using it like a fencing foil to thrust and parry as oncoming pedestrians bore down on them. He considered himself an expert fencer, and liked to show off his form and footwork, movements that were sometimes punctuated with sudden and inexplicable cries of "Egad! Egad!" This was a manifestation of a happily cuckoo troubadour, one of the personas that he often adopted. And his costume—an apple-green shirt, a purple ascot, red socks in clodhoppers, a wide-brimmed fedora with the brim turned down rakishly on one side, a red Mephisto-phelian beard, red hair combed back from his forehead in a mountainous heap—made him look the very reincarnation of James McNeil Whistler, the quintessential Bohemian.

But when he answered Ford's question, he switched from the cuckoo troubadour to the persona of a cantankerous old cracker-barrel philosopher from mid-Western America: "Why, cat piss and cucumbers, Hueffer, don't you know them females ain't got a lick o' sense?"

Not only could Ezra speak seven languages, he could also speak at least five distinct dialects of English. Sometimes he even mixed the foreign languages and English dialects together so that a quote in Greek might be spoken with a cockney accent, the brogue of a Scottish warrior, or the drawl of the old coot from mid-Western America.

"But they do have brains, old boy. I mean, they do. So where did—"

"Brains?" Ezra cried, switching to the persona of a professional with a Harvard accent. "No, no, no. It's a scientific fact, my good man, the female's cranial cavity tends to disprove the theory that nature abhors a vacuum. No, no, no, their brains are between their legs."

"Oh, that's capital," Ford said. "Cruel, but . . ."

"Cruel? No, no, no. Cruelly put, perhaps, but actually complimentary, when you think about it. Who wants a woman with a head full of preconceived notions? Better to have Pygmalion's statue. But for Gawd's sake," he added in an urgent tone, "don't try to bring her to life! That always spoils everything."

He was thinking of his own beloved, his own intended, his very own Dorothy Shakespear, when he said that about a woman's cranial cavity, and he rather liked that about her. He liked her best when she just sat there like a lovely ornament, silent except for a song now and then, sweet and submissive. She shared Ezra's ideas about art, race, and literature, and those reasons, along with the fact of her tidy trust fund, made marriage with her fit perfectly into Ezra's plans for his literary future. Even after six years in England, during which time he published three small volumes of poetry and one book of essays, he still wasn't making enough money to live on without help from the old folks at home, who sent him about eighty dollars every month, though they couldn't afford it, and they hinted now and then that maybe it was time for Ezra to think about getting a job.

What! A job? Why, shit fire and save matches, could they be serious? He had a destiny to fulfill—that of becoming the greatest poet since Dante—and his own mother and father were suggesting that he go out and get a job? Ridiculous! But then, of course, they were so sweet and loving, he had to forgive his father for being weak and his mother for being stupid.

Still, maybe they were right. They were getting on in life, after all, and needed all the money they could scrape up for themselves, so maybe it was time for Ezra to stop being a burden to the old folks. Even so, he refused to consider a job. That wasn't the answer; getting married was. Dorothy's father had arranged for her to receive an annuity of 150 pounds a year, which was enough to keep them going and gave him the freedom to write as he pleased, without having to write home for money from the old folks. It would be enough to free him from having to worry about selling his writings. If publishers and readers didn't like his poetry and essays, to hell with them.

But it was a measure of how apprehensive he was about husbandly duties that caused him to hesitate for five whole years before he actually got around to proposing to Dorothy. During those years neither of them seemed in any hurry to bed the other, so they just went along under the assumption that they would one day be married, as if the marriage had been arranged beforehand, as if it were their destiny as revealed in Yeats' tarot cards. And the closest Ezra got to sex with her during all that time was a furtive kiss or two, and even then it was like kissing a statue, or a sister.

This frigidity on her part didn't really bother Ezra. He figured that when he had to have sex, he could either masturbate, as was his practice, or go out and find himself a mistress. He assumed, naturally, that after the wedding, when he would have full rights to her body, she might learn to like sex, or at least tolerate it, though she was not at all encouraging. Indeed, about a month before they were to be married, she summoned up all her strength, boldness, and determination to warn Ezra that . . . well, the physical side of marriage not only held no attraction for her, it made her rather sick with disgust to think about it.

Ezra tut-tutted her maidenly primness. He continued to express confidence that the whole messy thing would work itself out after the wedding. After all, he wasn't exactly a novice at this sex game. He had deflowered a virgin or two in his time. He'd had his share of mistresses. Why, even Dorothy's mother, Olivia, whose greatest claim to fame was that she had once been the mistress of William Butler Yeats, had, on occasion, offered herself to Ezra, perhaps just in case he one day fulfilled his promise of supplanting Yeats as the world's greatest living poet. And it wasn't for nothing that Ezra—if he did say so himself—was probably the world's leading expert on the medieval Eleusinian Mysteries, in which knowledge and wisdom were held to be the result of coitus between the Eleusinian priests and young women. It was these extensive studies in medieval sexuality that supplied the basis for Ezra's theories about geniuses requiring constant sexual outlet because their brains were composed of primordial clots of jism.

They were married in St. Mary Abbots on April 20, 1914, and immediately departed by train for Stone Cottage in Sussex, where Ezra had spent the previous winter being secretary to W.B. Yeats. Yeats had since returned to London, and had offered it to Ezra and Dorothy for their honeymoon. It was a four-room cottage, with a heath in front and a forest in back, a rainy, gloomy place, with the menace of the heath and the moors confining the newlyweds indoors and to their separate rooms.

Yes, separate rooms, right from the start. They did try sleeping together their first night at the cottage, but Ezra's ineptness ruined whatever chance they had of becoming lovers, and finally Dorothy pulled her nightgown tightly around her throat and retreated to a separate bedroom and locked the door. He beat on her door later that night, and begged to be let in. She told him to go away.

Trying to get back into her good graces, he fixed breakfast for her the next morning and took it to her on a tray. She let him in, and took the tea, but waved the food away. She was sitting on the stone ledge of a casement window, gazing pensively out at the dripping rain and the misty moors.

"I'm sorry about last night," she said, with tears in her eyes. "I . . . I just can't do it. I'm afraid, dear Ezzy, that ours will have to be a marriage of comrades, not of . . . conjugal mates. I simply will not be able to sleep with you, ever."

That didn't come as a surprise to Ezra—or even as bad news, really. Of course he was disappointed, because he needed sex in order to be creative, but, hell, he didn't need her for that. If she didn't allow him his conjugal rights, that would be tantamount to giving him permission to have mistresses. He liked that idea. He'd had plenty of mistresses before, but to have them as a married man sounded so dashing, so cavalier, so sophisticated.

"But what about brats?" he asked. "You don't want any?"

At the moment he was struck by how beautiful she was. Sitting on the stone window ledge, with the casement framing her like a picture, with her slightly disheveled honey-colored hair catching the pale light, her beauty seemed ethereal, the beauty of an angel.

"I loathe children," she said.

"So you've said, yes, but I didn't know how serious you might be."

Jerking her eyes toward him, as if prepared for a surprise, she said, "And you? Do you want children?"

"Me? Ha! I might consent to breed if I were convinced of the reasonableness of reproducing the species. Or, better yet, as my contribution I'd subsidize a stud farm of young peasants. But for myself? No, I wouldn't enjoy a brat, I'm afraid, with its puking, pissing, its diapers, its bottles, its damp pieces of biscuit . . ."

"Then we're agreed on that," she said. "Are we agreed on the other?—that our marriage will be one of . . . comrades? And nobody need know that we . . ."

He shrugged. "If that's the way you want it. I've got my work to do. Luckily enough, I even brought some along on this trip. Don't know what I could have been thinking of. Translating Remy de Gourmont's *Philosophy of Love* as a matter of fact. Must write a translator's note, too, to go with it, about my theory of brain matter being clotted genital fluid. So I have plenty to do. How about you? If I work, will you be lonely?"

"No," she said with a smile of blessed relief. "I brought some watercolors with me, I'll do a few paintings of the moors."

They were to stay at the cottage for two weeks, and everything went along splendidly for the first week, but then Ezra came down with a mild case of the grippe. Happy for some wifely tasks to perform, Dorothy took good care of her husband: kept him tucked into bed, with a hot-water bottle at his feet, hot soup on a tray, and an empty chamber pot beneath his bed. She also read to him for an hour or two every day, and when he had recovered enough to write his own poems, she always asked him to read them to her. One day he read his latest creation in a sententious voice:

> The rain ploppeth, the slop sloppeth
> The cold stoppeth
> > my circulation.
> The stove wheezeth, my nose breezeth,
> O Jheezeth!
> > Flu and damnation.

She laughed. It was good to hear her laugh. It was the first time she had laughed since their honeymoon began. Then she came over and sat down on the edge of his bed, smiling but slightly sad.

"Oh, Ezzy, I'm sorry I'm not the wife you wanted. You're a brilliant poet. You're wonderful, you really are. I'm always amazed at your genius. You deserve a better wife than me."

"What's this, have I complained?"

"No, but I'm feeling guilty. I'm feeling badly because there's nothing I can do for you that a wife should."

"Oh, sure, there is: just keep calling me brilliant. Keep telling

me that I'm a genius, that I'm wonderful. That's all I need, someone to idolize me."

She leaned over and gave him a quick kiss on the forehead.
"Well, you are my idol, you know. And the one thing I know I
can do fairly well, I'm going to do for you: I'm going out to do a
watercolor of the cottage." Nodding toward the window, she
added, "The rain's stopped and the sun's come out a little. If I
hurry, perhaps I can finish the picture before the sun disappears
again."

About an hour later, he got up and went to stand at the window. What a pretty sight it was: Dorothy at her easel, with the
moors in the background. She saw him in the window and
waved with a paintbrush. And once again, he was startled to
realize how beautiful she was. A shaft of sunlight had broken
through the ragged clouds and fell on her like a stage light,
shimmering nimbuslike in the wispy edges of her hair, and he
realized that this, indeed, was all he wanted and needed from
her, just her presence, her beauty, her shimmering sensibility,
her trust fund.

So the pattern was set. After they took up residence in London,
Ezra's first full-time mistress was a young painter from Australia
named Stella Bowen, who later became Ford Madox Hueffer's
common-law wife. Ezra's second mistress was Kitty Cannell, the
separated wife of his poet friend, Skip Cannell, a lovely woman
who had been a professional dancer. Then the novelist Mary
Butts. Then the violinist Olga Rudge. Then . . . well, the list
went on, and by the time he and Dorothy had moved to Paris in
1921, he had acquired the reputation in literary circles of being
quite a randy old goat.

In all those years he'd never had sex with his wife, and Dorothy objected to his affairs and peccadilloes only when he was
not discreet. As for herself, she was not without male admirers.
She never encouraged them, never seemed tempted to come
down from her tower of ethereal isolation, not even when men
gave signs of being at least a little in love with her.

Hemingway was one of them. After their first introductory
meeting, Hemingway came to Ezra's apartment quite often during that summer of 1922, for a party, or a literary talk, or for

Ezra's criticisms of his poems and stories, but Ezra hadn't noticed that Hemingway was smitten with Dorothy until one day when Hem came to give him a boxing lesson. He and Hem had made a deal: He would help Hem with his writing if Hem would give him boxing lessons now and then. And during these visits, as well as the social visits when Hem was accompanied by Hadley, Hem seemed to go out of his way to be sweet and nice to Dorothy. At first Ezra thought it was just some sort of incongruous gallantry (incongruous, because Hemingway seldom if ever showed any gallantry toward his own wife—never opened doors for her, never helped her take her coat off, never held a chair for her, never lit her cigarettes, never deferred to her in any way)—but on this day, Ezra noticed how he looked at Dorothy. They—Ezra and Hem—had been pushing the furniture aside to make room for the boxing when Dorothy entered the room, on her way out to do some shopping. She and Hem greeted each other with the sweet, bright smiles of infatuated schoolchildren, and when Dorothy left the apartment, Hem went to stand at the window and watch her walk up the street toward Boulevard du Montparnasse, and on his face was an expression that could only be called wistful longing. It was then that Ezra realized that Hem was a little in love with Dorothy.

"Gee," Hem said in a wistful tone, "Dorothy must have been a wonderful beauty when you first met her."

Also wistful, Ezra said in a voice full of years and vague discontents, "Oh, she was, she was." Pause. "A beautiful picture. I fell in love with a beautiful picture that never came to life."

There was a long silence. Then, snapping out of the brown study brought on by Hem's remark, Ezra pulled off his shirt as he said, "Incidentally, did I tell you? There's to be a little *recital musicale* at Natalie Barney's this Friday. A reception for Margaret Anderson and Jane Heap. Would you care to come?"

"A lesbian salon?" Hem asked, pulling off his own shirt and pulling on the boxing gloves. "I doubt I'd be welcome."

"Oh, I'm sure you'd be more than welcome—a fine specimen of masculinity like yourself! Let them pussy-bumping bitches see what they're missing. Be an eye-opener for you, too, wouldn't it, being among all those lusty lesbos? Colette often comes and sometimes can't resist ripping off her clothes and doing a little bare-assed dance."

Hem looked as if he were interested in the idea, perhaps even excited about it. "Yeah, that sounds swell," he said after giving the matter some thought. "Yeah, I'd like to go." Then, as an afterthought: "Hadley might want to come, too, would that be all right, you think?"

"Of course. Why not? But do be veddy, veddy careful with her, me bucko. Fresh meat for the lesbo lionesses, you know! If you don't keep an eye on them, they might eat her up."

Having put on their boxing gloves, Ezra took a fencer's stance and said like a fencer, "En garde," then charged at Hem with the jerky, uncoordinated movements of a puppet. Hemingway easily parried Ezra's punches, and brought Ezra's charge to a sudden stop with a right hook to his head.

"Keep that left up," he said. "Raise your left shoulder a little to protect your chin."

Inept but game, Ezra came charging in again, bulling his way through Hem's defenses to land a few punches on Hemingway's head. And Hem again brought Ezra's charge to a sudden stop by throwing a hard left uppercut to his unprotected solar plexus. Ezra fell back, panting, but with enough breath left to utter in wide-eyed consternation, "Egad! Egad!"

"Keep your elbows in, protect your gut," Hem instructed. "You're boxing like a fencer."

Back in the days when Ezra had belonged to the fencing club at the University of Pennsylvania, his friend and fellow student, William Carlos Williams, had observed that Ezra fenced like a boxer; now Hem was telling him that he boxed like a fencer. But whatever else he was, he was game. He came back in, thrusting his jabs the way he might thrust a fencing foil. Hem took it easy on him for the most part, but when Ezra swarmed over him in a desperate effort to land a telling blow, Hem swung a hard right to Ezra's unprotected jaw, and knocked him down. Ezra hit the floor with a bone-jarring thump.

"I told you to keep your left up," Hem said apologetically. "You okay?"

Yes, he was all right—just shook up a bit, that was all. But out of breath and tired, he remained spread-eagle on the floor on his back for a little while. Hem, also out of breath, sat down on a trunk to rest. Except for the sounds of their panting, they were silent until Hem made a few throat-clearing mutters, then said, "Uh, about this, uh, party at Natalie Barney's . . . you think Djuna Barnes might be there?"

"Of course she will," Ezra said, as if it were a foregone conclusion. "She comes to all of Natalie's lesbic functions. She and Natalie were once lovers, they say. Maybe still are, far's I know. But what's this—interested in Djuna the puma, are you?"

"She's sure a beautiful woman."

"Sure as hell is. Got it in mind to try to fuck her? I tried once. At one of Ford's parties. Enticed her into a storage room for a little smooching."

"How'd you make out?"

"Well, she wasn't too cuddly, I can tell you."

"What did you expect? She's a lesbian—right?"

Ezra sat up, then raised himself to his knees as he said, "So it would seem, but rumor has it that she took on both men and women back in her Greenwich Village days. Laurence Vail, Edmund Wilson, that Provincetown playwright, what's his name?— Eugene O'Neill. They all had affairs with her. Even Charlie Chaplin, that little kike. It's only after she came to Paris and met Natalie Barney that she turned totally queer."

"That Thelma Wood . . . her current lover, I guess . . . she once asked me to teach her how to box."

"Well, cat piss and cucumbers, me bucko! That would be something, wouldn't it? Wonder how she'd be in the clinches? And have you volunteered your services?"

"No, I've been avoiding her. I don't want to hurt a woman."

"Maybe you wouldn't have to. She's a notorious barroom brawler, you know, is our Thelma Wood. Gets a real thrill out of fighting, apparently. Maybe it's like sex with her. Maybe she'd like to fight and fuck at the same time. Could be interesting. If I were you, I'd find out."

Once on his feet, Ezra made a couple of kangaroo leaps, banged his gloves together, and said, "Come on, let's go another round. I'm just beginning to catch on to this mug's game."

11

Hadley

WHEN ERNEST TOLD Hadley that Ezra Pound had invited him to a musical recital at Natalie Barney's Friday evening, he added, "Of course you're invited to come, too," somewhat sheepishly, as if he had a guilty conscience. "But in case you don't want to go, I told Ezra you hadn't been feeling well lately. Told him you had a bad cold."

"Yes," she said. "I'd like to go. I've heard a lot about Natalie Barney's salon. I've often thought I'd like to see it for myself."

"You're sure you're up to it?"

"Of course I'm sure."

She wouldn't have missed it for anything. While not as fascinated with lesbians as Ernest seemed to be, she nevertheless wanted to get a good look at what was probably the most famous lesbian salon in modern history.

It didn't look like much from the outside. The entrance to 20 rue Jacob was only a couple of blocks from the Hotel Angleterre, where Hadley and Ernest had stayed when they first arrived in Paris. Ernest knocked on a pedestrian's door in a huge wooden carriage gate, and the servant who opened the door, dressed in the quaint livery of a nineteenth-century footman, provided the first indication that they had arrived at an unusual place.

"De la part de qui venez-vous?" the servant asked.

The mention of Ezra Pound's name gained them entrance into

the deep cobblestone courtyard, at the end of which was a small, two-story pavilion on the edge of an overgrown garden. This was where Natalie Barney lived and hosted her regular Friday cultural soirees and her Saturday lesbian parties. In the courtyard around the pavilion and on the building's ironwork balconies, guests gathered in the afternoon sun, and their elegantly unconventional clothes often made gender identification difficult, if not, in some cases, impossible.

Natalie Barney detached herself from a small group in the courtyard and met Ernest and Hadley with a smile. After introductions, Ernest mentioned Ezra Pound, and Natalie gestured toward the drawing room that opened onto the courtyard through huge French doors. It was there, she said, where the musical recital would be held, and there where they would find their friend Ezra.

An American heiress who had come to Paris in the early 1900s, Natalie Barney was tall and willowy, in her middle forties, and had a billowing cloud of blond hair. Hadley, who conventionally equated lesbianism with masculinity, was surprised—pleasantly so—to see that Natalie Barney had not adopted any masculine characteristics. She was still a fine-looking woman, though Hadley saw nothing in her of the allure that had reportedly driven legions of women wild with desire. It was said that Natalie was—or had been, in her younger years—a veritable female Don Juan, a notorious seducer of Paris' most beautiful and desirable women. It was said that she listed among former lovers Isadora Duncan, Romaine Brooks, Marie Laurencin, Mata Hari, Colette, Dolly Wilde, Djuna Barnes, and Renee Vivian, to name only the most famous few. It had been with Renee Vivian that Natalie traveled to the island of Lesbos, where they built a shrine to Sappho.

Many of these former lovers were present at the musical recital, even though this was one of Natalie's "Fridays," a salon to which males were also welcomed, especially those who were the foremost writers and thinkers of their day. Hadley had heard it said that Natalie's "Saturdays" were attended only by females, and it was on these exclusive occasions that the initiates performed

nude dances and poetry readings and spirited musicales, all celebrating the loves of Lesbos.

Natalie guided Hadley and Ernest to the opened French doors
leading off the courtyard and into the drawing room, a room
with an enormous domed ceiling of stained glass. The decor was
that of the belle epoque, a decadent ambience produced by tapestries, towering mirrors in gold frames ornately carved with
cupids and naked nymphs, velvet-covered love seats, and tasseled and beaded lamp shades, pervaded by smells of incense
and potpourri. The chandeliers were glass grapes in shades of
green and amber. In each corner of the room was a divan, and
on each divan, a well-known personality or beauty presided
over his or her court. On one divan was Jean Cocteau, flanked
by his lover, nineteen-year-old Raymond Radiguet, on one side
and Princess Edmond de Polignac of Monaco on the other. Un-
knowns sat at their feet. Another of the divans was occupied by
Sylvia Beach, Adrienne Monnier, and a small, dark-haired man
that Hadley didn't know. There was room on the divan for one
more person, and Sylvia signaled for Ernest and Hadley to join
them. Hadley took the seat and Ernest sat near her on the arm
of the divan. After warm greetings all around, Adrienne introduced them to the man next to her, André Gide. The pretty
young man who sat on the floor at Gide's feet, apparently his
lover, was introduced as Antoine.

In a spotlighted location between the two other divans was a
piano, where the two musicians who were to perform had taken
their places. One was Olga Rudge, the violinist who was ru-
mored to be Ezra Pound's mistress, and Hadley was surprised to
see how young and lovely she was. Ezra had never impressed
Hadley as the kind of man who would attract beautiful, cultured,
young women, but if his wife, Dorothy, and this lovely young
Olga Rudge were any indication, why, then, he would have to
be accorded the charisma of a Svengali. Olga's piano accompanist was Renata Borgatti, who had lately been gaining renown in
Europe as a brilliant Chopin interpreter, and while she was neither as young nor as good-looking as Olga Rudge, she was nevertheless quite handsome in a masculine way.

Ezra was on the divan closest to the piano. As usual, he was scrunched so far down in the chair that he was virtually sitting on his shoulders. He was surrounded by disciples and admirers, among whom Dorothy Pound was nowhere to be seen. Ezra waved to Ernest, and called out that he wanted to talk to him after the performance.

Among those sitting in straight-back chairs or on the floor, Hadley recognized Max Jacob, Marie Laurencin, and Mina Loy. There were others in the room that Hadley recognized by sight but didn't know by name. Among them Adrienne pointed out the novelist Radcliffe Hall, another of Natalie's former lovers, who dressed entirely as a man, with short hair, a top hat, a monocle, and a big cigar. Dolly Wilde, Oscar's niece, was dressed in Oscar's old clothes and hat, and it was said that she looked so much like her late uncle that some people thought she was Oscar, come back from the dead.

There were many other women dressed in men's clothes, but the woman that Ernest paid most attention to was not mannish in her dress. Djuna Barnes, sitting near the piano in a straight-back chair, was elegantly feminine and quite beautiful, in spite of her short hair—hair as short and sleek and red as the pelt of a thoroughbred bay mare. On an ottoman next to her chair sat Thelma Wood and another woman.

"This is your first time here?" Sylvia asked.

"Yes," Hadley said, looking around. "And I'm amazed." She gestured toward the stained-glass dome. "Was this once a chapel?"

"I don't know, but it's said that Louis XIV built it for his mistresses—a sort of seraglio, I suppose."

"And the furniture looks rather turn-of-the-century Turkish, doesn't it?" Adrienne asked in French, an observation overheard by André Gide, who added in a gossipy undertone, "Yes, Natalie has carried on the tradition wonderfully, hasn't she? The stained glass and this decor make the place a sort of cross between a chapel and a bordello."

"One is not sure whether to pray or lay," Adrienne said, using both French and English to get the rhyme. As usual in her gray robe and white blouse, she looked like a voluptuous abbess, and Sylvia, in her velvet jacket and enormous foulard bow, resembled a Renaissance page boy. As for Hadley and Ernest, Hadley wore her best dress and a pair of tatty shoes, Ernest wore his three-piece Brooks Brothers suit and unpolished shoes—clothes that made them appear to be the most conventional people present.

As soon as Olga Rudge got her violin tuned to the piano, Natalie introduced the two musicians, and the performance began. They played a modern piece by Satie, then a Mozart sonata, and ended with a piece by Franz Liszt. Olga proved to be a consummate violinist. A passionate and fiercely energetic young woman, she seemed to be a stark contrast in character to quiet and remote Dorothy, Ezra's stay-at-home wife. And the attraction between her and Ezra was obvious in the way she played toward him, as if hurling the notes at him. Between pieces, he applauded madly and called, "Brava! Brava!"

But it was Olga's piano accompanist, Renata Borgatti, who riveted Hadley's attention. As a pianist herself, she could appreciate Renata's musical abilities, and she also marveled at how much the woman looked like Franz Liszt. Dressed in men's clothes of a *fin de siecle* cut, without makeup, and with a haircut like that of Liszt in the old paintings, she became Liszt as she played the sonata, or at least as Hadley imagined Liszt must have been: flamboyant technique and passionate feeling, her hands moving so fast they became a blur, her hair flying.

And perhaps she sensed Hadley looking at her, for once, between pieces, when she and Olga were acknowledging the applause, Renata raked her eyes over the audience, as if looking for someone in particular, as if she would recognize who it was that had been staring at her so intensely, and when her eyes met Hadley's, she looked no further. Their eyes locked for a moment, seeking some kind of recognition, and then Hadley blushed and dropped her gaze.

When the performance ended, Ernest went to talk to Ezra and to be introduced to Olga Rudge. Feeling vaguely apprehensive by the look that had passed between Renata Borgatti and herself, Hadley avoided the spontaneous little social groups that gathered in the drawing room. Instead, she made her way into the dining room where refreshments were being served on a large oval table. There were little triangular cucumber sandwiches, strawberry and raspberry tarts, with plenty of champagne and tea. Although the texture of the sandwiches was like damp little handkerchiefs, they were delicious and the champagne was the best money could buy.

Hadley had been in the dining room for perhaps ten minutes before Ernest found her. With him was Renata Borgatti.

"There you are, Hash," he said. "Here's someone I want you to meet." He introduced Hadley to Renata, and said, "I told her you were a pianist, too, and how good you are, and maybe you two could play a duet."

Flushed with embarrassment, Hadley protested, "Oh, God, Tatie, I'm not good enough to turn her pages, let alone play with her."

As she gulped a glass of champagne, Renata said, "Oh, I can't believe that. Sylvia Beach told me about you. Said she heard you play, and you had the talent to be a concert pianist."

"Oh, that," Hadley mumbled. "That was just living room stuff. She and Adrienne came to dinner at our apartment one evening, and after dinner I . . . . It was nothing."

"Oh, don't believe her. She's really very good, and I'm proud of her," Ernest said, and he meant it. Hadley was touched, not just by his faith in her, but that he should make a public announcement of it. Until she had met him, nobody in her life had ever told her that she was something to be proud of. Nobody but Ernest had ever tried to show her off, the way he did in public places—hotel lobbies, restaurants, parties—when he would beg her to play the piano. Sometimes, trembling with the fear of disgracing herself, she would do her best and no matter how badly she thought she played, he always applauded and said he was proud of her. She loved him for that.

"Ernest is slightly biased, I'm glad to say," Hadley said.

"Well, Sylvia isn't—at least not to the point of impairing her judgment, not to the point she'd sacrifice truth to flattery," Renata said, devouring one of the sandwiches and tossing off another glass of champagne. Her appetite seemed as robust as her piano playing. "If she says you're good, I believe her. Maybe we could play a four-handed piece?"

"Oh, my God," Hadley groaned, intimidated by the prospect.

As if having accomplished his purpose, Ernest, without excusing himself, picked up two glasses of champagne and went back into the drawing room. Hadley had a hunch that he was carrying the second glass to Djuna Barnes.

With Renata making conversation by asking Hadley about her favorite piano pieces, they had their glasses refilled once again by one of the maids, and then they drifted away from the table to the windows facing the garden. The twilight filtering through the thick green foliage was almost aqueous, as if they were under water, which contributed to Hadley's feeling of unreality.

"And what does your husband do?" Renata asked as she lit Hadley's cigarette.

With the conversation centered on herself, Hadley had no chance to find out about Renata, though there were some things she was certainly curious to know, such as why was Renata being so aggressively friendly to her? And did she expect Hadley to respond to her as if she—Renata—were a man? She certainly looked like a man—that is, an aesthete, quite good-looking, quite charming man—but she didn't stir in Hadley the sexual response that a man might have.

Hadley tried to steer the conversation away from herself by making some favorable comments about the house, and when Renata learned that Hadley had not seen the rest of it, she offered to give her a tour.

As they passed through the gay pandemonium of the crowded drawing room, Hadley saw Ernest in an intense tête-à-tête with Djuna Barnes. Djuna was standing with her back to the wall, and Ernest, facing her, was leaning against the wall on one outstretched arm, as if he had her trapped right where he wanted her. Thelma Wood was nowhere in sight. Hadley's baser inclination was to stay in the drawing room and keep an eye on Ernest and Djuna, but she surmounted her jealousy as she mounted the stairs, following Renata, and was diverted from her apprehensions about Ernest by her growing apprehensions about Renata.

As the two of them made their way through the upstairs bedrooms and Natalie's office, they met a few lesbian couples here and there, some of whom were having intimate conversations in dark corners, and in one bedroom Renata interrupted a couple who were passionately kissing.

"Oops, excuse us," she said, and before she closed the door, Hadley recognized that the couple was Thelma Wood and the elegantly feminine woman with whom she had shared the ottoman during the recital.

"Who's that she was with?" Hadley asked in a confidential whisper.

"Edna," Renata said, and when she saw that the single name meant nothing to Hadley, she added, "Edna St. Vincent Millay—the American poet? You haven't met her?"

"No. I'd like to, but now isn't the time to be introduced, obviously."

"I didn't expect so much of this sort of thing today," Renata confessed in a guilty whisper. "Tomorrow is women's day." And as she showed Hadley the balcony of the second bedroom, she said, "Any possibility of you coming tomorrow?"

Hadley gulped. "Without Ernest?"

"Of course. No men allowed on women's day. Can you come?" She had a clean seductive voice, with an almost imperceptible Italian accent.

Feeling that a flat refusal might appear to be rude, Hadley smiled as she said, "Oh, I don't think so. I hate to sound old-fashioned, but I'm a married woman." Trying to deflect her attention, Hadley gestured toward a small building in the garden behind the house. "Is that the Temple à l'Amitié that I've heard so much about?"

"Indeed it is."

It was a miniature Greek temple dedicated to the pleasures of Sappho. Hadley had hoped to get a look at this temple, and there it was: a classic, Doric-columned building with *à l'Amitié* carved into the stone over the entrance.

"The legendary Temple of Love, where, out of the sight of males, sapphic relationships are celebrated and ritualized," Renata said. "Would you like to see it before it gets too dark? Come along, I'll show it to you." She reached for Hadley's hand—just a touch—as they turned and walked back to the staircase.

Ernest and Djuna Barnes were no longer in the drawing room.

Hadley assumed they were in the dining room, and as an excuse to find out, she told Renata she would get another glass of champagne.

But they weren't in the dining room, either. Hadley hoped they hadn't managed to somehow slip by unseen upstairs into one of the bedrooms. Disguising her growing apprehensions with a debonair air, Hadley let Renata lead her down the pathway through the garden toward the Temple of Love. Each had a cigarette in one hand and a glass of champagne in the other.

Renata imparted what little she knew about the history of the temple. The garden had once belonged to Racine, she said, and the temple had been built sometime under the *Directoire,* just after the revolution.

"Natalie's lived here for about twelve years now, and many lesbian loves have been pledged here since she moved in," she said as they stepped inside. Four guests had just finished their visit and were walking away, leaving Renata and Hadley alone. The temple was a single room which, like the main house, was exquisitely and ornately furnished in a decor that suggested a courtesan's receiving room, a royal whorehouse.

As Hadley looked around, Renata watched her intently. Hadley shivered, whether from the chilly evening air or from apprehension, she didn't know.

"Are you cold?" Renata asked, and with a sort of token tenderness pulled Hadley's sweater tighter around her neck. Hadley almost giggled with nervousness, suspecting that Renata was getting ready to kiss her. But before Renata began any movement, Hadley heard a voice, and her smile vanished. It was Ernest's voice. He and Djuna Barnes were approaching the temple from the rear, walking slow and talking fast.

"But Djuna, I really want to see you sometime. Couldn't we have dinner together sometime?"

They were still talking when they went past the temple, with Djuna saying, "But I don't see the—"

Then they saw Hadley and Renata. They turned to face them, and the expression on Ernest's face was unforgettable, that of a boy getting caught by Mummy while doing something naughty.

"Oh. Hello," Ernest said, in his best fancy-meeting-you-here voice.

"Hi," Hadley said, and then as she said, "We . . . Renata and I . . . we were just looking over the temple," Ernest said at the same time, "We were just . . . walking . . . the garden."

To escape the awkward and undignified scene, Djuna Barnes tossed her head as haughtily as a thoroughbred racehorse, and walked on.

"Uh . . . excuse me," Ernest said, showing a rare sense of politeness, "I'd better . . ." He followed Djuna.

Perhaps out of consideration for Hadley's discomfort and jealousy, Renata did not resume her maneuvering for a kiss. Hadley was thankful, because, upset as she was, she didn't know how she would have handled it. And yet, she regretted it, since she suspected that Ernest and Djuna had been kissing in the garden behind the temple, and a kiss from Renata would have been sweet revenge, and—who knew?—she might have enjoyed it. It certainly wouldn't have been the first time she had kissed another woman on the lips.

But instead of kissing, they went back to the party, where Hadley found Ernest talking to Ezra Pound and Olga Rudge. Djuna Barnes was nowhere to be seen.

"Well, did you get a date with her?" Hadley asked scornfully after they had left the party and found a taxi to take them home.

"A date?" Ernest apparently had decided on denial as the best defense. "For Pete's sake, Tiny, I wasn't asking her for a date— not the kind you're implying. I just wanted to see her again, to get to know her. She's a good writer, and . . ."

"And beautiful?" Hadley prompted.

"Yes. All right, then, sure, beautiful, too. But you got no call to be jealous."

"Jealous? Who says I'm jealous? Just because my husband takes me to a party, and fobs me off on somebody else so he can spend all his time fawning over a beautiful, elegant, intelligent woman—what's there to be jealous about?"

"Nothing," he said. "And, besides, what have you got to complain about? You were getting plenty of attention from that piano player, Renata What's-her-name, weren't you? Did she try to make a date with you?"

"Yes," Hadley said in a tone of flippant vengeance. "She invited me to come back to Natalie's tomorrow evening, when it's women only. How do you like that?"

"Are you going?"

Hadley was shocked. "What? You can ask that? You can sit there, calm as you please, and ask your own wife if she's going to a lesbian orgy?"

"Oh, hell, I bet they don't have orgies," Ernest said, then added with less certainty, "Do they? Anyway, you're a big girl, you could walk out anytime you wanted."

"Wait a minute," Hadley said, trying to figure this out. "You sound like you want me to go."

He shrugged. "How else am I going to learn what goes on there? They sure as hell aren't going to ask me. And Djuna . . . I was hoping she would tell me, she being a writer, and all, but she's too haughty. She isn't awed by anything. I think she's incapable of feeling awe." He said it as if he had found her tragic flaw.

"And why do you want to know what lesbians do?"

"I might want to write about them someday, and how can I if I don't know what they do?"

When they got home, there was still tension between them; some dissatisfaction that caused them to be withdrawn and sulky—Hadley withdrawn, Ernest sulky.

"I think I'm going out to get myself a drink," he said.

"Can I come, too?"

"No, honey, not this time. I just want to be alone for a while. Okay? Maybe do some writing in a café . . ."

Hadley had come to recognize this ruse. Ernest was using what the working-class men in America had institutionalized as a night out with the boys. He would go somewhere and meet some of his male friends and most likely get drunk. She supposed it was their way of reaffirming their masculinity.

"And what am I supposed to do?" Hadley felt petulant and, at the same time, ashamed of her petulance. "Sit around here and drink by myself?" But when he adopted the sullen look of a little boy who's been denied permission to go out and play, Hadley forced herself to sound indulgent as she said, "Oh, go ahead."

After he was gone, she poured herself a stiff drink of whiskey, and sat down at the piano to play a few random notes, trying to remember one of the musical pieces that Renata had played that day with such vigor and skill. Remembering how Renata played, remembering how she smelled, remembering the moment just before Ernest and Djuna Barnes showed up. She wondered what might have happened. And what would Ernest have said had he caught them kissing?

12

Hadley

HADLEY DIDN'T ACCEPT Renata Borgatti's invitation to attend the lesbian soiree at Natalie Barney's, and—as far as she knew, anyway—Ernest never succeeded in getting a date with Djuna Barnes. His infatuation for Djuna seemed to diminish considerably after he met Margaret Anderson at a party at Ezra's house. Margaret and her lover, Jane Heap, had just arrived in Paris, preceded by their reputations for being the owners and editors of *The Little Review,* the literary magazine that had first published segments of James Joyce's *Ulysses.* The two women had been convicted of obscenity in an American court, the famous decision resulting in Joyce's masterpiece being seized by U.S. customs agents. Unable to continue publishing *The Little Review* in such a climate of censorship, the two women had moved their magazine to Paris, where they were celebrated as martyrs to literature. Ezra Pound, the foreign editor of *The Little Review,* had sent the magazine the two offending segments of *Ulysses* and then did everything he could for the two women, including putting them in touch with John Quinn, a famous defense attorney. Quinn defended them in court without charging them a penny.

"He lost the case, of course," Margaret Anderson said.

The guests at the party welcoming the two editors to Paris

included many notable expatriate writers and artists and musicians. James Joyce came since he was a guest of honor, accompanied by his wife, Nora. Kitty Cannell, the estranged wife of the American poet Skipwith Cannell and one of Ezra's former mistresses, was there, as was Ezra's present mistress, Olga Rudge. Both Kitty and Olga got along just fine with Ezra's wife, Dorothy. Mike Strater, the painter, and his wife, Maggie, were there. Sylvia Beach had come, too, but Adrienne Monnier, who disliked Ezra, stayed home. Hilda Doolittle, the American poet H.D., who had been Ezra's first sweetheart back in the days when they were both students at the University of Pennsylvania, was there without her lesbian mate, Bryher, who—it was also said—couldn't stand to be in the same room with Ezra. Jean Cocteau, Raymond Radiguet, Natalie Barney, Mr. and Mrs. Louis Bromfield, and Kay Boyle were among the guests, as were the Hemingways. George Anthiel, a young avant-garde pianist and composer, a protégé of Margaret Anderson and Jane Heap, was there with bells on— literally, with bands of jingling bells strapped around his wrists and ankles, so that he could make music when he moved. The only prominent American literary figures missing from the party were Djuna Barnes and Gertrude Stein. Djuna had been invited, but didn't show up. Gertrude had not been invited.

Margaret Anderson was one of the most beautiful women in Paris. She had skin as smooth and poreless as a child's, she had violet-colored eyes, the dark ringlets of a Grecian goddess, and perfectly symmetrical features. It was, altogether, a beauty marked by an exquisite femininity. Jane Heap, her lover, a huge woman, who always wore men's clothes, combed her short hair like a man's, and smoked big black cigars.

Like Hadley and Djuna Barnes and Dorothy Pound, Margaret Anderson was at least eight years older than Ernest. But in spite of her great beauty, Margaret was not perfect. Hadley was glad to see that she was a rather dithery woman, a compulsive talker, a trait that ordinarily would have repelled Ernest, but such was her beauty that Ernest seemed willing to overlook the way she rattled on and on and on.

"Just think!" Margaret joyfully commanded her audience as she stood in the middle of the room, wearing the single white glove on her left hand that had become her *insigne*. She smoked cigarettes continually as she regaled the guests with rambling comments about the famous *Ulysses* obscenity trial. "Just think!" she said now, "the judges were so addlepated they wouldn't even let our lawyer read sections from the magazine. Quinn wanted to read the dirty passages in *Ulysses* to demonstrate that, while they may be dirty and even disgusting, they weren't obscene. But the judge! No, no, no! He couldn't read the passages while Jane and I were present because the language was too indecent for our delicate feminine ears. We were the ones who published it, for God's sake, but I guess the judges thought we'd done so without reading it, because they wouldn't let Quinn read it out loud in our presence!"

It was only when Ezra, who didn't like being in a crowd unless he himself was the center of attention, finally overpowered Margaret's chatter with some obtuse comments on the nature of justice in America, that Ernest finally got a chance to engage Margaret in private conversation. He followed her when she went to the toilet. From where Hadley sat on the floor in the front room, she could see Ernest waiting at the toilet door, and when Margaret came out, Hadley saw Ernest sort of enfold Margaret into his character, into his overpowering enthusiasms and puppylike excitement, as he was so capable of doing, quite as if he were wearing a cape and drew her into it. Hadley couldn't hear what was being said between them, but she could guess from Margaret's attentive but slightly embarrassed reactions that Ernest's words must be very flattering.

Because Margaret was the guest of honor and the star of the party, Ernest was able to monopolize her for only short periods, but he never missed a chance to get her alone, or whisper something in her bejeweled ear as they passed in the crowd of guests, or give her a look of adoration from across the room.

Hadley got drunk. Perhaps in an attempt to reclaim Ernest's attention, she drank too much wine, and got sick, and had to stagger to the toilet to throw up. When she came out of the toilet and found Ernest talking merrily with Dorothy Pound and Margaret and Nora Joyce in the small kitchen, he didn't even look at her until she gently tugged on his sleeve and said in the squeaky voice of a needy child, "Tatie, would you take me home, please? I'm sick."

Slightly annoyed by being interrupted in his conversation with three lovely women, all of whom he was a little in love with, he said, "How about some coffee? That'd fix you up."

"No, I have to go. . . ."

"Ah, Bones, damnit to hell, everybody's talking about going down to Les Halles and getting some onion soup, and I want to go with them. I'll tell you what," he added, getting a bright idea, "we'll go up to Montparnasse and get you a taxi. I'll be home later."

"Oh, no, Tatie, please, I couldn't make it up those stairs on my own."

But Ernest remained ungiving until Margaret said in an imperious tone, "Oh, for God's sake, Hemingway, take your wife home. Don't be like Leopold Bloom, sneaking around Nighttown while your wife is maybe going beddy-bye with a bugger like Blazes Boylan. You never can tell who'll be the next cuckold, can you, eh? Take her home."

He obeyed, though grudgingly. As they were saying good night to the other guests and apologizing for being unable to go with them to Les Halles, Ernest left no doubt whose fault it was.

At first Hadley hoped they would get a taxi on boulevard Montparnasse, but Ernest, perhaps as punishment, said they should walk home. He said walking would do her good. Sober her up. And he was right. After staggering along for a block or two, the exercise and fresh air began to clear Hadley's head, and soon she was no longer staggering, no longer sick to her stomach— had become sober enough, in fact, to feel guilty for having taken Ernest away from the party.

"I'm sorry, Wemedge," she said to a sulking Ernest. "You looked like you were having such a good time with Margaret."

He conceded that fact with a grunt.

"You were talking to her most of the evening."

Another grunt.

"What did you two talk about?"

"Oh, it was nothing," he said. "I was just telling her how much I admired her for publishing *The Little Review,* is all, and talked to her about me submitting some of my sketches for the next edition."

"Really?" Hadley said, trying to keep any signs of jealousy and possessiveness out of her voice. "Then I guess Jane Heap and Margaret got the wrong impression. From their looks of discomfort, I gathered that they thought you were flirting with Margaret."

"Oh, shit, that's ridiculous. Look, to make it as a writer, I have to butter up people like her, don't I? It was my career I was thinking about. That's all."

He was lying. Hadley knew it. But though his flirting sometimes caused her pangs of jealousy, she always found solace in her steadfast belief that he loved her. She knew he did. And as for her love for him, that never flagged, no matter what he did or didn't do. She was his feather cat and his poo and he was her wicky and her cuddly waxen puppy, and if he needed constant reassurance that he was attractive to other women, why, so be it—just as long as he came back home to her.

"Anyway, what're you talking about?" Ernest said after a moment's thought. "Why would I be flirting with her?"

"Because she's so very beautiful, of course."

"Yeah. Sure, she is. But she's also a lesbo."

"Oh," Hadley said with a goading but good-natured smile, "I was beginning to wonder if you'd noticed."

13

Margaret

MARGARET HAD NEVER met anyone quite like this Hemingway lad. It was downright embarrassing the way he pursued her at Ezra's party, telling her how lovely she was, and how he wanted so much to take her to dinner some evening soon or take her dancing or show her Paris.

"Why?" Margaret had asked, wondering what he thought he would get out of it.

"For the same reason I like to sit in front of a Cezanne or a Goya—to get to know you better, to experience you, to absorb you," he said. "As lovely as you are, you should be absorbed like a work of art."

Well, who could help but be flattered? Within fifteen minutes of meeting her, he had boasted that, though he made his living as a writer, he was a professional boxer, that he had once been a lieutenant who led Arditi troops into battle on the Italian front during the War, and that he had been wounded by 242 pieces of shrapnel. Did she want to see his scars?

"I don't think that will be necessary," Margaret said. "I believe you. However, I can't quite believe you're a boxer. You have no scar tissue on your face, your ears are not cauliflowered, and your nose, by the look of it, has never been broken."

"I'm a good defensive fighter, I don't get hit a lot," he said. "Besides, I'm tough. You want to hit me to find out?" He pointed to his abdomen. "Go ahead, hit me with your fist. Go on. As hard as you can."

Margaret had never in her life hit anyone with her fist. Was this due to cowardice? To a fear of reprisal? She had never really thought about it; but she was tempted to take advantage of Hemingway's permission—no, his encouragement—to do so now with impunity. Well, why not? She might never get another chance like this. So she carefully put down her cigarette and her glass of wine, made a fist by curling the four fingers of her right hand around her thumb, and got set to thump him a good one.

"Wait a minute," he snapped. "That's not how to make a fist—you'll break your thumb like that. Here." He took her hand and showed her how to make a fist, with the fingers curled into her palm and the thumb curled over them on the outside. "Now stand like this"—taking her by the shoulders and showing her how to stand—"in order to put the whole weight of your body behind the blow. Now hit me with everything you've got. Go ahead."

She hit him, but she couldn't bring herself to do it as hard as she could. She didn't want to hurt him. It was an odd sensation. *Smack!* It was like . . . like what? Like nothing she had ever felt before. And he didn't even flinch.

"Oh, come on," he said. "Is that the best you can do? Hit me again, and this time put the weight of your body behind it."

Since all the party-goers in their immediate vicinity had stopped to look at them, Margaret, who loved to be the center of attention, had the added incentive to sock Hemingway with everything she had, to hurt him, and then reap the award of applause that she was sure to get from the onlookers. So she drew her fist back and hit Hemingway with all her strength. She was shocked to find that she had hurt herself more than she had hurt him. Her hand throbbed while he stood there, smirking, saying, "See? I told you." He banged himself in the stomach. "Solid muscle."

Hemingway was not what Margaret would have considered an attractive male. The males in her social circles were poets and musicians, always sensitive and vulnerable and often effete, so she didn't quite know how to handle Hemingway's aggressive masculinity, his bully-boy manners. But for that very reason she was beginning to find him both fascinating and repellent—as a snake might both fascinate and repel—and so she no longer tried to shoo him away. Still, she was glad enough to be rid of him when his wife got drunk and prevailed upon him to take her home.

She had put him completely out of mind by the time she and Jane Heap and the Joyces and the Pounds and some others from the party had gone to Les Halles for early-morning onion soup and wine and gaiety among the produce market's cacophony of rattling and creaking horse carts, shouts of workers and vendors, the laughter of drunken all-night revelers. Among the market's many smells were those of food cooking and fresh horse droppings and the moist earth clotted around the roots of the farm produce being unloaded and arranged for display in the stalls.

Margaret took it for granted that Hemingway's odd interest in her would end with the party, or at least as soon as someone informed him that her sexual interest did not extend to men, but two days later, as she, Jane Heap, Djuna Barnes, Laurence Vail and his wife, Peggy Guggenheim, were all having drinks at the Café Select, Ernest came shadowboxing along the street, and when he saw Margaret, he stopped and approached the table. Dressed in dirty tennis shoes and rumpled clothes, unshaven and uncombed, he appeared to be a rather disruptable character, and Laurence Vail, a bitchy snob, was annoyed by the intruder.

"Who is this?" he asked. "The Jack Dempsey of Montparnasse?"

Hemingway gave Laurence a straight look. "What's it to you?"

Laurence Vail was known to be a man who was easily aroused to violence. When drunk or displeased, he had been known to knock people about, throw bottles, overturn tables. In addition, being married to the immensely wealthy Peggy Guggenheim had given Laurence an arrogance and air of social superiority that few people challenged, especially loutish-looking boulevardiers like Hemingway. So it was no surprise to anyone when Laurence warned, "Say, I don't think I like your attitude."

"Want to make something of it?" Hemingway said, and if his readiness to do battle was a bluff, it was a convincing one.

Laurence snorted his disdain. "Well, they told me around the Quarter you were quite a show-off, but I didn't believe it till now."

Hemingway said in a hard, level voice, "They told me around the Quarter that you're a goddamn phony, and I've always believed it."

"Come, come, you lads," Jane chided, puffing on her cigar and chuckling dryly. "No fighting. You're in the presence of ladies."

Laurence had bunched his muscles, ready to rise to Hemingway's threat, but Jane's admonition checked his movement, giving him an excuse to back down gracefully. He and Hemingway continued to stare at each other for a moment longer, but it was Laurence who first dropped his gaze.

Considering that the contretemps was over and that he had won, Hemingway's expression changed from combativeness to gentle beseeching as he said to Margaret, "I've been looking for you. Can I talk to you for a minute?"

It was obviously a request for a private chat, and though intrigued and puzzled, Margaret wasn't sure what to do. She glanced at both Djuna and Jane for some signal. Though she and Jane were lovers and mates, their relationship was not the dominant-submissive paradigm of heterosexual marriages. By agreement, they were equals, and free, and forever friends, no matter what, and there would be no question of jealousy or betrayal if Margaret acceded to Hemingway's request; so Margaret's glance wasn't asking for permission, it was merely asking for advice. And Jane, who seemed as intrigued and puzzled by Hemingway's request as Margaret herself, shrugged, leaving it entirely up to Margaret.

"All right," Margaret said, and she and Hemingway moved into the interior of the Select, where they stood at the bar and drank *fin,* which Hemingway paid for. Margaret held the glass in her left hand, the one on which she always wore a white glove, and in her gloveless right hand she held a long cigarette holder.

"I been looking for you," Hemingway said in a slightly sheepish voice.

"So you said," Margaret responded. "Why?"

"I can't . . . I haven't been able to get you off my mind,"

Hemingway said, as if diagnosing an ailment. "I think about you all the time. Listen, isn't there some way we could . . . slip off together?"

"Tonight?"

"Gee, that would be lovely, if we could."

"We can't. Jane, Djuna, and I are going to La Monocle," Margaret said, naming the famous lesbian nightclub where males were not allowed. "Anyway, what's the point? What do you want of me, if I may be so blunt?"

To Hemingway's credit, he seemed embarrassed when he murmured, "I just want to . . . to be with you. I can't get you off my mind, I think I . . . I just have this fierce urge to make love to you."

"Don't be absurd," Margaret blurted. Her first impulse was to laugh, but she quickly perceived that this was not as ridiculous as it was pathetic, so she added sympathetically, "Listen, don't you know? Don't you realize that I'm . . . that I don't make love to men?"

"Oh, yeah. Sure, I see this . . . this woman you're always with, this Jane Heap. She looks like a man, talks like a man, and acts like a man. The only difference between her and me is, I've got between my legs what it takes to be a man, and she hasn't."

Margaret allowed herself a derisive little laugh, uncertain if she should be amused or offended. With her beauty, she had been the object of many men's desires, but most of them had been disuaded—some even disgusted—when they learned that she was a lesbian. But Hemingway's desires didn't in the least seem blunted. He reached out to put his arm around her waist and pull her close to him.

She extricated herself, saying, "No, no, excuse me, I've got to go," and then she patted his unshaven cheek with sympathy and flattered fondness when she saw how disappointed he was by her rejection. "Sorry. Good night, and thank you for the drink. Ezra says he's going to give me some of your poems and sketches for *The Little Review,* so I'll be talking to you about them, but I think we'd better forget about any other kind of relationship, don't you?" And without giving him a chance to protest or plead, she turned and went back to the sidewalk table, leaving Hemingway at the bar.

Laurence Vail and Peggy Guggenheim were no longer at the table. Djuna and Jane ceased all conversation and gave Margaret their full attention when she, looking a little agog, resumed her seat at the table.

"So?" Jane asked in a voice that anticipated amusement. "What was that all about?"

"My God," Margaret said, sticking a new cigarette into her holder, "the man is quite mad. Says he wants to make love to me, in spite of me being a woman's woman."

Djuna smiled. "Oh, I see you don't know about Hemingway. He doesn't want to make love to you in spite of you being a lesbian, but because of it."

"What?" Margaret said, confused. "Why would he want to do that?"

"Because, my dear, he's one of us," Djuna said.

"One of us? Whatever do you mean?"

"I mean he's only attracted to lesbians."

"Oh, God, Djuna, how droll! You're drunk and having a joke."

"I'm not joking," Djuna said. "I've had some experience with that lad."

14

Hadley

HADLEY LEARNED MANY things about Ernest that summer in Paris. She learned what he was like when he was productive, and what he was like when he wasn't, and what the differences were between them. She learned that he was a thrill-seeker, not a thinker. Indeed, he seemed to be something of an anti-intellectual. You never heard him discussing Nietzsche or Plato, and he looked down on people who did. The people he admired were professional soldiers, boxers, aviators, bullfighters, big-game hunters, explorers, conquerors—men of action, rather than men of intellect or spirit or even men of words. He identified himself as a writer only among people who might admire writers; among working men and sportsmen, he was a boxer or, at most, a hard-bitten reporter.

She learned that he not only liked emotional highs, he thrived on them. On ordinary days of routine and drudgery, he became depressed, restless. The times when he was most productive were times of emotional highs, which he sought through love experiences with women or physical confrontations with men. He needed someone to love, and he needed someone to hate. It wasn't the kind of feeling that made the difference, it was feeling itself. Descartes had said, "I think, therefore I am," but Ernest would have said, "I feel, therefore I am." Like Lord Byron, with whom he shared many other qualities, Ernest would have said,

"Feeling is all!"—even if what he felt was pain. And if feelings lacked intensity, he would create tension as a substitute for intensity. At parties, he would get drunk and make passes at pretty women, and if the party got dull, he would stir things up by provoking quarrels, and sometimes he would insult you, then laugh to demonstrate that his insults were only good-natured raillery, then charm you to disarm you of any anger. Strife was preferable to the boredom of peace, and the thrill that came with fear was better than no thrill at all. Under certain circumstances, the thrill produced by fear could be the best thrill. It was this constant search for excitement that brought about his trip to Constantinople and his and Hadley's first big fight.

War broke out between Greece and Turkey in September 1922. Every day Ernest devoured the newspaper accounts of the war, and he talked to Hadley about it—ostensibly talked to her, that is; he was really talking to himself, imaging the war, getting excited about how Mustapha Kemal, the Turkish leader, was making a slow, strategic advance toward Constantinople, which was then under the protection of the Allied Armies that had won the World War. Constantinople's polyglot population—Turks, Christians, Jews, White Russians, and Greeks—were on the verge of panic. They feared that Kemal would at least impose a rigid Islamic regime on the city; at worst, he might carry out a bloodbath in retaliation for the massacre of the Turks at Smyrna three years earlier. The headlines blared the news that Smyrna was in flames, and the fire and the Turkish bombardment had killed more than 1,000 people and left more than 60,000 Armenian and Turk refugees struggling toward Constantinople. There were rumors of cholera epidemics and massacres.

"Looks like it might become a war between Turkey and the Allies," Ernest said, savoring the excitement. "That would mean another World War."

Hadley knew he was itching to go, and if the *Star* had asked him to go as their correspondent, she might have been a little less resistant to the idea; but it was Ernest himself who deliberately proposed the assignment. He sent the editor at the *Star* a list of expenses, asking only 200 dollars for travel and nine dollars a day for living expenses, which was not enough for two people. When the cable from the *Star* arrived, accepting Ernest's proposition and authorizing the expenses, Hadley complained, "So you're going to leave me here again."

Hadley and Ernest had just sat down to a dinner that Marie Cocotte had prepared before she went home for the day when the courier delivered the cable from the *Star*.

"What the hell do you expect? You can't go with me."

"Why not?" Hadley demanded, pushing away her plate. She had lost her appetite.

Ernest was incredulous. "Goddamnit, there's a war going on, that's why. This won't be a nice hiking trip into the Argon Forest, or a skiing trip to Chamby. Read the papers, for shit's sake. Where I'm going, there are massacres and epidemics. It could even become a new World War."

"Then I don't want you to go. What if you got killed, or injured? What would I do? I don't want you to leave me here alone again. I was here all by myself when you went to Genoa for three weeks, and God only knows how long you'd be gone this time. You said I could go with you next time, or you wouldn't go."

"Sure, but that was . . . I meant, if I went to another conference, like Genoa, sure, you could go, but a war? I didn't mean a war."

"Then I don't want you to go," Hadley said, becoming adamant.

"Well, I am going," he declared, "and that's that. I'm a correspondent, it's what I have to do to make a living, and—"

"Hack work!" Hadley cried. "That's all it is, hack work for a damned newspaper that'll be used to line garbage cans the next day. Why don't you do what Gertrude and Pound advised you— quit writing that newspaper stuff, write the great fiction you're capable of?"

Ernest threw down his fork. "Because we have to eat, that's why."

"No, that's not why," Hadley said, directly contradicting him for one of the few times since she had known him. "We could live on my money, just like Pound lives on Dorothy's, and Gertrude lives on her family's trust fund. It would only be till you started selling your stories. So it's not because you need the money, is it? It's because you need the excitement, and you don't want to have me tagging along."

"We've been through this before," Ernest snapped, becoming more angry. "I've said all I'm going to."

"Well, I haven't," Hadley said. "I don't want to be left alone in Paris again while you go gallivanting around exotic parts of the world, having adventures and wasting time and talent on news-paper writing that you should be devoting to serious fiction. Maybe even getting yourself killed."

But though she kept arguing until their dinner got cold, she couldn't make him understand how she felt about being left alone.

"I don't want you to go because I'm nothing without you," she said in a pleading tone. While the flattery of her dependence made Ernest momentarily more sympathetic, it didn't make him more understanding. She tried to explain that all her life she had fulfilled other people's expectations of her. Before her father had put a gun to his head and blew his brains out, he had always expected Hadley to be Daddy's little girl, a docile child who would bring him his pipe and tobacco and house slippers and never give him cause for displeasure. And she became that child. Her mother's expectations had made her into a prisoner, a spin-ster, an invalid too timid and weak to break the slave's bonds of loyalty to old ways and old masters. And Ernest had freed her from those bonds, had given her the gift of life, had brought her to live in Paris as the wife of a man who was a skier, an adven-turer, a boxer, a tennis player, a mountain climber, a hobnobber with literary legends the likes of Sherwood Anderson, James Joyce, Gertrude Stein, and Ezra Pound, among whom she was sure he would someday be acknowledged as a great writer. And his expectations for Hadley had made her an extension of him-self. He had defined her. And when he left her alone, as he had when he went to Genoa on assignment for the *Star*, she was nobody. Undefined, she was nothing more than a child cast adrift in the wilderness of a great city.

"And you don't care!" she cried, as frustrated and furious as she had ever been in her life. The quarrel continued into the night

and began again the next morning when Ernest, under her baleful stare, declared his intention had not changed, he was going
to Constantinople.

"I suppose if I were your precious Agnes, you wouldn't go,"
Hadley jeered.

"That's a low blow," he said. "And you're not going to get me
to stay by being a copperplated bitch."

"Well, then, to hell with you!" she cried, and when he came
home drunk and belligerent that afternoon and began packing
his bags, she said, "Go on, get yourself killed, see if I give a
damn! But don't be surprised if I'm not here when you get back."

"The way you're acting right now, I hope you're not," he
shouted.

"Well, if I'm not, maybe you can get your precious Agnes back.
You'd like that, wouldn't you?" Even in her rage, she knew that
this was going too far, but she couldn't stop herself. It was like
running downhill and she had to run faster and faster to keep
from falling on her face. They hadn't had sex for the last three
weeks, not even on their wedding anniversary. And Hadley's
own rage and self-disgust and compulsion to hurt him came to a
crescendo when she sneered, "And maybe with her you can at
least get it up again. With your precious Agnes, you can—"

Her voice was cut off by a slap. For the first time since they had
known each other, Ernest struck her, a forceful blow across the
face with the back of his hand. Her head felt as if fireworks had
gone off in it. She staggered and grabbed a chair and held on to
keep from falling while she waited for her vision to clear of
multicolored pinpoints of light. And when she could see again,
she looked at him with the fear and incredulity of someone who
had seen for the first time a lover's true face.

He, too, seemed surprised by the blow, and for a moment he
had the confused look of someone who was vacillating between
self-righteousness and remorse. Had Hadley shown some contrition and a willingness to reconcile, his guilt might have tri-
umphed over his rage, and they both would have ended up in
tears, begging each other's forgiveness; but Hadley couldn't do
it. For once in her life, she couldn't accommodate. All she felt
toward him at the moment, with her stinging, aching cheek, with

her vision blurred by tears, was disgust. And when she spoke again, the words came out of her mouth without being bidden, as if the blow from the back of his hand had opened up the dark chamber where she had stored all the hurts she'd ever had to take from others in her life: "Oh, you big man. . . . Does it make you feel like a *big man* to hit me? Go ahead, if it makes you feel good, do it again."

And with that, all Ernest's inclination toward shame and contrition vanished. The self-righteous rage took over completely, and he drew back his hand as if to strike her again.

"Go on!" she goaded. "I can't defend myself. There's no one here to stop you."

"Damn you. Damn you," he muttered, and hurried out of the apartment.

15

Mike Strater

HIS MIDDLE NAME was Hyacinth. His full name was Henry Hyacinth Strater, but he was called Mike by everyone who knew him, though it was his middle name that was important to Hemingway. Hem learned of the name one evening at Ezra and Dorothy's apartment, when Mike and Hem got to discussing middle names in general. The name F. Scott Fitzgerald had come up in conversation because Mike had known Scott at Princeton, and Hem made the crack that he didn't like men who parted their names on the side.

"If your first name was Francis, you'd probably do the same thing." Mike said. "*I* wouldn't, of course, because even Francis is preferable to Hyacinth."

"Hyacinth?" Hem said. "Your middle name is Hyacinth?"

He seemed to consider it an almost personal affront that someone named Hyacinth could be as big and masculine and normal-looking as Hemingway himself was.

Mike tilted his head with mea culpa resignation. "Afraid so."

Ezra piped in with, "How in the name of holy soda crackers did you get tagged with a fairy moniker like that 'un?"

"My mother promised her Aunt Hyacinth that she'd name her child after her, and my mother was a woman of her word. When I came out with balls, it didn't matter, I still got christened Henry Hyacinth."

"Jeeees-us," Hemingway said, as if he couldn't imagine a worse fate for an innocent baby with balls.

Mike realized that he had said the wrong thing. Revealing such a thing to Hem was making himself vulnerable to being needled. Mike had known Hem only for a short while, but he and his wife, Maggie, had played tennis with Hem and Hadley a few times at the courts on boulevard Arago, and it had become obvious during the games that Hem would take advantage of any perceived weakness in an opponent. In the game of life, as in the game of tennis, everybody who wasn't on Hem's side was against him, and his need to win, to beat his opponents in whatever he did, transformed a leisurely afternoon game of tennis into a war, take no prisoners, give no quarter.

And how he hated to lose! If he missed an easy shot, or double faulted on the serve, he would become furious and sometimes throw his racquet. At such times he was treated as if he were an unpredictable grizzly bear, best regarded with polite silence to prevent becoming an object of his fury.

And he lost a lot. Actually, he was rather a poor tennis player. He was clumsy and uncoordinated and there was something wrong with his eyesight, though he wore no glasses. Neither was Mike a good player, nor was Maggie, but they were in it for exercise and fun; Hemingway was in it to win. And since he had a tendency to blame others for his problems, Hadley often caught hell whenever they lost a game.

Poor Hadley. She was the best tennis player of the four, but she usually took the blame when she and Hem lost. One day, after the game was over, and the Hemingways had once again lost to Maggie and Mike, the four of them were at the benches, putting their racquets away and toweling off, when Hem said to Mike in a sulky undertone, "Women! Sometimes I don't think they should even be allowed to play ball games. You ever see them play baseball? Awful! Destroy your faith in the game."

Hadley and Maggie were only a few steps away, drying off and chatting about Maggie's baby, and they heard what Hem said— as he obviously intended for them to, even though he tried to forestall any critical retorts by his confidential undertone. Then he added, "Sometimes I think the only balls a woman should be allowed to play with are a man's."

A glance at the women confirmed that they had heard the remark. Hadley blushed, Maggie bridled.

"Well, Mr. Hemingway," Maggie said in an icy voice, "if you want to get your balls played with, why don't you just hang 'em out here." She swatted the air with her racquet. "Nothing would give me greater pleasure than to whack 'em a few times."

Hem, perhaps feeling chastised for being such a bad sport, asked Maggie and Mike to join him and Hadley for a lunch at a nearby bistro, but Maggie had the ready excuse of having to hurry home and take care of the baby. She and Mike had a six-month-old boy who was being looked after by a French wet-nurse. They had a house out in the Hameau Beranger, near the Auteuil racetrack, and it was a long ride on the streetcar. To his credit, Hem tried to make amends by apologizing for being so difficult on the tennis court, but that didn't placate Maggie.

"I've had it with that man," she announced after she and Mike got on the streetcar at Place Denfert Rochereau, leaving a downcast Hem and Hadley to wait for a streetcar going the other way. "I'm never going to play tennis with them again."

"But what about Hadley?" Mike said. "You like her, don't you? Seems like an awfully nice woman to me."

"Well, I could like her," Maggie said, "if I didn't feel sorry for her."

"Why should you? For the way she is with him?"

"I know men like him. A woman doesn't exist for him as a separate personality, but only as an extension of his own personality."

"Maybe she likes it like that—so what?"

"I can't be a friend of hers if I can't respect her, no matter how nice she is, and I can't respect anybody who kowtows to a bully."

"Well, the bully himself is coming over Tuesday to spar a few rounds. Hope that won't be a problem."

"I'll be polite, and as long as he's a guest in our house I'll be hospitable, but as for playing tennis with him again—never."

Mike and Hem had begun boxing soon after they met at Ezra

Pound's apartment. Along with about a dozen other young artists, writers, musicians, and poets, Mike and Hem were considered to be Ezra's protégés. Mike was an artist, a portrait
painter—not a Rembrandt, but not bad. He had studied art at
Princeton, where he had known F. Scott Fitzgerald, who fixed
on Mike for a while as hero material, and even put him into his
first novel, *This Side of Paradise,* as a character named Burne
Holiday. Fitzgerald had admired Mike greatly for being—among
other things—a sensational prankster, a scholar, a class presi-
dent, a football star, a political revolutionary, a boxer, and an
artist. In *This Side of Paradise,* Fitzgerald had said of Mike that
he seemed to be climbing heights where others would be forever unable to get a foothold. But, finally, the most revolutionary
thing Mike ever did was to give up everything except his wife
and child and trust fund and move to Paris to become a painter.
It was Harold Loeb in Greenwich Village, where Maggie and
Mike lived for a while after they were married, who told Mike to
get in touch with Ezra Pound when he got to Paris.

Mike had heard of Hem before he ever met him at Ezra's—
heard that he was a professional boxer, and naturally, being the
only two boxers among Ezra's stable of protégés, he and Hem
had struck up a friendship as soon as they met. However, there
were reservations on Hem's part.

"Well, if you learned to box in college, you must be a very
smart fighter, so how about us sparring a few rounds someday
soon?"

"Sure," Mike said, assessing his chances of winning such a
sparring match, or at least surviving it without any permanent
damage. Hem had bragged that he had been a sparring partner
for the likes of Harry Greb, Sam Langford, and Tommy Gibbons.

"Only they didn't learn their skills in college. Like me, they
learned theirs in the school of hard knocks," Hem said, and went
on to boast that he had actually whipped Henry "Young" Cuddy
in a three-round exhibition match on board the *Leopoldina*
when he and Hadley were on their way over from America last
year. "You've heard of Young Cuddy?" Hem smiled to take the
sting of effrontery out of his ridicule. "Or did he come along too
late to be taught in your college courses?"

"A little too late for that, I'm afraid," Mike said. "But I saw him fight Eugene Bullard here in Paris last January. Must have been just after you beat him on the ship. But he beat Bullard, so he has to be a pretty good boxer."

Hem's bragging and ridicule were meant to be intimidating, and well it might have been, except that the lack of damage to Hem's handsome face belied his having been a professional sparring partner. Mike had heard around the Quarter that Hemingway, besides being a heavyweight boxer, was suspected of being a braggart and a poseur.

Mike was just as tall and weighed about as much as Hem did—six feet, 200 pounds—and Mike figured that with what he had learned about boxing at Princeton, he could probably hold his own with Hem in a sparring match.

He was right. A few days after the party at Ezra's, Hem came to Mike's house, bringing his lavender trunks and his own boxing gloves. Mike had converted an unused potting shed and hothouse into a sort of makeshift gym. Hanging from the ceiling were punching bags made of army duffel bags filled with sawdust, and on the floor was a canvas mat about the size of a boxing ring. It was nothing fancy, but it was well-lighted and had good ventilation during the summertime, and it kept Mike and Hem out of Maggie's way.

During their first sparring session the two of them were cautious. As Mike suspected, Hem was not nearly good enough to have been a professional boxer, and Hem found out that Mike's college-class boxing was not as sissified as he had anticipated. They boxed for a long time—about thirty or forty minutes—without a break, and neither of them established dominance. Hem's advantage was strength and a mauling, clubbing style that might have been more effective if they had been in a ring and he could have bulled Mike into a corner. But there were no ropes around the mat, and Hem was clumsy with his feet, so Mike easily evaded his bull-like rushes. After the second or third sparring match, Mike looked forward to Hem's rushes because they provided him with an excellent opportunity to shift from a right-handed stance to left-handed.

Mike was a natural southpaw, but he could box right-handed

or left-handed, and the one maneuver he had that Hem never caught on to was the Fitzsimmons shift. It had been originated by Bob Fitzsimmons, who used it to knock out Gentleman Jim Corbett and win the heavyweight championship back in 1897. Mike boxed right-handed until Hem became aggressive, then he would shift to southpaw. Confused and thrown off his rhythm, Hem could be clobbered. Mike would hit him with a right jab, come in with a left cross to the abdomen, and swarm all over him. When Mike finished with the flurry, he would switch back to the right-handed stance. Hem never did get wise to what Mike was doing.

"Hyacinth!" he sneered when he was more than usually disgusted with the outcome of their sparring matches. He simply couldn't reconcile himself to the fact that someone named Hyacinth could hold his own against him in a sparring match.

Though Hem hated not being able to beat Mike, they became good friends during that summer. Hem often stayed for lunch after the sparring was done, and because he had no bathing facilities at his own apartment, he sometimes used Mike and Maggie's big copperplated tub.

Mike began painting a portrait of Hem. He called it "The Boxer." It was a full-face pose of a young man in a gray sweatshirt, gazing pensively at something out of the picture. Both Hem and Mike liked the portrait, and Hem, in a burst of generosity and friendship, said that Mike was a swell painter and a swell guy.

But one day toward the end of September, Hem arrived for their weekly workout in an unusually belligerent mood. Mike had often seen Hem annoyed and offended, but never had he seen him so hateful as he was that day. Maggie and the baby weren't at home, so they went into the workout room right away, and Mike asked what was eating him.

"Goddamn women," Hem growled. "Once a man gets married he's absolutely bitched. I've been assigned to cover the war in Constantinople for the *Star,* and Hadley's throwing a fit." It was apparent that he'd had more than a few drinks, and his anger had an alcoholic edge.

"Maybe we should forget about working out today," Mike said.

"No, no," Hem said. "I want to. Do me good. Be my last chance for a while."

After they put on the gloves, Mike quickly learned that Hem intended to take his hostility out on him. Without even warming up, Hem charged. He had already hit Mike a couple of times before Mike realized that Hem was really trying to hurt him. And he did hurt him. A straight right hand cut the inside of his bottom lip. He could feel the sting of the cut and taste the blood.

"Hey, take it easy," Mike said, backpedaling, sidestepping, trying to get out of the way of Hem's wild but strong punches.

"Come on, college boy, let's see what you're made of," Hem taunted, and came rushing in again.

This time Mike was ready for him. He did his Fitzsimmons shift, and caught Hem with a quick right to the face and then a hard left cross to his abdomen. Hem grunted with pain and loss of breath, and his nose spurted blood. The blood dribbled down over his mustache and into the hairs on his chest.

Thinking that Hem might have gotten the message that Mike wasn't going to let himself be used for a punching bag, Mike backed off and said halfheartedly, "Sorry . . ." Blood was oozing out of Mike's mouth and down his chin. "What d'you say, let's knock off and get cleaned up—okay?"

"Come on, Hyacinth," Hem said. "You didn't hurt me. You're not afraid of a little blood, are you?"

Once again he lunged at Mike, and this time there was a look in his eyes that frightened Mike. It was as if anger had carried Hem beyond the limits of control, as if he no longer cared about pain and damage and the rules of the game—the eyes of a killer.

Neither of them was wearing any protective gear; none was called for in a friendly sparring match, so who would have thought that Hem would actually try to hit Mike in the testicles? Not Mike. It was such a surprise the first time Hem tried it that Mike automatically assumed it was an accident, a blow which, luckily enough, missed, hitting his flank.

"Hey!" Mike cried. "Low blow! Watch it, goddamnit."

But without hesitation Hem tried it again, and this time Mike knew it was deliberate, and this time the blow connected with its target. It was a blinding, searing explosion of pain that sent him writhing on the floor, in the most excruciating agony.

Hem was standing over him for a moment with a frightened, regretful look on his face. Then he dropped to one knee beside Mike, and said, "Oh, gee, Mike, I'm sorry, I didn't . . . what can I do? Shall I call a doctor? Shall I? I didn't mean . . ."

After a few moments, the agony began to subside, allowing Mike a small feeling of euphoric relief, and his eyes became sufficiently clear to see Hem's bloody face hanging over him, his eyes moist with tears, saying, "Oh, gee, Mike, I'm sorry. I didn't mean to hurt you, honest, I . . ."

Other than expletives, the first words Mike was able to utter were, "You bastard, you did that on purpose."

"No, no, I didn't, I swear. I didn't mean to hit you there."

"Go on, get out of here," Mike said in a strangled voice, still on the floor, the slow, blessed relief of diminishing agony allowing him to relax a little.

"Gee, Mike," Hem said with what seemed to be sincere contrition, "I hope you're not mad at me."

"Go on," Mike said. "Get out of here before I hit you over the head with a fucking barbell." He managed to pull off the boxing gloves, then flung them at him.

Hem seemed to get a little huffy because Mike wouldn't readily accept his apologies, and that huffiness—a sort of okay-if-that's-the-way-you-want-it martyrdom—gave him the impetus to gather his things and leave with Mike still on the mat. Mike was glad that Maggie and the baby weren't home. It gave him time to get his face washed and then crawl into bed with a groan of blissful relief and peace. He dreaded having to tell Maggie what had happened, knowing she would be furious.

"That son of a bitch!" she said. "And you call him a friend? Just wait till I see him again."

"That may not be for a while," Mike said. "He's on his way to Constantinople to cover the war there."

"Good. I hope he gets killed, that son of a bitch."

16

Hadley

HADLEY STAYED STRONG by nursing her anger and outrage, and if Ernest didn't change his mind about going to Constantinople, she vowed she wouldn't speak to him again before he left. If he changed his mind about going, they could make up and beg each other's forgiveness.

So during the three days Ernest went about preparing for the trip—getting visas to Greece and Turkey, exchanging money, buying train tickets—the two of them didn't speak or meet each other's eyes. They didn't even say good-bye. The only thing Ernest said as he was going out the door with his bags was, "If you want to reach me, you can cable in care of the Anglo-American Newspaper Alliance in Constantinople. I left the address on the table." Then he was gone.

Hadley went to bed and cried, off and on, for two days. Marie Cocotte brought her cigarettes and coffee in bed and, warning her that she would get sick if she didn't eat something, managed to get her to take a little soup and an egg now and then. She was still dragging herself around the apartment, drinking heavily, unbathed, her hair uncombed, dressed in nothing but an old bathrobe, when Renata Borgatti came to visit her. Renata said she had heard that Ernest had gone off to report on some war or other in Asia Minor, and she thought she might drop by to see if Hadley was lonely or bored.

"That was good of you," Hadley said, inviting her in. "I've been depressed as hell, and half-drunk most of the time, so I hope you don't mind the shambles."

"Oh, my apartment is always in a shambles, too, so—"

"I didn't mean the apartment," Hadley said.

"Poor Hadley," Renata said, looking her over. "I'm sorry I didn't come sooner. I've been thinking about you."

"Have you?"

"About your piano playing, yes. Sylvia Beach tells me you play exquisitely, and only lack the confidence to pursue music professionally. I thought maybe I could help you."

"That's good of you, Renata, but that's the last thing on my mind at the moment. Would you join me in a drink? Whiskey and soda?"

"Yes. Yes, I would, thanks. And I'd like to hear what is on your mind, if you could use someone to talk to."

It was unlike Hadley to unburden herself to someone who was practically a stranger, but as they had their drinks and smoked cigarettes and talked, she found herself confiding her most personal problems to Renata. The confidences were easy because Renata had a quality of being both sympathetic and discreet, a sort of detached compassion. The very look of her—an unruffled self-assurance, an urbane, nonjudgmental attitude—allowed Hadley to shed a few tears as she told how Ernest had struck her.

After Hadley had finished with her story, and after their second whiskey and soda and many cigarettes, Renata said, "I know what we should do. We have to get you cleaned up and get you out of here for an evening. Let's have dinner, then go to Le Monocle, eh? I'm supposed to meet some friends there tonight. You need to get out of here for a while. Come with me, do."

Hadley was shy about meeting new people without Ernest around for guidance, but after having spent four or five days (she had lost count) in her gloomy solitude, she was ready for some diversion, so she agreed. She washed and got dressed. She wore her best clothes, but she still looked like a rag doll next to Renata, handsome Renata, with her sleek Beau Brummell suit and silver-headed cane.

Renata took Hadley to dinner at the Brasserie Lipp, where

Ernest and Hadley could seldom afford to dine, and then they took a taxi to the nightclub Le Monocle. Hadley had heard of the famous lesbian bar, but of course had never been there. Men were not allowed in Le Monocle neither as guests, workers, or musicians. The "doorman" was a woman dressed in a man's uniform, the band was made up of women in tuxedos, the "barmen" were women who wore ties and shirts, and all of them had short haircuts. The customers were women whose costumes ran the gamut from the most elaborately feminine feathered hats and frilly gowns to the harshly masculine caps and striped French sailors' jerseys and ill-fitting pants of apache hoodlums.

Hadley and Renata were met at the hatcheck booth by a short-haired woman in a tuxedo who had the build of a wrestler and a basso profundo voice. Renata introduced her as Lulu de Montparnasse, the owner of the place, and Hadley wondered at first if it were possible that Lulu might really be a man who was pretending to be a woman pretending to be a man. Though intimidating in size, she was pleasant and hospitable, and when Renata asked if they could have a table where they could be inconspicuous, Lulu said in French, "For you, Renata, anything. Are you playing concerts these days? I look forward to hearing you again."

"I leave in a few days for a two-month tour of Italy," Renata said, raising her voice to be heard above the band's jazzy rendition of "Let Me Call You Sweetheart."

"Ah! Let me know when you have another concert in Paris, will you?"

"Oh, oui, bien entendu," Renata said.

Skirting the dance floor, on which couples danced cheek to cheek and breast to breast, Lulu led the way to a table in a darkened corner, then snapped her fingers at a tuxedo-clad barmaid who, balancing a tray on one hand, was threading her way between the crowded tables.

"Give Renata and her friend a champagne cocktail on the house," she ordered.

"Thank you, Lulu," Renata said. "And if some friends come and ask for me, send them to our table, will you?"

The friends, as Renata explained to Hadley in English after Lulu was gone, were Nancy Cunard and a couple of new Americans who had only recently arrived in Paris, Janet Flanner and Solita Solano. Did Hadley know them?

"No. But I've often heard Nancy Cunard's name mentioned."

"In some scandalous way, no doubt," Renata said with an appreciative chuckle.

"I believe it was usually in connection with Ezra Pound."

"Yes, she's having an affair with him—when she can squeeze him in between Louis Aragon and her black stevedore from Senegal, not to mention her nights out with her lady lovers."

"Sounds rather busy," Hadley said.

The barmaid in the tuxedo brought their champagne cocktails.

"That's our Nancy," Renata said admiringly. "Would you like to dance?"

"Me? Dance?" Hadley was uncomfortable with the idea, but she didn't want to be a prude, or make others think that she had come here just to gawk, so she said, "Well . . . okay." She started to ask which of them would lead, but the question would have served only to cover her nervousness, for there was never any question, of course, that Renata would lead.

They danced to a slow French love song, and Renata proved to be an excellent dancer. She and Hadley were about the same height, and their breasts prevented them from dancing cheek to cheek without pressing their breasts together, and Hadley was too self-conscious for that, and Renata sensed it, so theirs was a chaste embrace. But Hadley liked the way Renata danced (it was so much better than the way Ernest stumbled around a dance floor), and she liked the touch of her, and the fresh, sweet way she smelled. Ernest had never had a fondness for frequent bathing, and the lack of plumbing in their apartment furnished him with a ready excuse to go unbathed. Hadley didn't mind too much because she equated the strong smell of his body with the strength of his masculinity, but she had to admit it was very nice to dance with someone who could not only dance gracefully but smelled good, too.

They had one more dance and one more drink—whiskey this time—before Renata's friends showed up. They were a frenetic threesome in their middle thirties who had already had plenty to drink and were hurrying to have more. They were all politely interested in Hadley, but they talked circles around her. She would have felt like the left-out wallflower she had once been had not Renata continually made sure she was included in every volley of their jolly conversation.

Nancy Cunard, the heiress to the Cunard shipping line fortune, was the leader of the three. A boy-slim woman in a silver lamé dress, her blond hair cut short, with clacking ivory bracelets ringing both arms from her wrists to her elbows, she had the cold, sharp-edged look of a metallic doll.

"Janet and Solita just got in from Athens and Rome," Nancy said, lighting a cigarette, "and I wanted to show them this place, then go on to the Bal Négre. Would you like to join us?"

"The Bal Négre?" Hadley asked. "What's that?"

"An interracial nightclub," Renata said. "Where white men go to meet Negro women, and white women go to meet Negro men. If you want to do the Charleston or the Black Bottom shimmy, it's the place to go."

"Or get bedded by a beautiful black man," Nancy suggested.

"I'm afraid I've lost all interest in men, white or black," Solita Solano said. "My ex-husband was the last man who'll ever get a chance to beat me."

"Your husband beat you?" Hadley asked incredulously, as if she couldn't imagine a man doing such a thing to his wife.

"Regularly," Solita said. "Until I crawled out my window one night in Manila and ran away."

"How long ago was that?" Renata asked.

"Nine years, when I was twenty-seven. Married the bastard when I was sixteen, just to spite my parents and get away from home. An engineer he was, twice my age. Built roads in Malaysia and the Philippines." She placed a hand on Janet Flanner's shoulder. "Met Jan in New York, haven't missed a man since."

Janet smiled. She was the oldest one of the three—in her late thirties, Hadley guessed—and the least good-looking, and her hair, also cut short, was turning gray.

As the evening wore on, Hadley gathered from bits and pieces of their conversation that Nancy Cunard, who had a palazzo in Venice and an apartment on the Isle St. Louis, considered herself a poet, while Janet, though an aspiring novelist, was about to begin writing a regular column about Paris for the *New Yorker* magazine, and Solita Solano, who was also working on a novel, had just finished an article for the *National Geographic* on Constantinople.

"Constantinople?" Hadley said. "You were there?"

"A few weeks ago," Solita replied.

"My husband just went there to report on the war," Hadley said, and thought she saw a look of commiseration flicker across Solita's and Janet's faces.

"Oh, dear," Solita said, "it's awful there now, simply awful. I'm sorry for him."

This sent a shudder through Hadley, to think that Ernest was in some hellish scene of war, miserable and desperate, having left without her blessing or even a good-bye, and here she was, selfish and self-indulgent, having a good time in a lesbian nightclub. And then, unbidden by any particular word or deed, she experienced the sudden, sickening fear that Ernest might not come back to her. This was the first time that the possibility had touched her in all its horror, and it left her weak with dread.

"Renata, I'm sorry, I . . . I'd better go home," she said. "I shouldn't be here having a good time, when only God knows what poor Ernest might be going through right now."

"Oh, if he's a journalist, he'll be all right," Janet said. "We didn't mean to alarm you."

"Yes," Renata agreed, "and no matter what he's going through, how would your being at home help him?"

"But I feel guilty," Hadley said. "You understand, don't you?"

Renata smiled affectionately. "Of course. Well, come on, I'll see you home."

"No, no," Hadley insisted. "You stay, enjoy yourself. I'll get a taxi."

After Hadley shook hands and said good night to Nancy, Solita, and Janet, Renata walked her out of the club and to the curb and asked the woman in the doorman's uniform to whistle for a taxi. Renata took Hadley's hand and gently pressed it, saying, "I'm sorry you have to leave, but I understand. Look here, I'm going to be gone for two months to Italy, but when I get back, I'd like to see you again, if I may. I'd like for us to be friends."

"Yes, I'd like that," Hadley answered apprehensively, for she sensed that Renata was trying at that moment to gauge how receptive Hadley might be to a good-night kiss. But no doubt sensing Hadley's ambivalence about the prospect, Renata settled for an affectionate squeeze of her hand as the taxi pulled up to the curb.

When Hadley got back home, the first thing she did was write a cablegram that she would send to Ernest the first thing tomorrow morning:

> I love you STOP
> Please forgive me STOP
> Letter follows.

Then she wrote the letter, telling Ernest that she didn't know what could have gotten into her to make her be such a bitch about his going away.

> I could say it was due to a number of things, including the onset of my period, but nothing excuses the way I acted, the terrible things I said, my dear, dear tiny wax puppy. If you will please forgive me, I promise that for the rest of my life I will always remember that what is good for you is good for me. You have been a gift of the gods for me, Nesto, and everything in me is for you, or I can't be any good. When I think of you, I feel like someone in a crowd adoring someone up on a raised place, and I feel so ashamed that I said things that brought you down to a level of bitterness and violence. You once pulled me out of the darkness, and for an inexplicable and most regrettable moment I fell back into that darkness, and pulled you in with me.

She went on with total sincerity. She meant every word of it, and it seemed impossible for her to exaggerate her love for him. No one could love anyone more than she loved Ernest

Hemingway. And that was how she ended the letter, adding a postscript that his feather kitty longed to have her wax puppy home again so she could wrap all her limbs around him and show him how much she loved him.

The next day, she sent the cablegram and posted the letter at the same time, then undertook to carefully balance patience with tingling anticipation. She busied herself with cleaning the apartment and rearranging the furniture, repairing tears in her clothes and stockings, painting the kitchen, playing her piano, writing long, loving letters to Ernest (and wondering why she never got an answer), reading books from Sylvia's lending library, and counting days.

Soon she had counted to twenty-eight. Not one cablegram or letter had she received from Ernest. Had he gotten hers? Was he sick somewhere? Dying, maybe? Or already dead? Without knowing that she loved him more than life itself? And just before it got so bad that she herself became sick with the fear that he would never return, she received a cablegram from him, sent from Sofia, Bulgaria, saying that he would be home sometime soon. He sent his love, but he didn't mention getting her cablegram or any of her letters. The next day she got another cablegram, this one from Trieste, telling her that he would arrive in Paris at the Gare de Lyon at 6:35 A.M. on October 25 on the Simplon Orient Express.

She was there on the quai when the Express pulled in. She looked for him among the passengers debarking from the second-class cars and, as the moments mounted and he didn't appear, she became frantic. She ran alongside the cars, looking in the windows at the stragglers, but then she turned around and there he was, fretfully dragging his bags out of a car onto the quai, and she barely recognized him. Rather than a returning war correspondent, he looked like a war refugee from some Godforsaken outpost of the world.

She ran to him and threw her arms around him, never so glad to see anyone. They kissed and hugged, and then she drew back to get a look at him. All his hair was gone.

"My god, what happened to your hair?"

"Lice," he said. "Had to shave it off."

His face was covered with red splotches, as if he had broken out in a rash.

"Bug bites," he explained.

The whites of his eyes had turned yellow.

"Malaria," he said.

He had lost so much weight that his clothes hung on him as on a scarecrow.

"Dysentery."

He grimaced and groaned when he tried to pick up his bags.

"Hemorrhoids," he said.

"Oh, my poor Poo," she said. "Never mind, we'll get a porter to carry them. Come on, let's get you home."

In the taxi, he told her that he hadn't received her cablegram or any of her letters.

"But that doesn't surprise me," he said. "The telegraph wires have all been cut and hang like ribbons from a maypole, and the mail doesn't get through because most of the railroads have been blown up and all the trucks were being used to haul war materials. Total chaos. You can't imagine the conditions. . . . Anyway, I sure wish I had gotten them. All this time I've been wondering if you'd be here when I got back. I prayed you would be. . . ."

"Oh, darling, how awful for you. For me, too. I've been wondering the same thing—if you'd ever come back to me. In all my letters, I asked you to forgive me, and told you how much I loved you, and promised never, ever to stand in your way again."

She comforted him, cooed to him, promised that everything would be all right now, and when she got him home, she put him into bed and began the ministrations that would, over a period of many days, bring him back to health. But before dropping into a deep sleep of exhaustion, he dug into one of his bags and brought out an antique ivory-and-amber necklace, a family heirloom of a once wealthy White Russian family whose last member, reduced to being a waiter in a Constantinople café, had sold it to Ernest for a pittance.

Hadley loved the necklace. She vowed she would keep it for the rest of her life as a symbol of how devalued beautiful things and love could become during times of crises and upheaval.

In spite of Ernest's exhaustion and medical complaints, not even the days of their honeymoon on Lake Walloon in Northern Michigan were as happy as those first days of his return to Paris. He spent most of his time in bed, and Hadley frequently joined him there for a nap or lovemaking, whichever he preferred, and he often preferred the lovemaking, since the trip to Constantinople had revived his virility. She hardly understood how the experience, as horrible as he said it had been, could have such a felicitous effect, but then she read one of his dispatches to the *Star* in which he described Constantinople as a city of fear—the "gut-wrenching fear-thrill," as he described it, of those who cannot get away, who cannot flee from the horror of the oncoming army of cutthroats—and Hadley wondered if this description might explain the resurgence of Ernest's virility, since he, more than anyone else she had ever known, found in gut-wrenching fear a source of thrills.

But then she found something else that might illuminate the subject. After his fourth day in bed, Ernest forced himself to get up and take out his notebooks and write his final dispatch. And when he left the apartment to cable the dispatch to the *Star,* he left his blue notebooks on the table. Curious about the details of his trip, Hadley began leafing through them. For a number of reasons she did this without any thought about privacy. They were just notes for newspaper articles, after all, and Ernest always asked her to read everything he wrote, and certainly if he left the notebooks there on the table he wouldn't mind her looking at them. These reasons required no rationalization; they were simply taken for granted.

As usual with anything Ernest wrote, she found the notes fascinating. In them were depicted a Greek refugee column twenty miles long, leaving Adrianople in a driving rain, a ghastly, shambling procession of the homeless, abandoning their farms and villages, fleeing with only what they could carry in a desperate effort to save their lives.

Peasants. Brightly colored costumes, bedraggled by rain
and mud. All worldly possessions on their backs or in carts
pulled by mud-covered buffaloes and bullocks. Old
farmer carrying pig on shoulders. A chicken dangling from
a scythe. Old woman without shoes, carrying a sick child.
Families in carts loaded with household belongings,
soaked bedding—sewing machines, mattresses, pots and
pans, furniture. Roadside strewn with discarded furniture.
Dead bullock. Men pulling carts in rain. Greek troops on
horseback, driving them on. Woman in cart giving birth
under a blanket while a girl—daughter?—looks on and
cries.

There were three notebooks filled with such heartbreaking details. Hadley didn't have a chance to read them all, for she had
work to do, but she skipped through them, reading a page here,
a page there, until something in the October 18 entry caught her
eye.

Galata. Den of iniquity, halfway up hill from port. Whorehouses. Cribs. Dance halls. Drunks in gutters with rats and
skinny dogs rummaging through rubbish. All night
drunken roar from bars and whorehouses. Whored all the
time to kill loneliness. Dancing with Armenian slut. British
soldier claims she is his girl. Fuck you, Jack. Invites me to
settle it outside. Crowd follows, some cheering me, some
cheering him. Caught him on the jaw but he kept coming.
He hit me in the gut, and the eye, hard. Got him with left
hook that staggered him. Fell against me and my coat tore.
Then I swung the right and put him down. Head hit cob-
blestones. Ran with the girl. Got taxi back to her place.
Her body hot in bed, breasts heavy in the hand and buttocks you didn't need to put a pillow under.

Hadley had to look away from the page and blink to clear her
eyes of tears.
So he had been unfaithful to her. "Whored all the time." But
even so, that wasn't what hurt the most. "Buttocks you needn't

put a pillow under"—that was the detail that felt like a slap in the face. He had obviously compared the woman's buttocks to hers. He had asked her many times during sex to put a pillow there, and she had been glad to do it, but she hadn't known that she needed it—whatever that need might be.

Her instinctive urge to deny all this led her to wonder if perhaps the whoring had been just another of his fantasies, one of those instances when what is imagined becomes real. But fantasy or fact, why had he left it on the table? Had he expected her to read it? Wanted her to? Was it his way of confessing without feeling guilty? And if she accused him of it, he could take the moral high ground with a counter accusation that she had been snooping.

And what, indeed, would be her reaction when he returned home? Should she fling the notebook at him with an accusation of infidelity? But what would that accomplish? It wouldn't change the fact—if fact it was—that he had been unfaithful. It would only open wounds that might never heal. Besides, the mere thought of recriminations evoked in her that terrible feeling of fear that she had experienced that night at Le Monocle, the sickening horror that he might never return to her.

No. She would close the notebooks and pretend she had never read them. And when he came back, she would not greet him with tears or accusations. She would act as if nothing had happened. So he had been whoring in Constantinople to kill his anger and loneliness; she would not give him reasons to go whoring again. Please, God, let him come back, and she would greet him with a smile and make him a good lunch and love him and, rather than say things that might drive him away, she wondered what she could do to bind him closer to her.

A baby. That's what it would take, a baby. And that was what she wanted, too, what her body yearned for, a baby. But could Ernest be persuaded? Not likely. Even to have the slightest chance, she would have to wait for the optimal moment, and approach the subject cautiously.

But wait for how long? Days passed, a week passed, and she used her diaphragm when they made love, and kept her mouth shut about wanting a child. But the approach of November 9, her thirty-first birthday, was a bitter reminder that she was closer to the end of her childbearing years than to the beginning, so she decided she couldn't wait any longer. And there would probably never be a more optimal moment than the dinner he took her to at Michaud's on her birthday. For them it was splurging—the two seven-course dinners, plus wine and coffee, came to nearly five dollars—but Ernest was feeling expansive because he had just that day received the 400 dollars that the *Star* owed him for the Constantinople dispatches. In addition, Hadley had recently received a 750-dollar quarterly payment from her trust fund. With the franc having fallen to eighteen to one, its lowest point of the year, Ernest felt no qualms about treating himself and Hadley to an expensive birthday dinner. When he was full of oysters on the half-shell and duck a l'orange and Pouilly-Fuissé and was talking excitedly about them taking another skiing trip to Chamby, Hadley said, "I'd like that. As a birthday present, there's only one thing I'd like better."

"What's that?" he said, showing off by blowing perfect smoke rings.

"I'd like to have a baby."

"A baby?" He stiffened as if he had been stabbed in the back. "Good God, that's all we need! Are you pregnant?"

"No, no, no. Now, calm down—"

"You didn't miss your last period, did you?" He fumbled through scraps of paper from his pockets and pulled out a little notebook, which he leafed through while Hadley tried to reassure him that she wasn't pregnant, but he wasn't satisfied until he could jab his finger at the page in the notebook where he kept statistics on her menstrual cycle, and say, "There! You didn't miss your period last month. Gee, why're you scaring me by talking about having babies?"

"I'm not talking about having a baby," she said, flustered by his extreme reaction. "I wasn't proposing, I was just . . . But someday we will have babies, won't we?"

"Sure, someday. But I'm too young to be a father now."

"Oh, I don't know," she said, trying to lighten the subject with a little humor, "all you have to be is old enough to plant the seeds." She patted her abdomen. "And you're very good at that, my dear."

"Now, cut it out, Tiny. Don't get me nervous about that. I'm telling you, I'm too young to be a father."

Maybe so. Still a boy himself, he did not want to share his mummy with a rival. But how old would he have to be before he was ready for a child? She suspected that by the time he got old enough to be a father, she would be too old to be a mother. And she was determined not to let that happen. She wanted a child—his child—and she wanted it soon. Well, perhaps an accident could be arranged. Perhaps one night when they had drunk too much, she could plausibly forget to use her diaphragm. But, of course, even drunk he would probably consult that damned notebook of his, with all its data about her menstrual cycle. Well, maybe she could start feeding him false numbers. As erratic as their sex life was these days, it might work.

But before she could start mapping a plan, events intervened. First, Ernest came down with a bad case of the flu. He had been home no more than two weeks, recovering from malaria, only to develop a sore throat and congested lungs, which put him right back into bed, weak and despairing. Hadley nursed him through the illness with cool compresses and hot soup and aspirin, and by the end of the week he had improved.

That was when Frank Mason, the head of the Paris offices of the International News Services, sent Ernest a *pneumatique,* asking him to cover the upcoming Lausanne peace conference for the INS and the Universal News Service, both Hearst organizations. This was the peace conference that was supposed to end the war between Turkey and Greece, the war that Ernest had covered for the *Star.* So why didn't the editors of the *Star* ask Ernest to cover the conference for them? When Hadley asked Ernest this question, he was at first evasive, but finally confessed that he had double-crossed the *Star.* While he was in Asia Minor, reporting on the war under exclusive contract to the *Star,* he had also sold his dispatches under a pseudonym to the Hearst news agencies, and the editors of the *Star* had found out about the double cross, and therefore didn't trust Ernest to be their correspondent at the Lausanne peace conference.

"Ah, to hell with the *Star,*" he said. "I'll probably get better money from Mason, anyway."

"You're going, then?" Hadley asked.

"Of course. Why not? But this time you'll come with me. We'll stay at a first-class hotel. It'll be like a paid vacation. And after the conference is over, we'll go to Chamby for Christmas. There ought to be plenty of snow by then, and maybe we can get somebody to go with us—Bill and Sally Bird, maybe, and Chink, and maybe Lincoln Steffens—and we'll all have a real bang-up skiing holiday."

That sounded wonderful to Hadley, and she was certainly ready to go. But two days before they were scheduled to leave, it was Hadley's turn to come down with the flu. Now it was she, too weak even to stand up for long, who took to the bed, shivering and feverish and coughing up phlegm.

"I won't go without you," Ernest said, sitting on the side of the bed, putting a cool compress on her forehead.

"You must," she said in a cracked whisper. "You've already told them you'd go."

"I'll tell Mason to get somebody else to cover the bloody conference," he said. "I'm going to stay here and nurse you."

"That's sweet of you, Tatie, darling, but, no, you must go. Marie Cocotte can take care of me all right," Hadley said. She had vowed to herself that she would never again try to keep him from his writing assignments, and she looked upon this as a test of her resolve. "And when I get well, I'll join you, and we'll have a lovely Christmas in Chamby."

He seemed genuinely reluctant to go without her, but she argued that he should go. It was important to his writing career that he cover the peace conference, so he should not worry about her. Finally convinced by the wisdom of her reasoning, he prepared to leave on November 21. As he leaned over to give Hadley a good-bye kiss on the forehead, she held him at arm's length, warning him not to get close.

"We wouldn't want you to have a relapse," she said. "Goodbye, darling. Write me as soon as you get there, and as soon as I'm well enough, I'll come running to join you."

After he was gone, she began to wonder if she might never see him again. There were days when she was a little delirious, and there were nights when she had visions of all the people in the world who had died in the flu epidemic during the War, an epidemic that had taken more lives than the War itself. She was very much afraid that she would soon be joining the legions of the dead in their graves, rather than joining Ernest in Lausanne.

17

Bill Bird

SINCE BILL BIRD first met Ernest Hemingway at the economic conference in Genoa in April, he had often heard him talk about boxing. He had heard him tell stories about how he had, back in his Chicago days, been a sparring partner for some of the notable heavyweights of his time. Like most of the inhabitants of the Left Bank, Bird had also seen Ernest shadowboxing as he shuffled along boulevard du Montparnasse. After Bird and his wife, Sally, became friends with Ernest and Hadley in that Paris summer of '22, Ernest had asked Bird a few times to put on the gloves and spar with him.

Bird could hardly imagine it. He had never had any interest in boxing. He had never seen a boxing match, and had no desire to. He had nothing against it morally. If people enjoyed it, fine, let them have it. But he had dismissed it as a pastime practiced by brutes for brutes. Sally and he prided themselves on not being snobs, but they were also unapologetically proud of having refined tastes, whether in art, music, wine, dance, or drama. Their familiarity with these fields always reached the level of the cognoscente, and sometimes they were even skilled practitioners. In music, for instance, Sally had studied for years to be an opera singer, and had performed professionally in New York. She gave it up only to marry Bird and move with him to Paris in 1921, where he had opened a foreign bureau of the

Consolidated Press, a news service that he himself had founded with a partner in the States. But while Bird's vocation was journalism, his avocation was publishing fine books. Not long after he and Sally had settled in Paris, he used some inheritance money to purchase an ancient Mathieu hand press and install it at 29 Quai d'Anjou on the Ile St. Louis. He planned to publish books under the imprint of the Three Mountain Press, named for the three mountains of Paris: Montmartre, Montparnasse, and St. Genevieve. The books would be printed on large pages of fine paper, each book a work of art in itself.

It was when Bird first met Ernest in April in Genoa that he told him about the press, and when he asked Ernest's advice on how to go about getting some manuscripts that would be worthy of limited hand-set editions, Ernest suggested that he talk to Ezra Pound. When they got back to Paris, Ernest took Bird around to rue Notre Dame des Champs to meet Pound, who was quick to see an advantage to himself and to modern literature—two entities which were identical in his mind.

Not only did Ezra agree to supply the Three Mountain Press with manuscripts, he volunteered to become the general editor for a series of books, which would, he said in his grandiose way, be "an inquest into the state of contemporary English prose." Pound suggested that the series include a volume of Ezra's own poetry in the form of cantos; a book of essays by Ford Madox Hueffer on male-female relationships; a novel by Ezra's old friend in America, William Carlos Williams; a collection of poems from Pound's protégé in England, T.S. Eliot; and perhaps a collection of poems and short stories from their mutual friend Ernest Hemingway.

"Yours will be the last on Ezra's list to be published," Bird told Ernest one day while the two of them were having drinks at the Closerie des Lilas. "Probably early spring of next year. Think you could come up with enough by then to fill a volume?"

"You can depend on it," Ernest said. "I might even have a big chunk of my novel ready for publication by then. Not the parts about the War, but there are some sections in the book on fishing the rivers in northern Michigan that could stand alone as stories. I'm also working on a big boxing story that might be ready by then."

He sounded excited about the projected book, and smiled as if he had visions of seeing it in print. It was a constant source of amazement to Bird, the way Ernest's intensity about everything he did generated excitement in others. That must have been the reason why so many people were attracted to him. No matter who they were, everything they did seemed to take on a new importance when Ernest was involved. And this intensity and immediacy was why his stories, whether about traveling, trout fishing, food and drink, writing, or skiing, conveyed such excitement to the reader.

But boxing? Bird had never been able to understand how a civilized man could sit around and enjoy watching one man beat the hell out of another. Ernest's enthusiasm about the sport, however, made Bird wonder if maybe he was missing something. Ernest, after all, was a literate man—not a learned one, it was true, but a literate one, and a fine writer—so Bird felt he should make an effort to understand what he saw in boxing. But the one thing Bird refused to do was put the gloves on with him. A number of times that summer Ernest had asked Bird to spar a few rounds, promising to take it easy on him, but Bird would have felt as foolish with boxing gloves on as Ernest would have felt in a tutu.

Once when Bird went to Pound's apartment in rue Notre Dame des Champs, he found Ernest giving Pound a boxing lesson. The furniture in the room had been pushed back, and, stripped to their waists, the two writers were banging away at each other, sweating profusely in the muggy August air. Served a cup of tepid tea by Dorothy Pound, who seemed to find the pugilistic exhibition disgusting, Bird watched the boxers for a while and tried to discern the aesthetics of the activity. He failed.

The next time Bird saw Ernest box was during the peace conference in Lausanne. Bird had gone to cover the conference for Consolidated News of Paris, and Ernest was there for two Hearst news services. They both had rooms at the Hotel Beau Sèjour, along with the other newsmen who had converged on Lausanne from America and from across Europe: Lincoln Steffens, Guy

Hickok, George Slocombe, Max Eastman, G. Ward Price, among others. Ernest was the youngest and most inexperienced among them, but he was readily accepted and liked by everyone, and in Lincoln Steffens he found a particular champion for his writing. Along with two pairs of well-worn boxing gloves, Ernest had brought with him to Lausanne a short story that he had recently finished called "My Old Man." He passed the story around to anyone who had any interest in reading it, and Steffens liked it so much he offered to send it to a friend of his, the editor of *Cosmopolitan* magazine. Even though the story was clearly derived from Sherwood Anderson's racetrack tales, Bird also liked it, and he agreed with Steffens that Ernest had the surest future among the young writers currently at work in Europe.

Since reporters were not allowed to cover the actual sessions of the peace conference at the Hotel du Château at Ouchy, they had to rely on prepared statements and press briefings held at the various headquarters in different hotels around Lausanne. This arrangement made it unnecessary for all the newsmen to go chasing the same prepared statements and press briefings; only one or two of them usually went to the various headquarters, collected these statements, took notes on the briefings, and shared with the other reporters what little news could be gleaned from such scanty material. As a consequence, the newsmen were often at leisure, which they spent reading or playing poker or drinking. Ernest did all these things, but what he really wanted to do was box. He had discovered a public gymnasium only blocks from the hotel, but he couldn't get anyone among his colleagues to spar with him, in spite of his protestations that he wouldn't hurt them.

Then G. Ward Price finally agreed. None of the others thought such a bout would amount to much, since G. Ward Price seemed to be about as close as you could get to being a wet noodle in human form. He was thin, he was languid, and he had been terribly shot up during the War. Among his various wounds, he had lost one eye. He wore a black eye patch over the empty socket. Over the other eye, he wore a monocle. Furthermore, he was ten years older than Ernest and weighed fifty pounds less. Sure, he was one hell of a good reporter, a much respected correspondent for the *London Daily Mail;* he had even garnered a bit of fame by his coverage for *Century Magazine* of the Italian army's defeat and massive retreat from Caporetto in 1917; but where did he get the idea that he was a boxer? The notion was absurd.

No one who had read his war dispatches doubted that Price was a courageous man. It was said that during the Caporetto debacle he had continued writing his dispatches after he had been badly wounded by mortar fire, and when his pen ran out of ink he had filled it from his wound and continued writing his dispatches in his own blood. Though no doubt apocryphal (Price would never confirm or deny it), the story made a deep impression on Ernest. This was his kind of guy. And maybe it was this kind of courage that caused Price to agree to spar, for it was inconceivable that he might think boxing Ernest could be fun. Like Bird, he had never boxed before. He said so.

Ernest said, "That's all right, I'll teach you. And don't worry, I'll take it easy. I got a bum knee myself from my own war wounds, you know, and I got a bad eye from Sam Langford, and I'm just getting over the flu. So we won't do anything too strenuous."

None of the other newsmen were able to go to the gym the next day and watch Ernest and Price spar, but when Ernest came back saying that Price had trounced him, they assumed that he had let Price win. They asked Price, and he would neither confirm nor deny Ernest's account of their match. He only smiled a Mona Lisa smile, and let them believe what they wanted to believe. The next time Ernest and Price went to the gym, the story was the same. Ernest came back saying that Price had trounced him.

"For a guy who's blind in one eye, and can barely see out of the other one unless he's wearing that damned monocle, he's pretty good," Ernest conceded with honest admiration that evening in the hotel's dining room as he and George Slocombe and Bird were having dinner together. "Doesn't know a damned thing about boxing, of course, but he's a real tough cookie. He trounced me, all right."

Once again they assumed that Ernest was being magnanimous. He was, after all, a young man whose self-confidence bordered on cockiness, and so he could afford to let poor Price hold his own with him in the ring. But perhaps because the newsmen were fabulists at heart, they began to wonder if there could possibly be something to it. Like the story of Price writing his dispatches in his own blood, it appealed to their desires for myths, for fantastic happenings. Could G. Ward Price, this human wreck, actually have acquitted himself well against a brawny self-proclaimed professional like Ernest Hemingway?

"Yea, he's tough, all right," George Slocombe said, sawing at his steak with a knife. "Proved that during the War. Like this 'ere piece of meat, he is. Like leather. Should give the lie to the notion that poufs can't be tough, eh?"

Ernest frowned. "A pouf?" His eyes became hooded as his look of surprise turned to aversion. "A queer? You're saying Price is a queer?"

"Oh. Sorry. You didn't know? Spoken out of turn, have I? Thought everybody knew."

"No, I didn't know. If I'd known . . ." An expression of betrayal seemed to settle over Ernest's face. "Come to the gym tomorrow and see how tough he is," he said, and let the subject drop.

As the next day was Saturday, the peace conference and the delegation press briefings were not convening, so Guy Hickok, George Slocombe, and Bird, decided to amble down to the Lausanne gym and see for themselves whether or not Price could miraculously trounce Ernest—or, more accurately, whether Ernest would let Price survive for a few rounds.

The answer was no, on both counts. From the moment that the two of them climbed through the ropes and into the ring—Ernest in gym shoes and lavender trunks, Price wearing his black eye patch and his street pants but without his shoes and his shirt and his monocle—there was an ominous sense of doom. Perhaps it was because Ernest, rather than the smiling, extroverted fellow that they were used to, was glaring ferociously at Price and flexing his shoulders and legs like a bull getting ready to charge. As soon as Price gave the signal that he was ready to begin, Ernest rushed across the ring and hit him three or four times in the face, hard, and Price went down. His eye patch had been knocked askew and blood trickled from his nose.

"Sorry," Ernest said, but it was a mere formality, not an expression of regret. Indeed, he banged his gloves together and looked as if he couldn't wait for Price to get up so he could hit him again. There were a few other people in the gym—what appeared to be a wrestling class for college boys—and some of them stopped their own exercises to watch the boxing match.

Price got to his knees and—awkwardly because of the boxing gloves—tried to get his eye patch back in place. The droplets of blood from his nose fell onto his scrawny chest and the scars from his massive war wounds.

Bird half-expected Price to quit at that point, because that's what Bird himself would have done. But Price got to his feet and put up his guard as a signal that he was ready to have another go, and Ernest, as if being let off a leash, tore into him again, hitting him in the body to make him drop his guard, then crashing hard, lunging blows at his head and jaw. Price fell back against the ropes, which kept him from going down again, and tried to cover up as Ernest continued his vicious assault. And finally he did go down again, but by the time his knees had hit the canvas, he was clutching at the ropes, trying to pull himself up, and as soon as he was up ready to defend himself, Ernest knocked him down again, and he got up again. By this time his face was smeared with blood, his eye patch was askew, and his one good eye was glassy, as if he were out on his feet, but he wouldn't quit.

"That's enough!" Bird finally yelled, and climbed into the ring. "Come on, Ernest, what are you doing this for?" He touched Ernest's arm to nudge him away from Price, who was leaning back onto the ropes to keep from falling. "Can't you see he's beaten? What the hell are you trying to do, kill him?"

Bird hardly knew what kind of reaction to expect from Ernest, but he didn't expect the one he got. Ernest seemed offended that Bird would butt into what Ernest apparently considered a private affair. Panting heavily from all the blows he had thrown, he turned on Bird and snapped, "I'll take anything from you."

It seemed to Bird a strange thing to say. What did he mean by it? If Bird had had the chance to think about the remark, he might have made sense of it, or got Ernest to explain; but all his attention for the moment was focused on poor Price, who, as soon as Ernest's withering attack ceased, dropped to his knees on the canvas. He was holding his sides, grimacing as if in acute pain. George Slocombe, who had entered the ring with Bird, asked Price what was wrong, and Price grunted, "Pain. Bad pain."

"Where?" Bird asked, dropping to one knee beside him and reaching out to locate the source of the pain. As soon as he touched a rib, Price flinched.

"That's it," he said.

"Probably a broken rib," Bird said.

"Other side, too," Price said, and when Bird touched the lowest rib on the other side, Price jumped and gasped with pain.

"Two broken ribs, looks like," Bird said. "We'll have to get an ambulance."

"Must we?" Price asked. "I don't want to go to the hospital."

"If you've got broken ribs, Price, old boy, you'll have to go. Too easy for a broken rib to puncture a lung. Can't have that, can we?"

Ernest was now muttering half-hearted apologies, but nobody was listening. Hickok went to phone for an ambulance as Slocombe and Bird carefully eased Price's battered body around so he could lie down and minimize the risk of puncturing a lung. They took off his boxing gloves and tossed them to Ernest, then Bird lit a cigarette and gave it to Price. He also took out his handkerchief and gave him his to stanch the blood dribbling from his nose. A few of the Swiss wrestling students, and a man who looked as if he might be in charge of the gym, came over and asked if Price was all right, then they stood around, like gawkers at the scene of an accident, until the ambulance arrived. By that time Ernest had gone to the locker room to change into his street clothes, then returned with Price's clothes wrapped in a bundle. They didn't try to get Price dressed, but he did want his monocle. It turned out, however, that his one good eye was swelling up and turning black, so he couldn't hold the monocle in it. Looking grudgingly guilty, Ernest muttered a few more apologies, and then melded into the crowd, as if he were no more than a curious onlooker. Slocombe and Bird helped the ambulance attendants lift Price onto a stretcher, then they got into the ambulance to ride to the hospital with him, leaving Hickok and Ernest behind at the gym.

The doctor found that Price had not two but three cracked ribs, as well as a large number of contusions and abrasions.

"Did he get hit by a truck?" the doctor asked.

"Sort of," Bird said.

The doctor had to tape Price's ribs and keep him in the hospital overnight. A shot of morphine was the only thing that reconciled Price to staying in the hospital.

Slocombe and Bird went back to the hotel to shower and shave and have dinner in the hotel's dining room, where the lively talk among the newsmen was all about the beating that Price had taken from young Hemingway. Ernest himself was nowhere around. Bird didn't see him again until late that night when he went down to the hotel bar for a nightcap. Ernest was there, standing in the shadows at the dark end of the bar, sloshing down drinks. For his sake Bird hoped Ernest was getting drunk out of a sense of remorse for what he had done to poor Price, but as Bird approached him, he perceived that Ernest's mood was one of defiance, rather than remorse. It seemed to Bird a strange attitude for him to have, but he was beginning to realize that Ernest had a side that he had never seen before.

They had a drink together, and Ernest seemed willing to avoid the subject of Price altogether, but Bird finally brought it up by saying, "Well, so what was that all about today? Why did you clobber poor old Price that way?"

"Aw," Ernest said with a dismissive sneer, "I can't stand guys who part their names on the side, and I don't like guys who wear monocles."

He must have seen the amazement in Bird's face, and he certainly couldn't miss it in his voice when Bird said, "Good Lord! You mean to tell me you beat him up like that just because he parts his name on the side, as you quaintly put it, and wears a monocle?"

Ernest tilted his head, as if admitting that might be a possibility, but finally a look of confusion shadowed his face, and as if groping into some shadowed recesses deep within himself, he said, "Aw, those guys . . . I just can't help myself, when I see them . . . their simpering faces . . . I just want to hit 'em. I just want to smash their faces."

"Them?" Bird asked, trying to figure him; then it occurred to him: "Queers? You mean queers?"

"Yeah," Ernest grudgingly admitted. "That's who I mean. Whenever I see one . . . one of those cocksuckers . . . I feel like smashing his face."

"Why? As long as they don't try it with you, what do you care what they do?"

"Listen, they've tried it with me, lots of times. When I was sixteen and seventeen, riding the rails, sleeping in hobo jungles, I had to have a knife handy all the time. Those guys would come sneaking around at night. . . . One got me alone in a boxcar once, tried to rape me. I cut him up pretty bad. Queer buttfucker, I'll bet he never tried that with any other kid."

"But Price never tried anything with you, did he?"

"Nope," Ernest said, dismissing the subject. "How about another drink?"

"Actually, you didn't even know he was a fairy till Slocombe told you, did you?"

"No. But I should have." His voice took on a tone of personal betrayal as he shook his head and added, "It's just that I'd read the Caporetto stuff in *Century Magazine,* and I was thinking he was one of the best newspapermen of his time." With a snort of gratuitous sarcasm, he said, "The Monocled Prince of the Press!"

From this response, it became apparent to Bird that, along with the many other complicated reasons Ernest had for hating Price, he was envious of Price's achievements as a writer.

They had more drinks as the evening wore on, and the more they drank, the more the conversation seemed to keep coming back, time and again, to homosexuality. The repeated return to this subject was usually at Ernest's instigation, and—curiously— the hostility and repulsion he had originally expressed slowly receded.

"I mean, look," he said. "When I was young, I used to eat

worms, bird eggs, bugs, lizards—shit like that—alive, not because I was hungry, but because I'd heard that other people—
Indians, or people lost in the woods—they could survive on
such things, and I wanted to see for myself what they tasted like.
Wanted to see if I could do it, too. And it was the same with
experiences. I wanted to do everything—*everything* there was to
do. When I died, I didn't want there to be one experience I
hadn't had, one feeling I hadn't felt, one thought I hadn't
thought. See what I mean?" He shrugged. "But where does that
leave me with this fairy stuff?"

He looked at Bird as if he actually expected him to answer that.
But Bird couldn't because he sensed that Ernest was asking for
more than just theory or information. Bird remembered the
strange thing Ernest had said to him when he climbed into the
ring to stop him from continuing his beating of Price: "I'll take
anything from you"—as if he were giving Bird special dispensa-
tion, some kind of carte blanche to say or do anything. Bird still
didn't understand what he had meant.

"What do you think?" Ernest asked, downing his last cognac.
The bartender was waiting for them to leave so he could close
the bar. "You think it might be worth experimenting?"

Was he asking Bird an academic question, or was he actually
proposing that they experiment? Bird couldn't tell.

"I don't know," Bird said.

"Good night, gentlemen," the bartender said.

"Listen," Ernest said, "I don't feel like going to sleep now. I've
got some gin and vermouth in my room. Why don't you come
on up, we'll have another drink, continue the conversation?"

"No. No, thanks, I'd better get to bed. Got a lot of dispatches to
write tomorrow. But it's been interesting."

Ernest looked a little sulky, but after a moment he relaxed and
said good night. They went to their rooms.

18

Hadley

HADLEY HAD HOPED to join Ernest in Lausanne within a few days, but her flu got worse and she could hardly get off her back, let alone travel. She barely had enough strength to write him a letter, explaining that she was going to be delayed for a few days or a week because of her illness, and asking him to forgive her for letting him down. In return she had hoped to get a letter full of sunshine and optimism, a tonic for her depression, but what she got made her feel even worse. Along the left-hand margin of his handwritten letter she was addressed as "Dear sweet Mummy!" but in the letter's salutation she was addressed as

> Dearest Wicky Poo—My little feather Kitty. I'm so sad you're sick. I've got it too and I've felt awfully bum for days, dragging myself everywhere with a fever and coughing up stuff, and on my lousy pay can't take taxis.

By now she realized that this was going to be one of Ernest's standard letters of self-pity. And he went on with a long list of complaints about being overworked, harried, frustrated, hungry, and having to take leftovers at the table.

Hadley quite expected the letter to be spotted with tears. But he did finally get around to dealing with a few practicalities, such as the trip he had made to Chamby on Sunday (he didn't explain how, with such a harrowing schedule, he had managed to get a day off) to make reservations at the Gangswisch pension for himself and Hadley and all the people who were expected to join them there for Christmas. Then he returned to his complaints and concluded with:

> I love you Wicky—gee I wish I were home with my Poo.
> I'm your little wax puppy. Pups love mups

It occurred to Hadley that the castor oil worked on her the same way as Ernest's complaining worked on him: it seemed to be a cathartic that cleansed and renewed him. She knew that when the self-pity had cleansed his system, he would be on top of his game again, roistering and joyous, the axis around which others revolved.

Ernest's crybaby behavior had been learned when he was three and four years old, Hadley knew. It was his mother Grace who had confided this to Hadley during a visit that Grace made to the apartment of the newlywed Hemingways in Chicago. Grace said she had come to teach Hadley about love, wifely devotion, and tolerance, and as an illustration of the treatment Ernest might need from his wife, she mentioned—with teary nostalgia—how Ernest, her little summer girl, had often come to her conjugal bed with complaints of being a sick kitty who needed the feather softness of his sweet mummy's bosom to lie on and be comforted by baby talk until all was well again. Of course Ernest now referred to Grace as the Great American Bitch, but he still occasionally needed that mummy love and comfort that had been so healing for him so long ago.

As for Hadley's own need for comfort, she had to be satisfied with friends such as Dave and Barbara O'Neil, who had recently arrived from St. Louis and rented an elegant town house in rue Cothenet near the Bois de Boulogne. Back in St. Louis, Dave O'Neil, after making a fortune in the lumber business, had indulged his love of poetry by publishing a pamphlet that sold for a nickel from vending machines on St. Louis street corners and in train stations. Besides his own poetry, he had published poems by Ezra Pound, Robert McAlmon, Paul Mowrer, John Dos Passos, and T.S. Eliot, and so when he decided to retire and come to Paris to devote himself to writing poetry and living the literary life, his wealth and his connections allowed him to move quickly into Parisian literary circles.

Barbara O'Neil had been a dear friend of Hadley's in St. Louis, and their friendship blossomed anew in Paris, and when Barbara heard that Hadley was sick and Ernest had gone off somewhere on assignment, she cooked up a pot of chicken soup and brought it to the Hemingways' apartment. Marie Cocotte was doing a good job of keeping Hadley fed and comfortable, but Hadley appreciated the gesture, and readily accepted Barbara's offer to come by every day and read to her for an hour or two, often poems from Paul Mowrer's collection, *France in Love and War*.

By the first of December Hadley felt well enough to cable Ernest that she would be arriving in Lausanne on December 3. She had received a short letter from Lincoln Steffens who was also in Lausanne, telling her how much he admired Ernest's writing. He said he was confident that Ernest would someday be an important writer. Hadley figured that Ernest had put Steffens up to writing the letter, but wasn't it nice that a famous and busy man like Steffens would take time to write to her and reassure her of her husband's talent and future? Also, Steffens said he was looking forward to reading more of Ernest's stories, so Hadley wasn't surprised when she received a cable from Ernest asking her to bring all his manuscripts with her. She was sure that Mr. Steffens had asked to read the stories and poems, and she shared Ernest's excitement at the possibility that such an influential writer might agree to be Ernest's sponsor. So, after packing her clothes in a large suitcase with her skiing togs and mountain-climbing boots and various medicines and beauty aids, she went to the armoire where Ernest kept his work and gathered up all the typescripts, the handwritten originals, and the carbon copies of his unfinished novel, his short stories, sketches, and poems. She put them all in a small valise.

Barbara O'Neil and her daughter came by the next day to see

that Hadley got off all right. Barbara was a distinguished-looking woman of thirty-nine, handsome and slim, and her nineteen-year-old daughter, Barbara Too, was a copy of her mother. They and Dave O'Neil and their two sons, seventeen-year-old George and fifteen-year-old Horton, had accepted Hadley's and Ernest's invitation to join them in Chamby for Christmas, and the two Barbaras shared Hadley's mounting excitement about her departure for Lausanne. They helped her down the stairs with her luggage, and they waited on the wet street under umbrellas in the drizzling rain as Hadley went into the bal musette and brought out a slightly tipsy taxi driver whose Citroen cab was parked at the curb.

After hasty hugs from the O'Neil women, Hadley rode away with waves from the two Barbaras and cries of, "See you in Chamby!"

The long-awaited trip had begun! She felt wonderful—the weak, giddy wonderfulness of a person who has survived a grave sickness and awakened to a heightened appreciation of how lovely life can be. The taxi took her to the glass-domed Gare de Lyon, which once again struck Hadley as being the most beautiful railroad station in the world. The wooden benches on which travelers waited had polished brass fittings, the Train Bleu Restaurant upstairs was noted for its elegance and good food, and the impeccable red-jacketed porters who darted here and there were like bellboys in a hotel. Hadley accepted the services of one such porter, who took her luggage to where the well-lit Paris-Lausanne Express rested, sighing with steam. The quay, lined with potted palms, was wet and redolent with the familiar odor of damp coal smoke.

After the porter took her to her compartment and stored her luggage on the overhead racks, Hadley went to buy a newspaper and a bottle of water from pushcart vendors who patrolled the quay. But too nervous and excited to sit still for the thirty minutes until the train departed, she passed the time by strolling along the quay, vibrantly alive to all the sights and sounds of peddlers and passengers and steam-hissing locomotives chugging into and out of the station.

When the conductor called out for everyone to get aboard, Hadley hurried back to her compartment, happy with the promise that by this time tomorrow night she would be in her lover's arms, and all would once again be right with the world.

19

Lincoln Steffens

ERNEST AND LINCOLN Steffens were waiting on the platform when the Paris-Lausanne Express pulled in. Ernest had asked Lincoln to come along with him and meet Hadley. It was important to him that Hadley and Lincoln meet and like each other. He had asked Lincoln earlier to write to Hadley in Paris, telling her that he had read Ernest's work and believed that Ernest had a solid future as a writer of serious fiction. It involved no untruthfulness, and he gathered that Ernest was anxious for his wife to know from a professional source that he had the makings of a good writer. Lincoln found it charming that Ernest should be so concerned about his wife's belief in him. He was also pleased that Ernest had begun to look upon him as something of a father figure. At fifty-eight, Lincoln was certainly old enough to be Ernest's father, and Ernest had told Lincoln that he had been an orphan since he was sixteen. Understandably, then, the young man might be in need of some fatherly interest and approval. And now it seemed important to Ernest that Lincoln approve of Hadley, too.

He took it for granted that Hadley would rush smiling from the train to throw her arms around her husband's neck, but that expectation proved to be very much at odds with reality. When the Express rolled in and began disgorging its passengers, Ernest failed to locate his wife among them. He grew apprehensive.

Lincoln followed as Ernest hurried along the platform, looking into the windows of the compartments. They finally met her coming out of a car, followed by a porter with a single big suitcase.

She was crying. Her porter was so disconcerted by her tears that he sat her suitcase down and retreated without waiting for a tip. Instead of throwing her arms around Ernest's neck, Hadley sat on her suitcase and sobbed uncontrollably.

Ernest was shocked. "Wicky! What is it? What's the matter?"

She struggled to stand up. Wiping her red and swollen eyes on a handkerchief already soaked in tears, she fell against Ernest and said, "Oh, my God, Tatie, it's awful. I haven't had any sleep"—her voice was cut off by a sob, then she tried to resume—"all night. I've been crying ever since I left Paris." And she dissolved into another spasm of sobs.

Though in an agony of suspense, Ernest took her in his arms and tried to comfort her, saying, "What is it? What's wrong, sweetheart? Are you in pain? Shall we get an ambulance?"

"No. I'm in pain, God knows, but it's nothing that medicine would help. Oh, Tatie, how can you ever forgive me?"

"For what, goddamnit?" he said, showing the first signs of exasperation. "For what? Tell me!"

"Oh, I can't, it's too awful."

"For Christ's sake, has somebody died?"

"No, no, it's nothing like that," she said, her tear-smeared face twisted with sorrow. She took a deep breath, as if summoning up all her strength to tell him what was wrong, but she got no further than, "Oh, Tatie, I've . . . I've done a terrible—" But her words were once again lost in sobs.

Vacillating between impatience and tender concern, Ernest said, "Well, what could be so bad?" Forced to guess the worst, he said, "For Christ's sake, have you slept with a nigger?"

"Oh, how can you say that?" she cried.

"Well, then, what?"

Seeing that her handkerchief was wet and well-used, Lincoln offered her his.

"Thank you," she said, noticing him for the first time. "Are you . . . ? Are you Lincoln Steffens?"

He made a small bow of acknowledgment that somehow seemed to connect him to her unspeakable sorrow, for upon learning who he was, she sat down heavily on her suitcase, as if she were on the verge of collapse.

"It was for you that I was bringing them," she managed to say. "Your manuscripts," she said to Ernest.

"What about them?"

"Oh, darling, they were stolen! *All* of them! In Paris!"

Well! So it was finally out. Ernest seemed both relieved and appalled—relieved to finally find out what was wrong, and appalled to think that such a thing could happen. "Manuscripts?" he said. "Stolen? What do you mean?" But as if realizing for the first time where they were and that he and Hadley had become the center of attention of a few curious travelers, he said, "Look, let's get a taxi to the hotel, you can tell me on the way." He helped her to her feet and started to grab the suitcase.

"I'll get it," Lincoln said.

They found a taxi in front of the train station. Ernest and Hadley got into the back, Lincoln got into the front with the driver, and on their way to the Hotel Beau Sèjour they finally got a coherent story from Hadley. Her sobs had subsided from sheer exhaustion, and she managed to get through the tale without too many stumbles.

"The porter put the valise on the luggage rack in the compartment, and I went to get some water and a newspaper," Hadley said. "I walked around a little, till the conductor . . . the train . . . I got on, and the valise with your manuscripts . . . was gone. Stolen! I ran to get the conductor. I begged him not to leave till we could find out what . . . he got the station police. They held the train up for fifteen minutes while they questioned me, but . . . it was gone. Nobody had seen the thief take it. It was just gone. Oh, God, Tatie . . ."

"Look, it's not a catastrophe," Ernest said, trying to comfort her. "The carbons and original copies are—"

"Gone!" she cried. "I packed them all in the valise—everything."

"Oh, I can't believe it," Ernest said. "Why would you pack the carbons and original copies?"

"Well, I thought . . . you see, I thought if you were going to make changes in the originals, you'd want to make the changes in the copies, too, and . . . oh, damn, honey, I'm so sorry, it was just stupid to . . . pack them all in one valise, I can see that now, but . . . oh, God . . ."

"Three years of writing," Ernest said, trying to access the magnitude of the loss. "Three years. . . ."

But to Lincoln's surprise and Ernest's credit, he seemed less upset than Hadley. He was even tender and patient with her, trying to soothe her, trying to put a brave face on the loss.

"Well, as Chink says, never count casualities," he said. "I'll just have to start over."

"I'll be going back to Paris as soon as the conference winds down," Lincoln said. "Might be only a few more days. I can check out the lost-and-found at Gare de Lyon, see if the thief turned it in when he saw he had nothing but a valise full of language he couldn't even read."

"I appreciate that, Linc," Ernest said.

By the time they got to the hotel, Hadley had stopped her sporadic sobbing, but she didn't stop murmuring apologies. Ernest picked up his key at the desk and signed Hadley in. He now began to mumble like a man who had been stunned by a blow. It was impossible to predict what he would be like when he recovered from this stupor, but as a fellow writer Lincoln fancied he could appreciate the bitterness and defeat Ernest might feel. After all, the fact that Hadley had been so careless about her husband's work, his years of labor and heart-squeezed creativity, had demonstrated that she, for all Ernest's praise, had little understanding of his life as a writer. Indeed, knowing that most writers' wives were often jealous of their husbands' occupations, to which the husbands often assigned a higher priority than they did to their wives, it was not inconceivable to Lincoln that Hadley had unconsciously arranged for the valise to be stolen. And what, he wondered, would be the consequences of that?

20

Hadley

WELL, AS HADLEY was getting fond of saying to people who didn't understand Ernest or her devotion to him, he had more sides than could be configured in a geometry book. Just when you thought you had him figured out, he showed you a new side. That was what happened in Lausanne when she presented him with what was the worst disaster of his life. She had expected him to be so angry that he would berate her horribly, and then fall into a terrible self-pitying funk. And who could blame him? Losing his collection of stories and poems had been inexcusably careless on her part, and she had cried more over that one failing than over any other thing that had happened to her. Not even the death of her mother had brought on such a fit of sorrow. So she was more than surprised, she was amazed, to see him accept the disaster without a word of reproach. He was upset, naturally, but he put a brave face on it, and it was he who tried to comfort her.

His magnanimity made her love him even more, yes, but warily, suspiciously, since she knew he now had something that he could hold over her for the rest of her life. This was a man, after all, who never forgot an injury—never—and once he got down on a person, that person would never regain Ernest's respect or affection.

But the surest proof that Ernest was not going to punish her—

at least not yet—was his eagerness to be in bed with her that first night in Lausanne, his eagerness to lose himself passionately in her comforting embrace. His ardor cooled considerably, however, when she told him that she didn't have her diaphragm. She had left it in Paris.

"On purpose?" he asked accusingly, throwing the covers back and sitting up on the side of the bed. He turned on the bedside lamp and began rummaging through his clothes.

Struck by the fear that he was going to get dressed and storm out of the room, Hadley said, "Well, no, I guess it wasn't exactly on purpose, but . . . well, I've told you, I think it would be wonderful for us to have a baby."

"And, Hash, honey, how many times have I told you?—I'm too young to be a father." What he was looking for in his clothes was his pocket-sized notebook, the one in which he kept the vital data about Hadley's menstrual cycle. After quickly leafing through it and consulting some figures, he said, "Jesus, you're just on the cusp of your most fertile time."

"Well, we could do coitus interruptus, couldn't we?"

"You know I hate that," he said.

"I'm sorry," she said. "But I think it'll be all right. Really. I don't feel fertile at all. That flu thing threw my period off completely."

"You think it'd be all right?"

"I think so. I can usually tell when I'm in my fertile time, because of the sensitiveness of my nipples. I don't feel that way at all now."

"You think so?"

"I think so. Come on, Tatie, crawl back in here with me. I'm dying for you."

"Yeah," he said, accepting what he couldn't change. "But just in case, I'd better withdraw and you can finish me off by hand."

But once he started coming, he couldn't stop, as she knew he wouldn't. And after he had collapsed on top of her, she could feel the hairy pressure of his heaving chest pressing against her sensitive nipples.

He was very cross with himself for failing to withdraw. Usually after making love, he was mellow and even pensive as they smoked cigarettes, but that night he threw back the covers in a gesture of disgust and walked the floor, as though wondering how he had come to be trapped. Hadley tried to get him to come back to bed, but since she was the source of all his worries and troubles, he rejected her overtures until she was reduced to tears by her guilt for having lost his manuscripts and forgotten her diaphragm; then he could afford to put her feelings above his own and return to bed to comfort her by letting her share his sorrow.

The next morning, as they were having breakfast in bed, Ernest announced that he was going to Paris on the earliest train.

"I can't believe you actually put all the carbons and originals in that valise. I'll check the apartment, see what I can find," he said. "And who knows, the thief might have put the valise in the station's lost-and-found. Besides," he went on, "I want to get your diaphragm. It's too dangerous for us to make love without it. Where would it be?"

"In the drawer of the commode," Hadley said. "Oh, Tatie, can I come with you? I feel so awful about it, I . . . ."

"No use in both of us going. You stay here, do some Christmas shopping. I'll get one of the guys to cover the wire services for me, and I'll be back by tomorrow night."

21

Gertrude

HAVING JUST AWAKENED and come from her bed in the early afternoon, Gertrude sat on the low Renaissance chair, her bulk buttressed by brocaded pillows, her ankles crossed on an ottoman, and read the note that Hemingway had left with Hèléne, the *femme de ménage,* that morning.

> Just dropped by to see if you had left for your Christmas vacation in Provence. Am in town for the day, would like to see you if possible. Will drop by again this afternoon.

It was unsigned. Good! Gertrude always enjoyed a visit from Hemingway. It would not please Alice so much, of course, because Alice was jealous of what she saw as distinctly sexual undercurrents in Gertrude's and Hemingway's relationship. Gertrude pooh-poohed such concerns, but it flattered her nonetheless to think that a handsome, burly young man like Hemingway might be sexually attracted to her.

As she read the letters that Alice had culled for her from among the morning's mail, she smoked cigarettes in a long holder and drank strong, creamy coffee from a ceramic mug. Hèléne brought her a peeled and sectioned orange in a saucer. Gertrude sat the coffee down and lifted one of the orange sections to her mouth. She curled her lips sensuously around it and nibbled and sucked on it absently as she read a letter, then, swallowing, licked the juice from her plump fingers. Alice's typewriter could be heard from an adjoining room, as she transcribed Gertrude's output of the previous night.

"Pussy!" she called.

The typewriter sounds ceased, and Alice entered the room, clutching one of the school notebooks of blue-lined paper in which Gertrude always did her writing. As Alice approached, Gertrude was trying to scratch her back by pushing against the frame of the chair and twisting her torso.

"Would you scratch my back?" Gertrude asked. "I have an itch and it's driving me mad."

Alice slipped her hand down the back of Gertrude's robe and scratched.

"Ahhhhh," Gertrude sighed blissfully. "That's it, a little to the left, lower, oh, that's—ahhhh, yes, there, thank you, Pussy, you pretty thing."

Alice was not pretty, of course. Not at all. She was homely, almost ugly, poor woman. But when Gertrude called her pretty pussy, she wasn't describing Alice's face. The endearment was from a poem that Gertrude had written for Alice when they were on their honeymoon, so to speak, and since then Gertrude often recited it, as she did now while Alice was scratching her back. Enraptured by her words and the sound of her own voice, she said,

> Pussy how pretty you are . . .
> Kiss my lips. She did.
> Kiss my lips again she did.
> Kiss my lips over and over again she did.
> Pussy how pretty you are . . .

"You're the only one who ever thought so," Alice said sadly. "Is that enough?"

Gertrude made sounds of being satisfied with the scratching, so Alice withdrew her hand. "Yes, oh, thank you, but I am just not believing that as a girl, a child, somebody didn't tell you how pretty you were, your mother, surely."

"My mother!" Alice said wryly. "She was beautiful, my mother. As was a cousin of mine who lived with us in San Francisco. I used to watch her, this cousin, when she sat at a dressing table and brushed her long hair in the mirror, hair as black and sleek as a raven's wing. I was four or five years old then, with frizzy hair that hated a comb, and I'd watch her brush her beautiful hair, and my mouth would be gaping open in awe. Then one day my cousin turned around and looked at me as if I were a stranger, somebody she didn't know, had never noticed before, and said, 'Do you know, Alice, you are without a doubt the ugliest child I have ever seen.' "

"Ahhhggg!" Gertrude growled like an animal ready to rip and tear. "May she die a horrible death!"

"She did," Alice said. "She married a captain in the cavalry. He was caught sodomizing young stable boys. He was threatened with disgrace and ruin, so he killed his wife, then himself. Shot her in the head . . . that beautiful head. No more would she comb that beautiful black hair. And I—" She fluffed the edges of her own short, coarse hair—"I don't have enough to comb."

"But that was in another country," Gertrude said, "and, besides, the wench is dead. Who said that? Some playwright or other. Oh, Pussy, you're inspiring me! I can't wait to get back to writing plays again. I'll write one about you and your beautiful cousin, may her soul rot in hell."

"But for now," Alice said, sitting down on the arm of the chair and opening the school notebook, "I want to make sure I'm transcribing this correctly. Here, where you were writing last night, I'm not sure what this says. . . ." Alice pointed to a place in the notebook where the scrawled writing became particularly messy. " 'The pigeons'—something, something. 'Ass'?"

" 'The grass alas,' " Gertrude said. " 'Pigeons on the grass alas.' "

"Oh. Well, then." She closed the notebook and rose to go. "I'll get back to work, but I don't think I'll have time to finish this if Hemingway is coming to visit this afternoon."

"We'll try not to disturb you, dear."

"That's what I'm afraid of, all that whispering. It'll only make me listen harder, trying to hear what you're saying. I hope he doesn't stay long."

"You suspect we'll be whispering 'sweet nothings'? Oh, Pussy, how you do imagine things, don't you!"

"I know what I know, even if you and he don't know it: he'd like to take you to bed, that's what."

Gertrude flushed with pleasure even as she said, "Oh, pooh! I couldn't go to bed with a man, you know that. Besides, I'm old enough to be his mother."

"And that's probably one of your attractions for him. That head doctor from Vienna, he calls it an Oedipal complex, what Hemingway has for you."

"Malice, Alice," Gertrude said as a good-natured reminder of the defect in Alice's character that she had most assiduously to guard against.

"We'll see," Alice said, as if suspending judgment, and then with a tired sigh made her way back toward her labor of love.

Such a good soul she was. So devoted. So conscientious. Hardly a day passed that Gertrude didn't give thanks that she had met Alice. That had been—how long ago now? Fifteen years? Yes, fifteen years. And in all those years, they had been inseparable. Fifteen years of fidelity and trust and devotion. No marriage among heterosexuals could have gone better. And Gertrude congratulated herself for having seen, those many years ago, what a treasure Alice Toklas would make—having seen, and acted decisively to gather to herself the exclusive possession of that treasure, even if it meant wrecking the relationship that Alice had at the time with a young woman named Harriet Levy. The two of them—Alice and Harriet Levy—had come from San Francisco to Paris for an extended visit and had settled into rooms at the Hotel Magellan, near the Etoile, and, through mutual acquaintances, met Gertrude and her brother, Leo. And on that very first visit, it was obvious that Gertrude had been struck with that flattering device perennial to all romantic novels, *un coup de foudre*—love at first sight. Or perhaps love at first insight: Gertrude saw that Alice had a great need to love and to serve, and since Gertrude had a great need to be loved and to be served, what could be more natural? As the last child, the pampered baby of the Stein family, Gertrude had been raised to a life of unapologetic self-indulgence, made possible by having learned early that selfishness was a source of power, and she had come to accept as a credo that she was born to be pampered, that her needs would give purpose to the lives of those who were born to take care of her. So she and Alice had seemed made for each other.

All Gertrude had had to do was separate Alice from Harriet. On learning that Harriet suffered from religious mania, Gertrude had suggested that she kill herself. Alice was shocked. That seemed a bit extreme. But then Gertrude came up with another scheme: she invited both Alice and Harriet down to Fiesole in Tuscany, where Gertrude and her brother, Leo, had stayed when they first came to Europe. Alice and Harriet had agreed to the trip, and Gertrude had set them up in a villa, then persuaded Alice to accompany her on a walking tour of the countryside. Just a little jaunt. Leave Harriet behind.

They did. And, oh, what a tour! They walked from Perugia to Assisi, stopping at country inns every night. And because Gertrude, even on this journey, refused, as always, to get up before midday, they never got started until the sun was at its highest. Dressed in her usual brown corduroys, with her basket-hat bobbling on her high-piled hair, Gertrude trudged along, huffing and blowing and sweating and sighing, while Alice tagged along patiently, dressed in her usual black silk coat, black gloves, and black hat. The only extravagance Alice allowed herself were the lovely artificial flowers on her hat. But this costume proved too uncomfortable in the heat of the Italian noonday sun, so Alice went behind some bushes and discarded her silk combination and stockings. Later, lying on crushed grass and flowers under a Tuscany cedar tree, as the sun was sinking behind one horizon and a full moon was rising out of another, Gertrude kissed Alice and asked her if she would be her wife.

"Care for me," Gertrude had implored. "A wife hangs on her husband. That is what Shakespeare says, a loving wife hangs on her husband, that is what she does. What say you?"

"I will be your bride," Alice cried.

Gertrude coaxed Alice to undress in the moonlight, and for the first time called her Pussy, and Alice for the first time called Gertrude Lovey, and that night in the light of the full moon they gathered wild violets to replace the artificial flowers on Alice's hat.

Then, returning to Paris, they had to get rid of Gertrude's brother, Leo, so they could have 27 rue de Fleurus all to themselves. Leo was well ensconced there, and, having been the one who had found and rented the house in the first place, he had strong claims to it. But he was at that time involved in a lengthy relationship with an artists' model, who, Gertrude said, supplied Leo with what he most wanted and needed in life: an ear, into which he could pour his endless stream of zestful and opinionated lectures on art. Though a failed artist himself, he nonetheless claimed to know all about it. Having lived in Florence and studied the theories of art under none other than the renowned aesthetician Bernard Berenson, Leo was eager to spread the word about the modern artists, Paul Cezanne, Pablo Picasso, and Henri Matisse, to expound on the Impressionists and the Fauves, and naturally he tried to initiate his sister into the cognoscente. He let Gertrude tag along when he rummaged through the galleries of the modern art dealers, told her which pictures to buy, and even pooled his resources with hers now and then to buy a Renoir or perhaps a Gauguin.

She accepted his guidance readily enough, but Leo soon saw that her own critical judgment was not to be trusted. He told her so. He hinted that she was not intelligent enough to become a successful collector. Her naivete, he said, appeared to be insurmountable. And Gertrude, still the little sister in awe of the big brother, did not defend herself against such paternalistic domination.

Things changed when Gertrude began to take her writing seriously. She had first begun writing when she briefly attended Harvard Medical School, where she took part in laboratory experiments set up to investigate automatic writing. She subsequently adopted the method of writing as her own, and soon produced her first novel, *Quod Erat Demonstrandum,* or *Q.E.D.,* which Leo dismissed as being merely the self-indulgent babbling of someone who tried to make a style out of a lack of discipline.

And true to his prediction, no publisher would print the book. She had no better luck with her next novel, *Three Lives;* after being rejected by a number of publishers, Gertrude subsidized its publication by Grafton Press, and later it was reprinted by John Lane, a small English publisher, but it sold only a few copies, and attracted no attention or reviews, so John Lane declined to publish her next book, *Tender Buttons.* But never mind, Gertrude subsidized the publication of *Tender Buttons* through a small New York publishing firm devoted to "New Books for Exotic Tastes." It, too, was a critical and commercial failure, and as for *The Making of Americans,* a huge novel that she considered to be her masterpiece, the very seminal work of modern literature, not only did all the publishers refuse to print it, they often made fun of her writing style when they rejected it: "This is undoubtedly fine, Miss Stein, but we cannot see our way clear, clear our way to see, our way see clear, to publish it, publish it, publish it."

But did that daunt Gertrude? Not a bit. She sat right down and wrote another book, *Geography and Plays,* and when that, too, was turned down by the publishers, she had it printed at her own expense. She even sold one of Picasso's paintings, "Woman with a Fan," to pay for publishing her next novel, *Lucy Church Amiably.* The loss of the painting made Alice cry, but sacrifices had to be made, didn't they, to force the world to recognize Gertrude's genius?

"Genius?" Leo cried. "Oh, this is really beyond belief. It's bad enough that you're writing is damned nonsense," he told her, "but to add to that the conceit of being a genius—well! It's embarrassing, that's what it is, and I often find myself being embarrassed for you."

He mentioned the times during their Saturday evening soirees when visitors, perhaps prompted by a malicious desire to see Gertrude make a fool of herself, urged her to read from her writings, and then, upon leaving, some guests, who had kept straight faces during the reading, would be unable to contain their laughter when they believed themselves to be out of Gertrude's hearing.

Such incidents embarrassed Leo, and of course hurt Gertrude's feelings, but she persevered. She never let Leo's open contempt for her writing keep her from it. She reminded him of what he himself had often said, that geniuses were usually laughed at in their own time because they were ahead of their time.

"Look at Cezanne," she told him. "Look at Picasso. And what about Gauguin? What about Stravinsky? They were all laughed at, ridiculed, called mad, yes, they were called mad, too, because they were geniuses, and slowly I am knowing that I am a genius, too, and mad, too, perhaps, as all geniuses are mad—"

"It isn't that that drives me wild. It's the fact that you—an ill-educated, self-indulgent woman who is turning out the most god-almighty rubbish—you dare to place yourself among such masters as Gauguin and Cezanne? Yours is not the madness of genius, yours is an egoism that amounts to madness! You should see a doctor. There's a Jewish doctor in Vienna called Freud, specializes in women's neurosis. You should go and see him."

But did his opinions discourage or intimidate Gertrude? They did not. She had an unshakable faith in herself, in her destiny as the creator of a new and unprecedented literature. What's more, Alice agreed with her. The first time she heard Gertrude recite one of her poems, Alice knew—and acknowledged—that she was in the presence of a genius. And so convinced of Gertrude's genius was she that she was willing to offer up her life as a sacrifice to it. As a helpmate, a handmaiden, she would share in Gertrude's glory when it came at last.

Leo threw up his hands. With Alice there to reinforce Gertrude's delusions, he said, there was no chance of bringing her to her senses. So he quit and got himself another apartment. He took with him the paintings that he himself had collected, then he and Gertrude divided up the paintings they had collected together, after which they parted from one another, never to be close again.

Gertrude usurped his role as host and central figure of the Saturday evening soirees and it wasn't long before the guests began to consider themselves her friends, not his. She became the queen. And Alice was her lover, her caretaker, typist, cook, housekeeper, back scratcher, gardener, promoter, accountant, companion, confidante, protector, manager, muse, encourager, and even—with Gertrude's own money—her publisher.

That—the inability to find someone who liked her work well enough to publish it—was, Gertrude felt, the only thing that stood in the way of her attaining recognition. But she was absolutely convinced that it would happen someday, so she kept on turning it out, year after year, filling the copybooks. She created—quite literally—a closet literature, for the piles of manuscripts mounted, year after year, and were stuffed away in a Henry IV cabinet in the studio, a huge confused mass of words that nobody wanted to print and few people wanted to hear.

Not that her work was without admirers. Jean Cocteau sometimes attended her Saturday evening soirees, and if he wasn't on opium or preoccupied with his latest boy-lover, he usually found the opportunity to publicly praise Gertrude's genius. And young writers like Thornton Wilder and Glenway Wescott came to Paris to pay her homage.

But the writer whose admiration she valued most was Sherwood Anderson. He had been the first famous American writer to acknowledge her as a mentor. As the author of *Winesburg, Ohio* and *Poor White,* Anderson was at the height of his fame when he arrived in Paris in June 1921 and asked Sylvia Beach to introduce him to Gertrude Stein. Glad to be of service to such a gracious man, Sylvia had written a letter to Gertrude, asking if she could bring Mr. Sherwood Anderson around to meet her, adding, "He is so anxious to know you, for he says you have influenced him ever so much and that you stand as such a great master of words."

Well, this was what Gertrude desperately needed: living proof that she was who she thought she was. Yes, yes, do bring him around, and how do you do, sir? Please sit. She had gestured toward the ottoman near her chair, and Anderson, a big man with soft brown eyes set in a square face, with a lock of hair falling down his high forehead, lowered his bulk onto the ottoman at her feet. They had smoked cigarettes and drank hot tea served by Alice, and he had told her in low, honeyed tones what a wonderful writer she was—a genius, in fact. He had held his cigarette in an ivory holder; she held hers in a long ebony one, and they admired each other through the swirls of smoke.

"And how did you come in contact with my writing?" she asked after the get-acquainted pleasantries were over.

"Oh, a friend of mine picked up *Three Lives* in Paris years ago and brought it back to Chicago," he said, "and I read it. It excited me. Thought it contained some of the best writing ever done by an American. Then one day, oh, a year or so ago, there was a good deal of fuss and fun being made over *Tender Buttons* in the newspapers, and I managed to get a copy and thought it was wonderful—just wonderful. 'To dine is west.' That's the expression from the book that bowled me over, 'To dine is west.' A great revolution in the art of words! I saw that you were trying to do with language what the modern painters have done with images: You were reshaping, distorting, or otherwise arranging reality to reflect your own feelings. Am I right?"

"Yes, yes, yes," she said, enraptured. "Go on, tell me more."

"Whatever your intent might be, the results of your writings require your readers to pay particular attention to words, rather than to the content and motives that might lie behind them, and . . ."

A warm, effusive man, given to sentiments and hyperbole, he continued telling her what she wanted to hear, and before the meeting was over, she realized that Anderson was everything she could ever want in a brother—or in a lover, for that matter, had she ever considered taking a male lover. Failing either of those relationships, however, she was overjoyed to have him as a friend and admirer.

"You are so perceptive," she said, and "Ah, my friend," as the meeting was drawing to a close, "you cannot know what it means to me to have someone—and you have been the only one—who understands, who simply quite understands what it is all about. And to so charmingly and directly tell it to me! Ah, my friend, you cannot know how much I value this telling."

And after he had gone back to America, she showed that her gratitude was not mere politeness by writing a poem called, "A Valentine to Sherwood Anderson," which she sent to him for Valentine's Day.

Very fine is my valentine.
Very fine and very mine.
Very mine is my valentine very mine and very fine.
Very fine is my valentine and mine, very mine very fine
and mine is my valentine.

In Sherwood's next letter he thanked her for the beautiful valentine, and ended his letter with a simple, "Gee, I love you."

Sherwood Anderson was a sweet man. And some of the warmth Gertrude felt toward him was transferred to Hemingway, for whom Sherwood had written a letter of introduction, in which he had said that young Hemingway understood everything worthwhile in modern writing, and that she would find him a delightful friend—which had proved to be the case. Hemingway had come and sat on the ottoman at her feet and told her how much he admired her and her writing. On frequent visits to her house, he had read large sections of the novel she considered her masterpiece, *The Making of Americans,* and said it was great. He said publishers were damned fools not to publish it. And he was so moved by one passage that he asked her to read it aloud, which she was glad enough to do.

. . . or you write a book and while you write it you are ashamed for every one must think you are a silly one or a crazy one and yet you write it and you are ashamed, you know you will be laughed at or pitied by every one and you have a queer feeling and you are not very certain and you go on writing. Then some one says yes to it, to something you are liking, or doing or making and then never again can you have completely such a feeling of being afraid and ashamed that you had then when you were writing the thing.

"In that case," Hemingway had said that hot afternoon last summer, "in that case, consider that I have said yes to it, and so you should never again have the feeling of being afraid or ashamed that you had when you were writing it. It's the best stuff I've ever read."

It had brought tears of gratitude to Gertrude's eyes. Her own brother had said that her writing was embarrassing—"god-almighty rubbish"—and that people were laughing at her behind her back, or pitying her for being a fool. But here was a young man who was willing to sit at her feet and learn from her and tell her that her books were wonderful. It was too bad that Alice seemed to detect an ulterior motive in everything Hemingway said or did. True, Alice, the sly one, had discovered—bit by inadvertent bit—that Hemingway had lied to them shamelessly about his youth and about his war record, "And if he lies about those things, he'll lie about others," Alice argued. "So how can you ever believe him, trust him?"

Well, Gertrude didn't hold that against him. Boys would be boys. And even Alice managed some sympathy for Hemingway when he came up from Lausanne on that cold day in December and dropped by rue de Fleurus to tell Gertrude how his manuscripts had been stolen.

"Surely you have the carbons," Alice said as she served cakes and *eau-de-vie*. As a good secretary, she simply took it for granted that carbon copies would be tucked away somewhere in a safe, dry place.

"No," Hemingway said. "She put everything in the valise—carbons, originals, everything. I checked the lost-and-found at Gare de Lyon, but nobody had turned anything like that in, so I went by the apartment, hoping she'd missed something, but all that was left was the short story you didn't think was publishable—remember? 'Up in Michigan'? I'd put it in the bottom drawer of my desk in the Verlaine studio."

"Oh. Too bad," Alice said, a bit ambiguously.

"Lincoln Steffens had sent one of my stories to *Cosmopolitan*, so it and the 'Up in Michigan' story are the only ones I have left out of three years' work."

Gertrude was sitting in her big Renaissance chair, dressed in a long brown robe. Her rich brown hair was piled high on her head, on the very top of which she had placed a small decorative doily that Alice had crocheted, very much like the doily that Queen Victoria had often worn in photographs and paintings. She smoked a cigarette in a long holder, which she held like a scepter. Hemingway had taken his usual seat on the ottoman at her feet. He smoked cigarettes without a holder.

"Three years' work," Gertrude mused. "Consisting of what, my friend, what of what?" Taking the butt from her holder and extinguishing it in an ashtray, she then leaned forward and spread her legs and put her elbows on her knees like a washerwoman.

"Eleven short stories, a number of poems, and the novel that I'd been working on—the one you said I should do over."

Gertrude didn't tell him that he was perhaps better off for having lost such juvenilia. That's what she was thinking, but that would have been cold comfort for someone who was looking for warm sympathy. Alice went to stoke the cast-iron stove in the corner, then went into the kitchen.

"Do you remember the stories?"

He shrugged, hurt. "I guess, but I wouldn't know how to get them back."

"Leave them alone and they'll come home, wagging their tails behind them," Gertrude offered.

"I don't know. After this, I'm thinking about giving up writing altogether. Become a boxer, while I'm still young enough. Or a bootlegger. I could make a lot of money, running booze from Canada into the States."

Alice came back to fill their glasses and to check the temperature of their words. It was charming of Pussy to be jealous, it showed how much she prized Gertrude, still. Gertrude had a weakness for Hemingway. His extraordinary good looks and his barely concealed desire for her stirred within Gertrude's vitals the last, long-dormant vestiges of heterosexuality. This attraction manifested itself in the intense way she and Hemingway looked at each other, and in the peculiarly intense tones of their voices. It was idle speculation, of course, because Gertrude would never be unfaithful to Alice, especially not with a man, but she couldn't help wondering what might happen between her and Hemingway if Pussy weren't around. . . .

"Don't forget," Alice said, "we have to go to the bank before it closes, and put the car in the garage for service."

"What would I do without Alice to look after me?" Gertrude said to Hemingway. "So efficient. It's true, we're getting ready for our trip to Provence for Christmas. We are having so many things to do, so many things. Will you be in the city long?"

"No," Hemingway said. "I'll be going back to Lausanne on the night express."

"Will you be back in Paris for Christmas?"

"No, we're going to spend Christmas in Switzerland, at Chamby, wonderful place, skiing and bobsledding with a bunch of friends. It would be wonderful if you and Alice could join us for a few days. We could all have a jolly time."

"I, myself, and me?" Gertrude said. "On a pair of skis?" She laughed. Heaving her short but monumental body out of the deep chair, she took Hemingway's arm and escorted him to the door. "You might as well suggest I dance à la Isadora. By the by, she's back in Paris for a while, our Isadora is, if you'd like to meet our Isadora someday, she's so fond of handsome young men."

"You know Isadora Duncan?"

"Her brother Raymond lives just across the street, didn't you know? He makes my sandals. He wears togas. We're all from Oakland, you know, the Duncans and the Steins—Oakland, California, all from there, where there is no there there, that's why we are here, because there is a here here."

"Sure, I'd like to meet her."

"And I'm sure she would find you frightfully delightfully rightfully nightfully." Gertrude laughed her deep rich yolky laughter as she patted Hemingway's hairy wrist. "Yes. Oh, yes. So when we all get back in Paris, I'll see that you are introduced. Meanwhile, try not to worry about the lost stories, dear boy, the lost years, nothing is lost, ever, nothing except everything in the end, generations, decades, eons. Start again, and concentrate."

Hemingway thanked her warmly for her hospitality and advice, and left her germinating the thought to write one of her word portraits of him. She had written such word portraits of many people—Picasso and Mabel Dodge, T.S. Eliot, and others. Just as a painter would make portraits with paints, she would make portraits with words. So as soon as she and Alice returned from doing their chores in preparation for leaving for Provence,

Gertrude sat down at her Renaissance table, opened one of the student's blue notebooks and began.

Portrait of Hemingway, 1922
Accidents are reappearing for retribution. Accidents of loss are learning that what is done when is done and the lost lamb cries maaaaaama. War is hell is losing stories losing himself in many guises, that's what he does, many protective disguises of lost boy dejected lies lost. What is it darling. Nothing. Hell is war man that dies is nothing dearie lost in how do you do of boxer, bootlegger, hobo, fisherman, reporter, lamb in wolf's clothing crying maaaama for prairie mother bosom nothing at bosom but war. Is war hell, is hell war, hell is hell, was is war is was. So much losing himself before the lies of beginning of stories little lamb lost before the beginning of stories, after the ending of stories.

There, now. That was a good beginning, wasn't it?

22

Hadley

ERNEST RETURNED FROM Paris with only Hadley's diaphragm. Since the peace conference was drawing to a close, Lincoln Steffens and Bill Bird completed their work and returned to Paris, where they, too, got involved in trying to locate Ernest's stolen manuscripts. Ernest and Hadley stayed on in Lausanne for another week at the Hotel Beau Sèjour so he could finish filing his dispatches with the Hearst news services. As for his fictional work, Hadley expected him to brood openly and bitterly about the loss of his manuscripts, but he surprised her by doing just the opposite. He adopted an air of raffish gaiety. He laughed louder, drank more, danced more, and made love more often than usual, and talked about the wonderful skiing and bobsledding that lay ahead of them at Chamby.

Bird and Lincoln Steffens wrote from Paris that the only way to recover the manuscripts would be to advertise in the newspapers and put up posters around the Gare de Lyon with an offer of a large reward for the return of the valise. Ernest wired them to offer a reward of 150 francs, which amounted to ten dollars. Lincoln Steffens wired back that Ernest would have to offer more of an inducement to make the thief bring back what Ernest wanted and the thief didn't.

But to Hadley's astonishment Ernest was unwilling to offer more. She didn't argue with him about it, but she couldn't

understand why he would place so little value on the lost manuscripts. He kept telling people that the manuscripts represented
three years of hard work; was all that worth no more than ten
dollars? Why, ten dollars was no more than half a month's rent
on their Paris apartment, or the price of a month's ski pass on the
tramway up from Chamby to Les Avants. Did he value the lost
material so little?

Hadley wondered if he really wanted the manuscript back. But
if he didn't, what would he be gaining by losing them? An un-
ending source of sympathy and self-pity, for one thing; a source
of admiration from others for being able to face the loss with
such equanimity, for another; and (Hadley's particular worry)
something he could always hold over her.

Hadley did not want to believe this, and she realized that she
may be ascribing motives, rather than discovering them, but how
else explain his astonishing unwillingness to do what was necessary to try to recover his stolen manuscripts?

But even though she didn't understand his behavior, guilt-rid-
den Hadley was glad he handled his loss the way he did. His
enthusiasm made for a truly wonderful Christmas at Chamby.
The two of them went up to the Gangwisch pension on December 15 and were joined there by Chink Dorman-Smith the next
day. Chink took a room directly above Ernest and Hadley, and
the next morning at sunup, shortly after Ida, the pension's maid,
tiptoed into Ernest's and Hadley's room and closed the window
and built a fire in the big porcelain stove, Chink stamped on his
floor—their ceiling—the ski slopes were waiting. The snow that
had fallen during the night had ceased now, and the rising sun
reflected from the snow and the snow-laden trees in a rosy glow.

The three of them hurried their breakfasts, then strapped on
their rucksacks and carried their skis and ski poles over their
shoulders as they ran for the tram car that carried skiers up the
mountain. They shouted and cheered as the car stopped at each
platform crowded with skiers, all of whom were friendly and
giddy with excitement, their breaths making long plumes of vapor on the crisply cold morning air.

After passing through the village of Les Avants and the woods
of Chernaux, they reached the end of the tram line. The skiers

fanned out in the direction of the ski runs, but Ernest and Hadley and Chink, at Ernest's instigation, put on their skis, which were wrapped in seal skins so they could get a grip on the snow, and walked farther up the saddle of the Dent de Jaman. Each of them wore amber-shaded goggles against the glare of the snowfields.

They had taken off their sweaters when they started the climb, and by the time they reached the top, they were dripping with sweat. From here they could look out over many rugged mountain ranges, all glistening white, and now and then through openings in the trees they could see Lake Geneva far below, glinting like a blue mirror in the sun.

Ernest remembered that there was an old barn somewhere nearby, a log shelter for cattle that were herded there by peasants in the summer when the alpine meadows were green. When they found the barn half-buried in a bank of snow, they took shelter in it from the bright midday sun. From their rucksacks, they took their food and a bottle of white wine. The Gangwisch pension's cook had made lunches of cold chicken and sausages and cheeses, which they ate with gusto as they passed the bottle of wine between them, laughing and talking and loving life. They took their sweaters from their rucksacks and slipped them on again before they took the seal skins off their skis and waxed the skis for the seven-mile run down the slopes.

"What a beautiful day!" Chink said, glancing up at the cloudless blue sky as they prepared to start their run.

"We're very lucky," Hadley said. "Aren't we, Tatie? Aren't we lucky?"

"We're always lucky," Ernest said.

They pulled the amber-shaded goggles down over their eyes, took deep breaths, and pushed off with their ski poles. In one long, sinuous, heart-fluttering swoop, they dropped off the mountain, the powdered snow flying from their skis. There was no other sensation like it in the world.

Of the three, Chink was by far the best and most experienced skier, and Hadley had more natural athletic ability than Ernest did, but they had not gone half a mile before Hadley and Chink accepted what they knew already: Ernest simply was not going to be less than first in anything he attempted. Whenever Hadley or Chink got ahead of him on the slope, Ernest pushed himself beyond his abilities to try to overtake them, so that he stayed in the lead, not by superior skill but by taking dangerous chances that the other two would not take. To keep him from being so reckless, Hadley and Chink fell back and gave him the lead, without any loss of pride to themselves, since they, unlike Ernest, did not consider this a contest.

They took a few falls, none serious, but Ernest did frighten them once when they began to converge with other skiers and he had to swerve sharply to avoid a collision with one of them. Going too fast to stop, he suddenly dropped from sight over an embankment. When Hadley and Chink hurried to find out what had happened to him, they found him at the bottom of a deep gully, buried headfirst in the snow, with only his flailing legs sticking out. Hadley and Chink took off their skis and scrambled down the embankment to pull Ernest out of the deep snow, and when they saw that he wasn't hurt, they laughed. But Ernest was not amused. He had a keen sense of the ridiculous as long as he was not the object of the ridicule. He had regained his good humor by the time they got back to the Gangwisch chalet and devoured their dinner and fell into bed.

The next day, the three of them caught the train to Montreux, where they shopped for Christmas presents and pounds of fruit and candy to fill their Christmas stockings. Later, with their sacks and bundles pushed under a table in a beer hall, they drank and sang and danced to accordions and tubas.

And so the days passed, days of skiing or bobsledding, evenings in front of the chalet's open fireplace drinking hot rum and singing Christmas carols, and at night, when Ernest and Hadley were lying together in a big four-poster bed while a fine fire crackled in the porcelain stove, they watched through the frosted window as a cold full moon rose out of the snow-laden trees.

One evening Ernest trimmed Hadley's hair. Gertrude Stein had taught him how to do it, and Ernest became quite good at it, giving it the importance of a ritual. It seemed to stimulate his erotic imagination, and when Hadley asked him if he wanted her to trim *his* hair, he said, "No, I'm going to let my hair grow longer than yours," and that night as they snuggled under the goose-down comforter they spoke of trading sexes, he becoming the woman and she becoming the man.

"In a month your hair will be over your ears. Are you frightened?"

"Maybe."

"I am, too, a little. But we're going to do it, aren't we? We're really going to do it?"

"Sure."

When Hadley asked him what name she should call him when he was the woman, he told her to call him Catherine, and when he asked her what she was to be called when she was the man, she chose the name Peter.

These became their secret code names for each other. Ernest loved nicknames, of course, and used them extensively, affectionately or satirically, with people who were close to him. He treated names as if they held some sort of magical powers. And secret names were the holiest of all. Catherine and Peter were names that were never to be known to anybody else and, even between them, the names were to be used only in the most intimate and secret moments.

The arrival from Paris on December 23 of Barbara and Dave O'Neil and their three children completed Ernest's requirements for a more perfect holiday: more people to adulate him, and one person for him to despise. The adulators were all the O'Neils except Dave. Barbara and her nineteen-year-old daughter, Barbara Too, had succumbed to Ernest's male charms in Paris, and the two boys, George and Horton, tagged around after Ernest like wolf pups following the pack leader.

Dave O'Neil was the one Ernest picked on. Of course, Ernest believed that his hostility toward Dave was rational enough. He had reasons for despising him. In the first place, Dave had made a fortune as a businessman, and Ernest was envious. In spite of Hadley's trust fund, he still saw himself as a poor, struggling artist, and when he snidely asked Dave how to amass a fortune, Dave advised him, "Take care of the pennies, and the dollars will take care of themselves." For this Ernest, with forced good humor, labeled him a celto-kike.

And after Dave, a dilettante who considered himself a budding poet, prevailed upon Ernest to read a few of his poems, Ernest found the high ground from which to attack Dave's poetic pretensions unmercifully, and did so in front of everybody.

"Dave, you're an untalented amateur who tries to make a virtue of ignorance. You confuse obscurity with profundity. Your steady stream of strained metaphors tries to make a Taj Mahal out of a simple shithouse, and a simple romp in the hay becomes—how was it described? Yeah, here it is: the lovers 'splash their dreams in the dark pool of gratification.' Listen, Dave, the next time you get the urge to write another poem, I suggest you first consider the beauty of clean, white paper."

But Ernest ended his brutal criticisms with a wide, teeth-bared, mirthless smile that seemed to disarm any umbrage that Dave might naturally feel inclined to take. That smile, however phony, allowed Dave to believe that the criticisms were merely argumentative camaraderie, rather than outright insults. It was a fine line that Ernest was walking, but apparently he knew his man, for he got nothing but a weak, confused grin from Dave when he tested between his thumb and forefinger the texture of the paper on which Dave's poems were typed, and said, "But considering the quality of Swiss toilet paper, we might find a more suitable use for these pages."

This was said at a lunch table at the Grand Hotel in Les Avants, where the O'Neil family was staying. The group had spent the morning skiing and had come back to the hotel to enjoy an expensive lunch as Dave's guests.

"In fact, I have to go to the toilet before we get back on the slopes," Ernest said, "so why don't I just take a few pages along?" Getting up, he reached for the poems, giving Dave plenty of time to retrieve them, which he did with a comic cry of protest.

"Oh, come on, cut it out," Dave pleaded.

After Ernest had gone, Barbara asked her husband, "Don't you object to him calling your poems toilet paper?"

"What? Oh, no," Dave said, hiding his humiliation behind the same facade of camaraderie that Ernest had used to hide his hostility. "He's just kidding around. He's a good friend."

Hadley and Barbara exchanged glances. It was not their understanding that Ernest and Dave were good friends.

"Don't you think you're being a little hard on Dave?" Hadley asked Ernest that night when they were back in their room at the Chamby chalet, filling their Christmas stocking with candies and fruit.

"Why shouldn't I be hard on the jerk?" Ernest asked.

"Because he's the husband of an old and dear friend of mine, and it makes both Barbara and me uncomfortable, the way you humiliate him."

"Aw, I can't help it," Ernest said. "He's a jock-sniffer. I hate jock-sniffers."

"Jock-sniffer? What's that?"

"It's what boxers call some sycophant who hangs around gyms."

This was not an image that Hadley liked to apply to poor Dave. He didn't deserve it. Hadley felt like asking Ernest to be reasonable, but she knew that once Ernest took a dislike to someone, there was no reasoning with him.

Chink had to leave after New Year's Day, heading back to his army duty in Germany, and everyone was sad to see him go— particularly Ernest, with his need to be surrounded by friends. However, no sooner was Chink gone than Isabelle Simmons, one of Ernest's old girlfriends from Oak Park showed up. Isabelle had been on a tour of Europe, and when peremptorily summoned from Paris by a telegram from Ernest, she came to Chamby for a two-week skiing holiday. Hadley had never before met Isabelle, but liked her almost immediately, seeing that she was a strong, intelligent girl who had no intentions of supplanting Hadley in Ernest's affections. Then, a few days later, Janet Phelan, a friend of Hadley's from St. Louis, interrupted her vacation in Paris to come down and spend a few days with the Hemingways. Both the new women were young and good-looking and unattached, all of which suited Ernest splendidly. Moreover, the adulation that Isabelle—Izzy—had felt for Ernest back in those days in Oak Park when they were porch-swing neighbors and high school sweethearts, was quickly rekindled by Ernest's charms, while Janet Phelan, who had never before met Ernest, needed only a few days to become an admirer.

Knowing that Ernest's eagerness to have the attention of several admiring women was an innocent vanity, Hadley made light of it by referring to herself and Izzy and Janet as "Hemingway's harem." They even gave themselves nicknames: Hadley became Yasman, Izzy was Fatima, and Janet became Midina. And much to Ernest's delight, they sometimes addressed him in the third person as the Sultan.

"Is the Sultan pleased?" Fatima asked, referring to the progress made on the sweater for him that Hadley had begun and that each of the three women took turns knitting in the few idle moments that they didn't spend on the ski slopes or in the bars.

"The Sultan is pleased," Ernest said, joining in the game.

And as long as he took the game lightly, as long as it was merely an innocent vanity, Hadley was glad to play along, secure in her knowledge that Ernest was hers. But one day in the middle of January Ernest received a letter from a woman who had the power to threaten Hadley's hold on him. The letter came with a huge pile of mail that had been forwarded from Paris. Ida, the pension's maid, had brought the mail into Ernest's and Hadley's room and deposited it on the table, and because there were a number of packages among the letters, it was a little like a second Christmas. There were scarves and handkerchiefs and socks from the folks back home, and there were three copies of *Poetry: A Magazine of Verse,* published in Chicago by Harriet Monroe, a friend of Ezra Pound's. Ezra had sent six of Ernest's poems to the magazine, and there they were, in print, with Ernest's name on them. So at least six poems had escaped the thief in Gare de Lyon.

Unfortunately, the gratification of seeing the poems in print was dampened a little by a large manila envelope containing the manuscript of "My Old Man," the short story that Lincoln Steffens had sent to *Cosmopolitan.* It had been rejected.

"Oh, well," Ernest said, shrugging, "it wasn't their kind of story, anyway." After a moment's hesitation, he added, "But better not tell the celto-kike about the rejection. No use to give him a reason to crow."

Taking the letters from the top, Ernest read aloud parts of a letter that Gertrude Stein had sent from Provence, then he gave Hadley the letter to read in its entirety. The next one he opened was from Ezra Pound. Ezra and Dorothy were spending the winter in Rapallo, a little town on the Italian Riviera.

"Listen to this," Ernest said. "He calls the loss of my manuscripts an 'act of Gawd. As has been remarked,' he says, 'memory is the best critic. If the thing wobbles and won't reform, then it had no proper construction and never would have been right. All of which is probably cold comfort . . .' No shit?"

Taking a sip of hot rum from the mug on the table in front of him, Ernest recovered from his exasperation and continued with the letter.

"He wants us to come and visit them in Rapallo. Says it's quite a wonderful place. Mike and Maggie Strater are there, and he says Yeats may be coming down soon. Would you like to go? It's cheaper than Paris, he says. A couple can get by in a pension hotel for five hundred lire a week—about twenty-five dollars. And it's warm in the winter, he says."

"Well, I'd rather be just about anywhere than Paris in the winter," Hadley said. "And with Mike and Maggie there, we'd have company. Sounds nice."

"Let's do it, then," Ernest said decisively. "Maybe I could get some writing done there."

As usual after finishing a letter, he passed it on to Hadley, in case she wanted to read it. She happened to glance at him as he picked up the next letter in the pile, and the look on his face caught her attention. It was a strange look, as if he had gone cold all over, and then he quickly, furtively, slipped the thick letter underneath the pile. Hadley had never before seen him try to hide a letter, which of course only compounded her curiosity.

"Who was that letter from, dear?" she asked.

For a moment he had the guilty expression of a small boy caught in some forbidden act and looking for a way out, but he quickly saw that trying to deceive her would only make the matter worse, so he recovered the letter from the bottom of the pile.

"Agnes," he said.

"Agnes?" Hadley asked, trying to take it in. "Von Kurowsky?" And though he nodded and she needed no further confirmation, she said, "Your Red Cross nurse?"

"Yes." He opened the envelope.

"Why would she be writing you?"

"I wrote her a letter in November," Ernest said. "I don't know why. I thought she . . . It was after Bird said he was going to publish a book of my stories, and I guess I wanted her to know. I sent it to her family's address in the States. I didn't know if it would ever reach her."

But it had, and now the answer was in his hands. Until now neither of them had had any secret correspondence with anyone, and they had always read aloud to each other parts of any letters that the other might find interesting; but this time Hadley fell silent and allowed Ernest to read the many pages of Agnes' letter without the usual interruptions. She did glance at him as she read other letters, to see how he was taking it. He seemed agitated but utterly absorbed in the missive, and when he finished he sighed heavily, as if from relief at having successfully negotiated a minefield. He held onto the letter for a moment, trying to decide what to do with it, though he really didn't have much choice. Had he not offered to let Hadley read it, he would have been betraying a trust. So he handed it over to her, then drained his rum in one swallow and took his empty cup and turned toward the door.

"I'm going to get myself another hot rum," he said. "Want one?"

"Yes, please," she said, draining her cup and handing it to him.

After he was gone, Hadley turned her attention to the letter. The first thing she noticed was that it had been addressed to Ernest at the office of the Anglo-American Newspaper Alliance in Paris. So he had intended to keep any correspondence with Agnes a secret from her. It was only because the Newspaper Alliance had forwarded the letter to Chamby with Ernest's other mail that Hadley had learned of its existence. Agnes wrote of how pleased she was to hear from him and how it helped her get over the lingering hurt of the bitter letter he had written her after she had told him of her marriage plans. And she was so glad for him that he now had Hadley and just imagine what an antique she herself became.

Hadley was relieved to learn that Ernest had told Agnes about her, but then bit her bottom lip to learn that Agnes considered herself an antique. So Ernest had not told her that Hadley was one year older than she was.

The letter continued with a long account of Agnes' travels since she and Ernest had parted company three years ago. After returning to work at Bellevue Hospital in New York for a while, she had volunteered to be sent to Russia as a Red Cross nurse, but ended up in Bucharest, Rumania, instead, where she learned to speak Rumanian. From there her duties and her desire to travel had taken her back to Naples. There, while strolling along the streets one day with an Englishman, she caught sight of a young artillery officer in a carriage. Here he was, her former lover, passing by just like a character in a Henry James novel, with his villainous mother at his side. Agnes had recognized Duke Domenico Carracciolo immediately, but when he attempted to greet her, she pretended not to know him. All he got from her was a haughty toss of her head as she turned to her escort, smiling to herself, pleased that fate had given her one last chance to satisfy her wounded pride.

From Naples she traveled to Paris, which she had loved so much she became homesick for it as soon as she had to leave. In closing she wrote how good it was to have their old friendship back and when his book came out how proud she would be.

She wished that they might correspond occasionally, and signed herself, "Your old buddy."

What was Hadley to make of it? It was certainly not the letter of a long-lost lover. "Your old buddy. . . ." Hadley had to wonder if that was all they had ever been—just buddies, old wartime buddies. Was it possible that she and Ernest had never even been lovers? Was Ernest's great love affair with Agnes just another example of his inability to distinguish between memory and imagination?

The letter caused Hadley to feel no jealousy, no threat to her marriage. The fact that Ernest had written to Agnes and gave the Newspaper Alliance office as a return address caused her more concern than Agnes' letter itself. Obviously he had meant to deceive her. As far as she knew, he had never before done anything underhanded or secretive.

She looked for a chance to talk to him about it during the following days, but before she found an opportunity, Ernest had sunk into one of his sullen depressions, thereby ending the holiday mood, the loveliest holiday Hadley had ever known. A general feeling of loss had begun to pervade Chamby as the holiday vacationers began leaving—first the O'Neil family, then the girls of the Hemingway harem, Izzy and Janet, leaving Ernest like the last guest at a party that he didn't want to end.

Then in early February the snow turned to drizzling mist, ruining the skiing and bobsledding, and the good times had definitely come to an end—the good times and the lovemaking, too. For some reason—the absence of admiring women, perhaps, or Agnes' letter—Ernest suffered another period of impotence.

As for Hadley, she had missed her period. She didn't think much of it at the time. It seemed reasonable that the daily physical strain of skiing and bobsledding had disrupted her monthly rhythms. But by the time she was a whole month late, she began to feel changes taking place in her body. Because Ernest was in a funk and they hadn't been making love, he had neglected to make a monthly entry into his little notebook, so she waited until she had missed her second period before telling him. She wanted to be sure, for she didn't want to put him through the shock of it without being certain. So she waited until they were packing their things to go visit the Pounds in Italy.

"Tatie," she said. "I think there's something you ought to know before we get to Rapallo."

"What?" He was gathering and packing the poems and sketches he had done while they were at Chamby.

"I'm pregnant," she said.

23

Ezra

RAPALLO WAS A lovely little town, just the place Dorothy and Ezra Pound had been searching for in Italy, a place where they could have an extended rest, away from the maelstrom of a capital city. The town had once been a fashionable resort for elite English and other northern European travelers making the Grand Tour in the eighteenth and nineteenth centuries. But after the War, other resorts became more fashionable, and the steep rise of hills behind Rapallo left no room for the building of casinos and ballrooms demanded by the richer tourists, who moved on to richer resorts.

So the town was left a peaceful place, bordered by a placid sea on one side and mountains on the other. The mountains shut out all but the south wind, and the curve of the coast created a protected bay, though there was no harbor crowded with yachts, no wide swaths of yellow sandy beach to lure holiday bathers. Except for a few yards of sand, the waterfront was a shallow, gravelly shingle, bordered by an esplanade that was shaded by palm trees. Behind the town, mounting the hills, were villas and red-tile roofed cottages, with their terraced and trellised gardens, enclosed by flowering trees and eucalyptus that sweetly scented the birdsonged air.

Ezra and Dorothy settled into the Hotel Mignon. They took their meals at the café of the Albergo Rapallo, which occupied the ground floor of the hotel, fronting on the bay. When the sun was out, they usually ate on the café's seafront terrace. It was a good life, and easily affordable with Dorothy's trust fund, but it got a little lonely at times, so Ezra sent out invitations to any of his footloose followers who might be persuaded to visit. Mike and Maggie Strater came down from Paris and were staying at the Hotel Riviera Splendide, just a little way along the esplanade. Mike, however, had sprained his ankle playing tennis a few days after his arrival, so he couldn't accompany Ezra on a hike that Ezra wanted to make through the medieval kingdom of Romagna.

Ezra wanted to make the trip to research a fifteenth century ruler of Romagna called Sigismundo Pandolfo Malatesta. He wanted to write a canto about Sigismundo and his reign. The walking trip had been planned for February, regardless of rain, but Ezra delayed because he wanted a male companion for the tour. Dorothy was a compliant and amiable traveling partner, but intellectually she was dull.

So when Ezra received Hemingway's letter from Chamby, saying that he and Hadley were coming down to Italy for an extended stay, Ezra entertained the hope that he could persuade Hem and Hadley to come along on the walking tour.

In his letter accepting Ezra's invitation to Rapallo, Hem complained that the high altitude had adversely affected his sex glands, a matter he would like to discuss with Dr. Louis Berman, the New York endocrinologist who had authored a book called *The Glands Regulating Personality.* Ezra had reviewed the book for *New Age* magazine last year, and had recommended that Hem read it, along with Ezra's translation of Rémy de Gourmont's *The Natural Philosophy of Love.* Ezra had recommended Gourmont's book because of Hem's well-known disdain for fairies. Gourmont claimed that adultery and even homosexuality were perfectly natural, and the only true sexual perversion was chastity. The book had become very popular in Europe among such intellects as Havelock Ellis, Aldous Huxley, and D.H. Lawrence, but Hem's bourgeois background made him resist the notion that homosexuals were anything other than degenerates. As for Dr. Berman's book, Hem believed his thesis that the glands regulate personality, and was even willing to entertain Ezra's long-held belief that the brain had evolved from coagulated sperm, thereby making a direct correlation between sex and creativity, the creative thought being an act of fecundation like the male cast of human seed into the passive receptacle of the womb.

"Hot dog!" Ezra had cried when he first had this stroke of genius, lo, these many years ago, back in the days when he was a graduate fellow at the University of Pennsylvania. The passive receptacle of his sperm in that case was his first love, Hilda Doolittle, that tall, blond, bizarre nineteen-year-old beauty with a strong jaw and sky-blue eyes, whose father was a professor of astronomy at the university. The Doolittle family lived in Darby, a forested area not far from the university, where Hilda and Ezra could take long walks in the woods. Frequently they had been accompanied by their best friend, William Carlos Williams, a premed student at Penn, who sometimes brought his violin along and played it like the pipes of Pan as he and Hilda and Ezra gamboled in the glades and meadows and cried out their praises of nature. Ezra called Hilda "Dryad," his nymph of the woods, and she shortened his name to Ra, invoking the ancient Egyptian sun god.

"Oh, the grass! The grass!" Hilda cried.

"Oh, the flowers! The flowers!"

They picked wild daisies and strung them together to make diadems for their heads.

"The trees! Oh, the trees!" they cried as they danced.

"Oh, the sky, Ra, the sky! Look! The clouds!"

"Yes, yes, the clouds, yes! The sun!"

"Yes, yes, yes, the sky! Oh, sun! Oh, grass! Oh, trees! Oh! Oh! Oh!"

Hilda had a tree house in the backyard of her family home. She and Ezra often spent hours there, without Bill Williams, doing some heavy petting, practicing to become adepts in the pagan love cult of Eleusis. Hilda would listen raptly as Ezra instructed her in the Eleusinian Mysteries, which were based on the ritual sexual union of Eleusinian priests with young women, a union that produced knowledge, symbolized as light, which was then carried forward through the ages by the women. Then one fateful night in the tree house Ezra and Hilda—Ra and Dryad—felt they were at last ready to perform the sacrament of Eleusis. So they did, they fucked and found God. Or anyway Ezra did; Hilda wasn't so sure. She wanted to try again, but Ezra wasn't up to it.

"It's getting cold out here," he said. "Let's go in the house. I'm hungry."

Hilda's parents weren't home. Ezra and Hilda went inside and sat on the floor in front of the fireplace. Ezra peeled and ate an orange, and Hilda burst into song.

"Du meine Herzen, du mein Ruhe," she sang.

With orange juice dribbling down his chin, Ezra tried to join in.

"Oh, do shut up, Ezra," Hilda said. "You have no voice whatsoever. You sound like a billy goat munching tin cans."

"I don't want a wife, but if I did, would you be she?" Ezra asked.

"No, no, Ezra," Hilda said. "I'll never be your wife."

"Are you being funny?"

"You just said you didn't want a wife."

"I always say that, in case you don't want me."

"Anyhow, I love only me—me, me, me."

"Narcissus in the reeds. Narcissa. Do you wish you were a water lily?"

"No," she said. "I wish I were a green fire. I would run along a birch tree. I would make our pear tree out by the barn burst into flower." And as if imitating the pear tree bursting into flower, she once again burst into song, *"Du meine Herzen, du mein Ruhe,"* then abruptly broke off with, "Oh, do stop chucking orange peels into the fire, Ezra. You're making it smoke."

Nevertheless, they considered themselves engaged. One day they would be married. But not if Hilda's parents had anything to say about it. The elder Doolittles didn't want Ezra as a son-in-law. After all, he was jobless, without prospects, and dependent on his parents for support. Besides, the Doolittles thought him quite mad. They ordered him to be gone from their house and leave Hilda alone. Ezra asked Hilda to elope with him.

"But how would we live?" she wanted to know, though she had never given a thought to such things before.

Ezra promised that his father, though poor, would scrape up enough for them to live on until Ezra could make some money peddling his poems. However, Hilda was not so sure she wanted to marry Ezra—not because he lacked financial resources, but because she had recently begun her first lesbian affair. It happened in the tree house. She and her friend, Francis Gregg, became lovers. Ezra interpreted this as a betrayal of her Eleusinian vow to be the receptacle of his upspurting sperm, so he took off for Europe by himself, on money he mooched from his old gray-headed ma and pa.

When he got to England and became known among its literati, he wrote Hilda and invited her to come to London. She mistook the invitation as an offer to renew their engagement, and since her affair with Francis Gregg had been discovered and forbidden by her parents, she accepted Ezra's invitation and came to London—only to find Ezra engaged to Dorothy Shakespear. On the rebound, Hilda married one of Ezra's young writer protégés, Richard Aldington, who soon betrayed her by having an affair with Brigit Patmore, a young Irish writer who was a close friend of Ezra's. Miss Patmore had achieved some notoriety by helping D.H. Lawrence distribute copies of his banned *Lady Chatterly's Lover,* and this working relationship soon evolved into a sexual one, too, but it broke up when Lawrence began an affair with the New Zealand writer, Katherine Mansfield, and then Lawrence had broken off with Miss Mansfield in order to have an affair with Hilda Doolittle, who was by then rapidly becoming well-known as the poet H.D. Then Hilda broke off with Lawrence to have an affair with Katherine Mansfield, Lawrence's former lover, but soon Hilda left Miss Mansfield for a man named Cecil Gray, a music critic, who got her pregnant. After giving birth to a daughter, whom she named Francis Perdita after her first lesbian lover, Francis Gregg, Hilda—H.D.—published her first small volume of poetry, and began an affair with Brigit Patmore, the former paramour of D.H. Lawrence, Ezra Pound, and Richard Aldington—indeed, Miss Patmore being the very person who had broken up Hilda's marriage to Aldington in the first place. It was only later that Hilda established a long-term lesbian relationship with Annie Winifred Ellerman, known as

Bryher, an aspiring novelist who was the daughter of Sir John Ellerman, a shipping tycoon and the richest man in England.

Now, all these couplings, complex enough, became confused when Nancy Cunard was thrown into the mix, for she, a poet and the granddaughter of another famous shipping tycoon, had an affair with everybody, male and female alike—including Ezra, of course, and even including Aldous Huxley, whose lovemaking was, Nancy told everyone, like being crawled over by slugs.

And the fun had only begun. By the time Ezra's circle of friends and former lovers moved to Paris, the shifting alliances and couplings set a new standard for labyrinthian love affairs, and tended to prove Ezra's theories about sexual activity and creative output. Most of these people were geniuses, and with all the fucking and sucking that was going on, you'd think masterpieces would be popping up all over the place—as indeed they were.

Too bad Hemingway wasn't a part of it. But his admission in his letter to Ezra that he was practically sexless, and that he would like to discuss the matter with Dr. Berman, made Hem receptive to the hard-earned Eleusinian wisdom that Ezra was prepared to share with him to get his gonads going again.

However, when Ezra and Dorothy met Hem and Hadley as they got off the train at Rapallo's station, a day without sunshine, gray and gloomy, Ezra sensed that it was going to take more than a philosophical pep talk to set things right with Hem. As Hem and Hadley climbed down from the train with their rucksacks and a valise, they both looked suntanned and healthy, and Hadley looked happy. Hem didn't. Hadley was as chipper as an apple-cheeked summer girl, and Hem was as sulky as an errant boy being dragged off to the woodshed.

"Oh, what a beautiful place!" Hadley said of mist-shrouded Rapallo, trying to banish the gloomy weather with her sunny disposition. "Don't you think so, Nesto?"

"Don't look like much to me," Hem said.

"Just wait," Ezra said. "You'll love it. We got you booked into the Hotel Splendide, smack on the seafront. The Straters are there. They're looking forward to seeing you."

They walked back to the train's baggage car to collect the Hemingways' suitcases and skiing gear.

"Glad to see you brung them there boxing gloves," Ezra said, once again adopting for a moment the persona of the cantankerous old cuss. "How's about we begin my boxing lessons again?"

"Sure," Hem said.

Ezra signaled for a fiacre. After getting the luggage and gear into the vehicle, there wasn't room left for four passengers, so Ezra told the two women to get in and ride with the luggage.

"Hem and I'll walk. All right with you, Hem? Only a few blocks."

"Sure," Hem said. "Give me a chance to stretch my legs."

As the fiacre pulled away, Hem shouted to Hadley in a warning voice, "Now, watch that damned valise—the one with my manuscripts in it."

"Ah! The stolen manuscripts," Ezra said. "Terrible thing, by Gawd. But the six poems published in *Poetry* were saved, eh? Did Harriet Monroe, that old bitch, send you copies?"

"Yeah, a couple of copies—and a letter telling me how much she admired you. I get my poems published, you get the praise."

"That's only because I regularly write her insulting letters. Every time I want her to do something, I write her an insulting letter. And the more insulting it is, the more eagerly she does what she's told, and the more she admires me."

What Ezra didn't tell Hem was that Harriet Monroe, who was the editor and publisher of *Poetry,* had at first turned down Hem's six poems, and wouldn't have published them at all if Ezra hadn't written her an insulting letter, telling her that, except for the poetry he sent her, her damned magazine published nothing but perfumed cat piss, and unless she accepted his judgment and published the poems he sent her, without question or comment, he would resign as *Poetry*'s foreign editor. She had eagerly complied, and admired Ezra all the more for being masterful and for being such a good bamboozler.

And compared to Hem, Ezra looked the part of a bamboozler, too. Except for the hair growing down over his collar, Hem looked very conservative—even a little countrified—in his too-tight three-piece tweed suit and Tyrolean hat. Ezra, on the other hand, was his usual flamboyant self. He wore an earring in one ear, a sinister-looking Spanish hat with a wide brim rakishly turned down on one side, a blue cape flung cavalierly back over his shoulders, a loose collar and a careless cravat, a brown velour coat, apple-green pants, blue socks, and brown-and-white two-tone shoes. And, of course, he carried the malacca cane, which he used to clear a path between pedestrians on the crowded sidewalks.

"Egad! What was that in your letter about glandular malfunctions?" Ezra prodded in his usual way, anxious to get to the bottom of things bang-on. "Have you found that it was indeed the altitude of the alps, as you suspected? Or is it a depression brought on by brooding over your lost masterpieces?"

"Oh . . . that, and . . . other things," Hem answered evasively, then steeled himself and added in a tone edged with dread, "Hadley's pregnant."

"Ah, *sic transit gloria mundi,"* Ezra observed, grieving with the young man, for this could be a disaster for the gonads, all right. But the news didn't surprise him. He rather expected it. Given Hadley's bourgeois background and her age, he was surprised that she had waited this long to get her hooks firmly into Hem. "Planning to give up the life of the artiste, are you, me bucko, for the life of a family man?"

"It wasn't planned," Hem grunted. "It was an accident. She forgot her . . . stuff."

"Forgot, eh?" Ezra didn't believe that, not for a minute, especially in light of her having lost Hem's manuscripts. That loss was probably the result of an attempt—perhaps subconscious, perhaps not—to deprive Hem of a literary livelihood and keep him dependent on her trust fund. Add to that a child, and Hem was hooked for sure. The next thing you knew he would be thinking about returning to the States and getting a job.

"Does she want to have it?" Ezra asked.

"Yes."

"Do you?"

"No. I'm too young to be a father. But . . . well, there it is. Might as well try to get used to the idea."

"There are ways," Ezra said. "There are doctors. Expensive, but . . ."

"I don't know," Hem said.

"Will you be going back to the States?"

"I guess so. I'll have to get a job."

"Egad," Ezra said, recalling the early days in England when his old parents, no longer able to send him a monthly stipend sufficient for him to live on, had suggested he go out and get a job. What a horrible, whorish compromise for a poet to make! What kind of civilization was it that fed its poets and artists to the dogs of commerce? The only thing that had saved him from such a degrading fate was Dorothy Shakespear's trust fund. Too bad Hemingway hadn't married a woman with a bigger trust fund.

24

Hadley

THE HOTEL RIVIERA Splendide was a five-story stucco building of a weather-faded pastel ocher. Its windows had green wooden shutters. Wrought-iron railings enclosed its small balconies. From their room on the second floor, Hadley and Ernest could look down on the esplanade and watch the citizens and tourists promenading under the dripping palm trees, and they could see in the distance the statue of Columbus that commemorated his landing at Rapallo on his way home from Spain after having discovered America. And directly below their small balcony was the War memorial, a bronze sword-bearing angel atop a fifteen-foot high block of white marble, holding high an olive branch of peace. Fallen bronze soldiers lay strewn on the pedestal at the angel's feet. Veterans of the War, including Ernest, sometimes stood in respectful silence beneath the sword and the olive branch.

There were tennis courts behind the hotel. The Hemingways spent a great deal of their time on the courts during their first days in Rapallo, weather permitting. Mainly Ernest and Hadley played doubles against Ezra and Maggie Strater. Maggie did not like to play with Ernest, and told him so, but when he smiled charmingly and begged her to forgive him for his former trespasses and boorish behavior, she agreed—warily—to play with him once again. Sedate Dorothy Pound did not care for physical games, and Mike Strater was eager to get in the games but his sprained ankle kept him out. Ernest teased Mike about malingering in both tennis and boxing, with the predictable result that Mike was finally goaded into going out onto the tennis court before his ankle was healed. But after he hobbled around for a few moments, wincing with pain, Maggie persuaded him to stop.

"Well, Hyacinth, what's this?" Ernest asked in the tone of a jocose insult. "Letting a woman tell you when you can and can't play tennis and box?"

"Lay off, Ernest," Maggie said. "What satisfaction do you get out of beating a cripple?"

"Aw, he's not crippled, he's malingering."

But Maggie showed an unwavering solicitude for her husband's physical welfare—which, Hadley was sorry to see, was more than Ernest showed for *hers*. Rather than being solicitous about her delicate condition, Ernest encouraged Hadley to be more and more physically active. She suspected that he would have had her riding horses or jumping hurdles, if he could, with the ill-concealed hope of inducing a miscarriage. And Hadley's refusal to jeopardize her pregnancy in order to satisfy Ernest seemed to confirm his fears about becoming a father: his desires and demands would not always be uppermost in Hadley's mind, and he would have to compete with a child for her attention, and would sometimes lose.

However, since Hadley hated being physically inactive, she took a train to Milan one day to see a doctor who had been recommended to her by Maggie Strater. After ascertaining that Hadley was indeed pregnant, the doctor said he saw no reason why she couldn't continue to play vigorous sports, as long as she didn't fall down. And on the very afternoon that she returned to Rapallo and told Ernest what the doctor had said, he hustled her out onto the tennis court to play two fiercely competitive games of singles. Nor did it surprise her when he suggested the next day that they ought to think about leaving Rapallo for a little town high in the Dolomite Alps in northern Italy called Cortina de Ampézzo, where they could get in another month of skiing before the snow melted. Hadley told him she was agreeable, though she knew—as Ernest did, too—that skiing was the sport in which she would be most likely to take a fall.

It was becoming more evident every day just how much Ernest did not want a child. After the doctor in Milan had confirmed her pregnancy, and after the vigorous physical activity had not produced the miracle of a miscarriage, he began to connect her pregnancy with the loss of his manuscripts. While in Chamby, Ernest had been wonderfully uncritical and forgiving about the manuscripts, but now he began to complain about the loss every time the subject of the baby came up.

"Gee, Tiny, I just don't see how we can afford a baby," he said. "If I have to go back to the States and get a job, I'll never have time to replace those stories you lost."

Another time he said, "If you hadn't lost my novel, I might be able to sell it for enough money for us to afford a baby, but as it is . . ."

Hadley thought that his ploy was to build up her guilt about losing the manuscripts so that he could absolve her of it as a trade-off for losing the baby.

Hadley suspected that Mike and Ezra fed these fears in Ernest as a way of showing their sympathy for him. While painting a portrait of Ernest, Mike came to the Hemingways' hotel room almost every day for a week. He sat on a stool to rest his bum ankle, which was wrapped in a massive supporting bandage and covered by a well-worn fuzzy house slipper. With Ernest posed by a window in the best light, they often talked about the similarities between writing and painting, and sometimes they talked about sports, but sometimes Ernest would bring up the subject of Mike's and Maggie's child.

"Having a kid doesn't make it harder for you to paint?"

"Oh, sure, sometimes. But we get a nanny wherever we go, and we always get an apartment big enough to have a room for a nursery."

"Yeah, that's right, you've got money. You can afford to have a kid. You don't have to sell your paintings for a living."

Hadley would leave the room at such times and go for a walk around the picturesque little town. She would walk along the waterfront, watching the fishing boats and sailboats in the bay.

She would have cappuccino at a sidewalk café and watch black-skirted women with twig brooms sweeping the piazzas. She would stroll among the stalls of the open-air market where vendors filled their bins with local vegetables and fish wrapped in wet seaweed. Sometimes she would stand and watch old men and small boys with fishing poles on the concrete bridge across the canal bait their hooks with worms and fish for eels on the changing tide.

One day her return to the hotel room caused Ernest and Mike to fall silent. She had the distinct feeling that they had been talking about her, saying something they didn't want her to hear.

"Oh, it's you," Mike said lamely to fill the strained silence.

Hadley went to stand behind Mike and looked over his shoulder at the portrait of Ernest that was taking shape on the canvas.

"It's a wonderful likeness," she said. "Not at all like Picasso would have painted."

"Is that supposed to be a compliment?" Mike asked jokingly, and stood up to stretch. He stamped his left foot—the one with the sprained ankle—against the floor. "Leg's gone to sleep."

"Ah!" Ernest said, as if Mike had been found out. "So it's well enough for you to stamp on it now, huh? Then it's well enough for us to do a little boxing. Goddamnit, I'm getting tired of waiting. And now that Ezra's gone to Calabria to increase his carnal knowledge of Nancy Cunard, I won't even have the small satisfaction of beating him up. So come on, Hyacinth, that damned ankle's well enough now for you to box a few rounds, isn't it?"

"What do you mean? Ezra's gone off somewhere to meet Nancy Cunard?" Hadley asked as she picked up a book and went to lie on the bed. But they ignored her question, which wasn't unusual for Rapallo. Following Ezra's example, both Ernest and Mike now often ignored any contribution a woman might try to make to their conversations.

"Maybe in another day or two," Mike said to Ernest. "But I'd better finish this portrait first, 'cause your face may never look the same again after I get through pounding it."

Ernest adopted the same tone. "The sooner, the better. I've given up sleeping with Hadley just so I can knock you out."

Ernest had said it in a joking way that would lead Mike to

assume it wasn't true, whereas, it was quite true that they hadn't had sex for a couple of weeks, though she doubted it was for the reason claimed. Probably God alone knew the real reason for Ernest's impotence.

"What was that about Ezra going off to meet Nancy Cunard?" Hadley asked, refusing to be ignored.

"Yeah, he came by while you were out," Ernest said in a dutiful tone. "He got a wire from Nancy Cunard this morning, telling him to meet her in Reggio di Calabria for a little *woppian* tryst."

"And left Dorothy alone?"

"Well, it might have been a little awkward to take her with him, wouldn't it?"

"Does Dorothy know?"

"That he's with that Cunard tart?" Ernest shrugged. "Who can say? He's never bothered to keep his peccadilloes a secret from her, that I know of."

"You men," Hadley said, shaking her head, feeling so insecure that she was slightly queasy.

" 'You men'?" Ernest snarled. "What the hell do you mean, 'You men'? You saying we're all like Ezra?"

"No," she said. "I'm sorry."

"Well, then, shut up about 'you men.' "

He was right. Except for the time he went whoring in Constantinople, she had no reason to impugn his fidelity. Mike, however, was a different case. Like Ezra, he was a well-known womanizer around Paris, and Maggie, like Dorothy, didn't seem to care much, if at all. Hadley didn't understand such women, but she did feel sorry for them, especially for Dorothy. Hadley would have found it humiliating to have been left alone in Rapallo while her husband went gallivanting around Italy with a beautiful heiress, and knowing that her husband's friends were making jokes about it.

It was then, while listening to Ernest and Mike joking about Ezra catching up on his carnal knowledge of Cunard, that Hadley decided to pay Dorothy a sympathetic visit. But the next day, when Hadley went to the small apartment on Via Gramsci that the Pounds had recently rented, she felt that her sympathy was uncalled for.

"Yes?" Dorothy said, without inviting Hadley in. Though her face registered a slight puzzlement, she was, as usual, as cold and composed as a porcelain figurine. "Ezra isn't here," she added, as if automatically assuming that it was he Hadley had come to see. Dorothy had no friends of her own.

"I know," Hadley said, a little flustered. "It's you I came to see. I thought you might be lonely and we could . . . well, have a little chat?"

Dorothy's puzzlement seemed to increase, as if she were asking herself what she and Hadley could possibly have to chat about. They were not friends. They were always polite, but whenever Ernest and Hadley came to visit the Pounds at the Hotel Mignon, or, later, here in their small furnished apartment on Via Gramsci, it was assumed that Ezra was the one they had come to see, and Dorothy, after performing the rituals of a dutiful hostess, would usually retreat to the bedroom to lie down and read a book.

No one considered this to be rudeness on her part. Hadley often wished that she, too, could go home and curl up with a book. Had there been social interaction among the visitors she might have found some satisfaction in being there, but she knew that people weren't invited to the Pounds' house as guests; they were there as an audience for Ezra, which was not always a delightful thing to be, especially since Ezra had come to Fascist Italy. Here he seemed to have added smugness to his catalog of gaucheries. It was as if here in Rapallo, in a country under the heroic Fascist leadership of Benito Mussolini, Ezra felt safer and more secure than he had in Paris, sure in his convictions that he was right, by God, in his ideas about economics, race, politics, poetry, religion, history, painting, music—anything. You mention it, he knew it. And almost always there would come a point during the evening when Ezra, perhaps growing tired of spontaneous pontificating, would clutch a few of his poems or a few pages of his latest translation, settle down in a big chair, fix his pince-nez firmly on his nose, throw his head back, squint his eyes and look down his nose, chuckle, stroke his red Mephistophelian beard, and attempt to astonish his guests with the products of his creative genius.

No wonder Dorothy left the room. No one blamed her. But as a result, no one ever got to know her very well. Some would say that there was no Dorothy there to know, that she was merely a Victorian vessel that had been filled up with Ezra's crackpot ideas. But Hadley sensed there must be more to her than that. Beneath that porcelain exterior, Hadley wanted there to be a heart that felt the humiliation of being left alone in a strange town in a foreign land, where she had no real friends, while her husband, no doubt traveling on railway tickets purchased with her money, went off to tryst with one of his many beautiful and talented and wealthy mistresses.

"But if you don't feel like chatting . . ." Hadley said, giving her a graceful exit in case she didn't want Hadley's sympathy.

"Oh, well," Dorothy said. "Yes, I suppose . . ." She invited Hadley in with an expression of noblesse oblige. "Have a seat. Would you care for tea?"

Hadley took a seat in the living room while Dorothy fixed the tea in the small kitchen. When Dorothy returned, they quickly exhausted the gloomy, overcast weather as a topic of conversation, and then Dorothy said, "So what was it you wanted to chat about?"

It struck Hadley then that Dorothy had the idea that Hadley had come to her as a supplicant, as someone who needed a wiser and older woman to talk to.

"Oh . . . nothing. I just thought . . . now that Ezra's gone on a trip, you might not mind a little feminine company."

"Ah," Dorothy said. "I see." But she really didn't. She still seemed to think Hadley was looking for a way to broach some delicate subject of her own. "So you're going to have a baby," Dorothy ventured, in case that was what Hadley wanted to chat about. "I loathe children," she went on. "In Paris, you know, we won't even allow them in our apartment."

"Oh, dear," Hadley said, and then veered away from that topic by asking, "Is that where Ezra's gone? Back to Paris?"

"No. If it was Ernest who told you Ezra was gone, I suppose you know he went down to southern Italy to visit with Nancy Cunard. There's no need for you to be embarrassed about it. I'm not."

"Well, I must admire your savior faire," Hadley said. "If Ernest went off with another woman, I'm afraid I'd go out of my mind."

"Then you'd be very foolish," Dorothy said, and the look on her face seemed recognizably sympathetic, as if she had finally divined Hadley's problem and brought it out into the open. "It shouldn't bother you if Ernest has other women. If you had grown up among artists, as I did, you would know. My mother had a lover—W.B. Yeats—and my father knew about the affair, and tolerated it. No, my dear, even if an artist has a wife, you must expect him to have several sexual attachments. As Ezra says, an artist must be excited by more than one woman at a time for creative genius to flower."

"Why get married, then?" Hadley asked.

"Ezra says it ought to be illegal for an artist to marry, or nearly that. If the artist must marry, he should find someone more interested in art, or in his art, or in the part of him that is the artist, rather than in him. You see?"

"You really think so?"

"And after that, let them take tea together three times a week. If legalities require it, or if it's necessary to prevent gossip, the ceremony may be undergone." She fell silent for a moment, then added in a solicitous tone, "Does that answer your questions?"

"Yes, I think so."

"Just remember, if Ernest has another woman, it's for his art—not because he's tired of you, and you shouldn't mind. If you do, you should go back to the States and marry a doctor or a barber or a farmer or something."

"Thank you," Hadley said, letting Dorothy continue to believe they had been talking about her—Hadley's—troubles, not Dorothy's. "But look," Hadley added, finishing her tea, "do you mind if I ask you a personal question?"

"Not if you think the answer might be of some good to you."

"Do you love Ezra?"

"Yes, of course. Wholeheartedly."

"Can you tell me why?"

"Why?" Dorothy ruminated for a moment, then said, "He gave me life in a way that I never knew existed. He saved me from a dreary and boring life, perhaps as the wife of a doctor or a banker or God knows what. For that, I shall always love him, and be grateful to him. Do you understand?"

"Yes," Hadley said. "Yes, I do"—as well she should have, since she had fallen in love with Ernest for the same reason. Ernest had no doubt saved her from a horrid, stultifying life as a spinster; had taken her from the middle-class prison of St. Louis and given her the keys to the world. How odd to find that Ezra had gained Dorothy's love and loyalty by doing the same for her!

"So I don't mind his little flings with the others—Olga Rudge, Nancy Cunard, Kitty Cannell—whoever," Dorothy said. "It doesn't matter to me. I always have the last laugh." And as if to demonstrate, she laughed.

And for the second time within as many minutes, Hadley saw in Dorothy another odd similarity to herself. Dorothy's laugh was Ezra's laugh. It began as a bray, then diminished into a distinctive hiccupy chuckle—Ezra's laugh, exactly. It was then that Hadley realized that she hadn't been talking to Dorothy, she had been talking to Ezra. Everything Dorothy said had come out of Ezra's mouth. In many ways, Dorothy had become Ezra, or little more than an appendage of him, a mouthpiece for his words and ideas, his ventriloquist's dummy.

But wasn't that what Hadley had striven to be with Ernest?— the same person? Hadn't she cut her hair short while Ernest had let his grow long so they could look alike? She had told him, "I want to be one with you, I want to be you, I want us to be the same person, never again to be a separate one." Had passive Dorothy and dominant Ezra undergone the same transformation, right down to the laugh?

Though Hadley had gotten up to leave, and Dorothy was seeing her toward the door, she might have delayed and attempted to explore this latest revelation a little further, had they not been interrupted by an abrupt knock on the door—a man's knock, to judge by the aggressiveness of it. When Dorothy opened the door, her composure (one characteristic, at least, which she did *not* share with twitchy Ezra) was momentarily shattered by surprise.

"Why, Bob! What're you doing here?"

"Came to see you and old Ez," the young man said. "Got sick

and tired of Berlin, need to hide out for a while. Had an invitation from Ezra to mosey on down, pay him a visit. Checked in the Hotel Mignon. They said you'd moved here. Here I am. Where is he?"

"He's not here. He's on a trip to southern Italy."

"Rats! When'll he be back?"

"A week. Maybe two."

"Rats!" he said again, and looked at Hadley.

Dorothy said, "Do you know Hadley? Ernest Hemingway's wife?"

"Ain't had the pleasure. Howdy, Hadley." He held out a raw-boned hand.

"Hadley, Robert McAlmon," Dorothy said.

He appeared to be what he was, a man from the American heartland, a man who had done hard traveling and hard drinking. Wearing a wide-brimmed fedora and an expensive rumpled suit, he was short and skinny and rawboned, with depthless, intense Irish-blue eyes and thin lips, with a look as lonely as the rugged spaces of the West, used up and yet perpetually restless with the need to seek new lands. He appeared to be in his late twenties, but it was hard to tell. He wore in his left ear a turquoise earring that matched the hardness and color of his eyes.

"I've heard about you in Paris," Hadley said, shaking hands.

"Yeah? I know what they call me—Robert McAlimony. The guy with the rich in-laws. Joyce hung that on me. Okay, but anything more damning than that, I deny." He inhaled deeply from a cigarette held in nicotine-yellowed fingers, and blew the smoke from his nostrils like a dragon. "What else you heard about me?"

"Nothing damning," Hadley said. "Mostly that you were a writer, and one of Joyce's closest friends."

"Joyce! How the hell is the old man?" he asked, and his lack of deference was shocking. Hadley had believed that everybody was in awe of James Joyce; but within minutes after meeting McAlmon, she realized that he was incapable of awe toward another person. He must not have weighed more than 125 pounds, and had the small man's compensatory cockiness. "Haven't heard from him in a coon's age. How's his eyesight holding out? How's *Ulysses* doing?"

"The last I heard, he and his family were spending the winter in Nice," Hadley said. "That's about all I know. If you want to know more, you might talk to my husband."

"That sounds like a good idea," Dorothy said, rather transparent in her efforts to avoid being a hostess to McAlmon. "And since Ezra isn't here, you'll want a companion in Rapallo. Her husband, Ernest, is a writer, and a good one. Ezra has great faith in him. You'll want to meet him."

Hadley was quite willing to take McAlmon back to the Hotel Splendide and introduce him to Ernest. There seemed to be an absence of artifice and pretense in McAlmon's brash, American character, which she knew would appeal to Ernest, and, besides, he was rich—rich enough to help support James Joyce with a monthly stipend. She had heard Ernest speak enviously of the money McAlmon received from his father-in-law, Sir John Ellerman, who was said to be the richest man in England, when McAlmon entered into a marriage of convenience with Sir John's lesbian daughter, Bryher. For the sake of knowing where to apply one's energy and charm for the best chances of career advancement, Ernest had often said, "There are those people in the literary scene who count, and those who don't." Gertrude Stein was among those who counted, as was Ezra Pound, Sherwood Anderson, James Joyce, and since Hadley was confident that Ernest would likely include Robert McAlmon among them, she was happy to take him back to the hotel and introduce them.

They found Ernest in the hotel's dining room. They joined him at the table, and he and McAlmon got on well right from the start. A new friendship seemed to be solidified the moment McAlmon, in response to Ernest's complaint that the dining room served no whiskey, pulled a pint bottle of bourbon from the inside pocket of his coat. He poured half of its contents into Ernest's empty water glass, then turned up the bottle and drank the rest of it. Ernest admired men who could hold their liquor. In addition, McAlmon was as lively as a cricket, and irreverent as a hyena. To Ernest's surprise and secret delight, McAlmon indifferently dismissed Ernest's polite praise for his efforts to help Joyce get *Ulysses* ready for publication.

"Don't blame me for that mess," McAlmon said.

"You don't like it?" Ernest asked, with a tilt of his head to show his incredulity, impressed by McAlmon's lack of awe.

"I haven't read it, at least not all the way through. Have you? Has anybody?"

Ernest grinned. "Tell you the truth, no. I couldn't get all the way through it. I found parts of it pretty dull."

"It *is* dull. It takes one of those supermorons, an intellectual, to read it through."

And his irreverence didn't end there. Within half an hour Hadley and Ernest had learned that McAlmon thought all government was a farce, all religion was the shits, all people were fools or snobs or worse, Nancy Cunard was a ball-buster, Gertrude Stein was a case of arrested development, Picasso was a fraud, and the Pope was a pig fucker. But these opinions were given with such a playful lack of conviction that one could hardly take him seriously.

Besides, even though he thought all writing of any kind, either ancient or modern, was garbage, McAlmon had begun Contact Editions, a publishing venture financed by a $70,000 gift from his father-in-law, and he was looking for fresh young writers to publish. Did Ernest happen to have anything—a novel, a collection of stories—that McAlmon might consider?

This, of course, was Ernest's cue to tell, once again, how "Feather Kitty here"—jerking a thumb toward Hadley—"left all my manuscripts on a train in Paris and they got stolen. Three years' work . . ."

Which was Hadley's cue to leave. She went upstairs to their room, feeling restless and vaguely discontented. She had thought maybe she would wash some of her underwear, but the day was too overcast and muggy for the underwear to dry, so she looked for something else to do. She found a small stack of mail on the table. Ernest had opened the letters, and Hadley read the one from the concierge of their apartment in Paris, and the one from George O'Neil in the States, but found nothing of interest until she came upon a telegram to Ernest from John Bone, the feature editor of the *Toronto Star.*

YOUR IDEA FOR STORY ON RUHR INTERESTING
STOP WILL LET YOU KNOW

So! After telling Hadley that all he wanted to do for the next
eight months was write serious fiction, Ernest had once again
contacted the *Star* and proposed to write an article for them. And
since he had told Hadley nothing about it, she had to assume
that he had decided to go off on his own again, leaving her
sitting by herself in Rapallo or Paris.

But even if he had planned to take her with him, would she
want to go? She didn't think so. There was something in her that
yearned to be still.

She went for a walk. She walked around the town until she got
tired, then went into the public gardens and sat down on a
wrought-iron bench and watched the sea.

It began to rain. She had not brought an umbrella. She tried
standing close to the trunk of a palm tree, but the rain dribbled
through the fronds. When it started coming down hard, she
dashed for the hotel. She ran into the dim lobby and the hotel
keeper said from behind his desk, "Ah, Signora! You were
caught by the rain." He was an old man and very tall, a grandfa-
therly man of dignity and sincerity.

"Oh, I'm okay," she said. "Just my hair."

She went up to the room. Ernest was there, lying on the bed,
with a sheaf of manuscripts on the bedside table and the typed
pages of one manuscript strewn around him.

"Did you get wet?" he asked.

"Just my hair. I'm okay."

"What've you been doing?"

"Went for a walk. Terrible rain. I think I prefer the snow."

"I do, too," Ernest said. "I think we ought to go on to Cortina.
Skiing is more fun than this."

She went into the bathroom for a towel and dried her hair with
it. Ernest went on reading. Hadley went to the window and
looked out as she rubbed her damp short hair vigorously with
the towel. Down below their window on the hotel's terrace,
under a green lath table, crouched a black-and-white cat, trying
to make itself small to avoid the rain dripping through the table.

"Oh, there's a kitty down there," she said. "The poor thing's trying to keep dry under a table. I'm going down to get it."

"You'll get wet again," Ernest said from the bed, "Better let me do it," but made no move to get up.

"No, I'll do it," Hadley said, and kept the towel as she went down to the lobby, where the hotel keeper behind his desk looked at her with a grave, puzzled frown.

"Signora, is something wrong?"

"There's a cat outside under a table, trying to keep from getting wet. Does it belong to you?"

"No, Signora, there are many cats here that belong to no one."

"I'm going to get it." Hadley draped the towel over her head and opened the door and looked out. It was raining harder. The terrace tables were around to the right. She figured if she sidled along under the eaves, she might avoid getting soaked, but then an umbrella opened behind her. It was the maid who cleaned their room, sent by the hotel keeper.

"I will hold the umbrella for you," the maid said in Italian, smiling. "You must avoid getting wet."

With the maid walking close to her, holding the umbrella over both of them, Hadley hurried along the gravel path to the terrace beneath their window, where the cat would be. But the cat was no longer under the table, nor was it under any of the other tables. It had disappeared.

"Oh, it's gone," she said. "I wanted a kitty." A sudden sense of loss and loneliness caused her eyes to film over with tears. "The poor kitty, I wonder where it went."

"Signora, please," the maid said. "Let us go back inside. The cat will be fine."

"But I wanted it so much."

She went back into the hotel lobby, followed by the maid, who stopped in the doorway and closed the umbrella. Hadley thanked the maid and the hotel keeper, and mounted the stairs to their room, letting the towel drop from her head to her shoulders. Ernest was still on the bed, his head propped up on his elbow, reading the manuscript.

"Where's the cat?" he asked.

"When I got there, it was gone."

"Cats hate the rain," he said, and returned to his reading.

Hadley sat down at the dressing table and looked at herself in the mirror. Still with the feeling of loss and loneliness she had felt when she saw that the cat had disappeared, she said, "I wanted it so much. I don't know why, but I wanted that poor kitty so much. The padrone said she belonged to no one. The poor kitty has no home, no one to take care of her. I didn't want her to be in the rain. It's no fun for a kitty in the rain." To distract herself, she picked up a hairbrush and began running it through her short, damp hair. "What's that you're reading?"

"Some of McAlmon's stuff," he said, without taking his eyes from the page. "He wanted me to read it."

"Is it any good?"

"Some of his writing's damned good, but I don't know about him. This is some real degenerate shit—stories about bitchy transvestite drag queens in Paris, screeching queers in Venice, cocaine parties and bisexual orgies in Berlin. There's one here you ought to read, called 'Kicking Over the Traces.' About an itinerant preacher's son from South Dakota—that's what he is, you know, the son of a circuit-riding preacher—this guy goes to New York to become a writer and gets buggered. The guy who buggers him has a suspicious resemblance to Marsden Hartley."

"Is he one of them, you think?"

"Well, except for being bitchy sometimes, he doesn't look or act like a fairy. Seems like a rough and tough little character, in fact. But if these stories are written from personal experience . . . and they seem to be . . . well, what else can you think? Anyway, he's married to a lesbian—whatever that means."

"What's her name? Bryher?"

"That's what she calls herself, yeah. She lives in a big château on Lake Geneva, with Hilda Doolittle, Ezra's old girlfriend."

They fell silent. Hadley had become preoccupied by her reflection in the mirror. Ernest went back to his reading. "I wonder if they have short hair like mine," she asked absently.

"Who?" Ernest grunted without looking up.

"Those lesbian lovers—Bryher and what's-her-name? Hilda Doolittle?"

"I wouldn't know," Ernest said, annoyed with her for

interrupting him with such trivial questions. He shifted, propping his head up with his other arm, and returned to his reading.

"Tatie, I want to let my hair grow out."

He looked up at her. "Why? I like it like that. Don't I give you good haircuts?"

"I'm tired of looking like a boy. I like being Peter, but there's a woman's side to me that I like, too, and I want to be her now."

"You look damned good to me."

She ran the brush through her hair. "I want it to grow long so I can wear it in a chignon on the back of my head. I want it to fall around my shoulders when I take the pins out. And I'm tired of living in hotels where I can't have a kitty. I want a home."

"You want to go back to Paris?"

"I don't mean a furnished apartment. I want a home where I can have my own silverware, and eat off my own china, and have candles on the table. I want my own big bed, and my own linen. And I want to have long hair and I want some new clothes, and, damnit, I want a kitty." She had almost said, "And I want a baby," but had caught herself in time. She was still staring at herself in the mirror, but now her image had been blurred by the tears that once more filmed her eyes.

"What's the matter with you?" Ernest asked. "You know we can't afford those things, and I like your hair the way it is."

"Well, we can afford a kitty, can't we? If I can't have anything else, I can at least have a kitty, can't I?"

"Oh, shut up and get something to read," Ernest said.

25

McAlmon

McALMON FOUND RAPALLO to be boring, especially after sundown. But of course (he had to keep reminding himself) that was exactly what he needed. After a month of nerve-jangling, cocaine-intense hijinks in Berlin, he was badly in need of a rest. Even Paris was preferable to Berlin, though it, too, held too many temptations.

As Lake Geneva was on a direct line from Paris to Rapallo, McAlmon had stopped off in Switzerland for a short visit with his lawfully wedded wife. He had received a letter from Bryher just before he left Paris, telling him that they would have to meet soon to discuss family business matters, so he got off the Simplon Orient Express at Geneva and caught a local train to Montreux, where Bryher and Hilda lived in a secluded manor house in a woodsy setting.

Called the Riant Château, the mansion overlooked Lake Geneva, and had been chosen for the express purpose of providing a quiet country setting where H.D. could write her poetry and Bryher could write her novels and Perdita, Hilda's daughter, could grow up as a gentle Child of Nature.

In his travels around Europe, McAlmon had visited the Riant Château a few times during the last two years, and had always been made welcome—and why shouldn't he be? He had kept his part of the bargain he had made with Bryher. He and Bryher and Hilda had become good friends since that day in Greenwich Village two years ago when William Carlos Williams, who had known Hilda ever since he and Hilda and Ezra had been students together at the University of Pennsylvania, introduced McAlmon to Bryher and Hilda at a literary party. McAlmon didn't realize at the time that he was being looked over as a possible husband for Bryher. Had he known, he would have paid more attention. As it was, his first impression of Bryher was fast and not altogether flattering. She was a petite woman, fine-boned and blue-eyed, who looked to be in her late twenties. It struck McAlmon then that she looked a little like the portraits he had seen of Napoleon, with that same masculine hauteur. She wore a tweed jacket and skirt, severely cut. Her features, though never adorned with makeup, were finely shaped and proportioned, and her dark brown hair was cut like a boy's. She and the poet Amy Lowell, another guest at the party, were both smoking cigars. It always struck McAlmon as odd how many lesbians loved to suck on big black cigars.

The only conversation McAlmon remembered passing between himself and Bryher was her assertion that she was a novelist, and that she admired *Contact*. At that time, Williams and McAlmon were partners in publishing the little magazine. Williams was a young doctor with a family in New Jersey who couldn't contribute much to financing *Contact,* but McAlmon was living on a garbage scow on the Hudson and working at any number of odd jobs—posing for art students at the Cooper Union, working part-time in an advertising agency, training polo ponies on Long Island on weekends—all to keep himself and *Contact* financially afloat.

So he had been receptive to the proposition that Bryher made a few days after the party. It was on February 13, 1921, a day he would never forget. At Bryher's invitation, he had agreed to meet her and Hilda in a Greenwich Village café for lunch, and Bryher had been blunt.

"I'm looking for someone to marry," she said. "In name only," she hastened to add. "If I have a husband, my family will no longer try to control my life. As it is, I can't travel, or be away from home. I want to be free to live my life as I please. If you agree to marry me, I'll give you half of my allowance. That will be about six thousand dollars a year. And all that will be required of you is to join me for occasional visits to my parents' home in London. Other than that, we would lead strictly separate lives. How does that strike you?"

It was obvious, in spite of Hilda's having a baby and being the former wife of the English novelist Richard Aldington, that the two would be living together, but what did he care? He cared little for the institution of marriage, but he cared a great deal for the prospect of having six thousand dollars a year. For a long time he had wanted to go to Paris to meet James Joyce, and for an even longer time he had coveted freedom from having to earn a living so that he could write all the novels and stories and poems he wanted. So he didn't have to think about the proposition very long.

"When you want to do it?"

"Tomorrow morning," Bryher said.

"Okay. But what's the hurry? Don't you think we ought to have a game of tennis, or something? Get to know each other a little?"

"I know all I need to know," she said. "I've had a private detective investigating you. I've been informed that you can be trusted not to make any sexual demands on me. Besides, you come highly recommended by Bill Williams, and that's good enough for Hilda and me."

"Investigating me! Well, I'll be damned. Still, why tomorrow? Why the big hurry?"

"My father has ordered me back to London. I have to catch a ship leaving here tomorrow evening. If I'm not on that ship, he'll cut off my allowance."

They were married the next morning, February 14, Valentine's Day, in a civil ceremony at the City Hall in New York, with Bill Williams as best man and Hilda as maid of honor. It was only then that McAlmon learned that Bryher's real name was Annie Winifred Ellerman. In response to a telegram informing him of his daughter's marriage, her father, Sir John and Lady Hannah Ellerman, invited—*ordered* might be a more apt word—the newlyweds to come home to England for their honeymoon, and he booked them into the bridal suite on the White Star luxury liner

Celtic, which was due to sail for Europe within hours after the wedding.

And how did Sir John manage that on such short notice? He owned controlling interest in the whole White Star shipping fleet. That was how McAlmon first learned that his bride, albeit Jewish, was the daughter of an English Knight and his Lady, and that her father was England's richest man.

However, there were four people in the wedding party. Bryher arranged with the ship's captain for an extra first-class cabin next to the bridal suite, ostensibly for her dear friend Hilda and her child, but actually for McAlmon. Hilda stayed in the bridal suite with Bryher. For the sake of appearances, McAlmon often joined Bryher and Hilda for breakfast in the suite's sitting room. A crib was brought into the sitting room for the child, who was only two years old at the time and needed to be kept in a cage. And as a courtesy to his boss' daughter, the ship's captain assigned one of the ship's nurses to be a nanny and a warden for little Perdita, whom McAlmon had begun to refer to as the Lump, a name that both Bryher and Hilda were rapidly adopting. Thus, freed from having to look after the child, the three of them lolly-gagged their way across the Atlantic in coddled comfort, sailing from the New World toward a new and exciting life in the Old.

As the daughter and the son-in-law of the ship's owner, McAlmon and his bride were invited to dine at the captain's table every day, and McAlmon's lack of a tuxedo proved no excuse for declining. The purser supplied him with one. Still, he and Bryher didn't often go to the captain's table. Bryher didn't like all that folderol, and though McAlmon was admittedly envious of people with money, he was not a kowtower to privilege and power. The only thing in the Ellermans' world that he coveted was money—and not even that for its own sake, but for the sake of the freedom it could buy him, the freedom from circumstances, the freedom to do what and go where he damn well pleased.

And perversely enough, it was this very attitude that helped allay the natural suspicions that the Ellermans had about their new son-in-law. When McAlmon walked into the thirty-room mansion in Mayfair, like a grown-up Huckleberry Finn, the Ellermans first had to wonder if he were a social climber, a fortune hunter, or just an American country bumpkin on the make. But McAlmon made it clear right away that he didn't give a hoot for social position, and that he had no intention of trying to curry favor with the Ellermans. Her Ladyship, coquettish in spite of her advanced years, capitulated to his brash and independent charms almost immediately.

She was a pouter-pigeon dowager who was half-deaf and quite dithery, frequently peevish, and anxious to endear herself to the man her darling daughter had married, so solicitous of her son-in-law's well-being that she even came into the newlyweds' bed-room after they had gone to bed. For the sake of appearances it had been necessary to leave Hilda and the Lump at a nearby hotel, and Bryher and McAlmon had—naturally enough—been put into the same bedroom, which had only one bed. And they were going to have to sleep in that bed. A little apprehensive about this arrangement, Bryher, who had never before slept with a man, ordered her husband to wear pajamas.

"I don't have any," he said. "Never use them. Sleep in the buff, always."

She gave him a pair of hers, and insisted that he wear them. Even though they were a bit small, he put them on to ease her mind.

"But you don't have to worry," he told her. "I'm not going to claim my conjugal rights. We can even put a naked sword down the middle of the bed, if you're afraid I'll do something in my sleep."

They had only just got into bed and begun to read when some-one knocked on the door. They quickly shoved the books un-derneath the covers and tucked the covers under their necks to hide their pajamas. Without waiting to be invited, her Ladyship poked her head in the room and asked in the loud voice of a nearly deaf person, "Are you decent?"

"Yes, Mama," Bryher said peevishly, raising her voice. "What do you want?"

Her Ladyship, whimsical and sentimental, came in and ap-proached on tiptoe, as if on a secret mission. "I just had to come and see my darlings in bed together."

"Oh, Mama," Bryher said, exasperated.

But her Ladyship was not deterred in her mission. She went to Bryher first, leaned down and kissed her forehead, and said, "Now, dear, you've never tried to please your parents, no, you haven't, you naughty girl, but marriage is different. In marriage you must, you simply must try to please your husband in all things."

"Oh, Mama," Bryher said again, her exasperation edging toward anger.

Then her Ladyship toddled to McAlmon's side of the bed and leaned down to kiss his cheek, leaving him a little nonplussed.

"Dear boy," she said loudly, "I want to say how glad I am that our dear Annie has finally found a husband. We were beginning to worry. And now I hope you will put some sense into her at last. We—Sir John and I—we can now have hopes of a dear, sweet little grandchild, can we not? I'll take care of it," she added quickly, cutting off some objection that Bryher was going to make. "Neither of you would know how to take care of a child properly." And as if that subject were settled, she said with a small, nervous smile as she tiptoed out of the room like a clamorous cat burglar, "Good night, sleep tight, don't let the bedbugs bite."

"Well," Bryher said, "I think you've made a conquest of her, at least."

"Yeah? Well, what about that 'dear, sweet grandchild' shit?" McAlmon said, bringing his book—a play by G.B. Shaw—out from under the covers.

"Don't worry. I'd love to have a baby, but only if someone gave it to me, like a puppy dog. Having one myself would be too disgusting. I'd kill myself first."

"Listen," McAlmon said, "I must have heard you threaten to kill yourself at least three or four times now. Have you ever tried it?"

She showed him her wrists, both of which bore thin razor scars. "And I've taken an overdose of sleeping pills twice. Suicide's the only weapon I have against my father's tyranny. That's why you must get him to like you—so that we can leave here and Hilda and I can go live on the Continent, without losing my allowance. Otherwise, I'm going to kill myself."

McAlmon refused to take responsibility for her suicide, but he did manage to make Sir John like and accept him as a son-in-law. The key to that acceptance lay in the fact that Sir John, too, had once been a poor boy. Had he been born into the traditional English upper classes, no accommodation could have been possible, but, Sir John was a self-made man, and proud of it. He loved to tell how he had been born in Hull, a center of Jewish immigration from the Continent, and, like Horatio Alger, had worked hard, saved his pennies, was smart and ambitious—virtues which brought him to the attention of the Liverpool shipping magnate, Sir Frederick Leyland, who gave him a start as a shipping clerk. John was eighteen years old then; by the time he was thirty, he had joined the board of Leyland, and shortly thereafter became its chairman. By the time he was thirty-eight, he had started his own shipping line and was making deals with the likes of J. Pierpont Morgan. By the time he was fifty-four he had become one of the richest men in England. Next he became a major shareholder in *The Times* of London, and over the next few years he acquired a number of other newspapers and London magazines, including *The Illustrated London News, The Sphere, The Tattler,* and *The Sketch.* And with the political clout that came with the ownership of newspapers, it wasn't difficult to finagle himself a Knighthood.

McAlmon could have had the editorship of any of those magazines, had he wanted it. Indeed, if he had joined one of them and proved he could do the job, he could have eventually had the magazines themselves—plant, printing presses, and payroll. And—who could tell?—if he stayed around until Sir John popped off, why, Bryher and he might inherit the whole shebang. Imagine that! A poor country boy from South Dakota becoming Sir Robert McAlmon, a Knight of the Realm, and the richest man in England.

But he didn't want any of that. He didn't want to be editor of Sir John's magazines, and he wasn't interested in his money or his ships or his title. And that, when apparent to Sir John, was what dispelled any doubts or suspicions about McAlmon. McAlmon obviously wasn't going to take advantage of Sir John's wealth and position in order to further his own ambitions. All McAlmon wanted was to go to Paris and continue to publish

Contact, and maybe start a publishing house dedicated to printing books that no commercial publisher would touch.

So Sir John gave McAlmon $70,000 to set up his own publishing company in Paris. And if this wasn't enough to prove his fondness for his new son-in-law, he also gave McAlmon a diamond tiepin that had been a gift from his own mother.

Bryher was ecstatic. She could hardly wait to tell Hilda the news. She and McAlmon took one of the Ellermans' chauffeured Rolls Royces and went to the Hotel Washington, where Hilda and the Lump had been discreetly staying. Hilda visited the Ellermans' Mayfair mansion now and then and was welcomed as a friend and writing colleague of Bryher's, but it was only when Bryher went to the hotel that they could be affectionate. Otherwise they expressed their love in sealed notes carried in secret back and forth between the Hotel Washington and the Mayfair Mansion by Throckmorton, Jr., the youngest of the two Ellerman chauffeurs. Throckmorton, Jr., was the son of the Ellermans' other chauffeur, and he and Bryher had grown up together, and there was nothing he wouldn't do for her.

It was he who put the latest note from Hilda into Bryher's hand after she and McAlmon had gotten into the backseat. Bryher excitedly tore the envelope open and read the message, which McAlmon, too, could read with a casual sideways glance.

> This is just to say I love and love and love you. I missed not hearing this morning horribly, not a note came last night no doubt one will arrive *ce soir.* Come my darling, Fido, and be kissed and adored. Dear Heart, 1,001 kisses.

Once the Rolls Royce was out of sight of the Ellerman mansion, Bryher dug a celebratory cigar from her handbag and lit it. Then, rereading the note, savoring it, she told Throckmorton, Jr., to stop at a florist shop, where she bought an armload of flowers for Hilda. Next she had Throckmorton, Jr., drive to a confectionery store, where she bought Hilda a box of chocolates.

When they got to the hotel, Bryher took the stairs two at a time to Hilda's suite on the second floor, her hands full of flowers and sweets, her cigar clenched in her teeth. She rushed into Hilda's suite. The Lump was on the rug in the sitting room, mauling a biscuit. Hilda was in the bedroom, getting dressed.

Bryher called, "Cat! Cat! Guess what!" as she dashed into the bedroom. "We're going to Paris! Papa says we can go to Paris! We're free!"

McAlmon heard a squeak of joy from Hilda. He sat down on the rug and visited with the Lump while Bryher and Hilda carried on in the bedroom. He could hear what they were saying through the opened door. Hilda, speaking in the third person and using the masculine pronoun, as she often did, cooed, "Oh, Fido! How sweet to see, to smell, to touch, to taste Fido again. And how good of him to rush in, wagging his beautiful tail."

She actually said that. It seemed to confirm the generally accepted theory that love could make a sap out of anyone.

"And I have something for you, too," Hilda said, leading Bryher into the sitting room where the Lump and McAlmon were on the rug, the child looking stolidly at him with eyes so black they shone like undried ink. Hilda was carrying the huge bouquet cradled in her arms like an infant. Bryher had left her cigar in the bedroom.

"Bob!" Hilda said, and approached to put an appreciative hand on his shoulder and squeeze as she said, "You did it! You brought the Ellermans around—how very clever of you!"

"What? What?" Bryher demanded, looking around as if she might see what Hilda had for her. The more excited she became, the more infantile she became, demanding instant gratification.

"I want to make a bargain with you," Hilda told her. "Now that we're going to have our own home, I want you to take complete charge of Perdita's upbringing. In return, I want you to promise me to stop threatening to kill yourself. I want you to promise me to grow up and take care of the little girl."

Bryher was nearly incredulous. "You mean . . . you mean she'll be given to me, for my own? Exactly like a puppy?"

"Exactly like a puppy, yes."

Bryher swept the child up, claiming her for her very own. "Wonderful! Oh, how wonderful! And, yes, I do, I promise to take care of her, always. I'll educate her! I have some special ideas about education, you know. I'll start as soon as we get settled into our new home. I'll make a genius of her, wait and see!"

That did not seem to bode well for the Lump. However, McAlmon took some exculpatory comfort in his long-held belief that kids don't grow up because of their parents, they grow up in spite of them. In any case, it was no business of his. He had agreed that Bryher and he would lead separate lives, and he was determined to keep his end of the bargain.

He saw his little ersatz family often after they moved to Paris and he and they took up separate residences, but their get-togethers were usually no more than gossipy lunches or business meetings relative to the first two books McAlmon printed after forming Contact Publishing Company: a novel by Bryher called *Development,* and a collection of H.D.'s poems.

But Bryher and Hilda soon found the hectic, high-spirited, partying, bright-lights and boozing ambiance of Paris too hard on their nerves and too detrimental to their creativity, so they moved to Switzerland, to the Riant Château. Bryher used Shake-speare and Company as an address, with Sylvia Beach acting as post mistress, forwarding Bryher's mail from the Ellermans' to her in Switzerland, and making sure that Bryher's return letters to her parents had Paris postmarks.

So, when McAlmon, on his way to see Ezra Pound in Rapallo in February 1923, took a side trip to visit his wife, he arrived in Montreux in the afternoon and took a taxi to the Riant Château. He had been without sleep for nearly twenty-four hours and was looking forward to a nap before dinner, though experience did not augur well for the possibility. And when Clara, the English housekeeper, answered McAlmon's knock, she confirmed his apprehensions by rolling her eyes heavenward in an expression of comic despair at the sounds emanating from the loftier re-gions of the house: slamming doors, shouts, sobs, stamping feet, more slamming doors, shrieks, and more slamming doors.

How to explain love? Bryher's pet name for Hilda was Cat, and Hilda's pet name for Bryher was Fido, and that's how they got along, like cats and dogs. They loved each other madly, of course. Or at least they called it love, since they fulfilled each other's needs—Hilda's need to be taken care of like a child, and

Bryher's need to bestow on someone the bossy paternal affections that she had learned from her father. However, Bryher's mania for management and control didn't work well with someone like Hilda, who was high-strung and skittish.

"Oh, hello, Bob," Bryher said, coming down the stairs.

He hadn't seen her in a few months, but her voice held no more surprise or delight than if he had just returned from a trip to the store.

"You'll have to excuse Cat," she said. "She's upstairs in her study, having a nervous breakdown. I was just going to give Lump a geography test. Come along, see what wonderful progress she's made. Clara, take Bob's bags up to the mountain-view guest room." To McAlmon she explained, "Havelock's coming down from Paris sometime soon, and he always gets the lake-view room."

In his previous visits to the château, McAlmon had always been given the lake-view guest room, but he didn't mind giving it up to Havelock Ellis, who was an old and dear friend of Bryher's and Hilda's from London. McAlmon had met Dr. Ellis a few times, had liked and admired the man, and looked forward to seeing him at the Riant Château, since his would be a reasonable voice amid the nerve-rattling clamor of squabbling adults.

McAlmon followed Bryher into the schoolroom, where the four-year-old was sitting in a miniature chair in front of a miniature desk, hunting and pecking on the keyboard of a portable typewriter with two chubby forefingers. The fact that she could spell a few words and operate a typewriter at age four didn't surprise McAlmon. He had received a few typed letters from her in the recent past, letters that were marvels of Gertrude Steinian prose. Had there been critics around to impute significance to the gibberish, she might have been hailed as a child prodigy.

"Here's Uncle Bob," Bryher said. "Aren't you going to say hello to Uncle Bob."

The Lump refused to be interrupted. Beautiful in an unconventional way, the child had black hair and black eyes, and though she was not known to have any oriental ancestry, her eyes were slightly upturned at the corners, giving her the look of a miniature Japanese empress.

"Come along, Lump, do what you're told," Bryher ordered. She took the child's arm and lifted her to her feet. "I want Uncle Bob to see the results of my educational experiment. Name him all of the countries and main cities of Europe. Go on." To McAlmon, Bryher said, "She can do it easily. And for someone her age, she has an amazing grasp of history. Haven't you, Lump? Go on, name the countries and main cities."

The little girl trained to be a gentle Child of Nature stared resentfully at Bryher, then blurted out, "You're a liar. I'm not your experiment. I'm a wild Indian. I'll skin you alive."

But not only was Bryher undaunted by the response, she was delighted, for it was something that she herself might have said, which was another proof that, as Bryher often claimed, she and the Lump were twins. However, since she could not lightly countenance disobedience, Bryher said, "Hippo, hippo, if the Lump is naughty"—glancing at a coiled whip that hung on the wall, a whip made of hippopotamus hide.

"You're a liar," the Lump repeated.

Now, Bryher was nothing if not persistent. She had a capacity to persist in the face of denials, rebuffs, yells, weeping, begging, long after those who tried to deny or thwart her had forgotten the very idea upon which she was insisting. This monomaniacal persistence was the means by which she could reduce Hilda to a trembling, shrieking hysteria, after which she would show Hilda how loving and conciliatory she could be by saying, "There, there, it's a nice kitten, calm down, calm down," in tones calculated to keep Hilda in a fit of apoplectic rage. But in the Lump Bryher had met her match.

It was true that Bryher, with her mania for management and the symbolic threat of the hippopotamus whip, had set out to make a genius of the child, and had succeeded surprisingly well, because—luckily for her—the child turned out to have a fine native intelligence. And under Bryher's incessant bombardment of information, the child had, at the age of four, learned the rudiments of reading and writing and was able to memorize an amazing amount of geographical and historical data. The main goal and accomplishment of Bryher's educational efforts, however, was to instill in the child all of her own phobias, manias, prejudices, inhibitions, and complexes, including the one characteristic that would insure the child's survival, even in the face of Bryher's incessant pedagogic assaults: a regally disregarding disposition.

"Go away," the Lump said. "I go back to my story."

"What's it about?" Bryher asked.

"None of your business."

"Isn't she remarkable?" Bryher asked McAlmon. "An exemplary product of the right upbringing."

"Shit," the Lump said.

"Now, now, you know you're not supposed to use naughty words, especially not in front of visitors. The hippo, the hippo."

"Shit, fuck, piss, goddamn. I'll say all the naughty words I want to. Now go away."

Bryher said, "You'll have to excuse her, she's a little irritable today."

They left the Lump to her story, and as Bryher was walking McAlmon to his room upstairs, she informed him that they would probably have to put in an appearance at the Ellerman family home in England someday soon. Her mother was writing her letters, threatening to come to see her darlings in Paris if they continued to ignore the invitations for them to visit England.

"That would be a disaster," she said. "They mustn't find out we don't live together. And we might have to adopt a baby, or something. They're beginning to ask when they can expect a grandchild."

"Rats," McAlmon said.

Bryher pulled a cigar from the breast pocket of her jacket, unwrapped the cellophane, and licked the cigar to moisten it as she said, "That was my first reaction, too, but I've been thinking about it since then, and I thought—well, why not? The Lump might like a playmate. A little brother. We'd tell Mother and Father it was our natural child. But all you'd be expected to supply is a surname."

"A boy?"

"Yes. I always wanted to be a boy. I would've made a good one, too, and I think I could raise a good one—a son to carry on my name—Bryher."

McAlmon could visualize Bryher creating yet another miniature of herself—triplets! And this one, a boy with her name—which wasn't her real name, anyway. She had taken the name from one of the Isles of Scilly, where she had vacationed as a child.

"Rats," McAlmon said.

"Never mind, I'd see that the child had a governess and a nurse and of course I'd handle his education myself." She stopped for a moment in the hallway to light the cigar. "Nothing would be required of you—except the use of your surname, of course, and playing the role of father now and then when we took Little Bryher to England to see his grandparents." After a few puffs to get the cigar going, she added insinuatingly, "I'm sure Father would bestow a considerable sum of money upon his first grandson. It might mean you could afford to have a Rolls Royce, if you wanted one."

So this, too, came down to a bribe, as was often the case with Bryher's proposals. But the subject of fatherhood settled for him the matter of how long he would stay at Riant Château. Rather than be badgered by Bryher's frightful persistence, he would stay only long enough to take care of any business that she and he might have together—legitimate business, that is, because he didn't consider the business of her adopting a son to carry on her name to be legitimate. He thought about trying to make the argument that the kid might be better off growing up as an orphan, rather than being molded in her image, but that was a judgment McAlmon thought he wasn't qualified to make. Still, he couldn't agree to participate in such a cockeyed charade as going to London to visit the Ellermans with Bryher pretending to be pregnant, stuffing pillows of larger and larger size under her skirts as the pregnancy supposedly progressed.

"Good God," he said, "you don't think they'd let you stay in Paris and have the child, do you? They'd put you in chains, if necessary, to keep you in London, and what would you do when it came time for the kid to be born, pop out a pillow?"

"I could be here, and tell them it was born prematurely. Oh, why are you so negative? I don't ask much of you, do I? For the allowance I give you, I don't ask much in return, do I? So why don't you think of ways to help me do it, instead of thinking of all the reasons I shouldn't?"

"Look, if you really want a baby, maybe we could . . . you know . . . do something to get you pregnant. Artificial insemination, or something like that. I'd be glad to supply the sperm."

"Are you out of your mind? How disgusting! I don't want to be a *mother!* I want to be a *father!* Don't you see?"

"Well, then," he said, his argument weakening, "maybe Hilda and I . . . maybe, if we worked at it, maybe I could get her pregnant. I'm just trying to be helpful," he added hastily in view of her expression of jealous rage.

"Never mind that."

They had stopped near the door to Hilda's study, and before they resumed walking down the hallway toward the mountain-view guest room, the door to Hilda's room suddenly jerked open. Hilda stuck her head out.

"How dare you?" she cried to Bryher. "I won't have it! Do you hear me? I won't stand any more of your damned planning and arranging." Then she got momentary control of herself and tried to make her voice normal as she said to McAlmon, "Hello, Bob. Come and have tea with me in my study when you get settled in." Then she exploded with rage again as she yelled at Bryher, "And if you don't stop torturing me about Richard and Cecil, I'm going to leave and never come back!" And with that she slammed the door.

"She's a little upset," said Bryher, who was not usually given to understatement.

When they entered the guest room, Clara, the housekeeper, and Jeannette, the maid, were just finishing unpacking his bag and putting his clothes into an ornate ivory-inlaid chiffonier.

"Is there anything else I can do for you?" Clara asked.

"No, thanks," McAlmon said. "I just want to lie down for a little bit. I have a hard time sleeping on trains."

Glancing around like a general who expects to find incompetence everywhere, Bryher said, "Where's his water? Bring him a pitcher of water." And after the servants went out, she said, "Incidentally, I told you, didn't I—yes, I told you, Havelock's coming down from Paris for a visit soon. I've sent him the train fare. I want you to stay until he comes. You two get along so well, and I'm sure he'd like a man to talk to while he's here."

"Is that an order?" He took off his coat and tie and tossed them on a chair.

"Bob, I don't quibble over the money I give you every month, do I? Why should you quibble over words? I want you to be here when Havelock comes, that's all. Is that too much to ask?"

Unlacing his shoes and kicking them off, McAlmon said, "You're not asking, you're bargaining. For so much money, you expect so much in return, principally in submission. Look, I'll sleep on it, let you know," he added, "but I wouldn't count on it, if I were you."

Given her persistence he knew it wouldn't end there. She would have stayed in the room and kept browbeating him until she had worn him down and made him agree to everything she proposed, had he not known the one sure way to get rid of her: he began to take off the rest of his clothes, item by item. By the time he was out of his shirt and undershirt, she was backing nervously toward the door, and by the time he unbuckled his belt and unbuttoned his fly and was about to drop his pants, she was gone, her persistence floundering in incipient panic, leaving behind her nothing but an undulating wisp of cigar smoke.

Due to slamming doors and shouts in the upper hallways, McAlmon didn't get much of a nap that afternoon, and these disturbances convinced him to leave for Rapallo on the first connecting train. He rang for Clara and asked her to bring him the railroad timetables. When he learned that he could take a train to Italy at ten o'clock that night, he decided he would stay in his room until called for dinner, then announce that he was leaving, and flee.

His goal for the rest of the day was to avoid contact with anyone as much as possible, but while on his way to the bathroom, dressed in a robe and carrying his shaving gear, he was virtually snatched out of the hallway as he was going past Hilda's door. She pulled him into her study and slammed and locked the door behind him.

At thirty-seven, Hilda was still a handsome woman, tall and

slender and blonde, but at the moment she looked haggard, her hair in wild disarray.

"You've got to help me get away!" she said in a fierce whisper, with a glance toward the door, as if she suspected Bryher might have her ear to the keyhole. "Rescue me!"

"Look, Hilda, I'm not exactly the white-knight-to-the-rescue type, you know. What's going on? What's she doing that makes you want to get away?"

"He's driving me crazy!"—still using the masculine pronoun when referring to Bryher.

"But how, Hilda? What . . . what is it? What's going on?"

She pulled him to a sofa and sat him down beside her, holding his hands as if to keep him from bolting, saying, "He's neurotically jealous. He torments himself and me over my past love affairs, making me confess in greater and greater detail to acts of the most intimate nature. Can you imagine? 'Did he touch you there?' he asks me. 'How did it feel? Did you like it? How could you stand a man doing that to you? Didn't you find that disgusting? Aren't you ashamed?' And he won't stop until he's made me hysterical, tearing out my hair."

"Well," McAlmon said, feeling foolish at stating the obvious, "why don't you just leave?"

"I can't. He won't let me."

He glanced at her hands and feet. "I don't see any chains on you. And you're bigger than she is—so? What's stopping you?"

"Oh, it's not physical restraints, it's . . . he has powers over me."

"Powers? What powers?"

"Love," she said, and all the fight seemed to go out of her. "I love him. It's true. He's driving me crazy, but I love him." Tears had flooded her eyes.

"Hilda, my dear, how can I help you? I'm not a white knight, and I'm not a psychologist. Havelock Ellis is coming soon—why not talk to him about it?"

"Yes. Yes, I suppose I could."

She seemed to have forgotten the idea of being rescued, so McAlmon took his leave, with nothing more in mind than a nice hot bath and a shave, in preparation for getting out of this mad-house as soon as possible.

Bryher wasn't going to let him go so easily, however. When he told Clara to tell Bryher that he was going to catch the 10:00 P.M. train for Geneva, Bryher came to his room and, finding the door locked, jiggled the handle.

"Don't come in," McAlmon cried, "I'm masturbating."

When Clara came up to tell him that dinner was being served, he decided that courtesy required him to put in an appearance, so he went down to the dining room, and found that he and Bryher were to be the only ones at the table. The Lump wanted her dinner in her room, and Hilda had sent word that she wasn't hungry. And no sooner had the servants served and left the room than Bryher advanced the subject of adopting a baby. McAlmon deflected her by bringing up her treatment of Hilda.

"Hilda tells me you're still needling her about her former male lovers," he said as he picked at the pitiful, gray, tasteless mess that Bryher's cook tried to pass off as stew.

"I can't help it," Bryher said, with no sign of guilt or contrition. "All I do is try to understand how she did those things with those men. That's all. Is that so bad? I even pay Havelock to try to find out, and his services are quite expensive, I can tell you."

"What you want, my dear, is retroactive fidelity, and you don't have enough money to buy that." He pushed his plate away. "I'm not hungry. I think I'll go on down to Montreux, make sure I'm not late for the train. Is your chauffeur available, or should I start walking?"

After exhausting every dilatory tactic and argument she could to prevent his leaving, Bryher allowed him the use of her chauf-feured Mercedes Benz to take him to the train depot.

So, having escaped becoming a father, he boarded the train and settled into his seat in the first-class compartment with a sigh of relief, hoping for better things in Rapallo.

The trip, at least, was restful. In Geneva, he connected with the Simplon Orient Express, which took him through the Simplon Tunnel and into northern Italy. Dawn came with a wintry drizzle as the train followed the shores of Lago Maggiore and then past Stresa to Milan, where he once again had to change trains. The rain had stopped by the time the train got to Genoa, and there was intermittent sunshine all the way into Rapallo.

McAlmon liked the looks of the country. He liked the flashing views of Rapallo that he got through the olive trees between tunnels. It looked as if it might be a restful town, all right, and he was looking forward to male company. Ezra Pound was certainly eccentric in most ways, it was true, but his masculinity had never been in doubt, and so McAlmon had counted on him for the undemanding masculine companionship he would need in order to keep from expiring of boredom during his peaceful stay in Rapallo.

It came as something of a disappointment, then, to learn on his first day in town that his old friend Nancy Cunard had lured Ezra away to a rendezvous in southern Italy. That left McAlmon with Mike Strater and Ernest Hemingway for companionship, which was okay, because both of them seemed to be regular fellows. McAlmon had known Mike in Paris. There Mike was sometimes called Mike Straighter by the fairies, and Mike Satyr by the women, though there was nothing exaggerated or offensive about his masculinity. He was a simple and direct and clean-cut young American, a painter who was unpretentious, even modest—indeed, very much like the character Burne Holiday for which Mike had been used as a model by his old Princeton pal F. Scott Fitzgerald.

Hemingway, on the other hand, was not so easily pegged. During the days and evenings they spent together in Rapallo, Hemingway appeared at times deliberately hard-boiled and calloused, and sometimes he questioned people like a cop grilling a criminal, his peering eyes narrowed with suspicion, a potential snarl of scorn playing on his large-lipped mouth beneath the drill-sergeant's mustache. When entering a café or any place where he might be looked over, Hemingway walked with a tough-guy swagger. At other times, such as when he told McAlmon how Hadley had lost his manuscripts, his "complete works," as he called them, he appeared deliberately innocent, playing the sensitive boy who has been hurt but is trying to hide it, wanting to be admired for his stoical bravery in the face of such a loss.

As for his masculinity, the very way he exaggerated it made its authenticity suspect. McAlmon took that line of thought no further, but he couldn't help feeling a vague unease in Hemingway's presence, an unease that had its source in some shadowy sexual aura emanating from the young man.

Though McAlmon had never flaunted his own ambisexuality (a word he preferred to bisexuality, because of its hints of ambiguity and ambivalence), he had never made a secret of it, either, and over the years, he had become keenly attuned to the nature of sexual overtones. Indeed, so keen did this sense become that back in the days when he was a model, posing nude for art classes at the Cooper Union in New York, he could intuit which students, whether male or female, were becoming sexually aroused by some fantasy that his boyish body inspired. It had long ceased to surprise him that he had this sexual attraction for both men and women. As his friend William Carlos Williams had said of him in those days, he had the body that might have served for the original of Donatello's youthful Medici in armor in the niche of the Palazzo Vecchio in Florence.

In spite of this heightened sensitivity to sexual nuances, however, he didn't know quite what to make of Hemingway. There was nothing subtle about Hemingway's hatred of fairies. He contrived conversational opportunities to make his feelings on that subject quite clear, and, without a flicker of a doubt or a moment's hesitation, he took it for granted that McAlmon shared his views, perhaps for the purpose of forestalling any embarrassing admission McAlmon might make to the contrary. And McAlmon, having long ago given up wasting his time and energy trying to argue queer-haters into being men of reason and tolerance, let Hemingway assume that he took no exception to his views.

Where lesbianism was concerned, Hemingway showed an acute and well-disposed interest. It was common knowledge among the expatriate crowd in Paris that McAlmon was married to a lesbian, and though Hemingway never alluded to that fact openly, he did keep asking questions about Bryher that exceeded idle curiosity. And he usually clothed his curiosity in questions about Bryher's wealth.

"How's it feel to be married to a woman who's filthy rich?" was one of his questions, the bluntness of which was meant to be softened by his joshing tone of good-natured envy.

"She's neither filthy nor rich," McAlmon said, keeping his tone evasive without being defensive. "Her family's rich, she's not."

"Rich enough to live in a château in Switzerland," Hemingway said, and ordered another round of drinks, which McAlmon was expected to pay for.

"With her father's money," McAlmon said.

"What's the difference? If I had a château on Lake Geneva, I don't think I'd ever leave it. Doesn't your wife object to you wandering around Europe like you do?"

"We have an understanding," McAlmon said, still intentionally vague.

"I wish I had a rich wife who was so understanding. My wife is neither rich nor understanding. Every time I leave her alone somewhere, she raises hell. But, then, your wife isn't alone, is she? Doesn't she live with one of Ezra's former girlfriends?"

"Hilda Doolittle, yes—and Hilda's child."

"And what do they do all day, rattling around in a big château?"

"They write beautiful poems and good books," he said, and was tempted to add, "and mind their own business," but there was no sense in offending Hemingway needlessly when he could so easily—as McAlmon had found out in previous conversations—steer him away from any subject by simply directing his prurient interests at another target. Hemingway had an appetite for gossip, especially scandalous gossip, especially when it concerned rich people and lesbians, and McAlmon had only to bring up the name of Nancy Cunard, for instance, to snare his total attention. Furthermore, McAlmon didn't have to feel that he was compromising his friendship with Nancy by offering her up since Nancy, unlike Bryher and H.D., who were shy and private, took delight in shocking people. She had her affairs with both men and women, white or black, and didn't care who knew it. She once told McAlmon, if it weren't for getting thrown into the hoosegow, she wouldn't have hesitated to indulge in her sexual escapades in whatever public place she happened to be in when the mood took her.

"One day a friend of mine and I were having lunch at the Ritz," she once told McAlmon, "and my friend, having finished her lunch, crawled under the table, and there, concealed from view by the tablecloth, ate my pussy while I ate my *pâte brisée.*"

Hemingway couldn't get enough of this kind of thing. And McAlmon had lots of such stories to offer him—such as how Nancy one day got to feeling very amorous and there was no lover around at the moment to take care of her, so she called in the new maid, Faustina, to ask about Faustina's husband, the new butler.

"Does Guido fuck?" she asked.

Faustina didn't quite believe her ears, but after Nancy repeated the question in an impatient tone, the maid, who needed the job, blushed and tipped her head and said, *"Si, Signora."*

"Good. Send him up. I need one."

Guido, the butler, who also needed the job, did as he was bid.

Hemingway and McAlmon were strolling along the Rapallo seafront promenade when he told Hemingway this story, and Hemingway nudged him with an insinuating elbow, saying, "And what about you? You ever get any of that?"

"Not me. I'm a married man."

"Aw, go on," Hemingway said with friendly scorn.

But that was at least partially true. While McAlmon had never had an affair with Nancy Cunard, that circumstance was not due to his being married. What Nancy wanted for male lovers were men who were more than a match for her—masterful men, strong men. McAlmon was simply not her type, being too small and unbrutish, and God knows she wasn't his type. He was quite fond of her as a friend, and had great admiration for her severe beauty, her steely elegance, but he could never have handled her bitter, hostile, challenging femininity. His liaisons with women, once as numerous as his liaisons with men, had been diminishing over the last few years. He still considered himself to be ambisexual, but women who appealed to him seemed to be getting harder and harder to find.

He didn't discuss any of this with Hemingway. A couple of times Hemingway seemed to be edging toward a probe of McAlmon's own sexuality, but by then McAlmon had learned that scandalous gossip wasn't the only thing that could divert Hemingway from a conversational course. Boxing would do it, too—boxing and bullfighting. But Mike Strater had to be around to discuss bullfighting, since neither Hemingway nor McAlmon had ever seen a bullfight. Strater had, and he loved to hold forth on the beauties of the blood sport, and in Hemingway he had an avid listener. Sometimes Hemingway even took notes, like a reporter, as if he were going to write a story about what Strater had seen.

"I've got to go to Spain before I have to go back to the States," Hemingway said in a plaintive voice.

The three of them—Hemingway, Strater, and McAlmon—were sitting at a table in one of the cafés on Rapallo's seafront promenade. It was night and the café was empty except for the three men. Outside a light rain was falling.

"With a kid coming, I'll have to get a goddamned job, and who the hell knows when I might be able to get back to Spain to see one? Maybe never."

Hemingway was feeling sorry for himself again. Every time he had to face going back to the States and going to work and being a breadwinning father, he got that look of a hurt boy trying to put on a brave face.

"You've got the summer yet," Mike said. "That's when you can see the best bullfights."

"I've been thinking about taking a trip to Spain this summer myself," McAlmon said. "Seeing some bullfights. Gerty and Alice say they're crazy about them. Maybe we could go together?"

"Aw, shit, I can't afford it," Hemingway said. "With a kid coming . . . have to buy steamship tickets. . . ." He looked at McAlmon accusingly. "Too bad I'm not married to a steamship line heiress, I could travel for free." After a bitter pause, he added, "Of course, if I were married to a steamship line heiress, I wouldn't have to go back to the States at all, would I?"

The serving girl brought them more beers. Her apron covered her swelling pregnancy. She must not have been more than fifteen and was getting impatient for them to leave. McAlmon paid for the drinks.

"Let's drink up and go," Mike said. "She wants to get home to her husband."

"She hasn't got a husband," Hemingway said. "She's not married."

"How do you know?" Mike asked.

"No wedding ring. Around here when they get married, they wear wedding rings. She got knocked up, and has no husband, and now nobody will ever marry her—not in this country."

"Poor kid," McAlmon said. "Damned shame they don't allow girls that young to get rid of it. Ruin their lives, just because they can't get abortions in these backward Catholic countries. In Paris she could get one easy."

"Oh, yeah?" Hemingway said. "How do you know?"

"Knew a girl who got one. American girl. Came to Paris to be a poet, got knocked up by some lout, couldn't go back home, was going to kill herself," McAlmon said. "Djuna Barnes knew a doctor . . ."

"Really?" Hemingway fixed him with those piercing reporter's eyes. "It's dangerous, isn't it?"

"Not from what I hear," McAlmon said. "Not most of the time, anyway. It's perfectly simple. They just let the air in, then it's all perfectly natural."

"Yeah?" Hemingway said, his interest growing keener, as if he might open his notebook and start taking notes. "How much does it cost?"

"I don't know," McAlmon said. "I could find out from Djuna, if you really want to know."

Hemingway didn't say whether or not he wanted him to find out. They drank their beers. Between drinks, Hemingway chewed on his bottom lip, as if he were thinking hard, and pretty soon he said, "I don't know. If I did some more work for the *Star,* then went to the gym in Paris and worked as a sparring partner for a few weeks, maybe I could get the money together—for a trip to Spain—before I have to go back to the States."

"That's an idea," Mike said. "And maybe I could go with you chaps. I'd love to see some more bullfights."

Hemingway fixed Mike with an accusing look. "But if I do the sparring partner stuff, I have to get into shape, and how am I going to do that, here in Rapallo, unless you stop malingering with that damned ankle and spar some with me? With Ezra gone, and Mac here so small it'd be against the law to hit him, you're the only one left. So when are we going to do some sparring, for Christ's sake?"

This was getting to be a bore, the way Hemingway was always trying to get Mike to box a few rounds with him, in spite of Mike's bum ankle. In fact, everything about Rapallo was becoming boring to McAlmon, and he was beginning to think he'd had all the peace and quiet he could stand.

Hemingway had received a letter from Ezra. Dorothy had gone to meet Ezra in Firenze, and Ezra wrote and asked Hemingway if he would join him and Dorothy in a walking tour of some medieval battlefields in Romagna. Ezra claimed to be inspecting places that were associated with the career of Sigismundo Malatesta, about whom he was writing some cantos, and he wanted company. Hemingway and Hadley had been talking about leaving Rapallo and going to Cortina d'Ampézzo in the Dolomite Alps in hopes of more skiing before returning to Paris, but he agreed that they would meet Ezra and Dorothy and walk with them for a few days before going on to Cortina. Hemingway asked McAlmon if he would like to go on the walk with them.

"Nope," McAlmon said. "I got better things to do than walk in the rain and eat bad food and sleep in lumpy beds in poor Italian country inns during February, just to follow the trail of somebody I never heard of, and listen to old windbag Ezra spout off about esoteric medieval bullshit. No, thanks. Think I'll go on back to Paris, get some work done on the books I'm supposed to be publishing."

But he changed his mind the next day after he picked up a letter at the Poste Restante from Sylvia Beach. Shakespeare and Company had been serving as Contact Editions' official address, warehouse, and bank, and Sylvia was writing to tell him that he had a great backlog of letters and manuscripts waiting for him in Paris. In Sylvia's prim handwriting, the letter read,

This is rather a shot in the dark, I don't know if it will reach you. I've sent duplicates to Bryher in Switzerland, and to Nancy Cunard in Venice, hoping that at least one will find you. Darantiére in Dijon is waiting to schedule the printing for three Contact Editions books, the proofs of which are here, waiting for you. If you can give me an address where you will be sometime in the near future, I will forward them to you for proofreading. They are: Marsden Hartley's *Twenty-Five Poems,* William Carlos Williams' *Spring and All,* and your own collection of short stories.

But over and above these business matters, how are you? I think of you often, and I must confess that when Adrienne and I recently went for a holiday on the blustery north coast near Le Harve, I had a lot of time to think, and I had a thought that I am going to share with you, which is that I love you. I hope that this does not shock you. It did not come as a great surprise to me, for I have, as you perhaps know, been very fond of you for a long time, but if this timid confession of love comes as a surprise to you, and if you are not receptive to the idea, have no apprehensions. The feeling, if unrequited, will have passed by the time you return to Paris, and we need never mention it.

Sylvia Beach, that wonderful, kind, intelligent lady, whom he had thought to be happy in her relationship with Adrienne, with never a wink or a flirty smile or any encouragement from McAlmon . . . suddenly deciding that she was in love with him? It was enough to make him turn the envelope over and make sure that it was really addressed to him. And then all he could say was "Rats." It was flattering, sure, but it was also spooky and disconcerting. To be platonically married to one lesbian, and then have another one declare that she was in love with him, at a time when he was discovering that his own sexual attraction to women was weakening perceptibly . . . well!

But that settled one thing, anyway: he would not be going back to Paris any time soon. He would have to give Sylvia time to come to her senses before seeing her again. As for the letter,

he could just ignore it. He could go on to some other city—
Venice, for instance. One could assume from Ezra's letter to
Hemingway that his tryst with Nancy Cunard in southern Italy
had run its course, and if Nancy had gone back home to her
palazzo in Venice, he thought he might pay her a visit. He hadn't
seen her in a few months, and there were some interesting times
to be had in Venice, for sure.

So he made plans to leave Rapallo the next day on the noon
train to Milan. He delayed his departure for a day, however,
when he heard that Mike, in spite of his bum ankle, had finally
accepted Hemingway's challenge to a boxing match. It was Maggie Strater who told McAlmon about it when he went around to
say good-bye to her and Mike. Mike wasn't at home. He had
gone to the local gym to meet Hemingway for the match.

"Aren't you going to see it?" McAlmon asked.

"No, no, no. Ernest fights so dirty, I'd get furious. In their last
fight, he hit Mike a real haymaker in the balls. I'm telling you! It's
the God's truth! Right in the family jewels! After that, I went out
and bought Mike a protective cup. Even so, I can't watch it. If
Ernest started fighting dirty again, I'd probably pick up a chair
and brain him with it."

"What about Mike's ankle?"

"He says it's well enough for a little sparring. I don't believe
him, but what can you do? Boys will be boys."

This was something that McAlmon didn't want to miss. Mike
and Hemingway were both six footers and each weighed about
two hundred pounds. Mike had been a boxer at Princeton, and
Hemingway had told McAlmon within a few days of McAlmon's
arrival in Rapallo that he had once been a professional fighter
and a sparring partner for various heavyweights, and that he had
even whipped some professional boxer named Young Cuddy.
So it had the makings of a good match, if they mixed it up,
which McAlmon figured they probably would, given Hemingway's need to dominate and win.

So McAlmon went to the gym, where Mike and Hemingway
had already begun sparring. They were both wearing their tennis
shorts and tennis shoes. Mike's left shoe bulged over the supportive wrapping around his ankle, and Hemingway's right knee

was in a rubber support, the knee that was supposed to have
been so badly damaged in the War. But they weren't doing badly
for a couple of cripples. They were moving around at arm's
length, circling, measuring each other. There was no boxing ring
in the gym; they were using tumbling mats to simulate a ring.
McAlmon sat in one of the folding chairs that were lined up
against the wall. There were only three other men in the gym,
working out on weights or doing calisthenics.

Mike and Hemingway acknowledged McAlmon with a look or
a gesture, and Hemingway said in his cocky way, "Come to see
Hyacinth get knocked out, did you, Mac?"

"Just came to say so long before taking off for Venice,"
McAlmon said. "But go ahead, don't let me interrupt you. I'll just
sit here and watch."

They weren't timing themselves by rounds. It was just open-
ended sparring. Presumably part of the contest was to see who
could last the longest without a rest. Mike had quicker hands
and could hit Hemingway two or three times before Hemingway
could hit him once, but Hemingway didn't seem to care. He was
trying for the big one. He just wanted to get in close enough to
catch Mike with a lunging hook, or an overhand right, but by the
time he got set to throw one of his big ones, Mike would either
move out of range, or hit him with a stinging left jab, or just push
a glove into his face.

One of those jabs bloodied Hemingway's nose. It wasn't a real
gusher, but it didn't take long for Hemingway's mustache to be
soaked with blood. They stopped fighting as Hemingway drew
his glove across his mustache, looked at the blood on his glove,
and sneered.

Mike dropped his guard as he said, "Want to wash it off?"

Both of them were panting and in need of a break, but Hemingway didn't hesitate for a second. When Mike dropped his
guard, Hemingway caught him with a hard overhand right to the
head and a left hook to the body. Unable to get away from him,
Mike grabbed his arms and tied him up, but Hemingway got his
right hand free and drove the heel of the glove against Mike's
nose. They were practically wrestling for a moment, bleeding on

each other, before Mike jerked away and stepped back. He, too, drew his glove across his nose and looked at the blood.

"Want to go wash it off, Hyacinth?" Hemingway goaded, but didn't hesitate before he rushed in again. He was looking for the kill, using his fists and arms not for the purpose of punching, but as if they were clubs with which to beat Mike around the head and shoulders.

That was when Mike shifted from a right-handed to a south-paw stance. This brought Hemingway's charge to a halt as he tried to figure out how best to react to this new tactic, but before he could figure it out, Mike, grimacing with anger and vindictiveness, hit him square on the chin with a left hand that came all the way from his shoulder. The smack of the impact could be heard throughout the gym. Hemingway was staggered. His legs went rubbery. He almost went down. One more good blow would have put him down.

But Mike backed off. With some misguided impulse to sportsmanship, he dropped his hands and stood there, panting, waiting for Hemingway to recover. Had their positions been reversed, McAlmon had no doubt that Hemingway would have swarmed all over Mike, throwing everything he had at him, until Mike had gone down or cried uncle. But Mike not only allowed Hemingway to recover, he looked as if he would be quite willing to stop, if Hemingway gave him a signal.

But Hemingway wasn't about to quit—not as long as he was losing. He would just have to change his tactics. He would just have to take it easy until something happened that he could take advantage of—like Mike falling down from sheer exhaustion, say, or his sprained ankle getting so painful he would have to quit.

Mike's ankle didn't give him much trouble at first, but by the time they had gone eight or ten minutes, he was beginning to lose the coordination in his feet. You could see him wince now and then with the pain when he put all his weight on the left foot. Hemingway saw it, too, and sought to take advantage of it. In his clumsy, mauling way, he moved close and stepped on Mike's injured foot.

McAlmon could have accepted it as an accident—because who could believe that anyone would fight that dirty in what was supposed to be just a friendly sparring match?—except that he had seen Hemingway glance down at the foot just before he stepped on it. Hemingway had been measuring the distance. And he kept his foot on Mike's, pinning it to the canvas so that Mike couldn't step backward, as Hemingway got set to throw a haymaker. However, it seemed that he couldn't make up his mind which to throw, a right or a left, so he sort of threw both of them at the same time. His arms and fists formed a sort of battering ram as he lunged at Mike and pushed him. Unable to back up because Hemingway had his injured foot pinned to the floor, Mike fell over backward.

For a moment, McAlmon thought Mike was going to stay down. Both of them were panting heavily, gulping for oxygen. But energized by anger at being betrayed, Mike struggled to his feet, limping, and rushed at a surprised Hemingway, hit him with a right cross, and Hemingway went down, hard. Then, too tired to stand up any longer, Mike dropped to the canvas, too, and sprawled out in a spread-eagle position, panting, sweating, bleeding.

That was the only way it could have ended. Mike had no doubt won the fight, but by his gesture, he relieved Hemingway from the unacceptable onus of being a loser.

McAlmon had hoped that he might see Mike and Hemingway that evening in one of Rapallo's cafés and have a farewell dinner with them, or at least a drink, but neither of them showed up. Nor did they come out the next morning for breakfast. As McAlmon was preparing to leave on the noon train, he stopped by the Hemingways' hotel room, and knocked on the door. Hadley, still in her housecoat, let him in. Hemingway was in bed. His face had a few abrasions and bruises and he was holding an ice pack where his jaw was noticeably swollen.

"I just came by to say so long," McAlmon said. "I'm off to Venice for a while. See you back in Paris. Maybe we can get together for that trip to Spain this summer."

"I sure hope so," Hemingway said, moving his jaw tenderly. "And I hope to have enough material for a book by then, too. I'm going to hold you to that offer to publish it."

"You're on," McAlmon said.

"And, listen," he said, "after we get through walking with Ezra and Dorothy, we'll be going to Cortina d'Ampézzo for maybe a month of skiing. It's not too far north of Venice. Why don't you come up, do some skiing? Bring that Nancy Cunard with you."

It wasn't McAlmon he was inviting; he knew McAlmon wasn't a skier or a sportsman; it was Nancy Cunard he wanted to see.

"I'll mention it to her," McAlmon said. "Well, so long."

Hadley walked him to the door. She had a look of merriment on her face, like someone who has a secret she wants to share. McAlmon turned at the door to say so long, but she accompanied him out into the hallway and closed the door behind her. She crossed her arms under her breasts, as if trying to contain herself, and looked down at the floor as she said, "The doctor came by this morning." Then her shoulders began to shake and she made little sounds that could have been an attempt to suppress sobs.

"What is it?" McAlmon said. "Surely there's no serious injuries . . ."

Then Hadley emitted a small chuckle, and McAlmon realized that she was trying to suppress laughter.

"He won't be able to chew solid foods for a week," she said. "Maybe that'll put a stop to his silly ideas of being a boxer."

26

Hadley

ERNEST HAD BEEN told that Cortina d'Ampézzo was situated in a high-sided bowl in the ruggedly beautiful Italian Dolomites that made it especially good for spring skiing. And on the day Hadley and Ernest arrived—March 12—they could see that the snowpack was thick and the powdery snow was perfect. The town, with its enclosing ramparts of mountains and its Swiss-style architecture, reminded them of Chamby. There were Swiss-style hotels and beer halls and there was a charming baroque church with a 250-foot campanile on the bustling piazza.

The peak tourist season had passed, and the hotels were nearly empty. Hadley and Ernest took a room in the Hotel Bellevue on the Corso Italia a few blocks north of the piazza. The hotel was cheap, the food hardy, and there was a grand piano in the hotel lobby. The padrone encouraged Hadley to play the piano any-time she wanted. He said he liked her playing, and assumed that she was a professional pianist.

"You see?" Ernest said. "You are good. It's not just me who thinks so. You should try to be a concert pianist. It's not too late. You'd have to work hard, of course, and . . ."

And not have the baby—that was what he wanted to say. To judge by their arduous skiing schedule and the terrain over which they skied, he was still hoping for a miscarriage. Each day they got up before dawn, filled their rucksacks with food and wine for lunch, put the seal skins on their skis, and hiked up one of the nearby mountain slopes. At the top, they would have lunch, maybe take a nap, then come down, lickety-split, and some of the fields were scary. And wonderful and billowy and dangerous. But Hadley didn't oblige Ernest by having an accident that would have terminated the pregnancy.

"I'm gonna hate to leave all this, and go back home," he said to her one night after they had gotten into a big bed that had been made cozy by a warming pan filled with hot coals. "Won't you?"

"Sure," she said.

"So, do we have to? Even if you have the baby, the American Hospital in Paris seems modern enough to—"

"Even if I have it? What do you mean, even? Darling Tatie, we've been over this a dozen times. I want to have this baby, but I'd be very apprehensive about having it in Europe. The hospitals and doctors here just aren't as good as those back home. And I've told you, there may be . . . difficulties. Dr. Gellhorn told me I shouldn't even try to have a baby. He said it could be difficult for me. If it turns out that way, I want to be where I can depend on the very best medical help."

Dr. Gellhorn had been her gynecologist in St. Louis, the one who had fitted her for a diaphragm, and it was true that he had voiced apprehension about her trying to have a child. Perhaps she exaggerated the doctor's concern a little for the sake of quashing this interminable discussing with Ernest, but it was essentially true.

"Well, if it's dangerous, goddamnit, you shouldn't be having it," Ernest argued.

"With doctors I can trust, who know what they're doing, I won't be afraid," she said. "But, whether for medical reasons, or employment reasons, we'll have to go back to the States, where you can get a job as a reporter. Having a baby will be more than risky, it'll be expensive, too. It'll cost more than we could save from my trust fund and your freelance work here in Europe. So we'd better reconcile ourselves to it—okay, Wemedge? Come on, cheer up, honey. If this is our last skiing season in Europe, let's make the most of it—okay?"

He tried, but no matter how good the skiing was, and how

lovely the days, he wasn't having much fun. And it wasn't her pregnancy alone that was depressing him. He needed more company than just Hadley. They tried to recruit some by writing letters to everybody they knew in Europe who they thought might come. They touted Cortina and promised great skiing, but their letters failed.

Then one night Ernest and Hadley were in the hotel's salon, Ernest deep in a leather-upholstered chair, smoking cigarettes and drinking hot rum, dreamily listening to Hadley sweetly play "Malaguena" on the grand piano, when a taxi driver barged in the front door, loaded down with luggage and skis, followed by Renata Borgatti. She was dressed in a blue beret, a flowing cape, and black Spanish boots that clicked on the oak floor like castanets. She smoked a cigarette in a long holder. What a pleasant surprise!

But seeing them in the hotel was no surprise for Renata. "There you are!" she said. "I found you."

She bussed Hadley on both cheeks, shook hands with Ernest, and in answer to Hadley's blurted question about what in God's name was she doing here she said, "I was staying with Nancy Cunard in Venice for a few days, and Bob McAlmon came to visit. He said you two were up here, skiing. I decided I wanted to do some skiing, too. It's been years."

"Oh, wonderful!" Hadley said. "Isn't that wonderful, Tatie? Now we have a friend to ski with."

Ernest seemed genuinely pleased, but he didn't know Renata as well as Hadley did, so he was shy at first, and perhaps even a little intimidated by her panache. In Paris, Hadley had heard it said of Renata that she shouldn't have been a woman because for all good purpose, she was a man. Hadley had also heard it said that many women in Paris were ready to fall into her arms, if she wanted them. She had forgotten how handsome Renata was: tall and angular, with gray eyes, with black hair cut to frame the pale skin of her face.

The hotel's padrone was too polite to interrupt while they were renewing acquaintance, but as soon as Renata turned away to sign the register and be shown to a room, the padrone approached, bowing, and said in reverent tones, "Signorina

Borgatti, I give you greetings. Welcome to the Hotel Bellevue. You do me great honor, Signorina, to stay at my humble establishment. I was privileged to hear your concert in Ravenna only last month." He closed his fingertips to make a flower bud, kissed them, then tossed the opened flower into the air. *"Bella, Signorina, bella!* And your father, Guiseppi Borgatti. I often heard him sing. My profound condolences on his untimely death. Ah, a great man! A great singer!" He bowed again, deeply, and his eyes glistened with tears.

"Well, looks like we have a celebrity for a friend," Hadley said to Ernest after Renata had gone up to her room, followed by the padrone and a bellhop loaded down with her luggage and skiing equipment.

Her glory reflected on them. They had been treated quite well at the Bellevue before Renata came, but the padrone and the staff couldn't do enough after seeing that they were friends of the famous pianist. Ernest advanced this impression by telling the padrone a few lies, in private, about Renata being an old and dear friend of theirs from Paris, and letting it be known that she had come to the Bellevue specifically because Ernest and Hadley were there. Until Renata arrived, the Bellevue had seemed to be sinking into postseason doldrums, and Ernest and Hadley had definitely been into their own private doldrums. Renata proved to be the antidote they all needed.

The first day on the slopes revealed Renata to be a better than average skier, and her first after-dinner conversation kept Ernest up until after eleven o'clock. With only the three of them in the hotel's salon, they sat in front of the roaring log fire. Hadley knitted a sweater while Renata and Ernest drank brandy and smoked cigarettes and talked, mostly about sex. During a gossipy exchange about who was sleeping with whom in Venice and Paris, Ernest maneuvered Renata into a discussion of lesbianism by asking her, "But what does Natalie"—they were talking about Natalie Barney, Renata's friend and former lover—"say to people . . . what do you say to people who accuse you . . . accuse homosexuals of being . . . unnatural?"

"I tell them they're right," Renata said. "It can be shown, of course, that many lower animals are addicted to all sorts of so-called unnatural vices, but I agree that homosexuality has little worth in the natural scheme of things. But, Ernest, consider: it's been a long time since we humans have come down from the trees, and since then social life among us has become highly artificial. Take clothing, for instance, or books or pianos or houses or the cooking of food or machinery—none of these things grow on trees, or out of the ground. None of them exists in the so-called natural state. All of them—all—are inventions and refinements by humans, nature's most highly evolved beings. So, too, forms of intimacy little known in the natural state are to be regarded as improvements, as refinements, upon nature." She held her snifter up and studied the firelight through her brandy. "Like fine brandy. *N'est-ce pas?*"

Hadley didn't expect Ernest to be convinced by this argument, but he didn't offer much against it. All he said was, "But brandy won't bring the human species to an end, universal homosexuality would."

"Oh, *bien sur,* but of course, we must not encourage it to become universal," Renata said. "Like good brandy, it should be only for the privileged few. There'll always be those—quite enough to keep the stock replenished, I'm sure—who don't like brandy, those who like to breed. The bees have that problem solved. Let us develop queen bees, to replenish the hordes, while the rest of us go about our lives, doing the things we like to do, enjoying the most exquisite refinements upon nature."

Ernest tilted his head toward Hadley. "Would you make Tiny one of those queen bees?"

"I certainly would if she wanted to be one," Renata said with a bright smile. "What a batch of beautiful, robust children she would give birth to! Is that what you want, Hadley?"

"Not a batch, no, I don't think so, but at least one or two." She kept her eyes on her purl stitches as she added casually, "I already have one on the way, it seems."

"Yes, I know," Renata said. "I pretended not to, in case you wanted to keep it confidential a while longer, but actually Bob told me in Venice." She reached over and gave Hadley's arm a pat and a squeeze. "Well, congratulations! If you're happy with it, I'm happy for you. And I must say, the condition becomes you, Hadley—the apple cheeks, the twinkle in the eyes, the Mona Lisa smile! I've never seen you lovelier."

Ernest had never said that to her. But of course Renata was much more of a gentleman to her than Ernest ever was. Renata rushed to open doors for her, held her chair when they sat down at the table to eat, lit her cigarettes for her . . . things Ernest never did.

"She's attracted to you," Ernest said that night in bed. They had turned out the lights and were cuddling.

"You think so? Yes, I guess I sense that," Hadley said.

"She'd like to make love to you."

"You think so?"

"I know so. How would you feel about it? Would you like that?"

Hadley was distinctly apprehensive about answering that question. Sure, they had traded genders when making love, but they had never before gone this far, and Hadley was apprehensive because it was not only new territory; once you were there, could there be any coming back? But as Ernest talked, he began fondling her, kissing her all over, and she sensed that he wanted Hadley to be excited by the idea of Renata making love to her because her excitement would excite him. Whether that fantasy actually became exciting to Hadley, or whether Ernest's lovemaking led to her own excitement, she didn't know, but soon she was breathing hard and murmuring, "Yes. Yes. Oh, yes . . ." And she sensed that in his fantasy, Ernest had become Renata, doing the things to her that Renata would have done. Even the timbre of his voice had changed to sound like hers, or the voice he used when he became Catherine. It was the first time he had ever led Hadley to climax with his tongue in her, with no care for his own climax. Hadley found herself hoping that Renata, whose room was next to theirs, could hear her cries of climax and share in the experience, divining somehow that she was the one who had inspired it.

Hadley felt that this twist in their fantasy life could have led somewhere, had it been allowed to take its course, but that possibility was foreclosed the next morning when Ernest received a telegram from John Bone of the *Toronto Star*. The *Star* had apparently forgiven Ernest for having double-crossed them on the Constantinople assignment, for now they wanted him to make an immediate tour of the French-occupied German Ruhr and send back two to three feature stories a week for an announced, front-page series. This had been Ernest's idea. He had suggested it to the *Star* while he and Hadley were in Rapallo and not getting along well. Now they were in Cortina, having fun skiing and titillated by the possibilities with Renata, and Ernest didn't want to leave.

After the bellboy brought the telegram up from the Poste Restante, Hadley and Ernest looked at it for a long time. For more than three months now, ever since the Lausanne Conference, his only work had been fiction. In addition to making notes and doing drafts on a few short stories, he had written and polished six vignettes that Margaret Anderson said she would publish in the "Exile's Edition" of *The Little Review,* to be issued in Paris in April. Ernest had let his hair grow down over his collar, so that it was longer than Hadley's, and he had begun to think and act like a writer of fiction. Now this! What could he do?

"I'm going to have to go," he said sullenly. "It was my suggestion, after all. And it'll mean four or five hundred dollars for us. We'll need it for the passage back to the States."

"We could borrow the money," Hadley said.

"But we'd have to pay it back. Besides, I can't afford to get Bone mad at me again. If I turn him down on this, he'll probably turn me down for a full-time job when we get back. No. It's the shits, but I'll have to go. But I'll only be gone for a couple of weeks, I promise. That's what I'm going to tell Bone—a couple of weeks, no more. You can stay here. The higher slopes will still have some good snow on them when I get back, and there are some lovely trout streams around here. We can still have some fun."

"And I'm supposed to stay here for a couple of weeks? By myself? Not even being able to understand the damned dialects they speak here? Sure, that'll be lots of fun!"

"Renata knows the language. She can keep you company till I get back. If we go back to Paris now, we'll never come back here again, Tiny, and our skiing will be over for God knows how long, with a baby coming. Maybe forever."

Well, at least he had hit on the only arrangement that could have induced Hadley to stay in Cortina. "But what if Renata isn't planning to be here that long?"

"Well, I suggest you ask her."

She met Renata in the dining room at dinner, and Renata told her that she had no definite departure date in mind. Her next concert wasn't until April 10, in Bern, Switzerland, she said, and she was free until then, and would be happy to stay in Cortina and keep Hadley company until Ernest returned.

They had a small going-away party for Ernest that night, though the atmosphere was more like that of a wake. The hotel's padrone begged Renata as a favor to play Chopin's "Polonaise" on the grand piano in the salon, and that was the high point of the evening. After that, Hadley went with Ernest to their room to help him make a clean typescript of the vignettes he had written for Margaret Anderson. And to confirm her dread that he could never again pack a manuscript into a valise without thinking of his work she had lost in the Gare de Lyon, he said, "They're not much, but they're all I have ready for publication. If only those others hadn't been stolen. . . ."

Hadley had hoped they would make love that night, but Ernest was too glum for that, and the next morning they had to get up early so Ernest could catch the six o'clock train for Venice, where he would transfer to the Simplon Orient Express for Paris. He was going to Paris for clean shirts and to have his suit cleaned before going on to the Ruhr.

"I'll have to get a haircut, too," he groused as they stood on the station platform in the first light of dawn, waiting for the train. Flaky snow was falling. Ernest was wearing a beret that turned white under the snow, and the shoulders of his great coat were powdered with snowflakes.

Hadley ran her fingers through the long hair that fell over his collar. "I love your hair the way it is." She lowered her voice to an intimate whisper as she said, "How are you going to be my Catherine if you don't have long hair?"

"Well, there's no help for it," he said grudgingly, refusing to enter into her erotic intimacy. "When I get to the Ruhr, I'll have to look like a damned reporter again."

"Oh, Tatie, I'm so sorry," she said, feeling guilty. Even the train being late seemed to be her fault.

"You go on back," he said in a martyred tone. "You're cold. No use both of us standing here."

"No, I'll wait with you." She was willing to forego the discomfort. "We could go inside."

Inside the station house was a big stove that glowed with heat. Other passengers were inside, in the light of lamps, drinking coffee purchased from a vendor.

"No, I'll wait out here," he said, as if to spite the cold. Glancing upward, he added in a tone of sour envy, "Be great skiing tomorrow, if this keeps up."

"Oh, I'm sorry," Hadley said, finding herself in a position of being sorry there was going to be great skiing tomorrow if he wasn't going to be there to enjoy it.

When the train came, they kissed good-bye and he said he would be back in a couple of weeks, and as he stepped into the car he said in a begrudging tone, "Have fun."

Hadley waved at him once through the train window, then turned away and walked back to the hotel in the softly falling snow.

27

McAlmon

NANCY CUNARD HINTED to McAlmon that Ezra Pound's lovemaking during their recent tryst in Reggio di Calabria was less than memorable. But that hadn't come as a surprise to her, since she and Ezra had had a long dalliance in England a few years back, and his lack of sexual finesse hadn't mattered to her in Reggio because if she had been looking for good sex, she would have got herself a sailor. No; what she wanted from Ezra was his acumen as a poet and critic. Nancy Cunard loved to write poetry. And if she returned from her assignation with Ezra with no kudos for his sexual performances, she was full of praises for his editing abilities.

"It's no wonder," she told McAlmon, "that Eliot dedicated *The Waste Land* to Ezra. Ezra says he blue-penciled out about a third before Eliot published it, and I wouldn't doubt it. Look what he did to my poems."

She and McAlmon were lounging in the glass-enclosed solarium on the roof of Nancy's Venetian palazzo, sunbathing in the nude. McAlmon had been proofreading William Carlos Williams' book of poems, *Spring and All*, which Sylvia Beach had sent him from Paris. When he had sent Sylvia the cable asking her to forward his mail to Venice, he had neglected to mention the letter in which she had confessed her love for him. As Sylvia had said in her letter, if her love for him was unrequited, they need never mention it, and that was the tack McAlmon intended to take.

McAlmon put aside *Spring and All* when Nancy asked him to take a look at her poems, with the idea that if he liked them, he would consider publishing them in Contact Editions. McAlmon was impressed. Many were quite good. He also saw the wisdom and correctness of Pound's cuts and criticisms.

"Sure," McAlmon told her after reading the poems. "Clean them up, like Pound suggests, and, sure, I'll publish 'em." He sighed and raised himself up on one elbow to refill his glass from the bottle of champagne beside them in a bucket of ice. "But for now, I would like not to think about po'try and litchachure, if you don't mind. For the moment, I want nothing more than to be a Venetian hedonist."

He downed the bubbly, then snuggled down on his Arab rug to soak up the pale, thin sunlight of March that penetrated the glass walls of the solarium. Happy to have escaped the rains and boredom of Rapallo, he felt the sunlight stirring the ashes of old desires. He remembered the first lines of Eliot's *Waste Land,* about April being the cruelest month because it mixes memory with desire and stirs up new life in the dead land. That was how McAlmon felt now, restless with the need to burst forth with new life, even though April was still nearly a month away.

"I join you in that desire," Nancy murmured languidly, and stretched her naked body like a cat. She licked spilled champagne from her fingers, then closed her eyes against the sun.

McAlmon turned to contemplate Nancy's body lying next to him. With her eyes closed, she was unaware of McAlmon's inspection, so he took his time, noting her many physical attractions: a beautiful, slim, sun-browned body that had never been stretched by childbearing (she had got rid of that problem, once and for all, a few years ago in Paris by having a hysterectomy), and not yet ravaged by time (she was no more than thirty-five), and she had the fine features of a Michelangelo statue.

All these qualities—and yet she held no physical attraction for McAlmon. Nor did he apparently hold any for her. She had never made any seductive overtures toward him, or invited any from him. She apparently had concluded that he was exclusively a homosexual, and had accepted him simply as a good friend and a colleague, nothing more. He, however, did not consider himself exclusively homosexual. He liked to think he was still open to possibilities. But a love affair between him and Nancy would be, in spite of her many undeniable attractions, foolish. He would never be able to deal with her strident, pushy, castrating femininity. And just as well, for he valued her friendship, and long-term friendships with her were possible; long-term affairs were not.

As he was studying her, he noticed a man in a peignoir signaling to them from the roof of the palazzo directly across the San Barnaba canal.

"Who's that?" McAlmon asked.

Nancy opened her eyes and followed the direction of his gaze. Seeing the man, she raised up on her elbows.

"Oh, that's Cole," she said, and sat up straight. She had large breasts for her slim body, but they were firm and shapely. She waved at the man, and then entered into a mime of hand signals.

"He's inviting us to dine with them this evening," she said. "What do you say?"

McAlmon shrugged. "Suit yourself. Who are 'them'?"

Nancy made an *O* by placing the tips of her thumb and middle finger together to signal okay, and he raised seven fingers to indicate the time. After another signaled okay from her, the man waved and went back into the palazzo.

"That's Cole Porter," Nancy explained. "He and his wife, Linda, have had the Rezzonico for a year or so now. Nice people. Charming. Americans."

"Cole Porter?"

"You've heard of him? A composer—jazz, show tunes, that sort of thing."

"Sure. I've never met him, but he hangs out at Zelli's sometimes, and the black singers there often sing his stuff. But I had no idea that a jazz composer could be living here in Venice in a grand palazzo on the Grand Canal. How's he do it?"

"He has a rich wife. He has an inheritance of a million or more," Nancy said, "but Linda's divorce from her first husband brought her twice that much, and she doesn't mind spending it."

She went on to explain that the Cole Porter–Linda Lee Thomas marriage wasn't a simple marriage of convenience, it was a marriage between two people who, though they loved each other dearly, made no conjugal claims upon the other. As Nancy described them, Cole was a flaming faggot, and, as far as anybody knew, Linda was asexual.

"It looks a little like a mother-son relationship," Nancy conjectured, "and she spoils him outrageously. Last summer, when they were living in a villa on the Cap d'Antibes, she hired Stravinsky to come down from Paris and teach him harmony and composition. That's like hiring Picasso to teach your kid how to draw. Very costly, I should think, but anything for her darling boy."

Linda wanted Cole to compose "serious" music, Nancy said, rather than the Broadway show tunes that he preferred, and though she was willing to spend large sums to help him be "serious," he kept composing what he called "fun" music. And that was what he was engaged in that evening when Nancy and McAlmon crossed the San Barnaba Canal to the Porters' palazzo. When they were shown into the salon by the butler, Cole was at a grand piano, playing for a couple, Gerald Murphy and his wife, Sara. Cole and Gerald were old friends and fraternity brothers from Yale. Prior to moving to Venice, Cole and Linda had lived in a château on the French Riviera, and it was by their invitation that Gerald and Sara Murphy had visited Cap d'Antibes, fell in love with it, bought themselves a villa there, and now divided their time between Paris and the Riviera. Now Gerald had come to Venice to ask Cole to write a score for an avant-garde ballet.

As McAlmon learned during dinner, Gerald Murphy had been commissioned by the Ballet Suédois in Paris to create an American ballet, and he had worked out a story line to be called, *Within the Quota,* about a young Swedish immigrant's impressions of America. If it came to fruition, it would be presented later that year at the Théâtre des Champs-Élysées in Paris. Besides writing the story line, Gerald would also do the sets and costumes and paint a backdrop for the ballet.

McAlmon guessed Gerald to be in his middle thirties, and his wife, Sara, to be four or five years older than he. In spite of his rather mature age, Gerald was happy to claim that he was still an art student—a student of Fernand Léger, to be sure, and certainly not a student to starve in a garret. Gerald Murphy was wealthy, the heir to the Mark Cross Company fortune, and his talent as a painter was highly regarded by the avant-garde artists and gallery owners of Paris' Left Bank. So he was more than just an art student, or a rich dilettante playing at being an artist; he was a man with many proven artistic talents and ambitions. In addition, he and Sara were two of the most charming, classy people McAlmon had ever met.

Cole and Gerald talked about the Ballet Suédois production all through dinner. Cole seemed excited by the idea, but Linda, a lovely and gracious lady, cautioned Cole that the collaboration with Gerald would take time away from his "serious" composing. Cole's excitement admitted no impediments. He would have his way. The picture of epicene sophistication, as effervescent as the Perrier-Jouët champagne he loved so much, Cole Porter seemed in perpetual celebration of life.

Finished with dinner, Cole said to Gerald and Sara, "Oh, come on, I can't wait to begin," and hurried to his grand piano in the salon, saying, "We'll have a Swedish polka that transposes into jazz! With lots of jangly city rhythms! Oh, it'll be marvelous, darlings, marvelous!"

Nancy Cunard, finishing her espresso, also excused herself to follow Cole. McAlmon's appreciation for music in the making wasn't sufficient to draw him into the salon, and he had no wish to leave Linda alone at the table.

"Would you like some brandy and a cigar, Mr. McAlmon?" she asked, and when he gratefully accepted, she dispatched the hovering uniformed servant girl to supply him.

As a conversational gambit, McAlmon complimented Linda on the magnificence of her palazzo, and she, with obvious pride and pleasure, gave him a brief history of the structure, naming some of the archbishops and diplomats for whom it had served as a residence in the past.

"It's said that this was where Casanova himself was living when he was denounced and imprisoned by the Inquisition in 1755 for 'impiety, necromancy, profligacy, and licentiousness,' " she said in a tone that supplied the quotation marks. "Then Lord Byron lived here for a while."

Sensing that McAlmon's interest was not merely polite or pruri-ent, she then offered to give him a tour. With a Cuban cigar in one hand and a brandy snifter in the other, he was led into rooms whose ceilings were vaulted, frescoed, and gilded, em-bossed with the most florid moldings, all the product of work-manship that had lasted for more than two centuries. He walked under huge chandeliers that had been crafted by the artisans of the doges. He passed through massive mahogany doors that opened onto enormous rooms, the walls of which were covered with medieval tapestries, the floors with antique Oriental rugs. There was a great marble staircase with couchant lions for balus-trades. When they entered the master bedroom, Linda said, "This is the room, and that's the bed, in which Robert Browning died."

McAlmon had seen some palatial homes in his travels, includ-ing the Ellerman's mansion in London, but he had never seen anything to compare with the sensuous richness of this Venetian palazzo. Sir John Ellerman knew how to make money; Cole and Linda Porter knew how to spend it.

Cole was fortunate. To have married a woman as gracious as Linda, a woman who loved him tenderly and unconditionally, a woman who was rich enough to give him all this and require little in return. Most men would have considered that McAlmon himself had been lucky to have married a woman whose father was wealthy, but there had never been any love between McAlmon and Bryher, and certainly McAlmon received from her none of the satisfaction of being loved and pampered that Cole received from Linda.

During his monthlong stay in Nancy's Casa Maniella, McAlmon became friends with Cole and Linda. He dined at their palazzo occasionally, and attended the parties they threw for the socially prominent foreigners residing in Venice. But for him, the most memorable party was the one Cole gave while Linda was away on a trip to Paris. Since she had been unable to dissuade Cole from writing the score to the ballet *Within the Quota,* Linda had decided to support him in the endeavor, even to renting and decorating a flat in Paris where he could live and compose in palatial comfort while attending the rehearsals for the ballet. And while she was away, Cole's private gondolier paddled over to Nancy's palazzo one day to deliver an invitation.

"Cole's having an impromptu costume party tomorrow night," McAlmon told Nancy when he found her having breakfast early that afternoon. Infante, the servant girl, stood behind Nancy's chair as Nancy ladled caviar from a small wooden spatula onto a bit of buttered toast. "Will you be going?"

"I haven't been invited," she said.

"Of course you are."

"No. A costume party is Cole's code word for an all boy party. You can go either as a fem or a butch, but cock and balls are required by all."

McAlmon knew what that meant, having been to many such parties in Berlin, but he hadn't brought with him any clothes that could be made into a costume. Nancy said that if he wanted to go as a fem, she would be happy to loan him one of her more daring gowns. She and McAlmon were close to the same size, so the idea seemed feasible, and that afternoon, they went through her enormous wardrobe and he tried on a number of gowns. They finally settled for a flowing mauve chiffon backless evening dress that offered ample access to groping hands. Since the gown sagged in the breast area, Nancy talked him into wearing one of her brassieres stuffed with toilet paper. And the next evening, just before he left for the party, Nancy persuaded him to let her shave the hairs off his shoulders that had been exposed by the backless dress, after which she helped him to get dressed. She also supplied him with makeup and helped him apply it, getting a giggle out of the amount of kohl she put around his eyes and the bright, lacquer-gleaming lipstick she put on his mouth.

"Blot it before you kiss anybody," she warned. "It smears easily."

"I never kiss on the first date," he joked.

"Before you suck somebody off, then," she said.

"Oh, Nancy," he chided with a gesture of femininity. He was sitting at a dressing table, gazing at his reflection in the mirror, while Nancy stood behind him, trying to do something with his hair.

"You could use a wig," she said, "but I don't have any. Maybe Cole has one you can borrow."

"No, no, I like it this way. With my hair this short, I could pass for a lesbian."

"There won't be any lesbians at this party. This is strictly boys' night."

"But no roughhouse. I hate that stuff. With those young butches in Berlin, you never knew if you were going to be fighting or fucking, or both, maybe at the same time. Truth is, I'm getting too old for that sort of thing."

"No, not here. Cole likes the rough trade sometimes, but when he does, he usually goes down on the docks and picks up sailors. He gets beat up and robbed pretty often, but nothing like that'll be going on at this party. He's a frightful snob is our Cole, and very careful about who he invites into his home. Can't afford to have to call the coppers, you see."

"What about Linda? Does she know about this?"

"It only happens when she goes away, so I really can't say. She probably does, but chooses to ignore it, as long as Cole keeps it discreet." She stepped back to take a look at him in the mirror. "Well! Look at you! I think you're ready now."

Nancy's private gondola took McAlmon across the San Barnaba Canal to the landing at the Porters' palazzo, where the party had already begun. Cole, wrapped in a swath of gossamer, like an Indian Maharani, and wearing a black boa and dangling earrings, flitted about, greeting and entertaining and flirting with the twenty-five or thirty guests, and when he saw McAlmon his mascaraed eyes widened with delight.

"Oh, Bob, you look divine!" he cried. "Such nice tits!" He playfully squeezed one, then giggled. "Oh, there are so many sweet young things here I want you to meet. But first! Cocaine and champagne!" He guided McAlmon to a table, around which crowded a number of young drag queens and brute boys, all taking turns snorting huge lines of cocaine and drinking glasses of champagne. Dour middle-aged caterers dressed in tuxedos, looking as out of place as priests in a whorehouse, kept the cocaine plentiful on the table's glass top and passed out snorting straws to the guests. The caterers also made sure there were magnums of Perrier-Jouët cooling in antique pewter ice buckets, and that the glasses of the guests were kept full.

"Oh, Mario, there you are!" Cole said in Italian to one young man dressed in a pink ballerina's tutu. "Mario, sweetie pie, I want you to meet Bobby McAlmon, my next door neighbor. Oh, and you simply must get Bobby to tell you about Berlin someday!"

"Is it as wild as they say?" Mario asked excitedly in Italian. He was heavily made up and wore a blond wig.

"Oh, divinely depraved, my dear!" Cole said. "Simply and divinely depraved. Isn't that true, Bobby?"

"Divinely," McAlmon said.

A gramophone was playing jazz records in the background, and the guests were laughing and dancing about. After Cole and McAlmon had cocaine and champagne, Cole led him away to meet a young brute costumed in black leather pants, a fur vest, and a plumed Kaiser Wilhelm helmet. Pietro was his name. He looked McAlmon over approvingly and asked if he would like to dance.

"First another line or two of coke to get me in the mood," McAlmon said, and by the time he snorted more cocaine, then washed the lovely metallic taste down with champagne, Pietro was somewhere else.

At the center of a milling group, Cole was asking Mario when he was going to dance for everyone, and Mario said he would love to dance if Cole would play some adagio for him on the piano. Cole was quick to comply. With exaggerated mannerisms, his waved the ends of his boa like pompoms as he went to his grand piano, called for the gramophone to be turned off, then began to play one of his own compositions, while Mario swished about in a bad imitation of Nijinsky, to sighs and cries of delight from the others.

McAlmon was a passive observer of all this. True, he found the scene titillating, but it was the titillation of a small boy peeping through a keyhole at a forbidden scene, becoming erotically aroused by the scene, but knowing he could never be a part of it. Perhaps it was because of his upbringing as a Calvinist preacher's son, or perhaps it was because he, as a writer, was by nature an observer of life, a spectator, not an active participant. He had felt the same way when he experienced the perfumed decadence of the blue-lit bars and nightclubs of Berlin. The only time he had participated there was when he met a partner who needed his passivity as a provocation, as a way to excite both himself and McAlmon by playing McAlmon's master.

The same was true of Cole's party. McAlmon could have found among the many young men a lover for the evening, but as the party progressed and erotic play became more flagrant, his passivity put them off. Even Pietro gave up on him after a few dances and a couple of kisses, and went to find someone more responsive. McAlmon wasn't sure, but the likely truth was that he wanted to be seduced, even coerced. That would be a way to escape the moral responsibility.

Before he could insinuate that into any brute boy's head, and while many of the men had paired off and gone to find bedrooms and unoccupied sofas, while others were still dancing and snorting cocaine and drinking, one of the drag queens rushed into the salon from a side door, shrieking, *"Polizia! Polizia!"*

McAlmon heard the sounds of motorboats pulling up to the canal landing, motor cars in the side streets, booted feet pounding across marble floors, doors banged open, and policemen, in Fascist uniforms, waving batons and blowing whistles, apparently hoping to paralyze the guests with terror, ran into the salon.

They swarmed in, coralling the guests, pulling them out of hiding places, slapping the hysterical ones, lining them up along one wall. Though McAlmon didn't try to run or resist, he was grabbed and flung against the wall by a policeman, who shouted, "Get in line, you degenerate scum!"

The scene was still one of comic opera chaos when one of the police sergeants shouted, *"Silénzio!* Silence, all of you!" and then turned to salute a man who had just entered from the gondola landing. This was the Venetian chief of police himself, dressed in his florid, gold-braided uniform, followed by a retinué of lieutenants and lackeys. First his attention was called to the table that glistened with crystalline residue. One of the policemen drew a finger through the residue and tasted it on the tip of his tongue.

"Cocaine," he confirmed.

"Ha!" the chief said in a tone of operatic triumph. "Who is the master here?" On being told by one terrified young man that it was Signor Porter, the chief demanded, "Where is he? Where is this Signor Porter?" Getting no answer, he walked along the line of prisoners, asking the older ones, "Who are you? Are you Signor Porter? No? Who are you?" A lieutenant followed at his elbow, taking names in a notebook.

When he got to McAlmon, McAlmon told him his name, and the chief demanded, *"Lei da dov'è viene?"*

"Vengo dagli Stati Uniti."

"Americano!" the chief sneered. "This Signor Porter is an *Americano,* also, is he not? Which one is he?"

Cole wasn't among those lined up against the wall. He had apparently found a place to hide, but not for long. By the time the chief heard a few piteous requests from some of the young men not to be arrested, claiming the scandal would ruin their lives, Cole and Mario had been found and dragged into the majestic presence of the chief of police.

"Here he is," said the policeman who had Cole in one hand and Mario in the other. "I've got the degenerate dog. He and this one were hiding beneath a bed."

Cole was a pathetic mess. His eyes were wide with fear, his lipstick was smeared, he had lost one earring, and his hair, as if in evidence of how terrified he was, was mussed and standing on end. He had lost his boa, and his gossamer garment was half undone and trailing behind him, exposing his ass to the elements. But poor Mario was even worse. His tutu was gone. Except for the blond wig and heavy makeup, he was stark naked. When hauled in front of the chief, he bowed his head in mortification and tried to cover his genitals with his hands.

"So you are this Signora Porter," the chief said to Cole, and then added with scathing sarcasm, "the *man* of the palazzo—eh? The degenerate who corrupts our Venetian youth?" He tilted his head toward Mario as if to use him as an example of corrupted youth, but suddenly his face twisted with consternation. He lowered his head, trying to see Mario's downcast face. The lieutenant at the chief's side grabbed Mario's hair and attempted to jerk his head back, but the blond wig came off in his hand.

"Mario!" the chief cried. "Mario! Oh, my god!"

Cringing, hiding his genitals with his hands, Mario blushed and nodded. *"Sí, Papa."*

The chief became unhinged. "Oh, no!" he cried to the heavens. "No! No! Not my Mario! No! Oh, *impossibly! Impossibly! Mio figilo!* My own son . . . a . . . a pervert!" King Lear on the heath had little on him as he cried out to heaven about the perfidy of offspring, but then he apparently changed his mind about the impossibility that it was Mario, for he suddenly slapped him, hard. "You!" he shouted. "Your poor mother will die of shame!" He looked for a moment as if he was restraining himself from pummeling poor cringing Mario; then he turned on all the prisoners, and cried hysterically, "To jail! I will see that you all go to prison, you despicable perverts! To jail with them! Put them in chains! Kill them!"

But the cooler head of the lieutenant prevailed. When he said, "One moment, please, Chief, a word with you," the other policemen waited. The lieutenant showed the chief his notebook, saying in a voice that was only sometimes audible, ". . . give this some thought, sir . . . person here"—indicating a young drag queen— "the son of the Argentine ambassador . . . this young man . . . the grandson of the archbishop."

"Has the whole world become depraved? Let them go, then, but arrest the others. I will ask Il Duce to put them in front of a firing squad!"

"But, sir, think," said the lieutenant, still sotto voce, "If we arrest the others . . . bring them to trial . . . how can we keep Mario and these other two out of the scandal?"

"Aggghhhaaa!" the chief cried like a wounded beast, flailing his arms. "Get out, all of you! Leave! All of you, go! And you, and you," he shouted, stabbing his finger at McAlmon and Cole, "you foreigners get out of Venice! If I see either of you in Venice again, I will personally kill you! Get out of my city!"

Like the others who were hurriedly scattering for the exits, McAlmon headed for the nearest side door, which let out onto the Alberti walkway bordering the San Barnaba Canal. He glanced around for an available gondola to take him the thirty or so feet to Nancy's palazzo, but since there was no gondola near, he hesitated only long enough to take a deep breath before he jumped off the walkway. The water was foul, and cold, but he was a good swimmer; it took him only a few strokes to cross the canal.

Nancy and most of her servants were out on the landing, watching the raid. When McAlmon reached them, the butler pulled him out of the water. Across the way, amid shouts and cries, Cole's guests were piling into the overloaded gondolas, or jumping into the Grand Canal to swim away.

"Good Lord, Bob," Nancy chided as McAlmon stood before her, streaming water and shivering. "You shouldn't swim in the canal, it's nothing but a sewer."

"I've been in shit before," he said. "And now I'm getting out of this shit hole as fast as I can."

He stormed into the palazzo, streaming sewerage water across valuable rugs, with Nancy following close behind and giving orders to the servants to fix him a warm bath. Nancy was amused by the incident, and could hardly suppress a laugh when McAlmon went into his bedroom and turned on the lights and got a good look at himself in the dressing mirror. His water-logged bosom had slipped down to his waist, the chiffon dress was clinging to his body, his hair was streaming water, and his face was streaked with black trickles of kohl. He looked like something out of a Breugelian nightmare.

"I know it's not funny," she said apologetically, "but you do look a sight. And Cole? Did they let him go, too? I was afraid we'd be up all night, with lawyers and bail bondsmen, trying to get you chaps out of jail. What happened?"

She took a bathrobe from a closet and held it as he pulled off the dress and sandals, all the while explaining why they had let everyone go. "But they did tell Cole and me to get out of town, and that's exactly what I'm going to do, on the next train to anywhere. I've heard about what happens to fairies in Fascist jails. I don't know what Cole's going to do. I didn't stick around to find out."

"Oh, he'll be all right. When Linda gets back from Paris, she'll grease a few palms, as you Yanks say, and that'll be the end of it. She's gotten him out of such scrapes before, and the Fascist coppers are just as corrupt as they were in the old regime."

Maybe so, but McAlmon wasn't waiting around to find out. While he was having a bath and getting dressed in his traveling clothes, a servant was packing his bags, and Nancy found a railway timetable.

"Look," she said, "there's an Express arriving from Constantinople at midnight, on its way to Paris. If we hurry, you can make it."

She telephoned for a motorboat taxi, which picked McAlmon up from the landing, where Nancy gave him a good-bye hug, then the taxi whisked him off to the Venice train station. He got there only a few minutes before the train pulled out. Rushing to the ticket window, he bought a ticket for a first-class single compartment, and the porter who helped him aboard the Pullman car barely got off before the train jerked into motion.

McAlmon sat down on the compartment's plush sofa bed to collect himself. Then he spoke through the tube that provided direct communication with the car *conducteur*. In French, McAlmon asked if the wagon-salon-restaurant was still open. The answering voice told him that the restaurant itself was closed, but that the smoking lounge and library car, where one could buy drinks and *casse-croûte,* would be open all night. McAlmon left orders for his sofa to be converted to a bed, then made his way along the gently swaying cars to the lounge, which bore a striking resemblance to the ritziest continental *salons de société.* The wall panelings were of the finest woods and workmanship—teak and mahogany, inlaid with ebony and rosewood, carved into scrolls, scallops and friezes, cornices and borders, reaching to arched ceilings that were embellished with romantic paintings. The car was furnished with heavy leather armchairs and footstools and ornate standing ashtrays. There was an ornately carved bookcase at one end that contained both popular novels and works of literature, as well as travel guides, maps, and newspapers in French, Italian, German, and English. In an atmosphere heavy with cigar smoke a dozen men gathered in a convivial group, most of them in smoking jackets, talking, chuckling, perhaps planning seductions or financial deals.

Made self-conscious by his lack of evening clothes, McAlmon found an armchair in the end of the car farthest from the group of men. He ordered cognac and a Cuban cigar from a liveried waiter, and was leisurely perusing the *London Times,* enjoying the benefits of being rich, when another man entered the lounge. McAlmon would have paid no attention, except the man's clothes—an old, baggy, well-worn three-piece tweed suit and scruffy shoes—made him look even more out of place than McAlmon.

It was Ernest Hemingway.

"Well, I'll be damned," McAlmon said. "Look who's here."

"Yeah, Mac," Hemingway said. "Fancy meeting you here. You just get aboard in Venice?"

"Yeah. And you?"

Hemingway dropped into the armchair next to McAlmon's. "Just came down from Cortina, headed for the Ruhr. Newspaper assignment. Going through Paris. That where you're headed?"

The waiter, in his elaborate nineteenth-century costume, took Hemingway's order for a Scotch-and-water. The subtlety of tone as he said, *"Tres bein, monsieur,"* conveyed his judgment that Hemingway and McAlmon, though allowed to inhabit the car, were nevertheless not of the same class as the gentlemen who were appropriately dressed.

"Yeah, thought I'd better go back to Paris and get some books ready, if I'm going to keep calling myself a publisher," McAlmon said. "How's your writing coming? Doing anything that we could put into a book?"

With an irresolute tilt of his head, Hemingway said, "I've been polishing six sketches that I'm taking to Paris to give to *The Little Review.* You might want to read them."

"Sure. Why don't you bring 'em by my compartment in the morning? Compartment B, Xena car."

"You got a first-class compartment?" Hemingway said. "I might've known. I'm in second class."

The waiter brought Hemingway's Scotch-and-water.

Hemingway's tone prompted McAlmon to tell the waiter, "Put it on my tab, *garçon*. And bring me another cognac."

"*Tres bien, monsieur,*" said the waiter.

"Listen, Mac," Hemingway said in a confidential tone after downing half of the Scotch in one swallow, "there's something I want to talk to you about." He paused to summon up his determination, then said in a voice barely above a whisper, "In Rapallo—remember?—you mentioned Djuna knew someone in Paris, a doctor, who does abortions. You weren't just bullshitting? She really knows someone? A real doctor?"

"Well, as far's I know, he's a real doctor. I don't think he has a license to practice medicine in France, if that's what you mean, but he once practiced in America, they say. Dan Mahoney's his name—Doc Mahoney."

"What I was wondering is . . . you know, if he's trustworthy. Does he know what he's doing?"

"I don't know. You might ask Djuna Barnes. He once performed an abortion for her, and I guess she had no complaints. They became friends. Still are."

"And he's not some crazy wastrel with dirty fingernails—that sort?"

"Look, you read that story of mine called 'Miss Knight'? Remember? About the transvestite who hated one-night stands with uncircumcised men—'blind meat'? Well, that was Dan Mahoney."

"A transvestite?" Hemingway said. "A queer?"

The waiter brought McAlmon's cognac, and Ernest ordered another Scotch—a double.

"The queerest of the queer," McAlmon said, unable to resist the temptation to shock Hemingway a little.

"Good God," Hemingway said, as if he could hardly take in the enormity of the world's depravity. "Is everybody a goddamn queer?"

"Everyone except thee and me," McAlmon said breezily, "and sometimes I wonder about thee."

"What do you mean?" Hemingway asked.

"Just joking," McAlmon said. "Take it easy."

"Some joke," Hemingway said.

"In bad taste," McAlmon conceded. "But you can't blame me, can you, if sometimes me thinketh thou doth protest too much?"

"And what do you mean by that?" Hemingway asked.

"Nothing," McAlmon said. "Have a drink."

They both drained their glasses and ordered fresh drinks. The conversation had petered out by the time the train reached Verona, when McAlmon decided he had better try to get some sleep. He suggested to Hemingway that the three of them have breakfast together in the morning.

"The three of us?" Hemingway said suspiciously. "You got somebody with you?"

"No. I meant Hadley."

"Hadley? Hadley's not with me. I left her in Cortina. I'll be going back there as soon as this assignment's over. We're going to try to get in some more skiing, maybe some fishing, before we leave there. It's a wonderful place. Why don't you come and visit?"

Now it was McAlmon's turn to be slightly incredulous. "You left Hadley alone in Cortina?"

"Oh, no, of course not. Renata Borgatti's there to keep her company. She came up from Venice to do some skiing. But you know about that. You told her we were there. She's swell. We've all become pals."

McAlmon's incredulity didn't lessen, but it did change in kind from puzzlement to bemusement. He was having a hard time figuring out what was going on here. Had Hemingway actually left his wife alone in a quaint little isolated town in the Italian alps with Renata Borgatti, one of the most desirable and seductive lesbians in Paris, while he went off to write dispatches from a war zone in Germany? What did it mean? What did it portend? Like Hadley leaving his manuscripts where they could easily be stolen, was Hemingway trying to get rid of his wife by making it easy for someone to steal her away?

28

Alice B. Toklas

THERE CAME A knocking at the door at 27 rue de Fleurus one morning in the middle of March. Hèléne brought the news that Ernest Hemingway was at the door and wished to see M'dame. Gertrude had only just awoken and was having her morning coffee and brioche in the dining room as she perused the morning's mail. Alice would have told Hèléne to tell Hemingway to come back later in the day, but Gertrude said, "No, have him come up," because she must show her gratitude for the book review Hemingway had written about her most recent creative effort, *Geography and Plays,* a book which Gertrude had—once again—published at her own expense. Hemingway had written the review in Rapallo and sent it to the Paris edition of the *Chicago Tribune*. Published a couple of weeks ago on March 5, the review had been complimentary, declaring that "Gertrude Stein is probably the most first-rate intelligence employed in writing today." One could perhaps infer from this that Gertrude was a genius, but Alice wished that Hemingway had come right out and said it.

As Alice told Gertrude on the day the review ran, she was glad that Hemingway put her above such writers as Sinclair Lewis, H.G. Wells, and D.H. Lawrence; having granted that, however, Alice tried very carefully to convey to Gertrude the uneasiness she felt about the whole tone of the review.

"It's not so much a laudatory review of your book," she said, "as it is an attack on other writers. It's as if he, rather than putting you on a pedestal and genuflecting to your genius, is using you as a sharp stick with which to poke other writers in their pants. There's real venom here, Lovey, bitter, bitter venom, and I just hope that others don't hold it against you that he uses you to spread this venom. I mean, look at this, what he says about 'the unbelievably stupid young men who compile the *Dial.*' That's Scofield Thayer he's talking about—is that the Scofield Thayer we met? Is that the Scofield Thayer who just gave dear Sherwood Anderson the two-thousand-dollar *Dial* prize? Lovey, these are powerful people he's pissing on, and yet who is he? Nobody. He's never even had anything published, except some smutty little poems and some hack newspaper articles that nobody has ever read, and yet—what was it he says about D.H. Lawrence, whom you admire so much? Here it is: that he 'writes with the intelligence of a head waiter'! What is that but the piddle of a bitter, smart-alecky kid showing off?—using your book to draw attention to himself?"

Well, Alice may not have convinced Gertrude, but she had raised suspicion about Hemingway. Alice didn't like the man. She had an instinctive distrust of him, and she trusted her instincts. Hemingway seemed to have a shadow that one could sense but never really see, as if there were another Hemingway there who wouldn't come out. But of course she was always polite to him, always hospitable. She had to be for Gertrude's sake, who still had what she called a "weakness" for Hemingway. And while Gertrude was willing to believe that Hemingway's review of *Geography and Plays* was more about him than it was about her, she still felt she had to invite him in and express her gratitude for the review.

"I don't get enough favorable reviews to allow me to be ungrateful for those I do get," Gertrude said. "Invite him in," she said to Hèléne.

Hemingway said he had just come from Cortina d'Ampézzo, en route to Germany, where he was to write some articles for a newspaper on the French seizure of the Ruhr—information that caused her to be a trifle upset with him.

"But we've told you, haven't we told you, Hemingway, to stop wasting your time writing for newspapers? Why will you not listen? Will you have coffee?" To Alice: "Get Hemingway a cup of coffee."

"We need the money," Hemingway said, collapsing into a chair at the table next to Gertrude, and then seemed to summon up all his strength to face a fatal condition. "Hadley is . . . Hadley is . . . *enceinte*"—using French, as if that might make it less real.

"Oh, congratulations." But reading his face, Gertrude added, "But from the way you looky look, perhaps condolences would be more in order. You do not, I take it, do not want Hadley to be off-springing?"

"Damnit, I'm too young to be a father," he complained, like a boy protesting against an adult order, as if he wanted—expected?—Gertrude to do something about it.

"Oh, dear," Gertrude said. "That's sad. Isn't that sad?" she asked Alice.

"That's sad," Alice concurred, sincerely, for she thought it was sad to bring an unwanted child into the world. Having taken up some knitting, she took a chair at the far end of the table so that she could be apart and yet still remain close to the conversation. She had noticed how Gertrude's face lit up when Hemingway came into the room, and how Hemingway fell into a sort of slouchy familiarity in Gertrude's presence, an attitude that Gertrude would allow only to a few favorites.

She had seen it before—in Florence, for instance, when Mabel Dodge had tried to win Gertrude for herself, and, later, a woman named Mildred Avery had fallen in love with Gertrude, and then there had been Gertrude's attraction to that Etta Cone woman. None of these women had succeeded, of course, in coming between Gertrude and Alice. But this was something new. This was the first time Alice felt she had to fend off a man. And there was no use pooh-poohing her fears by telling her that men—real men—weren't sexually attracted to Gertrude, because here was one who obviously was. Of course, this begged the question, was he a real man? If the gossip in the lesbian community was correct, he was certainly different from most men, because Gertrude wasn't the first lesbian to attract his lustful looks. Alice had heard how Hemingway had run after Margaret Anderson, and Djuna Barnes had some stories to tell about how Hemingway had tried to get her into bed.

Still, those women were young and lovely in conventional ways; Gertrude was not. Besides being old enough to be Hemingway's mother, Gertrude had the sturdy physique of a peasant potato digger. So what could be the nature of Hemingway's attraction? Was it some sort of Oedipal mother love? It certainly seemed so. Whenever he came into Gertrude's presence, he came with either a small-boy swagger, as if looking for maternal admiration, or with a sulky look of self-pity, looking for maternal comfort.

As for Gertrude, she fell right into the maternal comforting mode. Alice would not have been surprised to see her chuck him under the chin, or pinch a bit of his cheek and shake it and say, "You naughty, naughty boy, you." Well, Alice had her eye on them.

Having him there for an hour or more was enough, and Alice was willing to get rid of him, so that Gertrude could get some writing done and she could go do some shopping, but Gertrude's maternal indulgence and her vanity as a writer allowed Hemingway to stay on and on, as long as he was responding to her as a matriarch and praising her as a writer, which he found ample reason to do, he claimed, after having read *Geography and Plays,* as if he had never read anything of hers before that.

"Hemmy—"

Now it was Hemmy, for God's sake!

"Hemmy, we do, oh, so appreciate your words of praise," Gertrude said, "but you know, Pussy and I, we both wondered— didn't we, Pussy?—we wondered why you would say such harsh things about that nice young man, Scofield Thayer—isn't that his name? The one who edits the *Dial?*—that he was—what was it you said in your review he was?—'unbelievably stupid'? He seemed like such a nice, bright young man to us, didn't he, Pussy? He came here one day, he wanted to meet us, and we thought he was terribly nice, and quite bright, quite right."

"Oh, him," Hemingway said, his voice hard with derision. "Well, I meant both him and that other editor at the *Dial,* Gilbert

Seldes. I hear Seldes has left the magazine now, his sphincter muscle no doubt having lost its attractive tautness."

Alice was shocked. That was one of the reasons she didn't like Hemingway, his language was so crude. And there was that venom again, the smart-alecky little boy thinking up dirty things to say about his betters. Gertrude, being a writer, claimed that there could not be such a thing as a dirty word, not in and of itself, but a glance from the corner of Alice's eye confirmed what Gertrude's long silence conveyed: that she, too, had been taken aback by Hemingway's imagery.

"What are you saying?" Gertrude finally asked. "That this Scofield Thayer and this other one—Seldes?—are pederasts?"

Seeing that he had perhaps gone too far, Hemingway toned his derision down a little when he said, "I suspect they are, yeah."

"Have you ever met them?" Alice asked.

"Nope," he said.

"Then how do you know they're unbelievably stupid?" Gertrude asked. "What could account for such severe judgments, Hemmy? Come on, 'fess up. What have they ever done to you?"

It took a long, expectant silence to drag it out of him, but finally he said in a bitter, sulking voice, "Ezra sent the *Dial* some of my poems last year, with a letter to Thayer, telling him he ought to publish them. They rejected them. Seldes sent me a rejection notice, and Thayer sent Ezra a letter saying I ought to stop writing poetry and stick to newspaper work."

Well, both Gertrude and Alice could understand that, at least. They had received many deriding rejections of Gertrude's work, and they, too, believed that the editors who sent such rejections were unbelievably stupid. However, they could not understand the imputation of pederasty for such stupidity. They could not see what one had to do with the other. They suspected that the pederasty had more to do with Hemingway than it had to do with Thayer and Seldes, and this suspicion was given credence later in the day when Hemingway read to them one of the poems he was going to submit to *The Little Review*. It happened that he was getting a haircut from Gertrude at the time of the reading. He had wanted from Gertrude both a haircut and a reading of the material that he had brought with him in a manila envelope, but she, at Alice's suggestion, agreed to give him a haircut only if he would read his material aloud to them while she was cutting his hair. That way they could get rid of him quicker. This he was glad enough to do. So, perched upon a stool, with a bath towel draped around his shoulders, he held forth while being nicely shorn by Gertrude's pampering and expert hands.

He read the six vignettes, which he had grouped together under the title, "In Our Time." After each vignette, he stopped to get Gertrude's reaction. Snipping away at his dark hair with the scissors, she gave her considered opinion of each piece, which was usually favorable, if only politely so. Nobody asked Alice's opinion, which was a good thing, because she could not have brought herself to say she liked the pieces, even for the sake of polite encouragement. Truthfully, she thought they were merely bits of pedestrian reportage, and the poems seemed, to her, little better than the smutty scrawls one might find on toilet walls.

"This is one I wrote about the Lausanne Peace Conference last year," he announced. "It's called 'They All Made Peace—What Is Peace?'"

Cast in the form of a disjunctive word play that Gertrude herself had originated, but without a glimmer of her genius, the poem—if it was to be called that—ran along in blunt disconnected statements, without merit or interest, until the few lines in which the major statesmen of the peace conference were depicted as pederasts:

> Lord Curzon likes young boys.
> So does Chicherin.
> So does Mustapha Kermal. He is good looking too. His eyes
> are too close together but he makes war. That is the way
> he is.

It went on and on in this vein, and when he finally finished with the thing, Gertrude chuckled wickedly. She combed one side of his hair, snipped a few uneven hairs, and stood back to inspect her handiwork as she said, "Well, Hemmy, there you are again, and again, and again. Tell us," she added in a parody of

seductiveness, "what is this preoccupation you have with pederasty? Why is it so much on your mind? Tell us, do, tell us, do, do,
do."

"I haven't got it on my mind," he said.

"Oh, come, come, you needn't be ashamed of it here. You're
among friends, and we are not prejudiced against pederasts, are
we, Pussy?"

"No, indeed," Alice said truthfully. "Some of my best friends
are pederasts. I'm quite fond of Gide, for instance, and Cocteau."

"But it's not on my mind, I tell you," Hemingway protested.

"We would wager that it was something that happened to you
in your youth," Gertrude ventured, refusing to accept Hemingway's denial. "Think back. Did some pederast fancy you when
you were a lad, a barefoot boy with cheeks of tan? Did he get to
you?"

"Hell, no," he said scornfully. "Sure, when I was a kid, riding
the rails across the country, sometimes staying in hobo camps,
sure, there were tramps who would try something with you if
you were a kid, but I carried a knife. I carried a knife, and I was
prepared to kill a man if he interfered with me."

"Interfered with you?" Gertrude asked. "What do you mean?"

"I mean, if he put his hands on me."

"You'd kill a man, just for putting his hands on you?"

"Well, it'd be according to where he put them, wouldn't it?"

"And if he touched you in the wrong place, you would kill a
man—actually kill a man?"

"Sure. Damn right."

"Did you ever? Kill a man? As a boy?"

It seemed that he had to search his memory for a moment, to
make sure, and then he said, "No, not as a boy. I never had to.
You had to know how to kill a man, though, and you had to
know you would do it, and if the queers knew you would do it,
they sensed it very quickly and let you alone."

Gertrude sighed, and snipped a few more hairs, saying, "It's
very sad, the way of male inverts, is it not? Men that way are to
be pitied."

"Pitied?" he said. "Why in the hell should they be pitied?"

"Because they are sick, and corrupted, and cannot help themselves. The act between men is ugly and repugnant and afterward, they are disgusted with themselves. That's why they take drugs and drink, to palliate this, and afterward they are disgusted with the act, and cannot love themselves or their partners in ugliness, and that's why they must always be seeking new partners. They can never really be happy, poor creatures."

"And it's not that way with women?" Hemingway challenged.

"No. With women, it's the opposite. What they do is not repulsive and disgusting, so they are not made unhappy by doing it. That's why they can lead happy lives together, without violence and drink and drugs."

"Really?" Hemingway said, with the keen interest of someone seeking rare information, but Gertrude signaled an end to the subject by stepping back to appraise the haircut. Seeing that it was good, she said, "There, Samson, Delilah has done her work." She brushed him off with a barber's brush, folded the towel with his hair clippings in it, and began making the signals that were meant to bring his visit to an end—and none too soon, as far as Alice was concerned. She had more important things to do than sit around all day, keeping an eye on those two.

Gertrude accepted his boyish thanks for the haircut and for giving him the benefit of her comments on his vignettes and poems, then said to him as she walked him toward the door, "I look forward to reading your things in *The Little Review.*"

"Oh, by the way," Hemingway said, "do you happen to know where I can find Margaret Anderson? I went by her apartment today, but nobody's there, and the neighbors say she and Jane Heap moved out a week or two ago. I want to make sure she gets this stuff."

"No, I haven't heard," Gertrude said, "but I'm sure you can leave it with Sylvia Beach, she'll get it to Miss Anderson."

"Yeah, but I'd really like to give it to her myself," he said.

Gertrude turned to Alice. "Pussy? Have you heard anything about Margaret Anderson and Jane Heap?"

Alice had no intention of volunteering any information, but since she had been asked, she said, "I hear they've moved out to Fontainebleau and become disciples of that mystical mountebank, Gurdjieff—the one who let poor Katherine Mansfield die of TB, telling her she could get well by smelling cows' breath."

"Gee, I wonder if that'll be the end of the magazine?"

"Well, if the stories are true," Alice said, "the first thing that charlatan does is take away all his disciples' money, then put them to work shoveling manure from the cowsheds. I'd like to see that—elegant Margaret Anderson shoveling cow manure."

Alice could not have found a more depressing note on which to send Hemingway away, except to remind him that his wife was pregnant, which she did by saying, "Will Hadley be needing me to knit some baby booties?"

He had turned at the door. Gertrude held his envelope while he slipped into his mackinaw. "Oh, well, you know I was kind of premature about that," he said, trying to take it back. "It isn't for sure yet. Maybe it's not true. Maybe I'm just worrying for nothing. Look, I'd appreciate it if you wouldn't tell anybody else about it—just in case it's a false alarm."

"Our lips are sealed," Gertrude said knowingly.

After he was gone, Gertrude laughed, the rich laughter that Alice loved so much. "Now I think I can finish my Portrait of Hemingway," she said, heading for her writing table. "It was his eyes, his passionately interested rather than interesting eyes, that betrayed the myopia of not seeing past his nose. Oh, I am so inspired, Pussy, do get me some tea, do, do, do, there's a good Pussy."

29

McAlmon

On his first night back in Paris, McAlmon donned evening clothes and had a fine dinner at Pruniers. Afterward, he took a taxi to Montmartre, to Zelli's Nightclub in rue Pigalle, a plush all-night jazz club, catering to a well-heeled international clientele of princes, pashas, movie stars, dukes, black-sheep scions of noble families, and the few members of the Left Bank literati who could afford dinner jackets, the door charge, and the customary champagne. An Italian from England named Joe Zelli owned the club, but the man who really made it go was a black American named Eugene Bullard, a man of many talents and accomplishments: an aviator, a professional boxer, a jazz drummer. As the only black pilot in the Lafayette Escadrille during the war, Bullard had become a national hero of France, and his fame brought with it the crucial connections Zelli needed to obtain the many licenses necessary to open and operate a nightclub in Paris. And as a musician with some managerial talent, Bullard soon found himself booking all the entertainers at Zelli's. It was he who was responsible for bringing over from America the thirty black jazz musicians who made up Zelli's Royal Box Dance Orchestra, of which Bullard himself was the drummer and leader. And because he was also a professional boxer, he proved to be an ideal bouncer when the need arose. Finally he gave up the drums to become the nightclub's factotum, with duties as manager and host.

Since coming to Paris, McAlmon had often frequented Zelli's to hear the jazz bands and blues singers, and he and Gene Bullard soon became friends. And when he visited Zelli's on his first night back from Venice, he was greeted by Bullard with a hearty handshake and a "Hey, Mac, you're back! Long time no see. Come on in." He ushered McAlmon to a very small but choice table near the bandstand. Tonight Mabel Mercer was singing with her own small combo.

Bullard joined McAlmon at the table for a glass of champagne, then excused himself to attend to business. After McAlmon had been at the table for a couple of hours, doing some serious drinking and enjoying the music and looking around for some young man who might like to join him for champagne or cocktails, he got a pleasant surprise: through the front door of Zelli's came Cole Porter. Cole and Linda were with a party of about ten people, the men in tuxedoes, the women in evening gowns and wraps of expensive furs, with diamonds galore on fingers, necks, and ears. Gene Bullard took over from the maître d' to usher the group to two reserved tables near the bandstand, only a few tables from McAlmon's. They were obviously a party of slumming swells, out for an evening of titillation. Among them McAlmon recognized Princess de Polignac, Duchess de Grammont, the movie star Rudolph Valentino, and Comte Max de Pourtales.

McAlmon waved to Cole through the crowd, and Cole, bubbling with the pleasant surprise of seeing McAlmon, left his party to make his way to him. Cole's dark hair was slicked down with pomade, he was dressed in elegant evening clothes, and he smoked a cigarette in a long, diamond-studded holder. His large, liquidy brown eyes were irrepressible.

"There you are, sweetie pie!" he said. "I'm glad to see you got out of Venice all right. My God, wasn't that a beastly scene! And, my dear, you should have seen what Mario and I were doing when the police burst in! Oh, my God!"

"How did you get here?" McAlmon asked, speaking loudly and close to Cole's perfumed ear in order to be heard above the music. "You couldn't've caught the Orient Express—or at least I didn't see you on it."

"No, no, no, I missed the last Express that night, but guess what! Oh, my dear, you won't believe it! I chartered a plane. There's an airport in Mestre. I'd never flown in a plane in my whole life, but I thought, what the hell, it's better than jail, so off I went. What a ride! They gave me goggles, a sheepskin jacket, and a silk scarf. At first I almost got sick on the smell of oil burning, but once we started over the Alps I forgot about everything else. Splendid! Wonderful! Flying over the Alps is something you must do before you die. There's no sensation besides coming that'll beat it. I'm going to write a song about it."

"So you probably beat me back to Paris."

"Oh, I'm sure I did. We made the trip in five hours! It cost a small fortune, but it was worth it. Look, are you by yourself?"

"So far," McAlmon said.

"Then come over and join our party, will you? Please. I want you to meet some of my friends. But, listen, don't mention that fiasco in Venice in front of Linda, please. She's still furious with me, and doesn't want to hear anymore about it."

Linda, lovely in a shimmering silver lamé gown with a silver fox wrap and a diamond tiara, welcomed McAlmon to the party. Without any formal introductions, Cole quickly made McAlmon known to the crowd, but he made a special effort to acquaint McAlmon with a bearded young bachelor in the group named Monte Woolley. Cole mentioned that Monte was a Broadway actor and director who had been a classmate of his at Yale. Perhaps Cole had in mind presenting McAlmon to Monte as a possible lover; if so, the effort was wasted. Monte had eyes only for Rudolph Valentino, but even after Valentino left the party early with Comte Max de Pourtales, Monte didn't settle for McAlmon.

Even so, McAlmon was quickly accepted as one of the gang, and he supplied his share of wit and laughter and hijinks as the party progressed. They all had a delightful and rather riotous time, although everyone fell into a reverently hushed silence whenever Mabel Mercer sang one of Cole Porter's songs. She dedicated one of the songs—"Love For Sale"—to Cole, and blew him a kiss from the stage.

Mabel Mercer joined the Porter party between sets, and after she had finished the show, she accompanied them back to their house at 13 rue Monsieur. McAlmon was happy to get his first look at the famous half-timbered Normandy farmhouse in an apple orchard, where the Porters lived in an art deco symphony of platinum-colored wallpaper, paintings and porcelain, zebra rugs on highly polished marble floors, red lacquered chairs with cushions covered in white kidskin, and settees covered in suede. The huge basement had been turned into a party room where the walls were covered with mirrors and the floor was of polished marble. Here they continued celebrating until dawn, with Cole at the piano and Mabel Mercer singing his songs.

Before McAlmon left to shamble drunkenly back to his own apartment in rue de Vaugirard, Cole took him aside and asked him if he would show him and his friend Monte Woolley where they might be able to pick up some rough trade.

"No faggot places," Cole said. "We're tired of those screeching bitches. What we want to meet are some real men."

"Sure," McAlmon said, "I can show you some of those places."

They made a date to meet at 10:00 the next night at the Café Falstaff, a well-known drinking place for American expatriates at 42 rue du Montparnasse. The three of them had a few drinks and talked about what Cole and Monte were looking for in the way of fun. McAlmon told them he knew of a bal musette in the Latin Quarter. It was a place where sailors hung out, as well as apaches and working men and poules, and the manager was never offended when a few fairies came in to try their luck.

"Oh, my God," Cole said when they pulled up in front of the Gipsy Bar, "doesn't it look wicked?"

"I can't wait to see what's inside," Monte said, scratching his beard. McAlmon had noticed that excitement always seemed to set Monte to scratching his beard.

Cole and Monte were both quite pleased with the low-class decor. They took a table in a dark corner just where the bar turned to meet the wall. From there, they could survey the clientele without being conspicuous. After a few drinks, Cole and

Monte began considering three Senagalese soldiers as possible pickups, but they were wary because if they picked up two or three men together, there was more likelihood of violence. When dealing with rough trade, it was less likely that one man by himself, no matter how masculine, would try to beat them up. So they decided to wait a little longer, to see if someone safer turned up.

And as they were waiting, who should come in into the Gipsy Bar, all alone, but McAlmon's buddy and fellow writer, Ernest Hemingway. He was carrying a manila envelope, and looked as if he had just had a rather severe haircut. McAlmon had last seen Hemingway yesterday, when they parted ways at the Gare D'Austerlitz. Hemingway had said that he was going to leave Paris almost immediately for the Ruhr, but apparently something had delayed him.

McAlmon's first impulse was to ask him to join them. But a recognition of the circumstances aborted that impulse so instead of hailing Hemingway, McAlmon pressed back into the shadows against the wall. Hemingway made his way to the bar and sat down only a few feet away from McAlmon without having seen him.

McAlmon's fear of discovery lasted only for a moment, and then he felt himself become ashamed of having been ashamed. And the realization that he had been a coward made him feel vindictive, so he smiled and said under his breath to Cole, "See this guy at the bar who just came in?"

Catching the excitement of secretiveness in McAlmon's lowered tone, Cole, too, lowered his voice as he said, "The big fellow with the mustache?" Both he and Monte looked Hemingway over, with Monte scratching his beard.

"That's him," McAlmon said. "I know him. Now, he's real rough trade, but he often comes here hoping to get picked up by a couple of randy fairies. Why don't you two give him the pitch, see what happens?"

"Oh, he looks positively divine, doesn't he, Monte?" Cole whispered.

"Yes," Monte agreed. "Well, come on, then, let's do it."

McAlmon prepared himself for the unexpected as he watched

Cole and Monte approach Hemingway, who was smoking a cig-arette and drinking a glass of brandy and looking disgruntled. From where McAlmon sat smirking in the shadows, he could see and hear everything. It was Monte who made the pitch.

"Hi, big fella," he said, scratching his beard.

Hemingway glared at them, first one, then the other, not at all friendly.

"Would you like to have a party?" Monte asked.

"What are you guys, a couple of cocksuckers?" Hemingway asked.

His sneering bluntness left Cole and Monte nonplussed for a moment. This was a little rougher than they had bargained for. However, after regaining their composure, Monte glanced at Cole with gleeful anticipation, scratched his beard, and turned back to Hemingway.

"Well . . . yes," he said. "And now that we've settled that, how about that party?"

30

Renata

RENATA HAD TWO identical blue berets. She gave one to Hadley. Then they went shopping in Cortina and Renata bought matching skiing sweaters. Their coloring and physiques were different, Renata's hair was black, Hadley's red, Renata's body was angular, Hadley's was rounded, so they could hardly pass for sisters, but the identical clothes did make them look as if they belonged together, which pleased them both.

Hadley had been sad and restless after Ernest left for the Ruhr, but in a couple of days her spirits began to bubble up again, and she agreed that she shouldn't mope around, wasting the sunshine and the snow. So she and Renata put on their hiking boots, packed food and wine into their rucksacks, carried their skis over their shoulders, and hiked up to Pocol Peak, from which there was a good ski run down to Cortina. There was a large cemetery on the hill. Some of the older graves were covered with slabs of granite, from which the wind had blown the snow and the sun had warmed the granite, so Renata and Hadley sat down on one of the slabs and lunched on sausages, cheese, bread, and wine. Afterward, made sleepy by the long hike and the sun and the wine, they each found a large slab to lie down on and take a nap.

Lying prone, resting her face on her hands, Renata read the names and dates on the tombstone.

"This is a man and his wife, named Osimo," she said. "Died in 1899, both on the same day. Who are you on?"

Hadley, who was lying on her back, with her rucksack under her head for a pillow, turned over and reached out and traced with a fingertip the letters carved into the tombstone. "Anna Marie Fabriano and bambina," she said. "1891—the year I was born. No name given for the bambina, no age. Wonder why? Maybe the child was stillborn, and so was never named, and the mother died in childbirth."

"Well, I suppose it's natural to be morbid while lying on a grave, but I refuse to imagine awful things, and I don't want you to, either. Let's be happy. Aren't you happy?"

Hadley looked up at the clouds in the blue sky. "Yes. At this moment, very happy, very much at peace," she said, and hurried on, as if discouraging a response from Renata, "I'm so glad you decided to come to Cortina to ski."

"Oh, I didn't come here to ski," Renata said. "Not entirely, anyway. My main reason for coming here was to see you."

"To see me?" Hadley was both intrigued and apprehensive. "Why?"

"Because I have a feeling for you. What is it you Americans say, a 'crush'? I have a crush on you," she said. "Are you not aware of that?"

Hadley was silent for a long moment, and finally murmured, "I don't know what to say."

"You need not say anything. I didn't tell you in order to draw you out, but only to have the truth known." She laid her head on her crossed arms and closed her eyes.

They slept for perhaps half an hour, then woke up and washed their faces with snow. Then Renata tossed a handful at Hadley, who, with a cry of fun-loving surprise, grabbed a handful of snow and threw it at Renata. Within seconds they were in a snowball fight, laughing and darting and ducking amid the tombstones.

Once while Renata was frantically making a snowball, Hadley ran up behind her and shoved some snow down the back of her collar, then dashed away, laughing, and Renata cried out with the shock of it, and chased Hadley around a family vault.

Pleading and laughing like a person being tickled, Hadley cried, "No! No! Oh, no, don't!" as Renata caught up with her and tried to shove a snowball down the front of her sweater. Hadley grappled with Renata's right hand, the hand that held the snowball, and Renata grabbed her around the neck with her left arm, to get her in a vise so she could push the snowball down her sweater, but the snowball fell apart before she succeeded, leaving them entangled, panting, laughing, subsiding into a silent joy of closeness, of touching. Renata didn't take her arm from around Hadley's neck, and Hadley didn't release Renata's hand. They looked at each other.

Had they been lovers, they would have kissed, but Renata didn't want to take advantage of a momentary weakness on Hadley's part. If they were to be lovers, it would be because Hadley wanted to, not because she had been seduced by Renata against her better judgment.

But they did embrace. That seemed to be Hadley's middleground way of dealing with the possibilities between them. She slipped her arms around Renata's waist and touched her cheek to Renata's and they stayed like that, holding each other, until Hadley made up her mind what she wanted to do.

"Come on," she said, pulling away, suddenly chipper again, "I'll race you down the mountain."

"No, no," Renata said. "No racing. In your condition, you cannot afford to be reckless. We'll go back at a leisurely pace. What's the hurry?"

"You're right," Hadley said, placing her skis for mounting, and added ruefully, "Ernest would have thought it was a good idea. He would have dared me to race."

Renata didn't step into that opening. Hadley had made it clear to Renata that Ernest didn't want the child, but whether he would go so far as to jeopardize Hadley's health to get rid of it, Renata didn't know. And she didn't want her fondness for Hadley to weigh in the balance of Hadley's problems with her husband.

They had an easy run down the mountain. Hadley didn't fall once. She was a good skier, graceful, with sure judgment. They got back to the Hotel Bellevue before sundown, just in time to share in a hearty meal of veal cacciatore and a carafe of good Chianti. Snow had begun to fall, and Renata gathered a pitcher full of the clean snow and mixed it with sugar and orange juice, and after the hotel staff and the other few guests had retired for the night, Hadley and Renata sat side by side on the sofa in front of the fire in the salon and sipped the orange snow and smoked cigarettes and talked softly in a silence broken only by their voices and the crackling and hissing of burning logs.

Hadley preferred the orange snow to alcohol because alcohol increased the chances for morning sickness. Renata had thought that morning sickness was an inevitable result of pregnancy, but Hadley said no, she never experienced it unless she had drunk too much alcohol the night before.

"I must be one of those women who are made for childbearing," she said. "So far I feel great."

"And you look great," Renata said. "Like a flower blooming."

"You ought to try it, Renata," Hadley joked. "It might suit you, too."

"Me? Become pregnant? Tosh! I've always hated the idea of love between men and women."

"Oh, Renata, but you don't know what you're missing," Hadley said.

"Don't I? I've been to bed with men—enough to know that it's a dominance game with them. Besides, even at the moment of supreme intimacy, no man knows what a woman really feels. It takes another woman to know that. So perhaps it's you, Hadley, who don't know what you're missing. Have you ever been made love to by a woman?"

Hadley blushed. She had a difficult time answering, but finally she said, "When I was young . . . there was a woman . . . and, later, in St. Louis, a girl. . . . But I always . . . I never enjoyed it, really, because of the guilt. I felt it was . . . my mother called it a perverted vice. Such women were freaks of nature, she said."

"If I thought that, if I thought I was a freak of nature, why, I'd fling myself off the nearest cliff. No, I believe that the kind of love one woman can give to another is something beyond ordinary love, something higher. It raises love out of the cycle of male dominance and bestial reproduction. It results in creation, not procreation. So, rather than a freak, I consider myself privileged to be constituted as I am."

Hadley leaned her head backward to rest on the back of the sofa, and sighed. The firelight flickered across her lovely face. Renata thought perhaps the moment had come to find out if they would be lovers. She laid her arm along the back of the sofa and brushed Hadley's cheek tenderly with her fingers. Hadley sighed with pleasure, and caught Renata's hand and lightly kissed her fingers. This seemed to Renata to be the signal she had been waiting for, but she didn't want to risk spoiling the tenderness of the moment by any blundering aggressiveness, so she waited, wanting to be sure and she was right to wait, for Hadley was not yet certain of herself.

"I'd better say good night," she said.

And for a few more days, that's how it was left: tentative, adrift, pushed and pulled. By April 10, the snow had turned to mush on the slopes and was unsuitable for skiing, and Renata considered leaving Cortina. Hadley pleaded with her not to go. She dreaded being alone. Ernest had promised to return from the Ruhr in a couple of weeks, but there had been no mail from him—not one letter—and he had been gone for nearly three weeks, and Hadley hoped to get a telegram from him every day, announcing that he was on his way back. In the meantime, without the skiing, there wasn't much to do in Cortina. Renata and Hadley talked about going to Venice for a few days. They could stay at Nancy Cunard's palazzo, Renata said, and find lots of fun things to do. But Hadley, though sorely tempted, was afraid that Ernest would come back while she was gone.

"I'd better stay here and wait for him, like a good little pregnant wife," she said.

They went for long walks in the daytime, and at night they often played four-handed pieces on the grand piano. Renata had refrained from playing the piano in the daytime or early evening because she always seemed to attract an audience. Even passersby in the street, who had heard that a well-known pianist was staying at the hotel, might stop and come in, or peek in the windows, if they heard her playing. But after everyone had retired for the night, she and Hadley could play softly without attracting attention.

It was hard to get Hadley to play by herself, so modest was she about her talent, and so intimidated by Renata's presence. But she took instructions gladly and quickly, and was pleased when Renata told her—quite truthfully—that she was technically accomplished.

One night as they both sat on the piano bench in front of the grand, Renata showed Hadley her technique of playing a Liszt lullaby. The only light in the salon was from seven small candles in a candelabra on the piano and the flickering fire in the fireplace. "You need to let go. You need to let the tender feelings in your heart go down through your arms and come out your fingertips as you touch the keys."

"Oh, I'm no good," Hadley declared, discouraged.

"Yes, you are," Renata said. "All you lack is passion. I think I can teach you how to let go."

"Could you?" she pleaded.

Renata reached across and put her left hand under Hadley's. "Let your fingers lie on top of mine, as if my fingers were yours. Now feel how I play these notes. . . ." Renata caressed soft, trembling notes from the keys. "See? The pressure? The hesitation? The modulation that reveals emotion?"

"I think so, yes," Hadley said, staring at their hands. "You have a wonderful touch."

Renata stopped making notes and let her hand lie still on the keyboard. Hadley didn't take her hand off Renata's. Renata looked at her. Hadley kept staring down at their touching hands. Renata leaned over and kissed Hadley lightly on her warm cheek. This was the second signal, and had Hadley chosen to ignore it, Renata would have left Cortina the next day, never having known what it was like to hold Hadley naked in her arms. But Hadley did respond. She slowly turned her face toward Renata, giving Renata the chance to kiss her mouth if she wanted to, and she wanted to, and did, and Hadley returned the kiss, a long, sensual kiss, and when they pulled apart, Renata whispered, "Hadley, I love you."

"Oh, and I love you, too, Renata, really I do," Hadley said. "But . . ."

"But?"

"It's hard to talk about. It's hard to understand. I love you, but it doesn't mean I love Ernest any less. He's everything to me, and always will be. I couldn't live without him."

Renata kissed her again, and touched the tip of her tongue to the corner of her mouth, and said, "Do you feel it would be a betrayal of him if you let me make love to you?"

A peculiar, crooked little smile curled Hadley's lips for a moment. "I don't know. I don't think so."

"He wouldn't be jealous?"

"I don't think so. It's funny, but . . . I don't think he sees women as rivals."

Renata kissed her again, lightly, tenderly, before she said, "Then how would he feel if you came with me to my room tonight, and we made love?"

With that crooked little smile again, a smile of irony and apprehension, rather than joy, her breath coming in short, quick gulps, Hadley said, "I don't know. I think . . . sometimes I think it excites him . . . the idea of me making love to a woman."

Renata slowly stood up, took the candelabra in one hand, and offered her other hand to Hadley. Hadley placed her hand in Renata's. They got up and, with the candles lighting their way, walked slowly down the hallway to Renata's room.

31

Dos Passos

HE FELT WONDERFUL, until Hemingway found him.

John Dos Passos was not generally an effusive man. He was bespectacled and balding (even though only twenty-seven years old), the very image of a myopic scholar deep in dusty tomes, studying things long dead and perhaps better left so. But that April day in Paris, he felt as if he had suddenly, by some accidental cross-wiring of Fate, become an incarnation of Dionysus. He felt spring tingling through his limbs like the sappy juices rising under the greening bark of the chestnut trees in the lovely Luxembourg Gardens, where he strolled, frisky as a chipmunk.

He had just come from the Théâtre de Champs Élysées, where he had helped his new friends, Gerald and Sara Murphy, Cole Porter, and Fernand Léger paint sets for the Ballet Russe's presentation of *Les Noces*. He had met the composer, Stravinsky; the choreographer, Balanchine; and the producer, Diaghilev. He had lunched with his old friends from New York and Harvard, Donald Ogden Stewart and e.e. cummings, and shared with them a bottle of fine wine, then went for a stroll with them along the Seine.

And now, as he walked alone through the Luxembourg Gardens on his way back to his humble studio in Montparnasse, with the chestnuts trees in bloom, he felt like stopping the first woman he met and asking her for a kiss. He felt like climbing a tree and conversing with the birds. He felt like taking off his clothing and jumping into the fountain to wash the winter off him. He felt like picking a flower and offering it to the first homely girl he saw.

He knew very well that the world was a lousy pesthouse of idiocy and corruption, a charnel house of pain and decay, a vale of tears and sorrows, but what the hell, it was spring, and he was in love with life. Actually, he was in love with a girl, too—Crystal Ross—but she was a student at the French university in Strasbourg, so he stood in front of the statue of Venus and tried, Pygmalion-like, to bring the statue to life so he could kiss it and whisper "I love you" before his heart burst from lack of declaring his love for someone or something.

"What the fuck are you doing, Dos Passos?" asked a man's gravelly voice behind him.

It was Hemingway—and what a depressing sight to see! He was unshaven, bleary-eyed, rumpled, drunk, and belligerent.

"I've gone crazy," Dos Passos said. "I'm spring struck. I'm love struck. I'm moonstruck. I'm trying to will this Venus to come to life. How about joining me?"

"Fuck it," Hemingway growled. "Come on. Have a drink with me. I need some company. I thought you were in North Africa or somewhere. When the hell did you get back in Paris?" He caught Dos Passos' arm and tugged him toward a wrought-iron bench.

"A week ago. I traveled from Tunisia to Syria. Wonderful, awful trip. Sylvia Beach told me you were in Italy."

"Was. Had to go to the Ruhr, write some newspaper horseshit. Just got back. Going back to Italy, if I can find Djuna Barnes. Don't suppose you've seen her anywhere? She's not at her apartment."

"Haven't seen her."

"Have to kill some time till she gets home, need some company," Hemingway said.

Since Dos Passos was in such a good mood, and Hemingway was obviously in such a lousy one, he would rather have foregone Hemingway's company. But Hemingway could be persuasive—intimidating, actually. One found oneself going along with what Hemingway proposed because of the strength of his

character. Dos Passos had been introduced to him the year before by Sylvia Beach at Shakespeare and Company. When Sylvia
heard that Dos Passos was from Chicago, had been an ambulance driver during the War, and was the author of a fairly successful novel, *Three Soldiers,* she said he would have to meet
Hemingway, they had so much in common. The only trouble
was, they were so entirely different—almost opposites: Hemingway, a big, loud-talking, take-charge, rough-and-ready kind of
fellow; Dos Passos, shy, retiring, soft-spoken, who only now and
then allowed his feelings to overflow into whimsy. But besides
being from Chicago, the two things they did have in common—
the love of good writing and the love of adventure—had been
enough to form a bond of friendship between them. Still, Dos
Passos always seemed to get sucked into the powerful orbit of
Hemingway's enthusiasms, and now he was afraid that Hemingway's bad moods might have just as strong a pull as his enthusiasms.

Dos Passos looked around for the gendarmes as Hemingway
pulled a pint of Scotch from the inside pocket of his rumpled
coat.

"Come on, let's have a drink."

"I don't think we're allowed to drink here," he offered.

"Fuck it," Hemingway said, nudging him with the bottle. "Have
a drink."

Dos Passos took the bottle, but didn't drink. "You think you
should have any more?" he asked Hemingway. "You're already
soused pretty good, aren't you?" Indeed, he had never seen
Hemingway so drunk. Hemingway hadn't staggered, it was true,
but his speech was slurred, and his eyes were bleary red. Unshaven and disheveled, he looked like a bum who had been
sleeping in back alleys.

"What I need is a friend to have a drink with me," Hemingway
growled.

Rather than risk antagonizing him, Dos Passos put the bottle to
his mouth and tipped it up, but put his tongue in the hole and
only pretended to drink.

"What's the matter, Hem?" he asked in an appeasing tone.
"Something bad happen in the Ruhr?"

Hemingway took the bottle back, rubbed his palm across the opening, then drank. The whiskers in the folds of his neck bobbled up and down as he swallowed. Then he passed the bottle back to Dos Passos, not just offering it to him, but shoving it at him, insisting.

"The Ruhr is the shits," Hemingway said. "Newspapers are the shits. Germany is the shits. Paris is the shits. Life is the shits. Death is the shits. I'm the shits. You're the shits."

"Well, that pretty much covers everything," Dos Passos said, holding on to the bottle without drinking.

"No, it doesn't. Alice Toklas is the shits. You know what she did? I went over to see Gertrude, the old bitch, and that crabby little hook-nosed kike, Alice—know what she said?"

"I shudder to think."

"Said I shouldn't come around rue de fucking Fleurus anymore when I'm drunk. Am I drunk? You think I'm drunk?"

"Well, gosh, Hem, I don't know, are you?"

"Fuck her," he said. "I always did want to, you know, you know? Fuck old Gertrude, I mean. That's what bothers the shit out of Alice. She knows I want to yence old Gertrude, and she knows Gertrude wants me to do it."

Dos Passos looked at his watch, then at the sun sinking into a bank of gray, cold clouds on the horizon. "Listen, Hem," he said, "it's going to be cold as soon as the sun goes down. I'm going to have to go back to my studio and get a coat." And while this was true, it was mainly an excuse to get away from Hemingway. He handed the bottle back to him, hoping he wouldn't notice that he hadn't taken another drink. "So I'll see you later."

"I'll go with you," Hemingway announced.

"Oh," Dos Passos said, intimidated by his authority. "Well, sure. Okay."

Hemingway put the bottle back in his coat pocket and they left the Gardens, headed toward Montparnasse. Hemingway was broodingly, sullenly silent for most of the way, and Dos Passos didn't know what to say or do to keep from being pulled into the mighty vortex of resentment he felt from Hemingway.

"Montparnasse is the shits," Hemingway said as they crossed the boulevard. "Bunch of phony fuckers."

Dos Passos was staying in a studio hotel in rue Delambre just behind the Café du Dôme. He had hoped that Hemingway would leave him at the street door, but Hemingway seemed to take it for granted that he was going up to Dos Passos' room with him. He stumbled in the dark a couple of times as they walked up the three flights of stairs, but he caught himself on the handrail.

The sundown chill of April evenings had permeated the room. Dos Passos wanted to build a charcoal fire in the small metal fireplace, but Hemingway said, "Oh, to hell with that. Come on, get your coat, let's go out and have some fun."

The electric light had revealed a room strewn with papers. The small table was covered with them—pages and pages of writing from a new novel. Gesturing toward the disorder, he said, "Oh, I think I'd better stay in, Hem. I haven't got any writing done today. I'd better stay here and do some."

Hemingway gave him a nakedly accusing look, and demanded, "Yeah? Well, what about me?"

"Uh . . . well, what about you, Hem?"

"What'm *I* supposed to do? Go out and get drunk by myself? You don't give a shit about what happens to me do you? No, you don't give a shit. Nobody gives a shit about me."

He sat down heavily on the unmade bed. He was on the verge of tears. Dos Passos was appalled. The man's capacity for self-pity was appalling. Dos Passos tried to mollify him by saying, "Oh, come on, Hem, that's not true. You have lots and lots of friends, and a wife who loves you very much. Where is Hadley?"

He had thought that a reminder of Hadley would be an antidote to Hemingway's mood, but it had just the opposite effect. Tears actually overflowed Hemingway's eyes. They trickled down his unshaven cheeks, and his lips quivered with an incipient sob. This belligerent drunk was rapidly dissolving into a crying drunk.

"Yeah, you're right, Tiny is wonderful. I don't deserve her. She's wonderful. But she's in Cortina. In Italy. And I don't have anybody to drink with. She's a great drinker. But she's pregnant, and I'm too young to be a father." He wiped the tears from his face with his sleeve, then pulled the Scotch bottle from his pocket, took a swig, and shoved it toward Dos Passos. "God-damnit, have a drink."

"No, thanks, Hem. I have to keep my head clear, if I'm going to do any writing."

"Fuck the writing!" he said, his bullying anger drying up his tears. "Have a drink. You goddamn prissy college boys! You're all alike. You can't drink. Have a drink, goddamnit! I don't want to drink alone. Only alcoholics drink alone, and I'm not an alcoholic. You think I'm an alcoholic, don't you?"

"No," Dos Passos said. "But maybe we should think about getting something to eat first. It's not good, drinking on an empty stomach. How long has it been since you've eaten?"

Hemingway stared into the middle distance for a moment with unfocused eyes, eyes that were once again puddling with tears, and then said solemnly, "Don't remember. Not since I saw . . . her yesterday, I guess."

"Her? Who? Gertrude Stein?"

A sneer broke through his stunned sadness. "No. To hell with that fat kike dyke." Then the faraway look returned as he re-peated, "Her . . . Agnes. You remember? I told you about a Red Cross nurse I fell in love with during the War, when I was wounded in Italy?"

"I remember you talked about her one night, yeah, sure, at Chez Rosalie's, I believe it was. You've met her again? Here in Paris?"

"I thought I did. Oh, Dos, it hurts! It's awful, the way I love that woman. I wrote her a letter, telling her how I'd never been able to kill it. She wrote me back . . . in December, it was . . . say-ing that I was better off without her, and that we ought to just be friends. But I can't stop loving her, Dos. In her letter she men-tioned her visits to Paris. She said she longed to stand at early twilight at the Place de la Concorde and see the little taxis spin-ning around those corners, and the soft lights, and the Tuileries fountain. Said she was homesick for the smell of chestnuts on a gray, damp fall day . . . for Pruniers, the Savoia, and her favor-ite little restaurant, Bernard's, behind the Madelaine. . . ."

Tears were overflowing his eyes again, and he softly began to sob as he said, "When I get to missing her, I go there . . . to those places . . . to Bernard's . . . hoping to see her. I went there yesterday, and I . . . I saw her. I saw her. She was leaving Bernard's. I got all faint and sick inside. I followed her along the Boulevard." Sniffling and snorting, he took another drink, emptying the bottle.

"Well? Was it she?"

"I don't know. I was afraid to catch up with her, afraid to lose the feeling it gave me."

So he wanted the feeling of being all faint and sick inside more than he wanted the truth. Dos Passos wondered if Hemingway saw the meaning of that—that what he wanted wasn't happiness, but pain—a drunk who wanted some reason to feel bad. Dos Passos found it disgusting, and was embarrassed when Hemingway finally began to sob like a brokenhearted boy. Dos Passos' natural inclination was to try to comfort him in some way, but he was so embarrassed for him that he couldn't touch him, afraid that if he sat down on the bed beside Hemingway and put a comforting arm around his shoulders and said, "There, there," Hemingway might let his head fall on his shoulder and cry like a baby, and Dos Passos didn't want to be any part of such a sordid display.

"Oh, Dos," Hemingway said, "if she ever came back into my life, I'd give up everything for her . . . everything."

"Then you're a fool," Dos Passos wanted to say, but didn't, because, fool or not, Hemingway's pain was real. As maudlin as his feelings were, he was nevertheless truly miserable. And as a friend, what could Dos Passos do to help alleviate that misery?

Nothing. He just sat there at the table, watching Hemingway blubber, and it was perhaps his lack of overt sympathy that finally brought Hemingway's sobbing to an end. Feeling nothing from Dos Passos, Hemingway finally looked up to find Dos Passos studying him. And perhaps because he saw the disgust and embarrassment in Dos Passos' eyes, Hemingway suddenly choked off his sobs with renewed rage. He flung the empty bottle across the studio floor. It bounced on the rug and didn't break, but it didn't need to break to convey all the resentment and rage engendered by the shame Hemingway must have felt at that moment.

"Fuck you!" Hemingway said, and struggled to his feet. He jerked his handkerchief from his hip pocket and wiped the tears from his face and then blew his nose, and stumbled toward the door. Jerking the door open, he turned back to glare at Dos Passos with murderous hostility as he said, "If you ever tell anybody about this, I'll kill you." Then he was gone, slamming the door behind him.

Dos Passos sighed with relief, and took stock of how depressed and emotionally dirty he felt. It seemed like a year or so ago, rather than merely an hour, that he had been having a delightful time in the Luxembourg Gardens, living in the sunshine and joyously making love to the statue of Venus. Now everything was gloomy and dark and cold. Now everything was—as Hemingway might have put it—the shits.

32

Djuna

THE GROWING NOTORIETY of *Ulysses* was bringing attention to some of James Joyce's earlier, lesser works. Djuna Barnes had written an article on Joyce for *Vanity Fair,* hailing him as the new and undisputed master of modern literature. So it was natural, then, that Joyce—always looking for an angle to spread his fame and hopefully make a little money—suggested to Djuna that she write another article, this time on *Exiles,* a play he had written in Trieste after writing *Portrait of the Artist as a Young Man.* The main characters in the play were a married couple, Richard and Bertha Rowen—thinly disguised versions of Jim and Nora Joyce themselves—and a man named Robert Hand, who, Jim admitted under off-the-record questioning, was modeled on a friend of the Joyces' in Trieste named Roberto Prezioso.

Djuna thought the play was second-rate Joyce because it was so obviously derivative of Joyce's only acknowledged modern master, Ibsen, and because it was so arcanely intellectual about its subject matter.

Still, she was willing to do what she could to publicize the play and perhaps get someone interested in producing it, so she agreed to write the article. Djuna spent the better part of an April afternoon interviewing Joyce at his flat. Nora and the children were not at home, so Djuna felt she could talk frankly to Jim about the play's subject matter, but Jim begged to disagree with her when she bluntly—perhaps even provocatively—said that the play was about homosexuality by proxy.

"No, no," Jim said, squirming in his big, overstuffed chair. "It's about the spiritual union of Richard and Robert, effected through the body of Bertha."

"Oh, come on, Jim, aren't you just trying to dress up sex in spiritual garments? Let me quote you something here from the second act, where Richard talks to Robert, telling him—encouraging him—to have an affair with Bertha." She found the place in the text, and read:

> In the very core of my ignoble heart I longed to be betrayed by you and by her—in the dark, in the night—secretly, meanly, craftily. By you, my best friend, and by her. I longed for that passionately and ignobly, to be dishonored for ever in love in lust.

She gave him a chiding look as she added, "That's what I call homosexuality by proxy; is that what you call 'spiritual union'?"

Joyce massaged his forehead with long, limber fingers. His eyes behind the thick lenses of his glasses shifted about. "But, of course, the bodily possession of Bertha by Robert would bring the two men into almost carnal contact, the two men, yes, and perhaps they desire this, to be united through the person and body of Bertha, which is the only way they could be united—carnally united, that is—without dissatisfaction and degradation—that is, carnally united man to man, as man to woman. But I don't see why anyone would want to make this point in an article about the play."

"Might be an angle that would interest playgoers," Djuna said. "But don't worry, Jim, you'll have copy approval of anything I write."

Nora returned to the flat before they had finished, and so they stopped for the afternoon, to keep from boring poor Nora with literary talk. Jim invited Djuna to join them for dinner that night at Fouquet's Restaurant, where they could continue the interview, if Djuna wished. It was around four o'clock when she left the Joyces' flat and went back to her own apartment in

Boulevard St. Germain. On arriving, she found a note that had been slipped under the door.

Djuna—would like to see you today, if I can. Hope to find you home this afternoon. Ernest Hemingway

This was a surprise. She thought she had sufficiently discouraged Hemingway from any hope he might have of them becoming lovers. And for the moment she couldn't think of any other reason he might have for wanting to see her. In any event, she put him out of mind as soon as she dropped her briefcase on a table and began looking around the apartment for any sign that Thelma had been there.

Thelma had been gone this time for more than a month, and there was simply no way of telling if and when she would be back. Sometimes her absences were only for a night or two, or for a few days, a week perhaps, according to how far she had gone and the strength of her self-destructive demons. Would she be in Tangiers? Rome? Amsterdam? Or still in Paris, wandering drunk from bar to bar, in the befouled beds of women or men she didn't even know, letting them do to her what they wanted, while she, in her drunken stupor, remained as silent and frigid as the dead?

Always before she had found her way back, with the relief of a child who has been lost, with the longing to be kept by one who knew herself to be astray.

But she would always leave again in a matter of time. And Djuna would go looking for her. She would make the rounds of the bars in Montparnasse that Thelma was known to frequent, and she would ask the people she knew, "Have you seen Thelma?" And they would look at her with pity in their eyes, as one would pity a shameless beggar, and say, "No, I'm sorry, Djuna." Or they might be ashamed for her, and say, "Yes, I saw her last night in such-and-such a bar," and Djuna would go there, and say, "Have you seen Thelma?"

Sometimes late at night, when the bars were closing and Djuna was too drunk to stagger home, she would sit on the curb, her feet in the gutter, leaning against a lamppost, and weep, and when late-night passersby would stare at her with pity and disgust, she would say, "I'm searching for my love. Do you know Thelma?"

Thelma had a little red topless Bugatti which she drove wildly through the streets. She had once gone over a bump so fast that the muffler was knocked off. She never replaced it, so you could hear the car from a great distance as it roared through the narrow streets of the Left Bank. Sometimes at night, when Djuna heard the car's roar, she would follow the sound, trying to find where Thelma had gone, and if she found the car parked somewhere, she would go into all the nearby bars and cafés, looking for her.

One afternoon, while she was on her way to see her friend, Doc Mahoney, with the desperate hope of securing from him some wisdom that would cure her sorrow, or, failing that, some drug to deaden it, she came upon the beat-up Bugatti parked at the curb in rue Bonaparte. Thelma was nowhere to be seen. Djuna got into the passenger seat to wait for her. She was prepared to sit there all night, if need be, but that proved unnecessary. In about an hour, she caught sight of Thelma staggering along the sidewalk, looking around as if she didn't know where she was, as if she had forgotten where she had parked the car.

She didn't seem at all relieved when she first spotted the car, nor did she seem surprised to see Djuna sitting in it. She seemed too disoriented, too deadened and indifferent to respond to anything.

Without a word of greeting, she walked up to the passenger's side of the car, groped into the pockets of her wrinkled and soiled slacks until she found the car keys, then tossed the keys to Djuna.

"You drive," she said. "I don't know where I'm going."

"Do you know where you've been?"

"In hell," she said, and looked it. Her freckled complexion had taken on the sick whiteness of whey, her short, curly, honey-blond hair was disheveled and unclean, her cheeks were hollow, her forehead furrowed with pain and perplexity, and she stank of unbathed bodies in unmade beds. She appeared much older than her twenty-eight years, a beautiful woman on her way to being a dissipated hag.

The only thing about her appearance that gave Djuna hope was the small silk scarf around her neck. It had been a Christmas present from Djuna, and it now was the only thing about her that tied them together, that gave Djuna some claim upon her.

Djuna scooted over into the driver's seat, and Thelma slumped down in the passenger's seat, her eyes closed, her head resting on the back of the seat. Djuna started driving in the direction of her apartment, her heart beating with the hope that Thelma would let her take her there. But as they were passing the church of St. Sulpice, Thelma cried, "Stop!"

Djuna's heart sank. "Why? Why do you want to stop? We're almost—"

"Stop!" she commanded, more forcefully this time. "Go back. The church. Let me out."

Djuna was afraid to let her out before she got her home, afraid that she would lose her again, but she knew that if she refused, Thelma would most likely jump out of the car while it was still moving, so she turned around and headed back toward St. Sulpice, saying in a concerned, placating voice, "What is it, darling? What do you—"

But Thelma remained silent, and as soon as Djuna found a parking place, Thelma, still without a word of explanation, got out walked lurching toward the church's front entrance.

Djuna got out and hurried after her. On the steps leading up to the Gothic doors, Thelma untied the silk scarf from around her neck and covered her head with it.

Djuna stopped just inside the vestibule when she saw Thelma dip her fingers into the holy water stoup and genuflect as she made the sign of the cross. Djuna was astonished. She had never known Thelma to be religious, let alone a Catholic, and yet here she was, going through the rituals like someone who had once practiced them.

Djuna stood in the doorway and watched as Thelma took the long walk down the aisle to the altar. A few worshipers were in the dimly lit church, but none paid any attention to Thelma as she, making an obvious effort not to stagger, went to the altar and the statue of the Virgin, at whose feet burned devotional candles like flowers of fire. The arms of the Madonna were outstretched to receive all those who needed Her comfort and solace. It was to Her that Thelma kneeled and bowed her covered head in prayer.

It was something that Djuna could never have expected to see, Thelma, a woman of demons and self-inflicted suffering, a woman of sensuality and violence, reeking of alcohol and sexual secretions, her freckled face lit by the flowering flames of the many candles, kneeling in supplication to the Virgin.

It was a picture Djuna knew she would someday have to paint. But for the moment she felt like a peeping Tom, as if this act of supplication was too intimate to be witnessed. So she left the church, and went out onto the front steps, where she waited for Thelma.

She stayed in the church for thirty minutes, and when she finally did emerge, she was weak and short of breath and pensive. She and Djuna looked at each other in silence for a long moment before Thelma asked in a child's pleading voice, "Can I come back?"

Djuna broke into tears, and embraced her. "Yes, my darling, you can come back. Please do. I beg you."

Djuna took Thelma back to the apartment. She helped her bathe, trying to wash away all the odors of degradation, and then she put her in their bed, and during her deep sleep, Djuna sat on the side of the bed, and kissed Thelma's face, and held her cold hands, and, in her delirium of love, whispered to her, "Die now. Die now and you will be at peace, and will not again be touched by dirty hands. Die now, so that you will never again take my heart and your body and let them be nosed by dogs. Die now and be mine forever."

Djuna knew that Thelma would leave her again, but she could not bring herself to save her by causing her to die. Besides, the first days of Thelma's return were always days of rebirth. A brilliant artist, Thelma began her silverpoint drawings again, and resumed sculpting. She had a small private income sufficient for her to live well and have her Bugatti, so there was no necessity to make a living with her art. She hoped to sell, of course, as confirmation that what she was doing had value, but her art was more a source of joy and self-expression than a means of making an income. Djuna, conversely, had to turn out stories and articles and plays in hopes of making enough money to support herself, and such work was often a source of resentment and tension for her. Still, after Thelma's return from each of her absences, for a while there was no pleasure greater than the way they loved each other.

Thelma loved with her hands—the big-knuckled hands of a man, the hands of a sculptor. Her touch was like the touch of the blind, who see with their fingers. In the night, her fingers would explore Djuna's body, going forward, hesitating, trembling. The sensuality of those fingers was greater than the sensuality of any male organ Djuna had ever experienced.

But knowing that Thelma could not bear to be happy for long, Djuna lived in dread of the day that always came, the day Thelma went out and didn't come back. Djuna found her at the Tois et As bar, drunk. She stayed with her, so that she would be there to pick her up when Thelma fell. Thelma was with some sailors. When Djuna tried to take someone's hands off of her, Thelma shouted at her, "Leave me alone! You're a devil! You make everything dirty! Leave me alone!"

"Do you mean that?" Djuna said, hurt to tears.

"Yes," Thelma said. "You make me feel dirty and ashamed and old!"

It was an uncontrollable impulse, born of weariness and misery, that caused Djuna to throw her drink in Thelma's face.

Thelma hit her. With a clenched fist, she hit Djuna in the mouth as a man would hit her, hard. Her knuckles split Djuna's lips. Djuna fell sprawling amid the cigarette butts and debris on the floor, horrified and ashamed. Bleeding from the mouth, she scrambled to her feet and ran out of the bar. Thelma followed her, and yelled at her as Djuna ran crying into the darkness, "You make everything dirty! Leave me alone! You're a devil!"

That had been a month ago, and it was the last time Djuna had seen Thelma. In her first fury, Djuna had emptied the apartment of Thelma's things, and tried to get her out of her life, but she still missed her. She still loved her. It wasn't as if she had any choice in the matter. She believed that fate had made that choice for her. Just as she'd had no choice in parents, she had to resign herself to loving the lover fate had given her. So in time, she began to look for Thelma again, her heart aching with pity for her, afraid of what she would find.

She soon learned that Thelma had left Paris again. Some said she had gone to Rome, but the most reliable report came from Bob McAlmon, who told her that he had recently seen Thelma in a lesbian bar in Berlin, drunk. Even so, each time Djuna returned to the apartment, she looked around for signs of her. And when she came back on the day of the Joyce interview and saw the note that had been slipped under her door, her heart jumped.

But it was only from Hemingway. Why would he want to see her? She vaguely remembered that the last time she had gossiped with McAlmon, he had mentioned that Hemingway had left his wife in Italy with Renata Borgatti and had gone off to do some newspaper work in the Ruhr.

He came again late that afternoon. Djuna opened the door to his shy knock, but didn't invite him in.

Hemingway glanced furtively up and down the empty hallway, then said in a low voice, "Excuse me. I hate to bother you, I hope I'm not interrupting your writing, but McAlmon said I should look you up."

"Why?" Djuna asked, not making it any easier for him.

He had apparently just come from a bath. He had nicked himself a couple of times while shaving, he smelled of shaving lotion, and his newly cut hair was plastered down with water. His appearance and demeanor were those of a bumpkin who had come a-courting.

"He told me you knew a doctor who . . . Hadley's pregnant, and . . ."

"Come in," Djuna said, and when he was inside and the door was closed, she spoke the word he was reluctant to use. "An abortionist? That's what you're looking for?"

"Yeah. I'm not sure . . . we're not sure that's what we want to do yet, but in case we decide, I thought I'd better look one up, make sure he's okay before we . . . And find out how much it'd cost, before we . . ."

"I'll have to take you to him." As she gathered up her interview notes and put them back in her briefcase, Djuna said, "He wouldn't talk to you otherwise, thinking you might be an informant for the police."

"Gee, I hate to interrupt your writing. I know how it is."

"And I know how it is to need an abortionist. Come on, we'll see if he's at home. We can walk, it's only a few blocks from here."

Since it wasn't likely that she would have time to return to her apartment before joining the Joyces for dinner, Djuna took her briefcase with her. She wore her cape and a turbanlike hat against the cool April evening air.

"Is this, uh, doctor . . . is he a real doctor?" Hemingway asked as they strode along boulevard St. Germain.

"He hasn't got a license to practice in France, if that's what you mean. He was a legitimate doctor in San Francisco though, before he decided he'd rather be a pauper in Paris than a rich man in America."

"And he's good?"

"You'll have to make up your own mind about that. He's eccentric, but he has a reputation for knowing what he's doing. And if you're looking for an abortion in France, you won't have a helluva lot of choices, will you?"

They turned into the narrow street that led into the Place St. Sulpice, a small square between the church and the Mairie du Luxembourg court, a bustling hub where tram lines ran in several directions. In rue Servandoni, just a few doors from the church, lived the doctor. Djuna tapped on the concierge's loge, and asked if Doctor Mahoney was in his room. In a slightly sarcastic tone, the concierge said that, to the best of his knowledge, neither Doctor Mahoney nor Madame Mahoney had as yet gone out for the evening, so Djuna and Hemingway trudged up the six flights to visit. The water-stained, paint-peeling walls and the threadbare runners and the stinking Turkish toilets on the stairwell landings all proclaimed poverty, which partially prepared one for the terribly impoverished disorder of the doctor's room.

When Djuna's rap on the door brought a shouted invitation from within to *"Entrez,"* Hemingway followed her into a room that was so small and so cluttered that they had to maneuver between piles of water-stained and dust-covered medical books and journals and newspapers to get to the bed and the dresser in the rear of the room. The drawers of the dresser stood partially open and from them hung various feminine garments—brassieres, stockings, laces, panties, and a girdle. On top of the dresser was scattered an assortment of perfume bottles, cream jars, powder boxes and puffs, along with a number of medical instruments, such as a pair of forceps, hypodermic needles, a catheter, and a broken scalpel.

On the narrow unmade iron bed at the back of the room, the doctor lay in all his feminine finery. With the dim light filtering through the room's one small, high window, the doctor had to strain to identify his visitors, and when he recognized Djuna, he pushed himself up to greet her. He was wearing a dowager's fluffy, old-fashioned, lace-larded dress that reached to his ankles. The gun-metal blue of his cheeks and chin was softened by layers of powder, his lips were rouged, his eyes heavily mascaraed, and his head was covered by a blond wig with pendant pigtailed curls that reached to his shoulders.

"Oh," he said, "you've just caught me taking a nap before going out for the night."

"Sorry to disturb you, Doc, but I have someone here who wanted to meet you." Djuna introduced Hemingway, but there was no shaking of hands. The frown on Hemingway's face betrayed his appalled disapproval of the doctor and the scene. "It's a matter of business," Djuna went on. "His wife is pregnant, and he doesn't want her to be."

"Oh, I see, I see," said Doc Mahoney, assuming a businesslike air. "Well, I charge one hundred dollars, payment in advance. Where's the patient? I would have to examine her before I agree to perform the operation."

Hemingway's voice caught in his throat and he had to clear it before saying, "She's . . . not here. She's in Italy at the moment. I was just . . . in case we decide. Is it safe?"

"I've never lost a patient yet," Doc said. "Can't afford to. More at stake than mere money."

"You don't do it here, surely," Hemingway said, as if such a thing could not be imagined.

"No, no. I do it in the comfort of the patient's own home. Or in a hotel room, if that is preferred."

"Well, I'll let you . . . let you know. We'll be back in Paris in a couple of weeks, I'll let you know."

"The sooner, the better," Doc said. "Every passing week makes it harder on the patient, and more dangerous for me. How far along is she now?"

But Hemingway, anxious to be gone, was already backing out of the room. "I'm not sure," he said. "I'll bring her back to Paris, and you can talk to her before we . . . make up our minds for sure."

"A three-hundred franc retainer would not be amiss," Doc wheedled.

"Yeah?" Hemingway said. "Well, we'd better wait till you talk to her."

"Two hundred?" he pleaded.

But Hemingway had left the room. Djuna took a twenty-franc note from her pocket and put it into Doc's hairy, nail-painted hand. It wasn't much, but it would buy him dinner.

Hemingway waited for Djuna in the hallway. Following her down the stairs, he said, "Is he crazy?"

"No more than the rest of us, I suspect," Djuna said.

"It's hard to believe that he could be a safe, responsible doctor."

"Just because he's queer doesn't mean he's irresponsible or careless," Djuna said, keeping her voice down. "He says he's never lost a patient, and as far as I know, that's true. But don't expect me to defend him. You wanted to meet him, I introduced you. Whether you use him or not is a matter of indifference to me."

When they left the building, Djuna stopped on the sidewalk to say, "Look, I'm going to Fouquet's to meet the Joyces for dinner and continue my interview with Jim. So I'll say good night here, and walk on up to Montparnasse."

She started to walk away, but Hemingway, who seemed a little at a loss, stayed with her, saying, "Joyce? Gee, it's been a long time since I've seen him. Listen, would it be all right if I walked up with you, and said hello to him? I mean, I wouldn't want to intrude."

Djuna stopped and gave it a moment's thought, then said, "Well, yes, come to think about it, that might be a good idea. I'm sure you'd be welcome to join us for dinner, too, if you haven't got anything else to do. Nora's going to be there, you see, and she hates literary talk. Maybe you could offer her a little diversion. Talk to her about Italy or boxing or something. Keep her from becoming too bored, while I finish my interview with Jim."

"Sure," Hemingway said. "I haven't got anything else to do. I'd be glad to. Thanks."

33

Nora

Nora was ever so glad that Djuna brought Hemingway along to dine with them at Fouquet's.

"I know how bored you are with all this literary talk," Djuna said. "While Jim and I discuss *Exiles,* maybe you and Hemingway could talk about Italy, or something."

She was right about Nora being bored. It was a constant source of amazement to her how such a to-do was being made about Jim's writing. Oh, how the intellectuals and wealthy art patrons loved to sing his praises and gave him money to support him and his family while he finished *Ulysses,* and Nora couldn't even get through the thing. She could never read the Molly Bloom section in its entirety, even though she knew Jim had used her as the model for Molly, that disgusting woman who sat around on a chamber pot and thought about how she would like to suck a young man's cock, or get a tongue stuck up her bottom. How could Jim have turned faithful Nora into such an adulteress, who gets fucked by her lover, and her husband knowing it, too, and not caring if she did, the disgusting man? Was this cuckoldry supposed to be funny? His admirers might think so. They were always talking about how funny the book was. Like the time that Sylvia Beach, Bob McAlmon, and Djuna Barnes came to the flat and talked all evening about the Irish wit and humor in Jim's books, and Nora finally said, "What's this about Irish wit and humor in your stories, Jim? Where is it? I'd like to read a page or two."

Well, they all looked embarrassed, but Nora didn't care, and Jim became condescending. Picking up an issue of *Perl-Romane,* a periodical that Nora always bought at railroad kiosks, he said to the guests, "This is the kind of sentimental trash my wife reads."

"Yes, I do," Nora said, unabashed. "Because the stories in there have love and adventure and endings. Why, this man," she said to the others, "doesn't even know how to end a story. Having some fat woman lying in bed and playing with herself ain't my idea of a proper end for a story, it's not."

Ignoring her, as if her opinion wasn't worth bothering about, Jim pulled one of Giorgio's favorite pulp westerns off the bookshelf, and said, "And this is what my son reads—cowpoke stories!"

"Yes, and they're wonderful, too," Giorgio said. He was sitting at the table, having hot cocoa and smoking cigarettes. "Those stories have horses and everything. I wish you could write one of them. You might make some money."

"Horses!" Jim snorted. "Giorgio's ambition is to work with horses. How odd it is, the father an intellectual, the son a stable boy. You know," he went on in a sort of bewildered way, "you can see that I have an effect upon people who come near me. Some imitate me, some hang on my every word. I even had one who fell on his knees and wanted to kiss the hand that created *Ulysses.* But my wife and my son seem impervious to any influence by me."

"No influence, is it?" Nora said. "Sure, and who, pray tell, influenced me to leave my family and my country and my religion, to follow you when you went off to seek your misfortune? The devil, d'you think? And whose influence was it that made me stay with you in that Godforsaken Trieste, when I was big with child and we didn't have a bite to eat in the house, so that when we woke up in the mornings, we had to turn over and try to go back to sleep to forget our hunger? Whose influence was that, Jim, I'd like to know?"

Ah, men! And there they were, in front of company, or Nora

would have told him a thing or two more about influences. Those who came to flatter him and tell him he was a great writer, and imitate him, and be influenced by him, and maybe even kiss the hand that wrote the book, what did they know about him? They would never know James Joyce the way she knew him. The critics said he had a dirty mind, judging from his books, but how little they knew! He wasn't much for carnal sinning these days, it was true, but there was a time when he wanted to live in it, wallow in it, gorge himself on it, like a pig in slops. It was his way of protesting against Ireland, the Church, God Himself, but it was also a way he had of making sex more exciting. He was always being thrilled by the possibility of being caught at it, being discovered in *flagrante de lecto,* as he was always saying in his bloody Latin. Fucking was what he meant. He was always telling people in public how crude speech offended him, but all it took was for Nora one night to tear off her chemise and get on top of Jim and put his prick into her cunt and ride him up and down, saying, "Fuck up, love! Fuck up!" to open a floodgate of prurience. The man went mad with lust. And after that he couldn't get enough of talking dirty. Oh, and it didn't take long for it to go past mere talking, either. One night he confessed to a wish to kiss her bottom, and put his tongue up her hole. She would never kiss a man there, no matter how much he begged her, it would be disgusting, but nothing could stop Jim. While wanting to kiss her bottom, he even pretended he couldn't find it in the dark, so he would have an excuse to ask her to break wind to guide him.

"I find this very repulsive, Jim," she had said, and he said, "I do, too, but that's as it should be! That's the excitement of it! You know what Cardinal Newman called a woman, don't you? A *saccus stercoris,* a bag of muck. Claimed he was trying to dissuade people from vice by naming its horrors, but he was only making it more spicy and attractive by forbidding it, by giving it the spice of a transgressed taboo. *O esca verminum, O massa pulveris!* What could be more exquisitely and deliriously vile? Fart for me! Make it the sound of a kiss!"

Poot.

"There," she said. "There's a kiss for you."

He would always feel terribly guilty afterward. He would treat her like a vile whore while having his way with her, but as soon as he was finished, he wanted her to play the saint, wanted her to be an object of pious adoration. He would say something like, "My prick is still hot and throbbing from the last brutal fucking I gave you, my little brown-arsed fuck bird, when a faint hymn is heard rising from the dim cloisters of my heart in tender, pitiful worship of you, my wonderful, innocent angel."

Wasn't that something? All flowery speech like that, after being so disgusting? Who could imagine such a man? Only by then he wasn't a man, he was a wayward and naughty boy who wanted to be loved and chastised. He insisted any number of times that he and she must tell each other everything, and not be ashamed of anything that went on between them, but afterward, ashamed of himself, as well as penitent, he would say, "How on God's Earth can you possibly love a thing like me? Instead of being comforted, I should be chastised," he said, only it would be a while yet before he actually wanted to be flogged.

The desire for being flogged didn't begin until after the dirty letters they exchanged when he went back to Ireland on a business trip. Yes: James Joyce as a businessman, if you can believe that. He got the idea that he might make some money by opening a cinema in Dublin, a theater where moving pictures could be shown. When the first such theater opened in Trieste in 1909, Jim took Nora to see them, the first moving pictures either of them had ever seen. On the screen a murderer threw his betrayed mistress into a river, and when the police came and were unable to find the culprit, Nora shouted out to the screen, "He's hiding behind the barrels, you bloody stupid peelers! Get him! Get him!"

Sure, the audience laughed at Nora's ignorance, but she had been so caught up in the thing, she forgot that it wasn't really happening. Sometimes Jim was embarrassed by such ignorance—adorably ignorant, he often said of her—but usually the way she blurted out everything she was feeling pleased him, and in this case, her reaction to the moving pictures gave him an idea. Since there was not a single moving pictures theater in all of Ireland, why not be the first to establish one, and maybe make enough money to keep them out of the poorhouse while he wrote his stories that nobody wanted to pay for? As an English teacher for the Berlitz language schools in Trieste, he had gotten to know a few Triestine businessmen. He talked to them about building a moving pictures theater in Dublin, and they all agreed that it might be worth investigating. So they invested enough money to pay Jim's round-trip passage to Ireland, where he would try to interest some Irish businessmen in joining them. Nora had two children by then, and there wasn't enough money for her to go along, so she had to stay in Trieste for the whole summer, with no one for company except Jim's younger brother, Stanislaus, who had come from Ireland to live with them and help support them as a family.

And it was in the letters that Nora and Jim sent back and forth from Dublin to Trieste that the dirty talk entered an extraordinary phase. Jim was always encouraging her to lead the way, telling her that he imagined things so dirty that he couldn't write them until he saw how she herself wrote, and he demanded that she put every sexual thought, however smutty, however shameful, into words, and he encouraged her in mad, lustful inventiveness by telling her how he dreamed of squirting semen on her face, of buggering her, of licking her rank red cunt, of doing all sorts of nasty things with her. When she compliantly wrote to remind him of the way she had used her fingers when they were fucking to tickle his balls or stick up his arse, he wrote back, "Talk dirtier! Talk dirtier, my darling brown-arsed fuck bird!"

Then he wanted more than talk. He wanted artifacts—namely, her drawers. He sent her money to buy the long-legged frilly undergarments he loved, and asked her to wear them until they were discolored by a brown stain. She sent the stained drawers back to him, and told him to masturbate as he was reading her letter, in which she said she wanted him to lick her cunt and fuck her arseways. Would he do that?

Oh, yes, he would do that, gladly, feverishly, foully, and told her he wanted to hear her farts spluttering out of her backside while he licked it, and he asked her to promise to shit in her drawers and let him fuck her then.

These letters went on for the whole summer that Jim was away in Ireland, and when he came back to Trieste—his moving pictures business having failed, perhaps because he couldn't keep his mind on it—he began to set into practice all the masturbation fantasies that they had concocted in their letters. The apprenticeship of obscenity had passed, and now Nora could comply with his every wish and fantasy. In bed together again, she amazed and thrilled him to the point of delirium by telling him how she wanted him to roger her arseways and wanted him to fuck her in the mouth and how she wanted to crawl under the dining table while he was at his dinner and unbutton him and pull out his Tiny O'Toole and suck it off like a teat. His Tiny O'Toole—that was what Nora named his prick. At first he was offended, hurt.

"Tiny, is it?" he asked. "So you've known bigger ones, I suppose?"

"Bigger, but not better," she said, playing the game. Actually, she had never been unfaithful to him, not since the first day they walked out together in Dublin, but she had discovered that he was aroused mightily by being called a cuckold, by having her tell him that, while he was away in Ireland, men had rogered her in the arse with cocks as big as a stallion's.

And on it went, and where would it end? There were still a few things that Nora found embarrassing, mainly those things having to do with excretory functions, such as his wish to see her in the water closet, with only her hat and stockings on, with a flower sticking out of her bottom. Imagine that! A flower sticking out of her arse! Oh, the dirty man! But she did it for him, and even let him persuade her to defecate while he lay on the floor of the toilet and watched. The toilet—the Turkish-style water closet with its floor-level hole, over which she squatted—gave him a perfect view of what he claimed would make him ecstatically happy: to see a fat brown turd protruding from her bottom. She did it, but she was too embarrassed to look at him afterward, and even her embarrassment pleased him.

But they at last reached the limits of how far she could go. She was complicit in his sexual games and forbidden explorations, not only because she rather enjoyed them herself, but because she knew that, in lieu of a marriage vow, the obscene exchanges bound them to each other, perhaps even more irrevocably than a marriage ceremony could. But when he said that if his filth offended her, she ought to bring him to his senses by punishing him, by flogging him, she said, "Jim, I can't hurt you. I can put up with all these crazy sexual pranks, but I could never bring myself to hurt you."

But he groveled. He implored. He called himself a swine; a low, disgusting wretch; a depraved monster; and claimed that what he needed to bring him to his senses was to be flogged.

"I need to feel you flog, flog, flog me viciously on my naked quivering flesh!" he cried.

She finally did it. She took a belt to him. She never did discover how far he would have gone, how much he would have endured, suffered, because she could never bring herself to really hurt him, but she at least gave him the token punishment that allowed him to groan and moan and sometimes cry out in the token pain of contrition. That didn't stop him from talking dirty again, or wanting to sniff her drawers, but it did relieve him of some of his guilt.

But of course there came a time when talking dirty and sniffing drawers wasn't enough for him. There always came a time when what they were doing wasn't enough. "Write dirtier! Flog harder! Talk dirtier!" Why, when he was writing his play, *Exiles,* which was about two men who share a woman between them, he had fantasies of his friend Roberto Prezioso being in the same bed with them, and all three of them doing it together, the two men fucking her at the same time, one in the arse, one in the cunt.

Then, when he began to write *Ulysses,* he began to get a thrill by imagining Nora getting fucked by other men, not just by Roberto, but by strangers. He began to encourage her to invite the advances of other men. He not only wanted to be called a cuckold, he wanted to be a cuckold.

Some small light was shed on this new twist of twisted desire when Jim prevailed upon Nora to read the part of *Ulysses* he was working on at the time. He called it the Penelope section, which, Nora gathered from what he and others had said in conversation, corresponded to the return of Ulysses from the Trojan War to find that his wife, Penelope, had been unfaithful to him. This was the part written from the point of view of Molly Bloom, the fat married woman who was the novel's heroine, but who was quite obviously Nora herself. There she was, with all the dirty things she had ever said, put down on the pages for God and everybody to see.

"Write dirtier!" he had said in his letters from Ireland. "Write dirtier!" And here he was, turning her letters into literature! There were Nora's words, coming out of the mouth of Molly Bloom, how she wanted to shout when she was coming, and Jim leaving out all the punctuation, just as Nora did in her letters. And this Molly Bloom character was having an adulterous affair with some man named Blazes Boylan, and Jim needed Nora to have an affair with some man so he would know what it was like for Molly's husband, Leopold Bloom, to be cuckolded.

Sure, she would pretend, she would go along with the fantasy, and even have fun with it, no matter how disgusting, but actually to go out and make advances to men, and go to bed with them? It wasn't in her nature. A coquette she was not, and never could be. She had never been unfaithful to Jim, and never would be under normal circumstances. But, crucified Jaysus, who could know what was normal with that man?

Well, what was she to do? She refused to be unfaithful to him. But what did that get her? Nothing. Without a constant increase in intensity and foulness Jim's interest in sex began to wane, and soon he seemed to lose all desire for Nora. After they had worn out the novelty of sinfulness, after they had used up the shock of talking dirty, had exhausted imagined violations, what was left? The monotony of monogamy.

Naturally, then, Nora began to think of having an affair. And why not? No reason why she shouldn't, except—who could she have an affair with? At forty, she was getting too matronly to play the vamp. For her to make advances to strangers would be ridiculous. And yet there was nobody within their circle of friends who might do, at least not until Hemingway came along. On the night of their first meeting—the night Hemingway brought Jim home drunk in a wheelbarrow—Nora had thought Hemingway a likely looking lad, and if she was ever going to be unfaithful to Jim, it would be with someone like Hemingway. The opposite of Jim, he was young, vigorous, and hairy, a man of action and muscle who had rather be out climbing mountains, or be in the boxing ring beating the bejabbers out of another man, than be sitting around all day in a smoky room talking about the finer points of Restoration literature, or the deeper meanings of ancient Greek mythology, or some such twaddle.

But she didn't seriously entertain the notion of Hemingway as a lover until one night at a dinner party at Sylvia Beach's flat, when Hemingway, drunk and boastful, offered to let Nora hit him in the stomach with her fist as hard as she could. What a peculiar sensation! Nora had never hit anyone with her fist, and to do it without fear or anger proved to be peculiarly exciting.

"Bedad, you must be a physical wonder, then, if the rest of you is as hard as your stomach," Nora said.

Thereafter she had a few nighttime masturbation fantasies about the lad, but she didn't come in contact with him again until Djuna brought him to join them that April evening.

"I brought Hemingway along," Djuna said. "He didn't have a dinner engagement, and his wife's out of town."

"That was thoughtful of you," Jim said. "It's been a while since we've seen each other."

"I know how bored you get with literary talk," Djuna said to Nora as they took their places at the table. "While I interview Jim, maybe you and Hemingway could talk about Italy, or something. He's just been down there, visiting with Ezra and Dorothy in Rapallo."

"Oh?" Nora said. "And how are dear Ezra and Dorothy?"

It was clear that Hemingway loved to gossip. He told them of Ezra's tryst with Nancy Cunard, and how McAlmon had gone to Venice to take over with Nancy where Ezra had left off. And as the gossiped, they dined on caviar with blinis, oysters on the half-shell, fresh salmon in cream, roast partridge, and champagne—all thanks to the beneficence of Jim's wealthy English patron, Harriet Weaver, whose generosity had kept the Joyces out of the poorhouse all these years. Miss Weaver had recently made Jim another gift—600 pounds this time, a small fortune, which was supposed to be spent on the medical bills for Jim's eye troubles, and on frugal living, but as long as Jim had money in his pocket, he was incapable of frugality. This mixture of improvidence and extravagance had caused his brother, Stanislaus, to place Jim among those he called the world's deserving poor—that is, those who deserve to be poor.

After they had finished dining and Djuna reminded him that they had to work, Jim said to Nora, "You and Hemingway might not want to stay around for this."

"And what're we supposed to do?" Nora asked.

"Maybe Hemingway has some suggestions," Jim said.

"What would you like to do?" Hemingway asked obligingly.

On an impulse born of boredom, champagne, and perverse defiance, Nora said, "Go dancing! Ah, sure, wouldn't it be lovely to go dancing now! It's been years, and Jim was never a dancer, anyway, unless it was an Irish jig."

"Well, they're having a costume ball at the Bal Bullier tonight," Hemingway said without his customary enthusiasm. "A festival—Féte de Nuit à Montparnasse—a benefit for poor artists. Every artist in Paris is probably going to be there. I thought I might go, try to shake this depression I've been in. You're welcome to come along, if you like."

His facial expression and tone of voice indicated that he was merely being polite, that he didn't expect Nora to accept the offer, but the news made her bubbly with delight.

"Oh, I'd love to go! A costume ball! For a good cause!" But then she frowned. "Oh, but what about costumes? They wouldn't let us in without costumes, would they?"

"You can buy masks at the door, and that's all that's required," Hemingway said, trying to make his tone merely informative, not proposive.

Nora brightened again. "Ah, sure, that would be wonderful, Mr. Hemingway. If you wouldn't mind escorting an old woman like myself to such a shindig. Jim would never be taking me to a costume ball, not if his life depended on it."

"Well, now's your chance," Jim said, glad to get rid of her. "If Hemingway doesn't mind?"

"Not at all," Hemingway said, though he didn't seem to know quite what to make of the turn of events.

So the four of them had after-dinner coffees and cognacs, after which Nora and Hemingway said good night to Jim and Djuna and caught a taxi for the Bal Bullier at the other end of boulevard du Montparnasse. Nora felt almost like a young girl going out on a date, going into a strange world where she didn't know the rules, and she was excited by the uncertainty.

And what a place the Bal Bullier turned out to be! On her travels around Paris, Nora had seen the huge building from the outside, but the size and grandeur of the ballroom's interior were more impressive than anything she had seen before. It was thronged with hundreds and hundreds of people in the most outlandish costumes, and Nora had to cling to Hemingway's arm to keep them from getting separated in the noisy gaiety of the surging, dancing crowd.

The masks that Nora and Hemingway purchased were made of papier-mâché and were held on by elastic bands, and though they covered only the upper portions of their faces, they were adequate to conceal their identities. From the moment Nora put on her golden mask and Hemingway put on his black one, she no longer called him by his last name. As if by unspoken agreement, she called him Ernest, and he called her Nora.

A dance orchestra, the musicians dressed in tuxedos, occupied a raised bandstand at one end of the ballroom. A mezzanine ran all the way around the building, on which were tables crowded with drinkers.

"Let's get a drink first," Ernest said, leading Nora toward the bar. They had to elbow their way through the crowd, and they might have had to wait for a long time to get a drink, except Ernest recognized one of the bartenders, a man who wore the costume of a cowboy. "Jules!" Ernest called, and lifted his black mask. "It's me."

"Ah, Hemingway!" Jules Pascin said. "*Ça va, mon ami?* What will you have?"

Ernest ordered double whiskey-and-sodas, and Jules, with a wet cigarette stuck in the side of his mouth, delivered them with only a little ash falling into their glasses.

After downing their drinks, they danced a few times, and stopped only when the band began playing tangos. Neither Nora nor Ernest knew how to tango. So they hailed Jules Pascin again, got more drinks, and went up on the mezzanine and claimed a table that someone was vacating. They watched the costumed crowd on the dance floor below for a while, ordered more drinks from a harried waiter in a clown's costume, and soon Nora began to feel quite drunk. She began to feel something else, too, that was harder to define, a feeling of freedom, of abandon that had something to do with the mask she wore. As long as the mask concealed her identity, she felt quite capable of anything—even dancing naked on a tabletop, if someone dared her to it, or if the impulse took her!

As for Ernest, he had mercurial moments of flirtatious friendliness, but the general direction of his mood was downward into apathy and indifference. Fearful that he might not make any unmistakable advances until she gave him an unmistakable sign of receptiveness, Nora finally reached under the table and gave his thigh a warm pat. It was a terribly bold thing for her to do, and she was able to do it only because of the drink and the mask. But it was for nothing. Ernest's only response was to drain his glass and ask if she would like another dance.

She hoped that the dance was merely a maneuver to get his arms around her and pull her close for a kiss. Many of the other dancers were kissing as they danced, and Nora hoped that Ernest might take a cue from them, but the waltz ended without a kiss, and Hemingway said, "This is too crowded for dancing."

"What would you like to do?"

"Get drunk. But not here. I don't want to fight my way to the bar for every drink. What d'you say we get out of here? Go somewhere where it's not so crowded?"

Hoping that this might be the first move toward a bedroom somewhere, Nora readily agreed. They made their way through the crowd and out of the Bal Bullier. The area just outside the main entrance was thronged with people in costumes, coming and going, fanning out into the nearby streets. Nora and Ernest, still wearing their masks, crossed the street and went into the Closerie des Lilas café, where they took a table in a dim corner.

Ernest had three or four drinks in quick succession, as if deliberately trying to get drunk as fast as possible, but the more he drank, the gloomier he became, until finally Nora, fearing that her fantasy of illicit sex was slipping away, asked him bluntly,

"What's the matter? You don't seem to be enjoying yourself very much."

Ernest pulled off his mask and dropped it on the table. "I'm sorry. I've got a lot of things on my mind. I know I'm not being very good company. I guess I should go home."

"Would you like me to go with you?"

There! Urged on by a desperate feeling that she was getting old and wouldn't have many more chances, she had gotten the words out, had asked Ernest a question that she had never asked another man except her husband.

Ernest seemed to blush a little as he smiled apologetically and said, "If you do that, I might want to take you to bed."

"Would that be a bad thing, do you think?"

"Might be for your husband."

"Ha!" she snorted. "Little he would care! When he was writing that bloody book, and Leopold Bloom was getting cuckolded, Jim wanted me to go out and have an affair with another man, so he would know what it was like, and could write about it."

"And did you?"

"I did not. Crucified Jaysus, it was enough that he was taking down all my words, and putting them in the mouth of that Molly Bloom character, without me sacrificing my virtue, too, for all the world like a whore in a peep show." She took a sip of her Irish whiskey, then said reflectively, "However, I must say, I gave the idea some thought, bedad if I didn't, and if I had met the right man . . ." She gave Ernest a straight look. "Who knows?"

In an agony of embarrassment, Ernest drained his whiskey-and-soda in one gulp, then squeezed the empty glass in both hands as he said, "Gee, Nora, I'm sorry. Ordinarily I'd jump at the chance, but I'm afraid I just wouldn't be very good company tonight."

Stung by the rejection, Nora groped for reasons. "How old are you?"

"Twenty-three. Why? What's that got to do with. . . ?"

"I'm forty," she said. "Seventeen years older than you—old enough to be your mother. Is that what it is?"

"No, no," he said, lighting another cigarette from the butt of the old one. "I like older women. No, I don't know what it is. It's just that . . . sometimes, when I get worried, or tense, or . . . shit, I don't know. I'm sorry. It doesn't have anything to do with you."

As her hopes settled into disappointment and shame, Nora said, "Well, then! I guess I'd better be getting home myself."

"I'll take you home," he said.

"No. You stay and get drunk, if that's what you've a mind to. I can get home by myself all right."

Ernest escorted her out of the café to an empty taxi at the curb, an old wartime Citroen without a top. After pulling off her mask and dropping it into a nearby trash can, Nora climbed into the backseat and closed the door. Ernest, disconsolate, stood beside the taxi, his hands jammed into his pockets, making no effort to touch Nora.

"Well, good night to you," she said. "And thanks for the dancing. It was fun."

"And, listen, I'm . . ." He shrugged and fell silent, as if on the verge of tears.

"Don't say it," Nora said. "Well, good night, then." She touched the taxi driver on the shoulder.

The taxi pulled away from the curb, leaving Ernest standing there, and leaving Nora to ride along the festive streets of Montparnasse and contemplate life's sad ironies. It had taken her years to work up the courage to have an affair, and look what had happened on her first try. Men! Who could fathom them? Crucified Jaysus, it was enough to make a woman want to become a lesbian.

34

Hadley

ERNEST SENT A telegram from Paris telling Hadley that he would be arriving in Cortina on April 12. Renata left Cortina the day before he was due to return. She went back to Venice. She said she would be returning to Paris sometime in the spring, and made Hadley promise to see her then, before she and Ernest went back to America.

The two of them had had a grand time together, but nothing they did could keep Hadley from missing Ernest. In her letters urging him to hurry back to Cortina, Hadley tempted him by telling him that his feather kitty was eagerly looking forward to putting all her four paws around her waxen puppy and making him squeal with joy.

But as soon as she saw him getting off the train, she knew that there was little chance that she would get even a smile out of him, let alone a squeal. Unshaven and red-eyed from too much liquor and too little sleep, he was obviously in one of his depressions, what he called his "black ass" moods. He was loaded down with his luggage and typewriter and the unjointed fishing rods and the fishing tackle box, and when the rods got caught in the door of the coach car, he jerked them loose at the risk of damaging them, which was an ominous measure of his impatience and irritability.

He set the gear down on the platform long enough to give

Hadley a hug and a kiss that held no ardency. They took a taxi to the hotel, and even though Hadley knew by now that the causes of his depressions weren't always knowable or discussable, she tried to get him to talk about inconsequential things—gossip from Paris, what he had seen and done in Germany—in hopes that he might inadvertently reveal the cause of his unhappiness. But without success.

She drew him a bath and scrubbed his back, but got no moans of appreciation, and she washed his cock with a warm, sudsy washcloth, but without any arousal. Once again he was experiencing a bout of impotence, as Hadley learned for sure that night when they got into bed and he turned his back on her. She had looked forward with both excitement and apprehension to talking to Ernest about Renata, hoping—expecting—that he would be drawn into the darker realms of Catherine-and-Peter excitement by hearing the details of the sensual things that Renata and she had done together. But he showed no interest in anything sexual. All he seemed interested in his first two days back in Cortina was lying in bed all day and looking up at the ceiling, or getting drunk and criticizing everybody and everything.

Finally, it came out and Hadley wasn't in the least surprised. He had made up his mind—got up the nerve—to ask her to have a surgical abortion. It was on the third day of his return. They had gone out for lunch to the Fascist café on the piazza across from the church and the campanile. Ernest was telling Hadley about all the people he had seen in Paris, and he mentioned that Djuna Barnes had taken him to meet a doctor—a real doctor, Ernest stressed, an American—who ended unwanted pregnancies.

"An abortionist?" Hadley asked.

"He's a real doctor," Ernest insisted. "An American. He'd do it for a hundred dollars."

"And that's what you want me to do?"

"Well, I wouldn't have you do it if you didn't want to."

"And you really want me to? Why don't you just say it?"

"Look, Tiny, I've never made a secret of it, this's the wrong time in our lives to get saddled with a kid, so, sure, I think it'd be best if you did it. But I don't want you to do it, unless you want to."

Hadley stared down at her plate of lasagna for a moment, then shoved it aside. She emptied her wineglass and lit a cigarette.

"It's a simple operation, Tiny. Why, it's not really an operation at all. It's just to let the air in, and then everything happens naturally." He continued eating his rare steak, but without gusto.

Hadley looked down at her hands resting in her lap. She was more than three months pregnant—nearly four—but she wasn't showing yet, not with her clothes on.

"I'd be with you all the time. Dr. Mahoney does it in the apartment, so you don't have to go anywhere, and you have a miscarriage. It's that simple."

"And afterward? You wouldn't feel bad about it afterward?"

"No. We'll be fine afterward. Just like we always were before you forgot your diaphragm and this happened."

"You really think so?"

"I know so. Gee, Tiny, it's the only thing that's messing up our lives, isn't it? It's the only thing that's made us unhappy."

"Made you unhappy," she corrected. "I'm happy with it. I feel fine."

"You're happy about having to go back to Toronto, and being the wife of a working stiff for the rest of your life, are you? Come on, you can't prefer that to Paris. Why, we're the envy of all the people we grew up with back in the States. We have friends here who're internationally famous, and can help me get started as a writer. We have a future in Paris. What would we have in Toronto? A dull life, a dull job, a squalling kid. . . ."

"And you think that's all it'll take to make everything all right and be happy?"

"I'm sure of it. And it's really simple, you don't have to worry about it, or be afraid. Lots of people we know have done it."

"Yeah," Hadley said, tapping her cigarette on the edge of the ashtray. "And afterward they were all so happy."

"Well, you don't have to do it if you don't want to."

"I don't want to."

"Then you don't have to," he said sullenly. "But you'd better think about it."

The waiter came and said something in Tyroler dialect, nodding toward Hadley's lasagna.

"He asks if you don't like the lasagna," Ernest said.

She pushed the plate toward the waiter. "No. Tell him to take it away and bring me a cognac. I think I'll get drunk."

Ernest pushed his own unfinished lunch toward the waiter, then drained his wineglass and handed it to the waiter. "Two cognacs, please," he said, and the waiter took the plates and glasses and went away. Two other waiters were standing in the back of the café, under a picture of Mussolini, looking at them. The picture of Mussolini was also looking at them. Ernest had once described Mussolini in a newspaper story as having "nigger eyes." Hadley had wondered what that meant—what were "nigger eyes"? But she never asked him because he didn't like having to explain his images.

"And if I do it, it'll be fine again, and you'll love me?" she asked.

"I love you now."

"But you won't love me if I don't do it."

"I didn't say that. Of course I will. I'll love you, no matter what. It's just that I can't . . . I can't do it when I'm so worried. Make love, I mean. You know how I am when I get worried."

Hadley sighed. "Well, I've always said that I'm you, so I guess I'll have to do it, if you really want me to. I've always said I'd do anything for you." She hesitated a moment before adding, "But I don't know about this. Tatie, we could get by."

"Of course we could 'get by.' But I want to do more than just get by. I want to get somewhere. I want to be a great writer, and that's a hard enough thing to do without having a baby to hold you back. Besides, I just want you. I don't want anyone else but us. That's the kind of life I want, just us." He shrugged. "Later . . . maybe someday. . . ."

"But it'll be too late for me later. I'll be too old. You'll find some younger woman to have children with."

"Oh, that's not true. You've got years and years yet. And I wouldn't want to have kids with anybody but you. You're all I want."

"All right, then."

"You'll do it?"

"I guess so."

"You won't regret it?"

"I already regret it."

"Then don't do it," he snapped.

"I'll do it, but stop talking about it, will you? I don't want to hear any more about it."

"All right, but I don't want you to do it if you don't feel right about it."

"Are you going to shut up, or not?"

"Okay, okay. I just wanted you to know."

The waiter brought the two cognacs. Under the baleful gaze of Mussolini, they drank in silence.

35

Hadley

As THEY WERE going up the path to the hotel, they met the old drunk who was the hotel's gardener. As if in a conspiracy, the gardener stopped Ernest and took him aside and whispered something to him as Hadley went on into the hotel. It was this mysterious conversation between the gardener and Ernest that set in motion an experience which Ernest transcribed into a short story he called "Out of Season." The events took place in no more than three hours that afternoon, and it took Ernest only a few hours later that evening to write the story.

He typed the story the next day, then gave it to Hadley to read. She read it while he went to the railway station in Cortina to buy their tickets back to Paris. Ernest had returned to Cortina in hopes of more skiing before the season was over, and he'd also had hopes of doing some trout fishing, but the skiing season had ended with a misty rain that turned the slopes to slush, and the hotel's padrone had told him that trout season wouldn't open for two more weeks, so Ernest and Hadley agreed that they might as well go on back to Paris as soon as practical and see Dr. Mahoney.

Hadley didn't like "Out of Season." The story annoyed her on a number of levels. It was a simple story about how the old gardener, anxious to make a few lire as a fishing guide, offered to show Ernest where he could catch some trout on the Bigontina

River just outside of town, even though trout season was not yet open. And that was exactly what happened in real life. The story was a literal rendition of the experience—more the work of a reporter than a creative writer. The only imagination shown in the story was what was left out, not what was put in. "Out of Season" was an example of what Ernest had recently conceptualized as an "iceberg theory" of writing fiction, in which only about ten percent of the mass of the story would be above the surface. He theorized that the writer could omit anything from a story if he knew what he omitted, and the omitted part would strengthen the story and make the reader feel something more than he understood.

For instance, the wife in "Out of Season," called Tiny was depicted as being sullen, bad-tempered, and shrewish, walking behind as the three characters are on their way to the river to do some out-of-season fishing.

This was how Hadley had actually acted, but Ernest didn't tell why. There were many reasons for her sullenness, the most immediate being that she had been asked to carry the fishing rods and follow the men at a distance. Ernest and the old drunk of a gardener had decided that, if spotted by the game police, she would be less likely than they to be suspected of fishing out of season. She hoped she would be caught so she could make a full confession, thereby publicly shame them for having a woman do what they were too cowardly to do.

But she wasn't stopped by the game police, and when they got near the edge of town, the gardener asked Hadley to walk with them. Hadley still held back until Ernest shouted "Oh, for Christ's sake, Tiny, stop sulking and come on up here with us."

In the story, Ernest called the drunk gardener Peduzzi, and as they pass the store, Peduzzi, with impertinent familiarity, tries to manipulate the young man into buying them some marsala. That had actually happened, but then Ernest wrote that marsala was what Max Beerbohm drank and why did Pedruzzi mention marsala?

Well, the reader might want to know who the hell Max Beerbohm was? And what did his drinking marsala have to do with anything? Perhaps only Hadley knew that the author had once met Max Beerbohm, an English humorist who lived near Rapallo, and probably not one person would know or care that Beerbohm was a fat old fairy whose favorite drink was marsala.

There is some more rigmarole about marsala, and before leaving the store where the marsala had been bought, the young gentleman apologizes to his wife for how he had spoken to her at lunch.

But the reader never finds out what they talked about at lunch, never learns what made Tiny so sullen and unhappy. This, too, was presumably omitted under Ernest's new iceberg theory of writing fiction. Or maybe he just didn't want to reveal to the reader that he had asked his wife to have an abortion.

That was another thing Hadley disliked about the story, the way Ernest always showed himself in the best possible light. For instance, when the young gentleman said, "Are you cold? I wish you'd worn another sweater," he seemed to be sympathizing with his wife; but what Ernest actually said to Hadley in a grudging voice was, "Are you cold? Why in hell didn't you put on another sweater, like I told you to?"

"I've got on three sweaters already," Hadley said.

The three of them walked on to the river, with the drunk gardener dismissing any possible trouble, and the young gentleman worrying that they might have been seen by the game police.

Hadley remembered saying, "Then why don't we go back? What have you got to prove? There's good reason for the fish being out of season. It's their spawning time, and if you catch the females before they spawn, there won't be any little ones for next year. Let's go back, Tatie, please."

Ernest flared with anger when he said, "Damnit, if you want to go back, go ahead. It's a rotten day, and we're not going to have any fun, anyway, with your killjoy attitude."

"All right, I will," Hadley snapped, and turned back toward town.

After that Ernest and the gardener realized that they had no lead weights, without which the bait would not sink below the surface of the muddy, roiling river, and they turned back.

In the story the young man was relieved to turn back. Hadley would have liked it better if Ernest's decision not to fish had

been made out of moral conviction, rather than letting an accident of circumstances make the decision for him.

There was a lot more about the story that she didn't like, such
as the lack of clarity in what it was about. However, she had no
intention of telling Ernest any of this. She knew that when he
gave her a story to read, what he wanted was praise, not criticism. That much she would give him, but the one thing she
would not give him was a chance to continue writing such
botched stories at the expense of an abortion. If this was the best
he could do at writing short stories, Hadley certainly wasn't going to forego having a baby just so he could keep writing them.

If it were true that Ernest was actually relieved when the lack
of sinkers prevented him from breaking the game law, then Hadley would take it upon herself to relieve him of breaking the law
against abortion.

So when he returned to the hotel after having purchased their
train tickets back to Paris, Hadley gave him the story, said she
thought it was fine, just fine, a good example of his new iceberg
theory of writing; then she told him, "Tatie, I've made a decision
about an abortion. I'm not going to have one. I'm going to have
the baby."

It took him a moment to adjust to the finality of that statement,
and then he shrugged. If not relieved, he at least seemed re-
signed.

36

McAlmon

BY LATE SPRING of 1923, everybody was returning to Paris. Mike and Maggie Strater were back, as were Ezra and Dorothy Pound. The Pounds had once again taken up residence in their apartment in rue Notre Dame des Champs, and the Hemingways, having returned from Cortina d'Ampézzo, were once more in their apartment in rue du Cardinal Lemoine. Even H.D. and Bryher, with the Lump in tow, had left their redoubt in Switzerland for an extended visit to Paris. Bryher had temporarily suspended her campaign to get McAlmon to agree to be the daddy of an adopted boy who would carry on Bryher's name, and had settled for the lesser goal of trying to get her husband to accompany her on a trip to England to see her parents, to make sure that the wool was still pulled snugly over their eyes. McAlmon, however, was resisting that ordeal of lies and subterfuges.

It was while he was searching for excuses that he decided to go to Spain. He told Bryher that he was sorry, but his plans had already been made, he was off to Spain to see some bullfights. And the moment he said it, it became true, he knew that was what he wanted to do. He had never been to Spain, had never seen a bullfight, and the stories Mike Strater had told in Rapallo had whetted his curiosity. Bullfights were the most brutal and barbaric sport still practiced anywhere in the civilized world, and there they were, just south of the border, so why not see if these rituals of blood and death were what was needed to pique his jaded appetite for stronger thrills, stronger wine?

Usually he was at a party or in a bar, drinking copiously, talking to friends, when the subject came up, and each time he talked about it, the plans became a little more concrete.

"They say the best bullfights are in Madrid and Ronda," someone told him.

"Oh, yeah? That's where I'm going," he said, having made up his mind on the spot.

"When are you leaving?"

"Oh, in a few days," he said.

"The height of the bullfighting season is in the summer, but they have some good ones beginning in May. The bulls are better then. Well-fed. Fresher."

"That's when I'm going," McAlmon decided. "See the bulls fresh. 'Cause after they been dead for a while, they ain't so fresh."

Thus the plans took shape. Actually, what he was waiting for was someone to volunteer to go with him. That was the missing ingredient, a traveling companion he could get along with for a few weeks. And it was a measure of how desperate he was for a companion that he asked T.S. Eliot if he'd like to go with him. McAlmon had gotten to know Eliot in London in 1921, when he was playing son-in-law to the Ellermans, and he rather liked Eliot, prissy though he was. So in April, when Eliot came to Paris to visit Ezra Pound, McAlmon dropped around Ezra's apartment to say howdy. He hadn't seen Eliot since the publication of *The Waste Land,* and he assumed that Eliot would be exhilarated by the great success of the poem; instead, McAlmon found him to be terribly depressed—understandably so, perhaps, since he had just returned from taking his wife, Vivian, to Montreux, where he had deposited her in a mental hospital—the same mental hospital where Eliot, suffering from what was diagnosed as a nervous breakdown, had been a patient in '21 while he was writing *The Waste Land.* Eliot didn't respond with any alacrity to McAlmon's invitation to go running off to Spain to take in a few bullfights.

"Oh, my word," he said in his affected English accent.

"Hmmmm. Well, don't suppose you'd want to go, Ezra?" McAlmon asked.

"Shit fire and save matches, boy," Ezra said in his affected American accent, "I got better things to do than see a bunch of damned fools kill a bunch of damned bulls."

McAlmon took James and Nora Joyce and Djuna Barnes to dinner at the Lutétia, and while he knew it would do no good asking them if they wanted to go to Spain with him, he extended an invitation as a matter of courtesy. Joyce was speechless at the prospect.

"Why don't you go, Jim?" Nora said. "I think you could do with a spot of that bullfighting."

Joyce remained speechless.

Djuna Barnes considered the idea, and said she would have to talk to Thelma about it. Thelma had recently returned from a long sojourn in Berlin, and Djuna wasn't sure she would want to go traveling again so soon. McAlmon didn't encourage her, however, since Djuna was at the moment wearing dark sunglasses over what was obviously the discolored residue of a black eye, presumably put there by Thelma Wood's knuckles, and the last thing McAlmon needed was to get stuck on a trip to Spain with a couple of battling lesbians.

McAlmon also had dinner with Cole Porter and Gerald and Sara Murphy, but Cole thought the idea of watching a poor bull get killed was just too ghastly, and Gerald Murphy, though interested, was too busy at the moment working on his and Cole's ballet to think about anything else.

Then one afternoon McAlmon ran into Hadley Hemingway and Renata Borgatti in the Tois et As bar, where McAlmon's good buddy, Jimmie Charters, was the bartender. Hadley had left Ernest at home alone, she said, so he could finish a short story he was working on. She and Renata had gone for a walk in the Luxembourg Gardens, then stopped in for an aperitif.

"Join us?" Renata asked.

Assuming that they were not having a tête-à-tête, McAlmon accepted the invitation. He had met Renata at Natalie Barney's, and had gotten to know her at Nancy Cunard's in Venice. While not friends, they were on friendly terms, so her casual invitation wasn't surprising; what was surprising was to see Hadley, a pregnant and respectable married woman, paling around Paris with Renata. However, he did not inquire into the singularity of that friendship, but contented himself with joining them for some banal afternoon chitchat.

"Spain!" Hadley said at the mention of McAlmon's plans. "Bull-fights! Oh, my god, Ernest would kill to get to see a bullfight! Oh, please, Mac, do take him with you. The poor man, we're going to have to move to Toronto in August, and he's afraid he'll never get to see a bullfight."

Though he didn't mention it to Hadley, McAlmon had reservations about Hemingway as a traveling companion. From their short acquaintance in Rapallo, McAlmon knew Hemingway's need to dominate every scene he was in. He knew that Hemingway would automatically take charge of itineraries, travel arrangements, hotels, and schedules. That was just the way he was. And, McAlmon guessed that Hemingway's enthusiasms would always carry the day against McAlmon's own more jaded and lackadaisical mode of adventuring. So conflict would be inevitable and since Hemingway was the stronger of the two, both physically and in character, McAlmon would sooner or later—and probably sooner than later—be faced with the decision either to break off the venture, or capitulate to Hemingway's dominance.

Still, he was willing to consider Hadley's request, so he accepted her invitation to dine with the Hemingways that evening. Hemingway and McAlmon hadn't talked since their train ride from Venice, but McAlmon, of course, had seen Hemingway once since they had returned to Paris, on the night in the Gipsy Bar when he had instigated the Cole Porter and Monte Woolley propositioning. Indignantly offended, Hemingway had huffed out of the bar, without having seen McAlmon in the shadows.

Hemingway greeted him heartily when McAlmon arrived at the shabby third-floor apartment, and he was wild for the idea of going to Spain. His enthusiasm brought him out of his chair like a trout rising from the water, but immediately he fell back again when he realized he couldn't go.

"Hell, I haven't got the money to do anything like that," he said plaintively. "As it is, we're going to have to borrow some money for our boat tickets back to America. But wouldn't that be something?—a couple of weeks bumming around Spain, seeing bullfights? Why, just the other day Gertrude was showing me a picture of her and Alice in the bullring at Valencia. They were sitting right in the first row of the *barrera* seats, with Joselito standing in front of them."

It was only because Hemingway seemed to assume that McAlmon knew who this Joselito was that McAlmon asked provocatively, "Joselito who?"

Hemingway gave him a disparaging look. "Joselito? You don't know who Joselito is? He was the greatest bullfighter who ever lived. He was gored that same year Gertrude and Alice had their picture taken with him, 1920. Died in the bullring."

"I drink to Joselito," McAlmon said, and drained the whiskey that Hemingway had served him when he came in. Hadley and the Hemingways' femme de ménage were in the tiny kitchen, cooking dinner. McAlmon had hoped that Hemingway would offer to refill his glass, but he didn't.

"I just can't afford it," Hemingway said, preoccupied, shaking his head sadly. "Probably be my last chance ever to see a bullfight, but . . . with a baby coming . . ."

It occurred to McAlmon that Hemingway's penury might provide McAlmon with a way to make him a docile and less dominating traveling companion. They might get along all right if McAlmon held the power of the purse over him. With that in mind, he said, "Well, if I could help out with the expenses . . ."

Nothing McAlmon could have said would have made Hemingway happier. "You mean it? You'd pay my way?"

That wasn't what he had said, of course, but Hemingway was so eager for McAlmon to confirm his version of the offer that McAlmon couldn't bring himself to snatch the vision of sugarplums away from him. Instead, he tilted his head, hoping that such a weak assent would warn Hemingway of qualifiers, but Hemingway, carried away by excitement, called to Hadley, "Did you hear that, Hash? Mac said he'd pay my way! Isn't that wonderful?"

"That's wonderful," Hadley said, poking her head into the

room and gazing at McAlmon quizzically, as if not quite able to believe it. "Well! How very generous of you, Mac."

"Oh, well, it's Sir Ellerman's money, anyway, isn't it?" Hemingway said. "And he's got enough of it, God knows."

McAlmon had the feeling that he had been suckered, but one thing that the guilt of having Sir Ellerman's money had taught him was how to be suckered and manipulated with a certain modicum of stoicism and perhaps even a little grace.

Hadley reacted well to her husband's assumption that there was no question of her coming along. She was pregnant, after all, and, by all appearances, close to being barefoot, so there wasn't any consideration of her accompanying the men. Her place was in the home, while her husband went gallivanting, seeing bullfights and attending festivals.

"Great!" Hemingway said, pouring McAlmon another whiskey. "When do we start?"

They started three days later. That was as soon as McAlmon could get the most pressing of his publishing company's business chores done. Hemingway spent those days trying to drum up a party to go along with them, but the only person who accepted Hemingway's invitation was William Bird. As he couldn't leave Paris immediately, he would join them in Madrid as soon as he finished some urgent typesetting for his Three Mountain Press.

"Probably in three or four days," Bird told Hemingway.

"We'll be in Aguilar's, a bullfighters' pensión in the Calle San Jeronimo," Hemingway told Bird as he and McAlmon were getting ready to board the train for Madrid. Bird had come to see them off. Hemingway had gotten the name of the pensión from Mike Strater, who wanted to go with them but couldn't because he had to fulfill a commission to paint the portrait of the American ambassador to France. However, Mike had given Hemingway a lot of information about where to go and where to stay in the cities that were known for their bullfights. Hemingway had written it down and, true to McAlmon's expectations, had taken charge of the itinerary. Without even bothering to consult McAlmon, who was paying for the train tickets and hotels, Hemingway had reserved a first-class double sleeping compartment for them and had sent a telegram to Aguilar's Pensión in Madrid, reserving a couple of rooms for the coming weekend. And McAlmon complied. Because he was beginning to realize that he needed Hemingway's take-charge enthusiasm just as much as Hemingway needed his money.

Hadley came to see them off at the Gare de Lyon, and while she was saddened to see her husband going on a trip without her, she didn't appear to begrudge his going. They seemed loving and at peace with each other. Saying good-bye, he called her Feather Kitty and she called him Beery Poppa, and at that moment McAlmon rather envied Hemingway his wife.

In the early afternoon of their second day, just after entering Spain, their train came to a rattling stop on the outskirts of a small town, and McAlmon smelled, and then saw, below the open window, the carcass of a dog. Movements beneath the dog's fur made it seem as if it were still alive, still breathing, but it was dead, all right, and the stench was overpowering. The pulsing movement beneath the dog's skin was caused by maggots feeding within the carcass.

Hemingway had the seat next to the door, where he had been reading a book on bullfighting. When he got a whiff of the dead dog, he fanned the air away from his nose, and said, "Damn, Mac, what've you been eating?"

When McAlmon got up and turned away, Hemingway scooted over on the seat to look out the window. The smell brought a grimace to his unshaven face, but the sight seemed to fascinate him.

"Ah, hell—a dog. That's nothing. During the war, a munitions factory near Milan blew up. Killed more than two hundred workers. Blew them to bits. Blew parts of them over the countryside. The Red Cross asked for volunteers to pick up the pieces. I volunteered. I was putting myself through a self-hardening process. As a writer, I wanted to learn how to write about violent death, without my feelings getting in the way.

"Well, that proved to be a good exercise for me. Most of the munition workers had been women. We found parts of them for miles around—an arm caught in a fence, a breast caught in the limb of a tree, a head with long hair found in a bush—all swarming with maggots, like that dog. The head of that woman in the bush?—her mouth was filled with maggots. And talk about stink! Hell, this is nothing compared to—"

Fighting down nausea, McAlmon left the compartment and hurried to the bar in the dining car, where he drank two shots of Hennessey's in quick succession, trying to get that sickening smell out of his nose and throat. Hemingway showed up in the bar in a few minutes, grinning.

"What's the matter, can't you take reality?" he asked, and ordered a glass of Hennessey's for himself, which of course he expected McAlmon to pay for.

"I don't need any lectures from you on death," McAlmon told him. "I've seen plenty of dead animals and people, too, in my time. Forget it."

"Hell, Mac, you write like a realist," he said. "Are you going to go romantic on us?"

"No, I just don't need to dwell on death—do you?"

"That's why I'm going to Spain and study the bullfights. Now that the wars are over, the bullring is the only place left where you can see violent death."

"You might find a slaughterhouse and sit on the fence of the killing chute for a while. That ought to give you your fill of watching violent death."

"It's not the same, and you know it, Mac. That's just slaughter. In the bullring, violent death is raised to the level of art." Fortifying himself with another cognac, he went on, "And that's what art is for, isn't it? To raise life to its highest point of intensity? That's what the bullfight does at the moment of the bull's death."

"Yeah? I'll bet the bull feels pretty intense, all right."

"Gee, Mac, you are a sentimental romantic, aren't you?"

"Yeah? Well, how would you know what happens at the moment of the bull's death? From something you read in a book?"

Hemingway bristled. "Hell, no, I don't have to get my knowledge of death from books. I hunted plenty when I was a kid up in Michigan, and I learned early that I never felt more alive than when I was killing something."

"Gives you a thrill, does it?"

"Yeah," Hemingway answered defiantly. "Yeah, it does. I never feel more alive than when I'm killing something. And if you weren't such a damned romantic, you'd know that's true for all men. Even soldiers. Sure, they may not admit it, but during war, after soldiers learn to kill, they get to liking it. I did, as long as it was the enemy I was killing. I'm one of the few who'll admit it openly. Hell, once when the Austrians broke through our lines up toward Caporetto, and we were told to hold the line in our sector at all costs, I had my men set up an ambush in a garden, and when an Austrian patrol tried to get past us, we waited until they began climbing over the garden wall. We held our fire until the first one got his leg over the wall, and then we potted him. Then a few more came over farther down the wall, and we shot them. They all came over, and we shot them, just like that. I killed ten of them myself. And I never felt more alive than when I was doing it."

He hesitated for a moment, ruminating, and then added, "Except maybe for the time when I was wounded. Got caught in the open, trying to carry a wounded Italian soldier back to the aid station. Got hit with a trench mortar, then a machine gun. At the hospital they dug 232 pieces of shrapnel and two machine-gun slugs out of my legs. Nothing like feeling your own life slipping out of your body to make you feel alive, intensely alive, I can tell you."

McAlmon had heard most of this before in Rapallo, and he didn't know whether it was true or not. He suspected it was mostly lies, but Hemingway always said it as if he believed it, so it was impossible to tell if he was a liar, or a braggart, or both. But one thing was for sure, he was a good sponger; while they were at the bar, he drank four snifters of Three Star Cognac, and it was McAlmon's money that bought it.

They arrived in Madrid on a chilly Friday just before midnight. On their way in a taxi to Aguilar's Pensión, they were surprised to see that the streets of Madrid were so lively. There were crowds on the sidewalks, and many cafés and cantinas were filled with music and noisy revelers. The taxi driver, who spoke a little English, said the festive air was because the first big *feria* of spring was in progress, and the first major *corrida de toros* since Easter was to take place two days hence, on Sunday, featuring two matadors who were favorites in Madrid, Nicanor Villalta, and Chicuelo. This news made Hemingway expansive with excitement, so that he, like a knight talking to his squire, instructed McAlmon to give the taxi driver a bigger than usual tip when they got out at the pensión.

Their first disappointment came when they learned from the desk clerk that there was only one room left.

"Oh, no. *No comprendo,"* Hemingway said in his tourist guide-book Spanish. *"Tengo dos reservas."*

"Lo siento, señor," said the desk clerk, but there it was: only one room had been reserved. There was no other room available. The others were all filled by the bullfighters and their entourages.

"Well, hell," Hemingway said to McAlmon, "if I'm going to study bullfighting, I've got to stay here with the bullfighters. Would you mind going to another hotel?"

"Damned right, I'd mind," McAlmon said. "I'm hungover, tired, and sleepy, and I'm not in the mood to go running around Madrid in the middle of the night, looking for an empty hotel room. How many beds does the room have?" he asked the desk clerk.

"Uno solo."

"Rats. Ask him to put another bed in the room," McAlmon told Hemingway.

Consulting his guidebook dictionary, Hemingway said, *"Podría poner otra cama en el cuarto?"*

No, the pensión had no more beds.

"Maybe the one there is big enough for two," McAlmon said. "We can make do tonight, I'll get another room tomorrow."

"Podría ver el cuarto?" Hemingway asked, and the desk clerk took them up to the third floor.

The room was of the bare-bones boardinghouse variety, but the bed was a double. Testing it, McAlmon found that the mattress was lumpy and the springs were squeaky, but "What the hell," he said, *"Esta bien."* He didn't ask Hemingway whether or not it suited him. If it didn't, then Hemingway would have to be the one to go looking for another room.

It worked out all right. Hemingway's snoring woke McAlmon a few times and he had to jab him in the ribs with an elbow and make him change his position before the snoring stopped, but they got through the night. Indeed, Hemingway, had a fine sleep, to judge by the way he woke up and hurried to get washed and dressed, impatient to go out into this wonderful new world of bullfighting and begin his study of violent death.

It was exhilarating to see, the way Hemingway took to this new world. It was as if he had come home after two or three reincarnated lives in foreign lands. As a boy, McAlmon had seen duck hatchlings when they were first introduced to water, and he had been amazed by the shock of recognition they so obviously experienced, the almost hysterical happiness at finding themselves in the element that they had been created for. So Hemingway seemed in the bullfight world of Madrid.

During a quick breakfast in the pensión's dining room, Hemingway used his broken Spanish to talk to the picadors and banderilleros at the adjoining tables, and he brought out his notebook to write down some of the answers they gave him. They themselves were quite blasé about bullfighting, but they smiled at one another to see Hemingway's naive enthusiasm, and they rewarded him by being open and informative. They told him what seats to get at the Plaza de Toros. They also told him about the *apartado,* the sorting and separating of the bulls in the corrals behind the bullring. With Hemingway taking notes as fast as he could write, they explained that the apartado was accomplished with the aid of steers and the use of runways and swinging doors to trap the fighting bulls in the individual pens where they stay until their turn comes to go out into the bullring and meet their deaths.

The apartado would take place just after noon on the following day, Sunday, and usually only matadors, their friends, and their colleagues would attend. Spectators were discouraged from attending by being charged five pesetas, but Hemingway figured McAlmon could afford that, so he made plans to go the next day.

After breakfast, McAlmon and Hemingway took a horse-drawn bus to the Plaza de Toros, where Hemingway bought tickets for the next day's bullfights. He had to deal with a *re-venta,* one of the ticket brokers who buys most of the unsubscribed seats, then resells the tickets to tourists and out-of-town visitors for twice the original price. And since Hemingway was going to be study-ing this ritual of violent death, he needed the best seat available, a ringside seat on the shady side of the bullring, just behind the barrera, so that no spectators would be between him and the bullfight. The price? Forty pesetas each.

"Jesus Christ," McAlmon protested. "For that price a man could live in a Madrid boardinghouse for a week."

"Well, sure," Hemingway said in a tone of voice that seemed to make McAlmon's fairness and generosity suspect, "but if we're going to do this, we should do it right—shouldn't we?"

"Okay, okay," McAlmon said, and paid for the tickets.

Next, following instructions that Hemingway picked up along the way, they took a horse-drawn bus back to the Puerta del Sol and found one of the nearby cafés whose walls were covered with posters advertising fiestas in Seville, Ronda, Valencia, Bil-bao, and Malaga. In his notebook, Hemingway wrote down the dates and places, and then they sat in the café and drank Domecq brandy and studied maps of Spain, figuring out an itin-erary that would take them to the major bullfights that were scheduled during the next four weeks. Hemingway was nothing if not ambitious.

By early evening they had found the Café Fornos, which was famous as a gathering place for bullfighters and their hangers-on. Among the hangers-on could be counted a number of whores. Amid the bustle of hurrying waiters, the noises of clink-ing glasses and talk and laughter and disputes and the scratchy sounds of music coming from an old phonograph, McAlmon and Hemingway talked to the customers and whores and McAlmon treated some of them to drinks, and before long Hemingway and McAlmon were accorded the courtesy titles of apprentice aficio-nados.

By dinnertime both Hemingway and McAlmon were drunk, but they both sobered up a little with a robust dinner of paella Valenciano, one of the most delicious meals either of them had ever had. With it they drank a bottle of chilled white Rioja wine, and finished with coffee and more Domecq brandy.

Sometime during the evening they were joined by a blond whore called Vicki, who took a liking to Hemingway. She sat on his lap and wheedled him out of drinks (which McAlmon paid for), and soon she was whispering something into his ear.

"She wants me to go with her to her house," Hemingway said. "I'm nuts about her. Why not? I already got a hard-on. She only charges ten pesetas. What d'you say? Could she be included in the expenses of the trip?"

In his alcohol-befuddled brain it took McAlmon a moment to realize that he was being asked to buy Hemingway a whore.

"Are you kidding?" McAlmon said. "You really expect me to pay for a whore? Maybe you'd like me to blow in her ear while you're fucking her?"

"That's it, how about if we both have her? At the same time. You take the front, I'll take the rear. What d'you say? Should I ask her? Two for the price of one?"

"Never mind," McAlmon said. "She ain't my type."

"And what is your type, Mac?" Hemingway asked. "If she looked more like a boy, would she be your type?"

"Lay off," McAlmon said.

Hemingway made a mirthless sound in his throat that was meant to be a chuckle. "What the hell, can't you take a joke?" To the whore, he said, *"No dinero,* Vicki. *Lo siento, mi dulce."*

Vicki stayed around long enough to cadge one more drink, then she went on her way with a backward glance of disdain.

McAlmon and Hemingway stayed in the café until the early-morning hours, drinking themselves into a stupor. McAlmon had seen Hemingway drunk before, but never this drunk, and while McAlmon prided himself on the amount of liquor he could drink without suffering any loss of control, he was staggering when they finally left the café and got a taxi. By the time they reached the pensión, McAlmon seemed to be slipping in and out of consciousness. He only vaguely remembered Hemingway digging his wallet from his pants' pocket to pay the taxi, and McAlmon didn't remember getting from the taxi into the room, though he did remember as he entered the room, half-carried by Hemingway, that he had forgotten to get himself a room in another hotel that day. But he didn't dwell on it as he hurriedly took off his clothes and flung them on the floor, trying to get into bed before he passed out. He had an impression of Hemingway dropping onto the bed beside him like a felled tree, immediately falling into a deep, snoring sleep.

Later McAlmon sensed he was in a dark room, naked, and some time had passed. And he was slightly made aware that someone was pawing at him. It took a moment of concentration to remember where he was, and that the person pawing at him must be Hemingway. Though still snoring, Hemingway was pulling McAlmon's naked buttocks against him, against his hard penis, hunching him, his snorts and snores becoming little grunts and whines.

McAlmon didn't do anything. He didn't resist. He went on pretending to be passed out as Hemingway shifted him around, drunkenly, roughly, almost contemptuously, so that he could mount him from behind. McAlmon submitted to the assault, even though he knew he could have stopped it if he had resisted; but he didn't because he found himself unable to resist. He had no conscious desire to be sodomized by Hemingway, but he had no will to resist, either. It was as if this were some preordained act that nullified his own will, and so he played his part. Indeed, he even enjoyed it, in a self-loathing, masochistic way.

It didn't take Hemingway long to finish in a violent climax, then he collapsed on top of McAlmon, where he stayed like a dead weight until his heavy panting subsided, after which he rolled off McAlmon with the same collapsing motion with which he had fallen onto the bed earlier, and once again was snoring in deep sleep by the time his head rolled back onto his pillow.

McAlmon lay for a long while, wondering and worrying about what he and Hemingway would do now, with this between them. This would have to change any relationship, completely and irrevocably. He dreaded the embarrassment of acknowledging the issue, and dealing with it, and wondered what agony of shame and conditioning they would have to overcome if they were to become lovers.

37

McAlmon

THE NEXT MORNING, Hemingway grumbled and groaned with a hangover as he got out of bed. He went into the Turkish toilet and sluiced himself off with a bucket of water, and when he came out he was as cheerful as could be expected.

"Boy, oh, boy," he said, "you could never guess what I dreamed last night. I dreamed I was in bed with Vicki—that Café Fornos whore, remember?—and did I ever give her a good yencing!"

So that was how he was going to play it—it had all been just a wet dream. Hemingway himself appeared to believe this. At first he seemed more self-consciously polite than usual, but otherwise there was no difference in his responses to McAlmon. As they had breakfast in the pensión's dining room, he talked about how God-awful drunk they had been last night.

"Yeah, I can hardly remember getting back to the room," McAlmon agreed.

"I can't remember much," Hemingway said, "except that dream and Miss Vicki! I'll have to tell her about it, if I see her today." He ordered a brandy with another cup of coffee. "On second thought, maybe I better not tell her—she might want to charge me for it."

But as the day wore on, Hemingway began to be short-tempered and even contemptuous toward McAlmon. At the bullring for the apartado, McAlmon found himself gazing through a space between the railings of the corral fence directly into the eyes of a frightfully big and belligerent fighting bull, he sought to calm the animal by saying, "Hello, bull," and Hemingway blew up. Taking McAlmon aside, he said in a fierce whisper, "Goddamnit, don't you know you're not supposed to talk to the bulls? You're not supposed to attract their attention in any way. If you get them excited, they may charge the corral, or the doors, or one another, and run the risk of injuring their horns or goring one another. That's why they charge five pesetas to see the apartado. They figure that anyone who has five pesetas to pay to see the bulls sorted will have enough sense not to talk to them before the fights."

"Well, excuse me all to hell," McAlmon said, not taking the rebuke with good grace. "It appears that I've got the pesetas and you've got the good sense, so tell me: How was I supposed to know that?"

"They told us when we came in, that's how. Goddamnit, if you'd bother to learn a little Spanish, you might pick up a few things, without me having to tell you."

"Well, you're sure as hell the expert when it comes to Spanish, ain't you? You and your travel book."

"Well, I make an effort, at least." He was sneering, trying to have the last word.

Though McAlmon could be combative when the need or the desire arose, he backed off from this tiff with Hemingway. He fell silent and let Hemingway have the last word, if it was so important to his pride. McAlmon's pride was at stake here, too, but more than anything else, he was puzzled by this harsh and insolent scolding by Hemingway, which did not seem justified by the ostensible cause. McAlmon had a hunch that Hemingway's ill-temper was not occasioned so much by McAlmon's saying hello to the bull as it was by McAlmon's having served as a surrogate Vicki in Hemingway's dream last night; previous to that, McAlmon didn't think Hemingway would have dared scold him in such a humiliating way.

And Hemingway's testiness got worse as the day wore on—toward McAlmon, and only toward McAlmon, for otherwise he was in high spirits, like that duckling that had just discovered water. And McAlmon had to acknowledge that Hemingway was an extremely quick learner. When he decided to find out everything he could about bullfighting, he went about it like a good reporter working on a story, as when he, while waiting for the bullfights to start, went down into the ring itself to talk to people. Then, with his bullfighting book under one arm and his notebook in his hand, he went into the patio de caballos, where the picadors and banderilleros waited to enter the ring, and went among the bullfighters, smiling, shaking hands, asking questions, taking notes, being charming. And McAlmon guessed that Hemingway had learned more Spanish in the last couple of days than he had learned in his life.

When the bullfights were about to begin, Hemingway came back to his seat just behind the barrier. He was practically panting from excitement as the three matadors and their entourages of picadors and banderilleros performed the ritual paseo—entering the ring to the stirring strains of a brass band playing "La Virgin de la Macareña."

Some Spaniards in the seats next to them were drinking wine from a *bota,* a container made of animal skin, the mouth of which never touched the drinkers' lips. By compressing the bota close to the open mouth, the drinker squirted a stream of wine, then kept the stream going as he gradually extended the bota to arm's length. When his mouth was almost full, the drinker would bring the bota nearly back to his lips before he stopped the stream.

"We're going to have to get one of those before the next bullfight," Hemingway decided.

Noting Hemingway's and McAlmon's interest in the bota, the owner offered them a drink from it. Hemingway was eagerly first, and he managed to keep the arching stream of wine going into his mouth, but McAlmon's hands were shaky from his hangover and he couldn't keep the stream steady. He got wine on his face and the front of his shirt. The people in the nearby seats laughed at his clumsiness, and he joined in the laughter, but Hemingway glared at McAlmon with aversion.

Chicuelo was the first matador to fight. Out of a compulsion to educate McAlmon, or out of a need to name things aloud, Hemingway kept up a running commentary on what he had learned from his books.

"That was a *veronica,*" he said, checking some illustration and naming one of the passes that Chicuelo made with his cape. "Look at that! A *chicuelina!* It's a pass that Chicuelo invented, the one that made him famous."

When the crowd began to shout *"Olé!"* at particularly well-executed passes, Hemingway joined in. "Olé! What a *rebolera!* Did you see that? Olé! Olé!"

Like an initiate into a new society, Hemingway wanted McAlmon to share his excitement, but he was quick to make him feel his scorn when McAlmon's reactions weren't the proper ones. The first time this happened was when Chicuelo's picador rode into the bullring on a sad old horse and made the horse take the full brunt of a charge by a maddened bull. The horse was lifted on the horns and came down into the violent chaos of the thrown picador trying to get out of the way of the flashing horns, of matadors trying to draw the bull away from the fallen man with their capes. Finally managing to thrash to his feet, the horse trotted off across the ring, frantic with fear, looking for a way out, trailing his entrails along the ground. He had been disemboweled so badly that he was stepping on his own guts as he ran. Soon he collapsed and began convulsing in his death throes.

"Oh those bastards!" McAlmon shouted when the horse was gored. He had jumped to his feet, but Hemingway grabbed his sleeve and pulled him back onto his seat.

"Sit down!" Hemingway commanded. "What the hell's the matter with you? It's just an old horse. They get killed in every bullfight."

"Yeah? Well, I don't like to see that. I used to train polo ponies, and I happen to like horses better than I do most people, and I think it's a shitty sport that lets them get disemboweled."

"I've told you, the bullfight is not a sport. It's a tragedy. A sport is a contest in which somebody wins; a bullfight is a contest between man and beast, and the beast has no chance of winning. The bull is in it to die. His death is inevitable, and that's why it's a tragedy. It's art."

"Art, fart," McAlmon said. "I don't give a damn about the bulls. At least they get a chance to go out fighting, something they were born to do, but what the hell does the horse get out of it? Why do they have to let the horses get killed?"

"The horses are for comic effect," Hemingway said with exaggerated patience, as if talking to a numskull.

"What? It's supposed to be funny?"

"They're not dignified. They're old and ugly and good for nothing else. If they hadn't been saved for the bullfights, they would've been dead a long time ago, in some glue factory. Now, they furnish a comic element when they gallop around the ring, spilling their guts."

"Comic element?" McAlmon said, as if unable to take it in.

"Sure. Didn't you hear the people laughing? The horses are a burlesque of tragedy, and the dignity of the tragedy is left for the death of the bulls."

"And you think that's funny? Man, this is carrying that self-hardening shit a little too far, ain't it?"

"Christ almighty, Mac, if you're going to be so obstinately stupid about it, why don't you just leave? Why spoil it for the rest of us?"

That was exactly what McAlmon should have done, with a parting suggestion that Hemingway go fuck himself. But before he got to his feet, he had second thoughts, and made the decision not to leave. He was now certain that Hemingway's growing contempt for him was connected with his dream of Vicki last night, and McAlmon wanted to see how these twisted emotions of guilt and desire played themselves out. He also realized that he needed Hemingway. That was the truth of it, he needed him. Hemingway needed McAlmon, too, of course, because of McAlmon's willingness to pay his expenses, but McAlmon needed Hemingway for something more important: his enthusiasm. Over the last years, since he'd had enough money to do about anything he wanted, McAlmon's adventures had been born of a desperation to escape boredom. He seemed to have used up his enthusiasm—something that Hemingway had in abundance. And now McAlmon recognized his need of Hemingway to buoy him and carry him along on these new adventures.

So he decided that he would meet Hemingway's growing derision with stoic indifference. Accordingly, he did not utter another word against the spectacle they were watching—he never again referred to it as a sport, though he could not bring himself to call it a tragedy. It certainly didn't fit the Aristotelian definition of tragedy, and McAlmon found it pretentious and phony to try to cover with the mantle of classic Greek theater this spectacle of brutishness and blood.

After Nicanor Villalta's corrida was over, Hemingway checked his notebook to see which one of the six bulls killed that day had been the bravest and best. He decided it was Chicuelo's second bull, a piebald bred by Vincente Martinez.

"Come on," he said. "I just decided what we're going to have for dinner."

McAlmon thought it was nice of him to decide what he—McAlmon—was going to have for dinner, and he was amused that Hemingway wouldn't disclose what he had decided on until they left the bullring with the crowd and, following directions, walked down a backstreet near the bullring into a slummy neighborhood filled with workers and beggars. The only cafés McAlmon could see were hardly more than booths where steaks were being grilled and chickens roasted over open charcoal fires. The smoke from the fires was thick and greasy, and the smell of raw sewage was heavy on the evening air. Ribby dogs sniffed through piles of rubbish in the gutters and prowled under the tables near the booths, looking for fallen scraps and getting kicked.

"You surely can't be looking for a place to eat around here," McAlmon said. "This is ptomaine city."

"Never mind," Hemingway responded. "Just come on."

Hemingway finally spotted a small slaughterhouse where the fighting bulls were butchered and loaded onto carts. The meat was tough and not prized, Hemingway explained, so it was sold from the carts in the poorer neighborhoods of Madrid.

"But there's a special part I want," Hemingway said, and

McAlmon realized what Hemingway was after even before they entered the old building.

The reek of blood and offal was overpowering. There, hanging head-down, with hooks through the tendons of their rear legs, were the last few bulls that had been killed in the ring. Men in blood-covered butchers' aprons were skinning the bodies and hacking at them with axes and cleavers. The viscera had been dumped into wheelbarrows, which were wheeled to a table where aproned women, flecked with blood and excrement, wrestled the slippery entrails onto a long table and cleaned the guts with wooden scrapers.

Near the door were two carts piled high with the meat and organs from the first bulls killed. Hemingway found the slaughterhouse foreman and told him what he wanted in his strained Spanish.

The foreman didn't seem surprised by the request. He asked questions of the butchers, then went to one of the loaded carts and dug among the slippery, shiny organs until he found the testicles of the piebald bull. He grabbed a sheet of newspaper from under a counter and wrapped them and gave them to Hemingway for two pesetas. Hemingway paid the man from his own pocket.

"I'm treating you to dinner tonight," he told McAlmon as they left the slaughterhouse.

They walked back up the street to the booths where the cooks were grilling over charcoal fires. Hemingway talked to one of the cooks for a moment, then handed him the blood-stained package.

"Roasted *cojones* coming up," Hemingway told McAlmon. "You ever had them before?"

"No," McAlmon said. "Have you?"

"Nope," Hemingway said. "But I've talked to people who have, and they say they're good, though no one's ever been able to describe the taste to me."

They sat at a dusty wooden table under a big tree. They were gawked at by children and sniffed at by passing dogs, and the waitress brought them a bottle of Valdapenas wine and a glowing lantern to ward off the encroaching darkness. Guitar music began in a cantina across the street, and old cars and wagons passing along the unpaved street stirred a fine dust into the odorous air.

"What made you think of them for dinner?" McAlmon asked.

"Cannibals eat the enemy warriors they kill, so they can acquire the dead warriors' bravery. I thought it might work with bulls, too. Why not?"

That was what McAlmon liked about Hemingway's exuberance: rather than ask, "Why?" he was more likely to ask, "Why not?"

The cook brought the crisply roasted cojones to their table on a platter with Spanish rice and tender young asparagus.

But though it was Hemingway's idea, he waited for McAlmon to take the first bite. And while McAlmon was chewing on the rubbery morsel, Hemingway sliced off a bite of his testicle and kept looking at McAlmon as he slowly raised it to his mouth, as if he were afraid that McAlmon might spit his own bite out. But with a second bite, they were beginning to get over their squeamishness.

"Never tasted anything quite like it," Hemingway said. "Have you?"

"A few times, yeah."

"What?" Hemingway said. "What's it taste like to you?"

"I'm trying to place it," McAlmon said, searching around for the elusive similarity, and then hit on it: "Sperm."

"What?" Hemingway said. "What do you mean?"

"Sperm. That's what it tastes like, sperm."

Hemingway's voice was hard with sarcasm as he said, "And just how the hell am I supposed to know what sperm tastes like?"

"It tastes like this," McAlmon said.

Hemingway must have known that McAlmon was bisexual. McAlmon had never made a secret of it, so Hemingway *had* to know, given his penchant for gossip about people he knew. McAlmon had to assume Hemingway was acting—pretending not to know, just as he was still pretending that nothing had happened between them last night. They finished the dinner in silence.

38

Hadley

ERNEST DIDN'T RETURN from Spain until the second week in June. For nearly a month, he and McAlmon and Bill Bird had gone from bullfight to bullfight, and when they finally came home, Ernest was a changed man. He was obsessed with bullfights. He could hardly talk about anything else. He brought Hadley a present of an old and very elegant black lace mantilla, but when he tore the wrapping off it to show her, he held it out to his side and used it as a bullfight cape.

"This is a *veronica,*" he said, demonstrating. "And this is a *gaonera.*"

"Well, let me see it," Hadley pleaded, taking the mantilla from him. "Oh, Tatie, this is wonderful! It must have cost a fortune! Where did you get the money?"

"Oh, I talked Mac into buying it with his wife's money," Ernest bragged. "He was such a pain in the ass by the time we left Seville, I was about ready to send him packing, and borrow the money from Bird to finish the trip. But when we got to Ronda, Mac figured he could maybe buy his way back into my good graces by giving me the money for the mantilla."

Hadley modeled the mantilla by putting it over her head and shoulders and folding it over the mound of her six months pregnancy. Looking at herself in the mirror on the chiffonier, she said, "Why, it makes me look absolutely saintly."

"Sure does," Ernest said. "You'd look wonderful at a bullfight, wearing that."

"Tatie, you and Mac didn't end on bad terms, did you? I mean, he's still going to publish a book of your stories and poems, isn't he?"

"Oh, sure," Ernest said, turning his attention to the stacks of mail that had been accumulating since he had been gone. "He's a queer, you know?"

"I'd heard he was, and you must have heard it, too."

"Yeah, but I didn't know whether to believe it or not. I mean he doesn't act queer so I guess I didn't want to believe he was."

"And how did you find out?"

"One day he was trying to tell me what sperm tastes like, for Christ's sake. He wasn't making a pass at me, or anything like that, so I let it go. But we had to share a hotel bed for three nights in Madrid, and I didn't get much sleep, wondering what he might try."

"Is this what you're looking for?" From the bedside table Hadley picked up a copy of *The Little Review*. "It came last week. I've been reading it."

"So it came out!" Ernest snatched it out of her hand and flipped through the pages until he found his own contribution: the six paragraph-sized vignettes, all about violent death, under the collective title, "In Our Time." "So now I'm a famous literary writer."

"Your sketches are the best things in the whole issue," Hadley said absently, still bewitched by the lovely mantilla.

"Well, looks like I'm going to have to get twelve or more of them ready before we leave here, so Bird will have something of mine to print. I have half a dozen notebooks filled with stuff about the bullfights, but I couldn't get any sketches written on the trip because Mac was always tempting us to spend every night in some cantina, watching those castanet-snapping dancers and listening to that damned flamingo music. He even dragged Bird and me out in the middle of the night to see some Gypsy caves in Grenada."

"Gypsies? Real Gypsies?"

"I guess they were real Gypsies, all right, but everything else about them was fake. Mac said we'd see some genuine Gypsies dancing there, but it turned out to be nothing but a tourist trap. Those Gypsy bastards overcharged us for everything, and tried to steal what we had left. It was disgusting. Mac was so drunk, he let one of the dancers drag him out onto the dirt dance floor, and he made a fool of himself, embarrassed us all by prancing around with a rose in his teeth."

"Well, sounds like he had fun, anyway. I hope you had as much fun with the bullfights."

"Oh, Tiny, it was the most exciting thing I've ever seen—just amazing. That's what I'd be, if I had my life to live over, a bull-fighter. Huh! Huh! Toro!" He pretended to have a cape in his hands, challenging an imaginary bull to charge, and when the bull did charge, Ernest guided him harmlessly and gracefully with the imaginary cape, while thousands cheered.

And it was a measure of how totally the bullfight had taken possession of his imagination and enthusiasm that he began making passes at imaginary bulls wherever he went. People in Montparnasse who had gotten used to seeing Ernest shadow-boxing now saw him walking along the street with a make-believe cape in his hands, fighting imaginary bulls. And when he got drunk he might, while crossing the street, wave an imaginary cape, call, "Huh! Huh! Toro!" and pass a car.

For a while it seemed that bullfighting would eclipse all his other interests, but his interest in boxing was revived when he got to see a fight between Emile Morelle, the French title holder, and the black African challenger, Battling Siki, for the light-heavyweight championship of France. The odd group that accompanied Ernest and Hadley to the fights at the Velodrome Buffalo arena was a testament to Ernest's ability to inspire in others enthusiasm. Ezra Pound was among the Velodrome group, in his madcap bohemian attire. Jane Heap was there, wearing her all-male attire, smoking a big black cigar. Mike Strater was there, too, without Maggie, and Robert McAlmon was there with his flask of brandy. But the oddest two among the group were Sylvia Beach and Adrienne Monnier, neither of whom had ever seen a boxing match before, and no doubt would never have seen one, had it not been for Ernest's persuasive charm. Ernest sat close to Sylvia and Adrienne so he could explain to them what they would need to know in order to understand and enjoy the bouts.

There were four preliminary bouts. McAlmon said he was a pal of one of the preliminary fighters, Eugene Bullard. Gene—as McAlmon called him—doubled as both manager and bouncer at Zelli's. He was to fight in the fourth preliminary against some French fighter named Jean Luc Pelletan.

"If he's as good a boxer as he is a bouncer, I'd bet a hundred francs on him to win," McAlmon said.

"Hell, I'll take that," Ernest said, also taking a long drink from McAlmon's brandy flask. "I know about your Bullard. He fought Young Cuddy last year, and lost, and I beat Young Cuddy in a match coming over on the boat from the States, so I could whip that nigger myself. Hundred francs, even money."

They bet, and by the time Bullard and Pelletan were into the third round of their six-round fight, it had become obvious that Pelletan and Ernest were going to lose. And Ernest didn't like to lose. So whenever Pelletan would make a valiant rally against Bullard's superior boxing skills and strength, Ernest would shout his encouragement, "Olé! Olé!" And when Pelletan was lucky enough to get Bullard in a corner and pummel him, Ernest, who had come to the fight about half drunk and was getting drunker with McAlmon's brandy, would shout, "Kill that nigger! Kill him!"

Once, between rounds, Bullard looked into the audience, as if trying to locate the source of the American voice that was calling him a nigger. Ernest and his group were sitting in the fourth row, and Bullard spotted him as the source of the slur, but his sweat-glistening face seemed to frown with puzzlement when he recognized McAlmon among the group. McAlmon made a palms-up gesture of helplessness and apology.

Bullard easily beat Pelletan on points. Ernest started to pay McAlmon the hundred francs, but said he would bet McAlmon the hundred francs, double or nothing, on the next fight, the main event, if McAlmon wanted the nigger again. Morelle would knock Battling Siki out in ten rounds, Ernest declared.

"I hope you know what you're doing," Hadley said. "We can't afford to lose that much money."

"Don't worry, it's in the bag," Ernest assured her. "Hell, I could whip Siki myself. I threw him and his pet lion out of Harry's Bar one night, and he didn't have any fight in him. He's a clown who's left all his fights in barrooms and the bedrooms of white women."

One of the reasons that Sylvia and Adrienne had let Ernest persuade them to come to this fight was because they were curious to see Battling Siki, an African from Senegal who had the reputation of being both a skilled boxer and a flamboyant clown. There had been so many stories in the newspapers that he had attained a level of fame far beyond boxing circles. The Paris *Tribune* had carried a picture of him, dressed in silks and satins, with diamonds on his fingers and gold in his teeth, "drinking his way," the story said, "into the championship." And the newspapers always followed with glee his boulevard antics, the best known of which was his habit of emphasizing his African origins by leading a pet lion around on a leash. There were pictures of him and his lion entering Montmartre cafés, much to the consternation of owners and customers.

"You threw him out of Harry's Bar?" Jane Heap asked, awed by the possibility.

"Yea," Ernest said. "Couple of months ago. He brought that lion into Harry's, and the damned thing scared most of Harry's customers away. Harry asked him to leave, and take his lion with him, but Siki pretended he didn't understand. I didn't give a damn, until the lion used the floor as a *pissoir*. That's when I threw him out, and his lion along with him."

"Mon Dieu," Adrienne said. *"Le lion aussi?* Were you not afraid?"

"Naw," Ernest said disdainfully, and winked at Hadley as he added, "Fwaid a nothin'."

When Battling Siki came down the aisle with his entourage, he was wearing a fake leopard skin robe and boxing trunks of a leopard skin design. On his lips was a grin, and on his arms were two young tarts—blondes, both of them, in cheap, flashy clothes. Many spectators in the Velodrome booed and hissed and called out, *"Singe Africain!"*

"All right," McAlmon said to Ernest, "I'll take Siki, double or nothing."

"Done," Ernest said.

Emile Morelle's entrance into the ring was not auspicious. Though the great favorite of the Velodrome crowd, by virtue of being white and French, he was a stolid and colorless man, a perfect foil for Battling Siki, who loved to turn a boxing match into a comedy act. The crowd, expecting to be offended by Siki's behavior, was not disappointed. Sometimes Siki, still grinning, jumped around in the ring, beating his chest and making silly noises, and during the third round, Siki outraged the audience by deliberately turning his back on Morelle and letting Morelle land a flurry of blows on his back and sides, all without any serious effect.

Again Ernest was unabashed in his loud support of his favorite, but it looked as if he was on his way to losing another hundred francs. Battling Siki was winning every round, and it seemed that the African could have knocked Morelle out anytime he wanted to stop his burlesque routines and get serious about becoming the light-heavyweight champion of France. That didn't happen until the sixth round. Siki came out of his corner, insolently waved bye-bye to Morelle, then knocked him down with a right uppercut, the first blow of the round. Morelle got up at the count of nine, then Siki knocked him down again. Morelle got up, backpedaled, staggered, hung on, covered up, but soon Siki knocked him down again. When he got up this time, the referee, presumably thinking about stopping the fight, talked to Morelle for a few seconds, then waved him back into the fight. Morelle crossed his arms in front of his face, leaving his body open for attack, and Siki took advantage of the opening. He hit Morelle's abdomen and this time when Morelle went down, he grabbed his groin and rolled around on the canvas, groaning with pain.

The referee stopped the fight and gave the victory to Morelle because of a low blow by Siki. Apparently nobody but the referee saw the low blow. Siki angrily protested that he had thrown no low blows, and that this was just a plot on the part of the white boxing officials to rob him of a championship that he had obviously won. And though most of the spectators hated Battling

Siki, they hated injustice more, and they roundly booed the referee's decision, and threw cushions and bottles into the ring.

Even Ernest said to McAlmon, "Well, the nigger was robbed, all right, but who am I to complain? Morelle officially won, so we're even."

Still, it was a sour victory. Ernest hated to be wrong, and he said he felt like climbing into the ring and knocking out Siki himself, just to show everyone that Siki could be beaten fair and square. After all, he had thrown Siki and his damned pet lion out of Harry's Bar, so he knew he could handle the nigger all right. However, he allowed Sylvia and Adrienne and Jane Heap to dissuade him from such a rash course of action. They mollified him by telling him how much they enjoyed the fights and how much they appreciated his explanations of pugilism's finer points, and after they left the Velodrome and were on their way back to Montparnasse in a taxi, Sylvia and Adrienne made him tell once again how he had thrown Battling Siki and his pet lion out of the bar, and they appeared to accept Ernest's assertion that he had actually done it.

Hadley, however, didn't believe a word of it. She had not betrayed any skepticism about the story in public, of course, and ordinarily would never have questioned his veracity even in private, but this particular story struck her as being so preposterous that it called into serious question Ernest's perception of reality. That he was an inveterate fantasist she had long ago accepted, dismissing the trait as a harmless way for him to feed his ego and attract attention, but she wondered if this story about Battling Siki and his lion indicated that he might be slipping over the line of harmless lies into mythomania; wondered if his refusal to distinguish memory from imagination and fantasy from fact might be a symptom of mental illness.

When they got back to their apartment that night, she broached the subject as she was getting ready for bed. The night was warm and the windows were open and the noises and smells of the Paris streets were making Ernest restless. Too drunk to work and too excited by the fights to go to sleep, he thought about going to the bal musette on the building's ground floor and having another drink, but Hadley sought to hold him by saying, "Tatie, there's something I'd like to talk to you about."

"Uh oh," he said, going on guard.

"Oh, it's nothing portentous," she said. "It's just something I'm curious about. That story you told tonight—you know, the one about throwing Battling Siki and his pet lion out of Harry's Bar . . ."

"What about it?" he asked defensively.

"Tatie, I know you well enough by now to know that . . . well, you would've told me that story as soon as it happened—if it had really happened."

"You saying I'm a liar?"

"Oh, Tatie, this is not an accusation. I loved you before I realized you tell lies, and I loved you after I realized you tell lies, but the fact is, sweetheart, you tell lies. Now, I don't care if you do— I just don't understand why you do. Why do you feel you have to? You're a marvelous man, the most marvelous man I've ever known, and most people feel that way about you. They're in awe of you. You don't have to tell lies to make us feel that way about you—all you have to do is be yourself."

Though persuaded that she wasn't criticizing him, Ernest was still defensive as he lit a cigarette and said, "Well, I guess I might tell a fib now and then. It just comes natural to me—like it does to all the best writers. They're all liars, if you want to come right down to it. It's their stock in trade, lies are. They get paid for lying, or inventing, and especially they lie when they're drunk, or to themselves, or to strangers. Sometimes writers lie unconsciously, then remember their lies with remorse, maybe even shame. But mostly a writer is a liar in full flower, as beautiful as a cherry tree or an apple tree in blossom. Nobody should ever try to change a liar by calling him one."

Hadley smiled. "And didn't anybody ever give you the sermon about George Washington chopping down the cherry tree and saying, 'I cannot tell a lie'?"

"Oh, sure. My grandfather was the first person to tell me that story—which, incidentally, I think is a lie. I was five years old at the time, and my grandfather asked me what I had done that day. I told him I had stopped a runaway horse. He said I was a liar, and predicted fame or a criminal career for me. But the funny thing is, to this day I don't know if it was a lie. Who knows? I could have stopped a runaway horse." He was silent for a moment, smoking the cigarette, and then continued. "That seems to be my criterion for truth—not what happened, but what could have happened. Like throwing Siki and his stinking lion out of Harry's Bar—it could have happened. And if it didn't happen that way, it's only because God didn't think of it. That's what we writers are for, to improve on the scheme of things, to do what God should have, to make things happen the way they ought to have happened."

Hadley sat down on his lap, kissed his unshaven cheek, and said tenderly, "I love you, Tatie. I think you're the most marvelous liar who ever lived. And forgive me, I should have known you were just improving on God's work."

39

McAlmon

MCALMON MET HEMINGWAY at the Café Select one day in early July
for a last conference before sending the manuscript of his book,
Three Stories and Ten Poems, off to the printer in Dijon. All
McAlmon thought he and Hemingway had to talk about was
technical stuff—the layout, the kind of print to be used—but
Hemingway flummoxed him by bringing along a new poem that
he wanted to include in the book. The poem was entitled "The
Soul of Spain," and it wasn't much worse than the other ten
poems in the book, but in this case a little more made a lot more
than a little difference. It was subtitled "[In the manner of Gertrude Stein]," as if Hemingway wanted to make sure that the
reader understood it to be a parody, thereby escaping any accusations of writing crap by claiming that he was merely parodying
the crap that somebody else wrote.

The first section of the poem read,

> In the rain in the rain in the rain in the rain in Spain.
> Does it rain in Spain?
> Oh yes my dear on the contrary and there are no bullfights.
> The dancers dance in long white pants
> It isn't right to yence your aunts
> Come Uncle, let's go home.
> Home is where the heart is, home is where the fart is.

Come let us fart in the home.
There is no art in a fart.
Still a fart may not be artless.
Let us fart and artless fart in the home.

This was enough to make McAlmon want to redefine the word *poem*. After all, the book's title claimed there were ten poems between its covers, and most of them were cutesy, sophomoric crap, but could this one even be called a poem? McAlmon realized that the dadaists called anything they wanted to a poem, but Hemingway was not a dadaist, and McAlmon wasn't publishing dadaist books. And, anyway, no dadaist would have been caught dead writing such shit house–wall stuff, the third section of which went like this:

Democracy is the shit.
Relativity is the shit.
Dictators are the shit.
Menken is the shit.
Waldo Frank is the shit.
The Broom is the shit.
Dada is the shit.
Dempsey is the shit.

McAlmon didn't tell Hemingway what he thought, for fear that Hemingway might sock him. McAlmon had learned that Hemingway was a highly opinionated man, especially when it came to his own worth, and to criticize his writing was the same as impugning his honor. Once in Spain, Hemingway had come close to attacking McAlmon because of a dispute they had over Hemingway's short story "My Old Man," one of the three in the book McAlmon was going to publish. McAlmon had told Hemingway that the story was obviously derived from Sherwood Anderson's "I'm a Fool," in which Anderson had assumed the attitude of an older person who insists on trying to think and write like a hurt child being brave. He and Hemingway had been in a cantina at the time, and Hemingway had given McAlmon a withering look across the table, and said, "Yeah? Well, I suppose the innocent voice of the good observer of life will always sound childlike to someone who is stupid or corrupt."

Hemingway left it like that, staring at McAlmon, daring him to respond. Had McAlmon tried to argue with him, he suspected that Hemingway would have hit him. In fact, he suspected that Hemingway had often come close to hitting him during that trip to Spain, and probably the only thing that stopped him was his ambition to have a book published. Now that Hemingway would soon be going back to America, getting a book published had become, by his own admission, the most important thing in the world to him. But even that hadn't stopped him from using McAlmon as a whipping boy for his verbal assaults. True, Hemingway never went so far that he couldn't mitigate his insults with a forced smile and a pretense to be joshing, but he once went far enough that Bill Bird came to McAlmon's defense and confronted Hemingway about his behavior.

Bird had taken McAlmon aside a couple of times and tried to warn him that Hemingway was taking advantage of him. Bird told McAlmon in private that Hemingway had more money than he pretended to have, but McAlmon shrugged it off.

Bird thought there was something more behind McAlmon's willingness to be Hemingway's patsy than merely a lackadaisical attitude. The way Hemingway treated McAlmon seemed to offend Bird personally. Then one night in Granada, after the bull-fights had been rained out and there was nothing else to do, McAlmon suggested that they visit some Gypsy caves on the outskirts of the city to hear flamenco music and see some dancing. Hemingway went, but he didn't enjoy himself, and he blamed McAlmon for having wasted his time on that damned "flamingo" crap. In his own defense, McAlmon suggested Hemingway might have a tin ear when it came to music, and Hemingway fired back with an accusation that McAlmon had a tin head, and that McAlmon was acting like a damned fool for getting friendly with the Gypsies, who were, in Hemingway's opinion, nothing but thugs and thieves.

Later that night in his hotel room, McAlmon found he couldn't sleep, so he took a flask of brandy down the hall to Bird's room. He knocked lightly on the door, hoping Bird was awake and wouldn't mind a little conversation, but there was no answer to the knock. Then Bird came out of Hemingway's room just down the hall. He looked peevish and resentful as he strode toward his own room, where McAlmon waited for him.

"I brought some brandy, in case you weren't asleep," McAlmon said.

"Come on in," Bird snapped as he unlocked the door.

"Am I disturbing you?" McAlmon asked, following him into the room.

"No. I'm already disturbed. I just had a talk with Ernest—about you, as a matter of fact. What the hell's he got against you, anyway? Why's he so insulting to you?"

McAlmon shrugged. "I don't know."

"He says it's because you're a goddamned jerk," Bird said, giving McAlmon two glasses for the brandy. "I told him, even if you were, you're still footing his bills and buying the Scotch. I asked him if he made a habit of accepting handouts, then biting the hand that feeds him? I never figured him for an ingrate."

"And what did he say to that?"

"He said . . . he chuckled in a sort of dry, bitter way, and said, 'You know, Bird, I'll take anything from you.'" Bird frowned, sipped the brandy, and shook his head. "That makes the second time he's said that to me . . . and I still don't know what the hell he means by it. Why should he take anything from me?"

They settled nothing that night, except to agree that Hemingway could sometimes be a puzzle and a pain in the ass, but the dispute between Bird and Hemingway had a beneficial result: Hemingway's attitude toward McAlmon changed. This made McAlmon think that Hemingway knew in his heart how badly he had been behaving toward him. In a gesture of reconciliation, Hemingway began to treat him with marked courtesy, which continued throughout the rest of the trip in Spain and after they returned to Paris.

However, when they met at the Café Select to discuss the manuscript and Hemingway asked him to include his new poem in the collection, McAlmon wasn't ready to test Hemingway's newfound courtesy by telling him, no, he wouldn't include the new poem because it was juvenile. Instead, McAlmon persuaded Hemingway not to include the poem because a title like *Three Stories and Eleven Poems* would sound odd, off-balance, and, besides, it would throw off the even-number pagination.

Hemingway listened and said, "Well, all right, you're the publisher," and McAlmon had to wonder, "Yes, but why?"—why was he the publisher? Now that it was almost ready for the printer, he had to admit to himself that he didn't even like the book. Of the three short stories, "My Old Man," "Out of Season," and "Up in Michigan," McAlmon liked only "Up in Michigan," and he liked only two or three of the poems.

In his search for an answer, it occurred to him that he was publishing the work, not because it was good and deserved to be published, but because Hemingway had written it. Had these stories and poems been sent to McAlmon from an unknown writer in London or Brooklyn, he wouldn't even have considered them, let alone joined in a competition with others like Bill Bird to see who would have the honor of publishing them first. Now explain that?

Hemingway himself had to be the key to it. Hemingway had the makings of a mythological man. Not because of his virtues but in spite of his faults, he was the kind of man who carried the day, whether as a soldier, a leader, a writer, a skier, a lover, a boxer. And, mind you, he didn't even have to be any of these things in order to make those who were in his company look upon him as a master of whatever he put his hand to. They all let him set the level of their expectations for whatever he and they did.

Was that a sufficient explanation of his power over McAlmon? Or should McAlmon have just come right out and confessed that he, like most of the other people who knew Hemingway, male or female, was a little in love with him? It was as simple as that, and yet it was not a simple love, of course, because nothing was simple where Hemingway was concerned. It was a love mixed with hate, where the conflicting feelings vied for dominance. McAlmon had to admit to himself that, whether it was love or hate he felt, he would have consented to be Hemingway's lover any time Hemingway desired him.

McAlmon couldn't offer himself to Hemingway outright, of course. That would only have driven him away in wrath and revulsion. Besides, McAlmon needed to escape the responsibility for such an act by being the passive partner, never the instigator. He needed the rationalization of being forced to do what he secretly wanted to do. McAlmon speculated that Hemingway might someday realize that the qualities he found so despicable, so unacceptable and hateful in other men, might be the very qualities he was trying to deny in himself. But if Hemingway was to escape insanity or suicide, those repressed qualities would someday have to come out, and McAlmon hoped that he would be around when that time came.

Meanwhile, he would act as Hemingway's publisher and—as it turned out—his boxing promoter. On that day in the Café Select, after they had settled the business of sending Hemingway's collection of stories and poems to the printer, Hemingway asked McAlmon about his pal Gene Bullard, who had fought on the Siki-Morelle card.

"Listen, would you mind asking him the next time you see him if he could use another sparring partner?"

"You're looking for the job?" McAlmon asked.

"Yeah. I could use the money, but more than anything else, I want to see if I could beat him. I mean, I beat Young Cuddy, and Young Cuddy beat him, so why not? And if I find out I can take him, I'd like to get a prelim bout with him at the Velodrome. I'm still thinking about turning pro, and that would make a good first fight, and I could make enough money to take Hadley and me home in style."

McAlmon told him, sure, he'd talk to Gene about it, and he didn't hesitate. He went to Zelli's that night. He went in early, before the jazz band started and the place got busy, so that Gene would have time to join him for a drink. McAlmon sat at the bar, and Gene was standing behind it, dressed in a tuxedo, looking sharp.

"A heavyweight?" Gene asked. "Naw, don't think so. I got plenty of heavyweight sparring partners, if I want 'em. I need somebody smaller and faster."

"This is the guy I was with at the Velodrome the other night," McAlmon said.

"The guy who kept yelling, 'Kill the nigger'?"

"Yep, he's the one."

Gene became interested. "He's got a big mouth."

"His ego is even bigger."

"He any good?"

"He says he is. Says he's sparred with Sam Langford and Henry Greb. Says he whipped Young Cuddy, and Young Cuddy whipped you."

"He a friend of yours?" Gene poured McAlmon another drink, and lit his cigarette with a silver lighter.

"Yeah, but just between me and you and the fence post, I wouldn't mind seeing him get his comeuppance."

Gene nodded. "I work out every Monday, Wednesday, and Friday between two and four at my Athletic Club, 15 rue Mansart. Bring him around, if you want to. We'll see if he's any good."

40

Bullard

Bullard was in the raised ring, in gym trunks and a sweatshirt, shadowboxing. Opal Cooper brought Hemingway to the ring.

"This here young gen'man say you expecting him," Opal said, habitually reverting to his days in America where any white man was automatically a gentleman.

But Bullard had higher standards. Hemingway, wearing old, worn-out tennis shoes, dressed in baggy pants and a threadbare shirt, with half-moons of sweat at his armpits, unshaven and in need of a haircut, carrying a scruffy old valise, looked more like a street bum than a gentleman.

"Who're you?" Bullard asked, though he guessed that this was the aspiring young writer and professed boxer that Bob McAlmon had said needed a comeuppance.

"Ernest Hemingway. Bob McAlmon sent me. Said you might be able to use a sparring partner."

"Where is Bob? Thought he was coming with you."

"He and his wife had to make a sudden trip to England. Beckoned by rich in-laws. Won't be back for a week or two, he said."

Bullard had stepped to the side of the ring, leaning on the top rope, looking down on Hemingway. Opal stood by, sucking on a toothpick, waiting to see if he would be needed.

"Bob says you got some experience as a sparring partner. He mentioned Sam Langford."

"Yeah," Hemingway said. "I sparred with Langford and Harry Greb in Chicago a few times, when they were preparing for fights there."

"Yeah? Sam's a friend of mine. We stayed at the same boarding-house when he came to London for fights, and I sparred some with him, too. And Bob tells me you beat Young Cuddy."

"Just a three-round exhibition match on the boat coming over, that's all. I took the decision." He shrugged, as if it were some-thing of no importance.

Bullard wondered if Bob had been wrong about the young man. Hemingway didn't seem the egotist that Bob had de-scribed. He seemed almost humble, even differential, charming, with a wide grin and an eager air. Sure, he looked like a bum, but maybe that was because he was poor. Bullard knew what it was like to be poor and on the bum. Nor did Hemingway im-press Bullard as being the kind who would yell out "Kill the nigger!" at a public prize fight. Could Bob McAlmon have been mistaken about that, too? Could Bob have been trying to manip-ulate Bullard into being an instrument of revenge for some pri-vate grudge of his own?

"Okay," Bullard said. "Ten francs a round, same as everywhere else in Paris. You got twelve-ounce gloves?"

Hemingway held up the scruffy leather valise.

Bullard pointed toward a door. "Locker room there. Suit up."

As Hemingway headed toward the locker room, Bullard pulled the sweatshirt over his head. Opal picked up some hand wrap-pings on the apron of the ring near the water bottle, and climbed into the ring. He put the wrappings on Bullard's hands, then pulled the gloves on, and taped the laces down. While waiting for Hemingway, Opal held the palms of his hands out, giving Bullard something to hit as he moved around the ring, warming up.

"Now, watch that hand," Opal warned, referring to Bullard's right hand, the one that had not healed right after being broken on the head of a big Egyptian heavyweight. "Can't afford to hurt that hand again—you hear?"

"Yeah, yeah, yeah," Bullard said, exasperated but still grateful for Opal's fussy concern.

Hemingway came into the ring dressed in new gym trunks but still wearing the old tennis shoes. Opal went to Hemingway's corner and tied the laces of his gloves and taped the laces down, then he climbed out of the ring and took his place near the bell. He pulled a stopwatch from his pocket.

"Okay?" he said, and at Bullard's nod, pulled the cord that tripped the spring-mounted hammer on the bell. "Round one."

Hemingway came out of his corner eagerly, as if he meant to make a fight of it. Most experienced sparring partners quickly developed a fighting style that nicely blended skill and forbearance, fighting just enough to engage, but not enrage, the emotions of the professional fighters, a method calculated to allow them to leave the ring with as little damage as possible in exchange for their meager earnings. A few, however, with overweening ambitions and dreams of glory, made a sparring session a contest from the moment the bell clanged for the first round. These few were either good or foolish, and it became obvious to Bullard before the first round was half over that Hemingway was foolish. He would never make a professional fighter. He had come into the ring stinking of whiskey. He hadn't staggered or showed any other sign of drunkenness, but the strong smell on his breath made Bullard wonder if Hemingway had stopped in a bar to work up some courage before coming to the gym. In addition, Hemingway was slow-footed, didn't have good coordination or quick reflexes, and made the common mistake of a street brawler who depends on his strength and lack of sportsmanship to win fights. True, those qualities were adequate to win most barroom brawls, but in the ring with a professional fighter, such qualities were worse than useless.

Bullard peppered Hemingway with left jabs to keep him off, and he was so much faster than Hemingway that he saw he could land a counterpunch, and be out of the way before Hemingway's punch ever completed its trajectory. Hemingway did sometimes bull his way past Bullard's defenses and maul him a little.

It was in the second round that Hemingway's bullying aggressiveness began to annoy Bullard. It was then, too, that Bullard found out Hemingway was defenseless against a right cross.

Bullard began to suspect that Hemingway must have defective eyesight in his left eye. It was as if he didn't see the punches coming. It was then that Bullard knew he could knock Hemingway out at any time he chose. But they were there to spar, not to brawl, and Bullard respected that limitation, even after it became apparent that Hemingway did not.

But by the third round Bullard was more than merely annoyed, he was disgusted with Hemingway's clumsy aggressiveness, which by now had begun to be just dirty fighting. Once during a clinch, Hemingway actually tried to knee Bullard in the groin, and in another clinch he brought his fist down on the back of Bullard's neck like a club. Bullard quickly punished him for such shenanigans. He hit Hemingway with an uppercut that sent him wobbling back onto the ropes, and then, as he was coming off the ropes, Bullard popped him, causing his nose to bleed, and then he hit him with another looping right cross, coming in from Hemingway's blind side, and Hemingway went down on one knee.

"Look, asshole," Bullard said to him as Hemingway held on to the middle rope, trying to clear his head, "you'd better stop fighting dirty, or I'll give you a few pointers on how it's really done."

Being called an asshole revealed another flaw in Hemingway's fighting qualities: he lost his temper. Springing to his feet, he charged after Bullard—another indication that he had never been a professional sparring partner or boxer. In a barroom or back-alley brawl, anger could be intimidating to an opponent, but anger meant loss of control and a dangerous disregard for consequences. He came bulling in to clinch Bullard again, blowing blood from his nose over Bullard's shoulder, and this time he raked the laces of his right glove up over Bullard's mouth and nose, abrading the skin, and it was then that Bullard completely lost patience with him. He drove Hemingway back with a flurry of lefts and rights, and then delivered another right to Hemingway's blind side that knocked him sprawling on the canvas.

Too disgusted to even speak directly to Hemingway, Bullard turned his back on him and said to Opal, "He's no good. Get him out of here. I wanted a sparring partner, not a wrestler or a punching bag. Pay him off and get him out of here."

As Hemingway struggled to get up, he said, "Yeah? Yeah? No good, huh? Shit! I'll show you, you black bastard, I'll show you!" He lunged across the ring toward Bullard.

It was being called a black bastard that cleared Bullard's head of anger, that caused him to face Hemingway with cold calculation. But rather than engage with him, Bullard danced out of the path of Hemingway's charge, and hit him with three or four straight jabs in the left eye, twisting his glove to tear the skin, and the eye immediately ballooned into a bruised, swollen mass.

"Oh, you'd better watch it, pretty boy," Bullard taunted as he glided away from Hemingway's flailing fists. "Hey, you're gonna kill somebody with that right someday, if you ever connect with it."

Goading and taunting Hemingway was half the fun of it; the other half was giving him a sound thrashing. Bullard wished Bob McAlmon was here to see Hemingway get a beating that soon brought him to a panting halt, hurt and humiliated. Both of his eyes were swelling to slits, and blood from his cut lips dribbed out of his mouth and down his chin and into the hairs on his chest.

Bullard went to a corner and reached through the ropes to grab the water bottle. He took a long drink from it, letting the water spill out of his mouth and down his chest, where it ran pink as it mixed with Hemingway's blood.

Opal said, "You want to keep on with this?"

Bullard shook his head. "Get him out of here. He can't fight."

Hanging onto the ropes in his corner, Hemingway said, "You're good at running; if you'd stand and fight, I'd show you."

Bullard sighed with mingled contempt and despair, and said to Opal, "Get this buckra bastard out of here before I break his goddamn head."

"Okay, you," Opal said as he climbed through the ropes, "get out of here while you're still in one piece. Go on, go take a shower. I'll pay you off at the front desk. And don't ever come back here, you hear?"

As Hemingway, full of resentment and pain, climbed out of the ring and headed for the locker room, Opal went to Bullard and began taking off his gloves.

"How's that hand?" As he took the wrappings off the right hand, he began shaking his head. "Now look at that. All swol' up again! Now it'll be a month or more before you be able to fight again. Damn!"

41

Hadley

THE NIGHT WAS hot and muggy and Hadley was lying on the bed in a thin chemise, reading F. Scott Fitzgerald's *The Beautiful and Damned* by the light of a gas lamp, when she heard Ernest coming up the stairs. She could tell by the stumbling way he slammed his feet down that he was blind drunk. He had missed dinner, which usually meant that he had been out drinking with friends. She was prepared to be cross with him, but when he stumbled into the apartment and she saw his face, she leaped out of bed, crying, "My God, Tatie, what happened to you?"

He had black eyes, a huge swelling on the left side of his face, and his lips were cut.

Ernest turned his back on her and shrugged, as if swaggering it off, and said, "Oh, nothing. I got in a fight with that nigger boxer Bullard today." He went into a little shuffle and threw a few shadowboxing punches, but stopped suddenly, wincing with pain, and grabbed his side. He staggered to a chair and lowered himself gently into it. Through the slits of his eyes, she thought she saw the glisten of tears. "But you should see the other guy." He tried to force a laugh, but the sound was cut off quickly by another wince of pain. "I knocked the black bastard out cold."

"Have you been to a doctor? Maybe you have a broken rib."

"Ah, it's nothing," he said. "Just sore, that's all. Be okay. What I need's another drink. Where's whiskey?"

Hadley wanted to tell him that the last thing he needed was another drink, but if that was what he was using as an anesthetic for the pain, why not? She went into the tiny kitchen and got a glass. From a bottle of whiskey in a cabinet, she poured a stiff drink, then put the bottle back in the cabinet. She took the drink to Ernest and knelt beside his chair. Her maternal impulse was to hold the glass to his swollen lips, but he took the glass and waved her away. He seemed to be making a superhuman effort to put a brave face on his condition, and Hadley sensed that any sympathy or solicitude from her would only weaken his supreme efforts against self-pity.

"What happened?" Hadley asked. "Didn't you have gloves on? Were you supposed to be sparring?"

"Yeah, but the nigger got mad as hell when I knocked him down the first time. So we got into a slugfest." He tried to chuckle, but the sound came out mirthless and hollow. "Sure, he got in some good licks, all right, and he butted me, too, and even gouged his thumb into my eye, like Harry Greb, and he hit me with his elbows. But I fixed his wagon. I don't think he'll be doing boxing in public for a while. I think I broke his nose and maybe his jaw."

"But look at you." Hadley struggled to repress the impulse to criticize him for being so careless with his handsomeness and his wonderful brain. "We should take you out to the American Hospital, get a doctor to look at you."

"No, no, no," he said irritably. "I'm okay, goddamnit." He drained his whiskey, handed her the empty glass, and lit a cigarette as he said scornfully, "Another whiskey. Just get it. That's all I need."

Hadley poured only a small amount of whiskey into the glass this time. Seeing him so drunk and agitated and angry, and yet at the same time trying to be so offhand and cavalier, Hadley became afraid for him. He seemed to be losing control, and if he got any drunker, she didn't know what he might do. And her feeling of dread became even more acute when she brought him the whiskey and noticed that he had pulled a bloody handkerchief from his pocket and was hurriedly trying to wipe away tears.

"Oh, Tatie, what is it, sweetheart? Is there something you're not telling me?"

"What d'you mean?" he asked accusingly, as if she had disparaged him in some way. He drained the whiskey in one gulp. "What're you getting at?"

"Nothing. I just thought . . . if you're crying, there must be—"

"Not crying!" he snapped, but at that very moment more tears overflowed his eyes. They seemed to be tears of anger, however, rather than tears of sorrow or self-pity. He drew back the whiskey glass and threw it across the room to smash against the wall. "You hear me, goddamnit? I'm not crying."

Some of the most disturbing memories of Hadley's life came from a time when she was a young girl and her father, an alcoholic, had come home on crying drunks. During the last years of his life, the life of a failed and broken-spirited man, her father had stayed drunk much of the time, but since the lives of the other members of the family weren't greatly disrupted by his drinking, no one paid much attention to him. It was only on a crying drunk that he upset the whole household. During these times there were always great arguments, things were thrown, with her father storming around the house, alternately laughing maniacally and crying piteously. Sometimes he would grab one of his daughters and pull her into his arms for a maudlin hug, telling her how much he adored her, while the daughter, terrified and disgusted, fought to get free. Then one night, after groveling on the floor in a fit of mingled self-disgust and self-pity, her father went up to his bedroom, took a revolver out of the drawer of the bedside table, stood in front of the dressing room mirror, placed the gun to his head, and pulled the trigger.

And now, watching Ernest struggle painfully out of his chair and stumble drunkenly around the room in a fit of anger and humiliation, with tears beginning to stream down his unshaven and disfigured face, Hadley felt once again the old dread and horror that she had felt while watching her father.

Ernest kicked at the furniture. "I'm not crying!" he cried. "Goddamnit, I'm not! Don't give a damn!"

He drew back his fist and slammed it against the stucco wall so hard that Hadley was afraid he would break it. When he drew his fist back to strike the wall again, she rushed to him and caught his arm.

"No! Tatie, don't!" she cried. "You'll only hurt yourself more."

He allowed her to stop him, but then he leaned his forehead against the wall and began to sob. It was as if he had dammed it up inside himself for as long as he could—perhaps years and years of frustrations and hurts and humiliations—and that night, with his forehead resting against the wall, the sobs and tears poured out in a flood.

So piteous was his sobbing that Hadley's eyes brimmed with sympathetic tears. She steadied his body as it shook and weaved.

"Oh, Tatie . . . Darling . . . Come. Sit on the bed. Let me hold you."

He allowed himself to be helped to the bed, where he sat down heavily on the edge, rested his elbows on his knees, and held his head in his hands as he sobbed.

Hadley put both arms around him, pulling him against her shoulder, cuddling him, saying, "Oh, sweetheart . . . what is it? Tell mummy, can't you, sweetheart? What's the matter?"

At first the words were lost in the sobs, but he repeated them again and again, so they finally began to be understandable: "He beat me. That bastard beat me. No good. Might as well face it. Not a good boxer. Not a good writer. Not a good son. Not a good husband. Not a good anything! It's all so shitty! It's all so shitty!"

"No, no, no," she said, comforting him as she would have comforted a helpless child. "Don't be so hard on yourself. You are a good boxer. And you're a wonderful writer, and a wonderful person, and I love you, and for me you're the bestest husband that ever could be, and don't you ever say that again."

"No, I'm not. I can't do anything."

"There, there," she said. "You'll feel better tomorrow."

42

Hadley

ERNEST USED THE following two weeks to write and polish the twelve vignettes he needed to complete the book Bill Bird was going to publish under the title *In Our Time*. During those two weeks, he stayed close to home or his studio, avoiding the cafés and parties of Montparnasse until his black eyes healed. He was a deeply brooding man during that time, and Hadley hoped that the depths of despair he had reached would result in some wisdom about the dangers of hubris. But Ernest would not have been Ernest unless he thought that nothing would be denied to him that he imagined to do. So by the time he was once more frequenting the bars and cafés and the racetracks and sporting arenas, he was once more shadowboxing as he shuffled down the streets, or was again demonstrating the fine points of bull-fighting at parties by playing the matador when he could get someone to play the bull.

Ernest had shown Hadley how to be the bull, and sometimes she volunteered to play the role at social gatherings so that Ernest could demonstrate to everyone how the matador worked. With candles held at the sides of her head for horns, Hadley would charge Ernest, and he, using a tablecloth or a towel for a cape, would shake it and challenge, "Huh! Huh! Toro! Toro!" And Hadley, though a little awkward with her bulging pregnancy, would bend low to simulate the bull and perhaps paw the floor to get into the spirit of it before she charged.

"And at the end, when he has the bull completely dominated, the matador uses the muleta to make the bull lower his head, like this, and then he goes right in over the horns for the kill. Buries the sword to the hilt, right between the bull's shoulders." He plunged the make-believe sword into Hadley's back. "That's when the matador and the bull are said to become one. That's what the Spaniards call 'The moment of truth—the moment of death.' "

Ernest told people that when he got to Toronto, he was going to buy a small bull, and when his son was born (there was never any doubt in his mind that his child was going to be a son), he would teach the boy the art of bullfighting from the time he could walk.

In many ways it was a sad summer for the Hemingways. Assuming that it would be their last summer in Paris, they forgave the city its heat and smells and noise. Things that they would have complained about before were now welcomed as they saved up memories for the coming days and years in the dark, church-bound city of Toronto, when they would say, "Remember that last summer in Paris, during the three days of the Bastille Celebration, when the band from the bal musette downstairs moved out onto the street and played all night? It was hot and we had the windows open, and there were fireworks over the Seine, and we could feel the baby moving?"

"Yes. And remember that day we walked through the Luxembourg Gardens and the sparrows were swirling through the chestnut trees like leaves in a storm? And the children were sailing their toy boats in the fountain? We threw coins in the fountain and made wishes, then told each other what we had wished for, and it was the same wish—that we'd come back to Paris someday."

"Yes. And remember . . ."

Storing up summer memories for the cold winters to come.

And especially they would remember that Sunday afternoon of August 5. Ernest had dribbled the day away in domestic trivialities, packing their things, crating their small paintings by Masson,

Kumae, and Dorothy Pound. He was working himself into a sour mood in the sweltering heat, but his mood changed to one of excitement and confidence when a messenger climbed the stairs to their apartment to deliver a package. Ernest ripped the paper off the package, and there it was: the proof sheets and cover design for the Contact Edition of *Three Stories and Ten Poems*.

That was a memorable day. Ernest had hoped that he could proofread the book and get it back to the printers in Dijon in time to have bound copies before they sailed for America, but that seemed unrealistic. They had bought tickets on the Cunard liner *Andania*, to sail for New York on August 16 from Cherbourg. So little time left for Paris.

But as if the hardworking printers in Dijon had conspired to make the author's wishes come true, Ernest received a *pneumatique* from Sylvia Beach on August 13, telling him and Hadley to hurry to the bookstore, she had a surprise for them.

In her eighth month of pregnancy, Hadley was in no condition to hurry anywhere, particularly in ninety-six degree heat, but she waddled down the stairs and got into the taxi that was owned and operated by the man who ran the bal musette on the ground floor, and the air blowing through the windows cooled her off a little as they bumped and rattled their way to Shakespeare and Company.

There, in the window of the bookstore, was a display of the first copies of the grayish-blue book, *Three Stories and Ten Poems*, by Ernest Hemingway. Ernest and Hadley looked at the display for a long time. Tears came to Hadley's eyes. Through the window they could see Sylvia behind the sales desk. She waved to them.

They went inside. In the cooling wind created by three electric fans, Sylvia handed Ernest his four author's copies, charged to McAlmon's account. Ernest opened the book to the dedication page to show Hadley: "This Book Is For Hadley."

She kissed him, thanked him, and shed a tear. The book was only fifty-eight pages long, and published in a limited edition of 300 copies—not much to show for the twenty months they had been in Paris, but though the book was small, they hoped it would mark a giant step in the writing career of Ernest

Hemingway. Both of them believed this little book was the beginning of a great career.

Sylvia congratulated Ernest, and wished him luck. "We've already sold two copies," she said. "And I expect to sell quite a few more before the day's over, and Bob will try to drum up a few orders from the bookstores in London."

"When'll he be back, do you know?" Ernest asked.

"No idea. You know our Bob, he's all whim." Noticing the worried frown on Ernest's face, she added, "Why? If it's a matter of business, you can tell me, you know, and I can pass it on to him."

"It's about money," Ernest said in a low voice.

"What about it?"

"I'm going to have to borrow a hundred dollars from someone, to tide us over till I get my first paycheck in Toronto."

"I think I can manage that," Sylvia said.

"Gee, could you? The exchange rate is eighteen-to-one now; if it falls below that by the time I get my first month's pay, I'll make up the difference."

"All right," Sylvia said as she took her cash box from the desk drawer and counted out 1,800 francs. "And if there's anything else I can do to help, let me know. What train are you leaving on? I'll come and see you off and bring you a basket of fruit."

"You've been a good friend to us," Hadley said. "You've been a good friend to everybody who needed a friend, and for that . . . thanks." She gave Sylvia a quick embrace. "Thanks, and God bless you."

Sylvia flushed with pleasure. "No thanks necessary. I'm just doing what makes me happy," she said, and then added in a less intimate tone, "Drop by and say good-bye to Adrienne, if you have time, will you?"

Leaving Shakespeare and Company, they crossed the street to Adrienne's bookstore, and chatted with her for a minute, saying their good-byes. Then they took a taxi back to their apartment and hurried to get ready to go to the going-away dinner that Gertrude Stein was giving for them that evening.

43

Picasso

GERTRUDE INVITED PICASSO and his wife, Olga Koklova, to dine with her and some of her friends. It was a good-bye dinner for the Hemingways, she said. Picasso hardly knew the Hemingways. He had seen them a number of times at Gertrude's, and they spoke, but that was all, and Olga could not even remember having seen the Hemingways anywhere, and, besides, she didn't like Gertrude Stein and Alice Toklas, so she refused to go to the dinner. She allowed Picasso to go, but only because she knew he would not be unfaithful with two ugly old lesbians. However, she threatened to shoot him if he didn't come straight home after the dinner. Olga was Russian. She had once been a ballerina with Diaghilev's Ballet Russe, and still acted the prima donna. She was madly jealous, and was very fond of the grand gesture. When she and Picasso first fell in love in Italy, she would say, "Oh, Pablo, I'm so happy I could kill myself!" Now she said, "I'm so unhappy I could kill myself—and if I do, I will take you with me, *cheri.*"

These days Picasso used any convenient excuse to get away from Olga. It was for that reason he accepted Gertrude's invitation to attend the going-away dinner for the Hemingways. Picasso only hoped that nobody at the dinner would want to talk about art. Gertrude's favorite topic of conversation was herself, but sometimes she wanted to talk about art. If Picasso wanted to talk about art, he would talk to Soutine or Pascin or Matisse or Léger or Cocteau or God. God would be best. He knew about art. Not as much as Picasso did, perhaps, but at least He could understand Picasso's ideas. But Hemingway knew nothing of art. Neither did Gertrude. She thought she did, but she didn't. Her brother, Leo, taught her everything he knew about art, and she still didn't know anything. But Picasso loved her. She was bizarre. When he was a child he always put the square peg in the round hole. He knew it didn't belong there, but he liked it there, so it stayed. Gertrude was like that. Alice was bizarre, too, and was a good cook. You could always get a good dinner at 27 rue de Fleurus.

Georges Braque was there. He brought his concertina. He couldn't play it very well, but that was all right. Henri Rousseau couldn't play a violin very well, either, but he could play bizarrely. Hemingway was there, hulky as a gladiator, with sinewy arms and strong body odor, sitting across the table from Max Jacob. When Max, a Jew, had seen Jesus on his wall one day in 1917, he had immediately converted to Catholicism and eventually left Paris to live in a cell in an abandoned monastery in Saint Benoît sur Loire. There he wrestled night and day with his demon of homosexuality, but now and then he got tired of wrestling and came back to Paris to surrender to sin and indulge his demon. And now, as they dined on *moules mariner,* salmon salad, and pasta, and drank white wine, Max gazed longingly across the table at the rough and brawny Hemingway.

"Why are you going back to your country?" Picasso asked Hemingway, though he didn't really care. It was only something to say.

"Money," Hemingway said.

"To hell with money," Picasso said.

"That's easy for you to say, but we have a child coming—as you can see. I have to make a living."

Hadley sat beside him, far gone with child. By looking at her, Picasso would have thought she was a lesbian. She had that masculine look, except she was pregnant. He suspected that, of the two of them, it was she who wanted to return to America.

Security. Picasso had noticed that every time a woman got pregnant, she began to think of security, a nest, a provider.

"Make a living?" Picasso said. "This sounds stupidly bourgeois."

Hemingway seemed to restrain himself. He was not an artist. He had said earlier that he would like to have been a bullfighter, but if he was too afraid of poverty to be an artist, he certainly would have been afraid of the bulls. Still, Gertrude had said he was a good writer. But how would she know? Was Gertrude a good writer? Picasso couldn't read English, so he had never read any of her books. Her brother, Leo, who taught her to like Picasso's paintings, said that she was a terrible writer, and knew nothing of art, and was stupid. On the other hand, Juan Gris said that he respected Gertrude's understanding of painting. But Juan Gris was a poor Spaniard who wanted to be accepted and flattered, so who could tell? Anyway, Picasso liked Gertrude. She was bizarre.

When the dinner was over, Gertrude asked Braque to play a song on his concertina. Braque said he would do so gladly if Max Jacob would do a dance à la Isadora. Max looked uncomfortable, as if he were being teased, but a number of voices joined Gertrude's to encourage him to perform, which he loved to do. It took a smattering of applause to convince him of their sincerity.

"Well, if you insist," he said, and added for the benefit of those at the table who had never seen him do one of his dances, "It's a little burlesque I do." It seemed to be an apology for the secret pleasure he took in his own foolishness.

The guests cleared an area where Max could dance. After taking off his shoes and his glasses, Max snatched up a tasseled silk *rebozo* that hung over an electric light shade, and announced that the name of his dance was "The Girl and Death." Then he began to move, dashing about with the tasseled *rebozo* held horizontal at arm's length above his head. Done as an imitation, not as a satire, of Isadora Duncan's style, the dance delighted everyone. Braque's concertina playing left a little to be desired, it was true, but his determination made up for what he lacked in ability, and he managed to supply Max with a bumpy rhythm for his flounces and whirls. Then Max fell down and died. The laughter and the applause marked the dance as a success.

By then there were others who were hungry for applause— Picasso, for one. So when Gertrude tried to keep the entertainment going by asking, "Who's next?," Picasso stood up.

"What?" Gertrude said. "You, Pablo? What're you going to do, paint a picture?"

"I am going to say a poem," Picasso said with enough pugnacity to make the others understand that he wasn't fooling. "It's a poem that was taught to me by an American yesterday. I remembered it. Every artist should remember it. It is called 'The Artist's Credo.' " And without waiting for anyone's encouragement or permission, he announced, "The Artist's Credo—

> The world is a big ball of shit,
> And we upon it try with all our might and wit
> To make it more pretty
> Than shitty."

An uncertain silence gripped the guests. It was well known among the guests that Alice didn't like vulgar language to be used in her presence. But Picasso assumed that he could get away with it because Alice believed him to be a genius. She had told him so when they first met. She said that a little bell had gone off in her head, the same as it had done when she first met Gertrude, announcing that she was in the presence of a genius. Picasso assumed that genius had its prerogatives. Still, everybody looked toward Gertrude and awaited her verdict.

Her first reaction, too, was uncertain. Then a smile slowly curled her lips, a chuckling sound came from her mouth, and she applauded. The others, relieved, also laughed and applauded. Picasso was the hit of the party. But Alice, perhaps as revenge for his presumption, and because she didn't want to see Gertrude upstaged and outshone, asked Gertrude to do something—read from one of her books, or tell a story, or recite a poem.

Gertrude shook her head, no, no, no. She didn't seem inclined to contribute anything to the evening's entertainment, until someone asked her to sing that song she loved so much, the one that had the same title as Gertrude's favorite novel, *The Trail of the Lonesome Pine.*

Gertrude's huge brown eyes lit up with delight, and she allowed herself to be persuaded to sing the song, with Braque accompanying her on the concertina. She sang without getting up. Her velvety smooth voice was perhaps not quite right for the song, which needed a hillbilly voice to get it's true flavor. But Gertrude gave it her best.

> In the Blue Ridge Mountains of Virginia,
> On the trail of the lonesome pine,
> In the pale moonshine
> Our hearts entwined
> Where she carved her name and I carved mine.
> Oh! June, like the mountains I'm blue,
> Like the pine, I'm lonesome for you.
> In the Blue Ridge Mountains of Virginia,
> On the trail of the Lonesome Pine.

Gertrude bowed regally from her chair in acknowledgment of the applause, and since nothing could top that, nobody else was asked to entertain. The rest of the evening was spent in what was supposed to be scintillating conversation, but was mostly just opinionated folderol. And when the Hemingways, the guests of good-bye honor, took their leave, most of the other guests left as well. There were manly handshakes between Gertrude and the Hemingways, with wishes for good luck, and thanks for everything, and please write, and we're sure we'll be hearing about your writing career.

Max Jacob and Picasso left with the Hemingways, intending to say good-bye when they got outside, but once in the street, they found that they were all going in the same direction, so they walked together. The Hemingways were going to the Café du Dôme for a one last sentimental drink, they said, and to say good-bye to any acquaintances they might meet, and Picasso was going to Montparnasse also, to see if he could find Jules Pascin, who always had lovely young models hanging on his arms, models that Pascin would gladly share with a fellow artist. Picasso and his wife, Olga Koklova, were not having sex these days. She had a pistol and was threatening to kill him for his infidelities, which was not a great inducement for him to go home and make love to her.

Going up Boulevard Raspail to the Dôme, Hemingway and Picasso walked in front. Hemingway wanted to talk about Spain and bullfighting, and Picasso wanted to talk about Gertrude Stein.

"Tell me, Hemingway," he said, "do you think she is a genius?"

"I don't know," Hemingway said. "*She* thinks she is, anyway."

"I know. She says the Jews have produced only three geniuses: Spinoza, Christ, and herself."

Hemingway chuckled. "So I've heard."

"And she tells me that there are two geniuses in art today, me in painting, she in literature," Picasso went on, hoping that Hemingway's own ego would push him into a truthful estimation of Gertrude's worth as a writer. "But I can't read English, so I don't know about her writing. I've never read any of her books. Have you?"

"The ones she's paid to have published, yeah," Hemingway said. "Even reviewed her last one, *Geography and Plays,* for the *Tribune.*"

"From what you have read, can you tell why she claims an artistic alliance with me? I confess this puzzles me."

"I don't know, but she says there's a similarity between the way she writes and the way you paint. Cubism. She claims to be using words 'cubistically.' She says that's the reason most people can't understand what she writes."

"That sounds silly to me," Picasso said. "With lines and colors, one can make patterns, but if you don't use words according to their meaning, they aren't words at all, *n'est-ce pas?* They are just sounds. You might as well grunt and fart and call it art."

"Some say that's what she's doing."

Hemingway didn't sound as if he were interested in defending her. Indeed, the small smile that played about his lips seemed to indicate that he shared the general perception that Gertrude was ridiculous. Maybe her claim to be the only living literary genius had aroused his ire.

When they got to the Dôme, Max and Picasso joined the Hemingways for a drink at a table on the terrace, but it was obvious that there was not going to be any more sustained conversation that night. Besides, it was all very conventional. The Hemingways spent their time saying good-byes to friends and acquaintances who stopped at the table. Kiki and Man Ray came by, as did Blaise Cendrars, Samuel Putnam and Flossie Martin, Mina Loy, and others.

Finally Max and Picasso got tired of the repetitive scene and decided to continue Picasso's search for Jules Pascin. Picasso was still hoping to find Pascin with more models than he could possibly get through in one night. If Picasso was going to be shot tomorrow by Olga, he at least wanted to die after experiencing one last night of blissful debauchery. God only knew what Max Jacob was looking for—a young man, certainly, but since Hemingway was obviously unavailable, perhaps a game of chess would do.

Picasso shook hands with Hemingway and his wife. *"Alors, au revoir,"* he said. "Perhaps we shall meet again someday. Perhaps you will come back to Paris someday, *n'est-ce pas?"*

"I hope so. Good-bye, and good luck," Hemingway said, the same as he had been saying to all the people who stopped at their table.

By the time Max and Picasso had crossed the rue Delambre, headed for Chez Rosalie, where Picasso hoped to find Pascin, he had put Hemingway completely out of his mind.

44

Hadley

WHEN HADLEY AND Ernest went to say good-bye to the Pounds the day before they were to leave for America, Ernest took along a copy of *Three Stories and Ten Poems* as a present for Ezra. Mike and Maggie Strater were at the Pounds, too, though the Straters' child was not there, children being unwelcome in the Pound domicile.

Ernest and Hadley stayed for a lunch that consisted of tea, scones, canned sardines, cheeses, and fresh fruit, and after lunch Ezra took advantage of his captive audience to read an essay he had been working on. It was called "Kongo Roux," the thesis being that the World War has been hatched by a conspiracy of Jews—*"totem de tribu* Sheeny, Yid, taboo," as he described them in bastard Latin.

Hadley found it quite puzzling how a man who, by general consensus, was considered to be a genius could seriously espouse such ignoble balderdash, but she said nothing, knowing that any opinion she might utter would be dismissed as that of an inferior being, a woman. It was the men who were the targets of Ezra's diatribe, and while Mike Strater didn't seem to take Ezra too seriously, Ernest was flattered by Ezra's obvious desire to have him as a disciple, so he gave Ezra his full attention. He listened as if to an oracle as Ezra moved restlessly about the room, his red hair swept back on his head like a woodpecker's crest, his Byronic collar open to his chest, his beard trembling as he expounded on the sickness of society, making a case against the Jews' misuse of capital, laying at their feet the corruption of civilization, the cunning way they had turned Western culture into "a botched civilization, an old bitch gone in the teeth."

Bored with it all, Hadley was ready to leave at any time, but she had to remind Ernest three or four times that they still had a lot of packing to do before she finally managed to pry him loose from his appreciation of Ezra's oracular ravings. But she didn't get away without her own private lecture from Ezra. As they were getting ready to leave, Ezra took Hadley aside and said, "Now, Hadley I have some advice I feel I ought to give you regarding your marriage. You mustn't try to change Ernest, you know. With him it would be a terrible mistake. After you have the baby, you won't be the same. Women's minds undergo a softening process when they become mothers, and they begin to try to change their husbands. They try to tame them. They try to make their husbands choose between domestic felicity and the conquesting, creative, adventuresome urge that is the very basis of maleness."

Hadley resented this advice, just as she privately resented the man who had presumed to voice it. Still, she couldn't help worrying about what he had said, and after she and Ernest had said good-bye to the Pounds and the Straters and caught a horse-drawn fiacre and were riding along boulevard du Montparnasse, headed back to their apartment, Hadley was seized with doubts and fears. When she saw the trees and the sidewalk cafés and the crowds of festive people along the boulevard, she knew they would never see the likes of this in America. Paris was the place to be if you were an artist. There was no other place like it on earth, perhaps never had been, perhaps would never be again.

And yet they were leaving.

Hadley couldn't hold back her tears. "Oh, Tatie, darling, I'm so sorry. I'm sorry we can't have everything. Forgive me if I've made the wrong choice. Will you?"

He took her hand. "Nothing to forgive," he said. "We made the choice, the both of us together. We'll live with it."

"But we were lucky to have been here, weren't we? We've had twenty months in Paris. We were lucky to have that, weren't we?"

"Of course, we're lucky," he said. "We're always lucky."

45

Sylvia

SYLVIA LEFT HER assistant, Myrsine, in charge of the bookstore. Hurrying up the street to the Place de l'Odeon, she found a taxi in front of the Café Voltaire. She urged the driver to get her to the Gare St. Lazare before 1:30, when the train carrying the Hemingways to their ship in Cherbourg was due to leave.

She made it with only a few minutes to spare. With the basket of fruit and flowers in one hand and two books in the other, she hurried along, looking for the Hemingways in the windows of the compartments and among the people still on the quay.

She found them in a second-class compartment in the middle of the train, storing their luggage. She called to them through the open window, and they, with expressions of pleasant surprise, came out of the car.

"There you are!" Hadley said.

"Gee, it was swell of you to come," Hemingway said with the boyish smile that hadn't changed since Sylvia had first seen him in Paris nearly two years ago.

The uniformed conductor on the quai used a megaphone to call out, *"Mesdames, messieurs! En voiture, s'il vous plaît."*

The passengers began boarding the train.

"I brought the basket of fruit," Sylvia said, handing it to Hemingway, "and a couple of books for the trip—two more of Bob's Contact Editions." She gave Hadley a copy of Mina Loy's *Lunar*

Baedecker and gave Hemingway a small volume of William Carlos Williams' poetry, *Spring and All.* "Hope you like them."

"And flowers!" Hadley said. "Oh, Sylvia, you're wonderful. You were one of our first friends in Paris." She gave Sylvia a quick embrace. "And now you'll be the last friend we see in Paris. Good-bye."

Hemingway shook her hand. "We'll write you as soon as we get settled."

"En voiture, messieurs, en voiture, s'il vous plaît."

"Better get aboard," Sylvia said.

They got aboard the train. The conductor followed them aboard and closed the door. Sylvia stood at the window of their compartment and after they put the books and basket of fruit on the seat, Hadley reached through the window to take Sylvia's hand.

"If we never meet again, Sylvia, I'll always treasure having known you," Hadley said.

There was a series of banging sounds between the cars as the couplings engaged, and the train inched into motion.

"Oh, we'll meet again, I'm sure," Sylvia said. "You'll be back one of these days."

"You think so?" Hadley asked.

The train began moving.

"I know so," Sylvia said, walking along beside the train. "You were Paris pilgrims. Everybody who's ever been a Paris pilgrim always comes back someday."

They waved as the train pulled out of the station.